FLIGHT

Also by Isabel Ashdown:

Glasshopper
Hurry Up and Wait
Summer of '76

Flight

ISABEL ASHDOWN

First published in 2015 by

Myriad Editions
59 Lansdowne Place
Brighton BN3 1FL

www.myriadeditions.com

1 3 5 7 9 10 8 6 4 2

A CIP catalogue record for this book is available
from the British Library

ISBN (pbk): 978-1-908434-60-9
ISBN (ebk): 978-1-908434-61-6

Designed and typeset in Sabon LT
by Linda McQueen, London

Printed and bound in Sweden by
ScandBook AB

For my children,
Alice and Samson, with love

'I thought how unpleasant it is to be locked out;
and I thought how it is worse, perhaps,
to be locked in.'

Virginia Woolf, *A Room of One's Own*

PROLOGUE

November 1994

Wren sits on the sofa in her softly lit lounge, her shadowed eyes fixed on the television, her baby at her breast. Her husband is beside her, one hand cradling a glass of red wine, the other loosely resting on his wife's shoulder, a ticket smoothed out across his knee. His toes stretch and press into the deep pile of the new carpet, and Wren's eyes are drawn to them as they flex up, flex down. Flex up, flex down. It's a little tic he's had ever since she first met him, something that, until now, she'd long since stopped noticing.

It's the first ever National Lottery draw, and this evening Robert returned from a squash match with a ticket, bought at the petrol station on the way home. With each number called, he expels an exaggerated grunt of disappointment. His thigh presses hot against hers and she can barely stand the intimacy of it. She resists a strong desire to pull away, to retreat into the cool corner at the other end of the sofa. When the last number is finally called, he sighs, neatly folding the ticket in half, once, twice, three times, four, then casually drops the paper nugget on the lamp stand beside him. He leans in to kiss the baby's soft crown, to kiss Wren.

Wren is frozen in position, incapable of movement, the infant having long dropped from her nipple, milk-drunk. She knows the numbers on the screen – recognises the birth dates and anniversaries as the ones she marked on her own ticket stub just this morning – and she dares not speak for fear of giving herself away.

Cautiously, she watches her husband from the sides of her eyes, as he pushes himself up from his seat and crosses the room.

'Oh, well, better luck next time,' he says, cheerily enough, and he heads upstairs, to run the shower, to wash the squash game from his skin. Wren studies the space he passed through, stares mutely at the gaping door, pulse hammering, muscles contracting beneath the broken wall of her softened stomach, and she knows she won't tell him. Not now, not tomorrow, not ten years from today.

Instead, she'll quietly pack her bags and, when the moment is right, she'll leave. Alone.

LAURA

Laura is drinking tea at the large oak table, watching Phoebe butter toast, when the phone rings. It sounds three times before she really hears it, so entirely captivated is she by the sight of the girl's thickening waist, her newly plump bosom.

'Are you going to get that?' Phoebe looks over her shoulder, holding up the knife. 'My hands are greasy.'

Laura puts down her mug and sprints into the hall, reaching the telephone just too late. She pauses to read the *To Do* list marked on the notebook by Robert, running her fingers over the swirling indentations of his clear handwriting: *Car tax due 1st December. Change internet provider. Order logs for next winter. Call builders re leaking gutter.* She picks up the pen and adds to the list in her own scrawl: *Book romantic getaway to the Maldives. Stock up on champagne. Run naked through Piccadilly Circus.*

'Who was it?' Phoebe calls from the kitchen, her mouth full.

'Don't know. They rang off before I got to it.' Laura returns to the table. 'They'll call back if it's important. So, what's the plan for today? Your dad said you need to start thinking about a job – or another course.'

Phoebe sighs heavily and flops into the seat opposite. She takes another bite from her toast, then reaches across to pick up Laura's glass of orange juice, drinking it down in one, and smirking as she does so.

'Phoebe! How many times? Get your own drink, you lazy mare!' Laura rises to fill the kettle, kissing Phoebe on the top of her head as she passes. 'Listen, I've been wanting to talk to you. Not the uni stuff – something else.'

Phoebe frowns, making a show of licking the crumbs from her empty plate, hiding her face.

'The thing is, you and Esteban – you became very close over the summer, didn't you?'

'Well, *this* is embarrassing.'

Laura gets up to pour the tea. 'Come on, Phoebs, you're twenty now. I don't need to talk to you like a child any more, do I?'

'S'pose not.' Phoebe shifts position, wrapping the zips of her hoodie across her body.

The phone rings again; Laura raises a halting hand as Phoebe pushes her chair out to stand. 'Leave it – let it ring.'

Phoebe looks exasperated but sits down all the same, placing her palms down on the table, impatiently rippling her fingertips against the wooden surface. The caller rings off.

'So. I'm assuming you and Esteban slept together?'

'Bloody hell, Laura! That's a bit personal, isn't it?'

'You were going out with him for, what, four months? And you spent every waking hour together during that time. It seems likely, pumpkin.'

Phoebe is doing her best to look offended, but weakens at Laura's use of her pet name. 'So what?'

Laura looks out through the glass doors of the kitchen, to the frosty sunlit garden beyond. A cluster of house sparrows dances beneath the feeders that surround the patio, bobbing and pecking at the fallen seeds and millet. 'Is it completely over between you two?'

'He won't say as much, but it is – you know he went back to Barcelona at the end of the summer, and there's no way he'll want to keep it going with me stuck over here. I'm not stupid. I mean, have you seen him? He could be a model. He'll have found a new girlfriend within a week.'

Laura places a hand over hers. 'Phoebe, love, were you careful when you were together? I can't help but notice that you've, well, filled out a little over the past few weeks, and – '

Phoebe snatches her hand away.

'Oh, my God, Laura – so I'm fat now? Christ, as if I don't feel shitty enough already.' She marches across the kitchen to bang her plate down beside the sink. 'And you and Dad putting all this pressure on me to get a job – it's no wonder I'm comfort-eating!'

'Give me a bit of credit, Phoebe. It's not that kind of weight I'm talking about and you know it.'

The colour rises to Phoebe's cheeks, her left hand instinctively drifting to her abdomen, the fingers resting there for a brief pause before she rushes from the room. Moments later the front door slams shut, and Laura is left alone in the stillness of the large, bright kitchen. Out in the hallway the telephone starts ringing again.

Robert was her first real love, though she barely knew it at the time. They lived on the same street in Surrey, a small suburban bore of a place, and their parents were passing acquaintances. Robert wasn't like the other boys in their little primary class, the boys who hung round the park in provincial packs; she could talk to him for hours about anything – about poetry, conkers, *Magpie*, hair nits, first crushes, fast cars, James Bond, the Bay City Rollers. It was like having another version of herself along the street; a better, cleverer, kinder version of herself.

At eight, so incensed was she that she couldn't join the Cubs with him that she would sneak along to the village hall each Tuesday evening, to hide among the cobwebs beneath the stage, watching through a dislodged wood-knot until the session ended an hour later. *I promise that I will do my best to do my duty to God and to the Queen, to help other people, and to keep the Cub Scout law.* Laura knew all the mottos, all the secret hand signals – she even persuaded Robert to steal a Navigator Badge from Akela, in acknowledgement of her secret missions beneath the hall stage. 'Good work,' she told him when he handed it over, and she rushed home that night to attach it to her duffel coat with small, careful stitches, one of the few skills she'd gained in her own short-lived career as a Brownie, along with boiling an egg and making a cup of tea without getting scalded.

Each Friday, they would walk home from school via Mr Wilkinson's sweet shop, spending an age dithering over the multicoloured jars and row after row of chocolate bars and prohibited gum. Their favourite combination was two ounces of sherbet pips and two ounces of fairy drops; Sweet and Sour, Laura called it, and before long they would ask for the mix by name, knowing that Mr Wilkinson would understand their request. 'The Terrible Twins,' he used to say when they appeared in the doorway with a ring of his shop bell. And it was true: they could pass for brother and sister despite Laura's brick-red hair. Robert's was dark and poker-straight with a fringe that grew too fast and subsequently hung across his left eye at all times, but beneath the fringe were a pair of amber-green eyes, so perfect a match for

Laura's that their mothers might have ordered them from the same catalogue. They barely spent a day apart, whether at school or at home, each becoming an extension of the other's family, free to come and go as they pleased. When Rob went into hospital to have his tonsils removed, it was Laura he asked for.

'Would you like some ice cream?' his mum had asked him from the side of his hospital bed.

'No,' he croaked. 'Want Laura.'

'Lucozade?'

'*Laura.*'

Lily, his older sister, was sent up the road to fetch her, and so when Rob returned home that evening Laura was already waiting at his bedside with the latest copy of *Whizzer and Chips*. His mum said it was the first time he had smiled since waking from the anaesthetic, and Laura felt like the most important person in the world. 'My throat is sore too,' she whispered into his ear as his mother tucked up the ends of his bedspread.

'How about some ice cream now?' his mum asked again as she left the room. They nodded in unison and Laura clambered on to the bed beside him, where they could sit shoulder to shoulder and pass the comic back and forth.

Despite his childish need of her throughout their youth, Laura was always the driving force, the one to make things happen. She wonders now if it was she who did all the running, she who kept them tethered together across the years, setting more store by their friendship than Robert ever did, chivvying him into joint adventures. 'You've got to have things to look forward to. *Fun* things,' Laura would chide when Robert wanted to take a more serious approach to their life ahead.

At the end of their final year in junior school, Rob was heading off to Norfolk for a two-week family holiday, whereas Laura had a long summer to endure at home in Gatebridge with her parents. 'I'll die of boredom,' she said. 'We *must* write every day.' The day before he set off, she turned up on his doorstep and provided him with seven notelets, seven envelopes and a strawberry-scented pen to ensure that he had no excuses.

'What about stamps?' he asked, looking as if he'd just been handed the burden of a school project.

Laura was furious at his lack of enthusiasm and returned home immediately to lift a fistful of change from her mother's purse, with which she bought seven stamps and a packet of Tic Tacs. The Irvings were eating dinner when she knocked at Rob's front door for a second time. She knew this because their dining table was located in the front window, where they ate every evening at six pm on the dot, in full view of the residents of Green Street.

'For the letters,' she said, holding up the stamps with one hand. With the other, she rattled the Tic Tacs underneath his nose and slapped them into his palm. 'For the journey.' Pointing her nose skywards, she made her way home without a backward glance, knowing she could expect a lilac-coloured envelope through her door within the next forty-eight hours.

Even now she can recall that first letter.

Dear Lolly,

Wish you were here. Norfolk is boring and Lily is annoying as usual. Will write again when something interesting happens.

Rob

Not even a kiss at the end. She wrote back immediately.

Dear Rob,

You win the award for the most lazy letter ever written in the history of letter-writing – ever. If nothing interesting is happening, then make something up!

Lots of love,

Laura xxx

ps I saw Tanya Sole holding hands with Grubby Greg this morning. She had her skirt tucked in her knickers hahahahaha.

pps Now that's how you write a letter.

ppps It's true, she really did have her skirt tucked in her pants.

Robert's second letter arrived by return, containing concocted tales of celebrity sightings and puppies saved from drowning, and Laura was happy with his progress, in particular with the inclusion of a small *x* at the foot of the page. *Much better*, she told him when she wrote back, and she counted off the days until he would return to their street, so that she might feel whole once again.

The voice at the end of the line sounds young, boyish even.

'We're trying to trace a Mrs Wren Irving, last known at this telephone number.'

Looking out across the leaf-blown panorama of their smart suburban street, Laura stands at the bedroom window and finds she has lost the power of speech.

'Hello? Am I speaking to Mrs Irving?'

The suggestion propels Laura to answer, though her reply comes out tongue-tied, her voice uneven. 'No – she doesn't – I mean, *no*. She's not here. She's no longer at this address – hasn't been for years. No.'

'You don't sound very certain,' the young man says; Laura detects the hint of a smile in his voice, and hates him for it instantly. 'Are you sure I'm not actually *speaking* to Wren Irving?'

'Who did you say you were?' she asks, sudden anger rearing up.

'Mike Woods. I'm a reporter. We're looking for Mrs Irving in connection with her Lottery win in the 1990s. Could that be you?'

'The Lottery? I've told you, *I'm not her*. The person you're looking for hasn't lived here for twenty years – and I can tell you she certainly wasn't a Lottery winner when she did. I'm sorry I can't help you any further.'

'Perhaps *Mr* Irving is available?'

'No.'

'So, I take it he still lives at this address?'

'I'm not answering these questions – I don't even know who you are.'

'*Mike Woods*. Now, as far as I can establish, they *are* still married, aren't they? Are you and he – ?'

Laura picks up a pen, flipping open a magazine to find a blank space to write in. She jots down his name, underscoring it fiercely. 'OK, Mike Woods. I've told you Mrs Irving no longer lives here. Her husband hasn't seen her for two decades, and really – the last thing he wants to do is have a conversation with some journalist about her last recorded movements.'

'Has she ever been reported as a missing person?' Mike Woods asks. 'Do you think she's dead or alive?'

Laura is almost floored by the question. '*Fuck you*,' she replies, and she returns the handset to its cradle, her heart hammering against the cage of her chest.

Without realising it, Laura had been on the lookout for a female friend for years, even before she first laid eyes on Wren in the college refectory on that grey day in October 1982. She had Robert, of course – she'd always have Robert – but she'd never really experienced the deep kinship of a sister, and she knew it was a missing part of her, something that ought to be filled. Just like the girls in her primary school, the girls in her senior years didn't really *get* her, not the way Robert did – and, to be fair, she didn't get them either. Theirs was a foreign language to her, and while she was never bullied, not really, neither side was interested in the other.

But then, there was Wren, alone and birdlike, in her black china doll slippers and tweedy overcoat, with her gentle wise smile – and Laura recognised her instantly as the missing piece. 'I like her,' she told Robert as they took their table by the window after chatting to her in the lunch queue. 'She's different.'

Robert nodded.

'Rob, she's like us.'

'What does that mean?'

Laura couldn't think of the answer. It wasn't a tangible thing; it was just a feeling, a sixth sense, if you believed in that kind of thing. It was the same feeling she had when she spent time with Rob: the comfort of profound familiarity, of security and warmth, of *simply knowing*.

They raised their arms in synchrony and waved at Wren across the room, beckoning her over to join them. At first, her expression somewhat aloof, she appeared not to notice them, until her face shifted and she crossed the room to slide her tray on to the table, sweeping the crumbs from the seat opposite.

'Will you be in our gang?' Laura asked her, purposely affecting an adolescent twang.

Wren was cool; she leant back, tipping the front legs of her chair off the floor to arch over and fetch the salt from the table behind. 'I'm not much of a crowd person. How big is the gang?' She raised the salt cellar, poised to sprinkle her rice. Robert ran his hands up through the front of his floppy fringe, betraying his embarrassment.

'It's very select,' Laura replied, now lowering her voice to a conspiratorial whisper. 'We like to keep the numbers down – weed out the riff-raff, you know?'

'I understand,' Wren said. 'So, just you two, then?'

Laura nodded.

'And me?'

'Correct – should you choose to accept our offer of membership.' She reached into her parka pocket and brought out a strip of Wrigley's gum. 'And there's a free gift if you sign up now.'

Wren took the gum, sliding it under her plate with a solemn nod. Robert's face relaxed enough to break into a wide smile.

'So, you're in?' Laura said, offering her hand across the plates of steaming curry.

Wren shrugged, and took her hand, giving it one firm shake. 'OK. I'm in.'

The headlights from Robert's car flood through the front windows as he pulls up on the drive outside, rousing Laura from her slumber in the darkness of the living room. She rises from the sofa, fuzzy-headed, and dashes to the kitchen to remove the supper from the oven, relieved to find that she hasn't let it overcook.

'Smells good!' he calls as he opens the front door, dropping his keys on the telephone stand in the hall. 'What've we got?'

Laura places the dish at the centre of the kitchen table, pushing her hair back and gesturing towards it like a game show hostess as he enters the room. 'Shepherd's pie – Laura-style, I'm afraid. We didn't have as much mince as I thought, so I had to improvise: I bulked it out with a can of baked beans.'

'Ah, that takes me back to our student days. You were always a dab hand at conjuring a meal out of nothing.' He fetches plates and cutlery, pausing to kiss Laura on the lips before laying the table. 'How was your day?'

She opens the fridge and brings out a bottle of white wine, snapping open the screw cap and pouring two large glasses. 'I don't know where to begin.' She indicates towards the table and Robert sits, removing his tie and ladling a large helping of supper on to his plate.

'Any veg?' he asks as he passes her the spoon.

Her face falls into a frown. 'I meant to do some broccoli to go with it. Damn. My mind's been all over the place today. Do you mind?'

Robert shakes his head, raising his face long enough for her to see his contented expression before he goes to work on his meal. 'Nope. This is perfect. So – what's up, then? You look worn out. Everything OK with Phoebe? Where is she, by the way?' He takes a large mouthful of pie.

Laura gazes across the domestic landscape of the table, at the benign concentration of Robert's sun-speckled face, and wonders how to put it all into words. *I think your daughter's pregnant, Robert. I think she's got herself in a bit of bother. I think Phoebe's having a baby and I wish it was me. Oh, and then there's the Wren thing…*

'She went out,' she answers. 'Actually, we had a bit of a falling-out. I guess she's gone round to Maisy or Hannah's for a bit.'

'Really? That's not like you two. What was it about?' He rests his fork on the side of his plate.

She almost says the words, almost tells him. But wouldn't Phoebe hate her for it? Isn't it Phoebe's right to tell him herself?

'It was my fault really. I was pressuring her about knuckling down to something now she's dropped out of uni, and she wasn't ready to talk about it. Anyway, it's probably better coming from you, Rob. You know how much she cares about your opinion. I'm pretty sure I'll only wind her up if I mention it again.'

He grimaces. 'And there was I thinking life would be a breeze by the time she was out of her teens. Honestly, when she left for Hull I had visions of you and me heading off on weekend city breaks and tours of the French vineyards. Mind you, looking at the abysmal state of our pensions, that plan doesn't seem too likely whether Phoebe's at home or not.'

'Please don't start on the pension conversation again, Rob. It's just too boring. We're well off, compared to lots of other people I know.'

'Actually, Ben in the finance office was saying that if your pensions are looking dodgy – and let's face it, most are – ISAs are the way to go. We ought to think about it – '

Laura puts her fork down, stretches her arm across the table, palm up. Robert pauses, smiles at her dead-eyed expression, and takes her hand in his. 'OK, OK, I'll stop. Just planning for a comfortable future, that's all.'

'Well, don't, please. It's boring. You're turning into your father.'

'In that case I'll stop right away.' He squeezes her fingers before reaching over for a top-up of wine.

After supper, they clear the table, and move into the living room with what's left of the wine. Robert pulls up a footstool and flicks through the television channels while Laura searches the bookshelves until she finds the photo album she's looking for – the oldest, most well-thumbed of the collection, the one labelled 'Kingston'. Sitting cross-legged on the sofa beside Robert, she cradles her glass in one hand, turning the leaves of the album with the other. Every couple of pages she pauses to study their young faces, noting the subtle changes in their hairstyles, their clothes, their eyes, as the years pass from the early days at college to their final term of those turbulent, delirious, distant days of youth.

Robert glances at the album on Laura's lap. 'There's something else you're not telling me,' he says, frowning. 'What is it, Laur?'

Laura gently closes the album, smoothing out the wrinkles of its vinyl cover. 'It's about Wren.'

'Wren?' Robert presses the mute button on the remote control, and the quiet of the room expands in the expectant pause.

'A journalist phoned today, looking for her. He was asking all sorts of questions, asking if we knew whether she was dead or alive. He said something about her winning some money on the Lottery. He was really pushy. And it got me thinking – what if he's got a point, Rob? What if she *is* dead? What if she died all alone – and neither of us was there for her?' Laura presses her face into Robert's wool-clad shoulder, the weight of her anxiety now given voice.

He shifts himself back to look directly into her eyes. 'She's not dead, Laura. Wren's no more dead than you or I.'

She hugs the photo album to her chest, as if the secrets are somehow stored within. 'But how can you be *sure*? What about her car? You said it was burnt out when the police found it.'

'Yes, but they were pretty certain it had been stolen – it's what joyriders do, drive around a bit then set a match to it. And that solicitor's letter made it quite clear that she'd decided to stay away, that there was no reason for us to fear for her safety. Anyway, don't you think we would have felt something if Wren had died? Don't you think we would just know?'

He's right, of course; this is Wren they're talking about, and somehow they would simply know.

From the earliest age, Laura was driven by a ferocious competitive streak when it came to the boys in her life, even with Robert, who she loved like a brother. Tired of the constant suggestion that boys were stronger, smarter, more interesting than girls, she did everything in her power to outrun them, outwit them, outsmart them. It wasn't just the boys in her class who held this opinion – it was the teachers, male *and* female, the stuffy besuited men on the telly, the man behind the counter in the local post office... even her own father. It seemed like madness to her young mind, a crazy, topsy-turvy lie of a thing, and she made it her mission to prove them all wrong.

'You'll never get a husband if you don't dress like a female,' her dad once told her. She was nine at the time. 'No one likes a tomboy.'

'Robert does,' she replied smartly, as her mother applied Germolene to the fresh skating graze across her left knee.

'I'm not talking about nancy-boy up the road. I'm talking about everyone else. Women should be feminine, look nice and pretty. You look as if you've been dragged through a hedge backwards.'

Laura dropped down off the dining table, stooping to inspect the clean dressing, stark against her grimy, tanned legs. 'Did I tell you I came top in the spelling test again? Twenty out of twenty.' She peered at her father through the thicket of her rich red fringe. 'That's three times in a row.'

He lowered his newspaper and gave her a curt nod. 'Nobody ever made a happy home with spelling prizes. Spelling doesn't cook the dinner, does it?'

'None of the *boys* got twenty out of twenty,' she replied, standing tall and planting her hands on her hips. 'Maybe *they* could cook the dinner.'

Her father slammed the newspaper into his lap, his face shifting into waves of irritation. 'How dare you speak to me...' he started, but he ran out of words as he glared into Laura's unflinching young face.

'George,' her mother said, raising her small hands as a peace offering, careful to keep her voice soft, 'a girl can do both, can't she? You know we're very proud of your school achievements, Lolly. Aren't we, Dad? And doing well at school won't make her any less of a homemaker, will it?'

Her dad returned to his newspaper and cleared his throat. 'Stick the kettle on, love,' he told her, and that was the end of the conversation, his point made as her mum obeyed his request. Laura straightened the buckles on her battered red rollerskates and rattled up the road to call on Robert.

'I'm never getting married,' she told him as he sat on the kerbside, lacing up his own skates. '*Never*. I'd rather poke my own eyes out with a saveloy.'

Robert laughed and held out his arm to be helped to his feet. 'You will. I bet you will. I bet you a pound that you'll get married and have six children.'

'Never!' she screamed, tearing up the street on her skates, wheeling her arms wildly as she picked up speed. 'Never, never, never!'

Every Saturday morning Laura cooks the same breakfast: poached eggs on smoked salmon, freshly squeezed juice and a large pot of espresso coffee. In their student days, this was the feast they'd reward themselves with if they had any spare cash – a rare treat. Back then, of course, Wren would cook, while Laura laid the tiny Formica table and Robert nipped along the street for the weekend papers. Fleetingly, as she scoots a knife around the edge of the poaching cup, Laura wishes that Wren were here now, to cook them their royal breakfast, to sit at the head of the table that's rightfully hers.

'Are you ready for your coffee?' she asks Robert as he brings in the newspapers. 'I'll heat up some more milk if you are.'

'Thanks,' he replies, reaching into his trouser pocket to fetch his mobile phone. 'Ah – message from Phoebe. She's on her way home now. Told you not to worry.'

Laura removes the jug from the microwave and pours steaming milk into Robert's Superdad mug. 'I wasn't worried. I just hate parting on a bad note, that's all.' She places the cup on the table in front of him, watching the milk and coffee swirl and blend around the spoon. 'I know it's a cliché, but she really is like a daughter to me. I couldn't bear it if she hated me, Rob.'

'She doesn't hate you, Laur. She's just a bit sensitive about the whole dropping-out thing at the moment – she was just sounding off, and it happened to be you who was in the room at the time.'

'OK.' Laura feels sick with the weight of her suspicions. She wonders what the right thing to do is – wonders if she's making a terrible mistake by not sharing her concerns with Robert. *It's Phoebe's secret*, she reminds herself again. And, at any rate, perhaps she's got it all completely wrong.

The first time Laura conceived, she was just fifteen. The boy, Niall, a wiry little Irish lad with black eyes and biceps like smooth pebbles, was with Quinn's Travelling Fair, which stopped on the common for a week each October. He was not much older than Laura, and they had first met on the waltzers after she'd quarrelled with Robert over which ride to go on next. Laura had wanted to stay put – she'd already spotted Niall giving her the eye – but Rob had wanted to move on to the shooting range. So he'd left her there, where, beneath the seductive charge of Niall's unwavering attention, she took another spin, and by the end of the ride they had arranged to meet behind the ghost train at nine – an arrangement they would repeat on every one of the six nights that followed. By the time Niall and Quinn's funfair had left, Laura was feeble-minded with passion and, for a few weeks at least, oblivious to the tiny cluster of cells that now grew and divided within her.

Finally, it was Rob who broke the news to her.

'Something's changed, Laur,' he said. 'You're different. You *look* different.'

In that instant she knew; of course, the signs were all there – the halt in her monthly cycle, the taut swell of her breasts, the voracious appetite. That night she locked herself in the bathroom with a half-bottle of vodka stolen from her dad's drinks cabinet and drank herself incoherent, all the while topping up the hot bathwater and praying for a miracle. Whether it was the combined power of prayer and liquor or nature's will, within days she collapsed in Rob's upstairs toilet and the tiny life slipped from her in a pool.

'Laura's got her period,' she heard him whisper to his mother outside the door, the hesitancy in his voice conveying his embarrassment. 'It's really heavy, she says – have you got anything?'

Rob's mum fussed about, discreetly providing sanitary napkins and paracetamol, encouraging Laura to lie down on Rob's bed until the pain passed. 'It's a woman's curse.' The older woman smiled as she placed sweet tea and chocolate biscuits on the bedside table. 'It gets much better once you've had kids, I promise you, sweetheart.'

By the time she walked back home that evening the worst of it seemed to be over, and, while relief was her abiding emotion, Laura felt the grief of loss: the loss of childhood, and the loss of a child.

By Sunday evening, without any mention of their earlier disagreement, things seem to have returned to normal between Laura and Phoebe. The following morning, when

Robert sets off for work, Laura drives her to the local college, to pick up a prospectus and look around the facilities. Apart from A-levels, which Phoebe already has, the main focus of the college is business and technology, with a few other subjects like hairdressing and mechanics thrown in for good measure. Laura tries to buoy her up as they pass suite after suite of computer screens and desks, but by the time they get back to the main foyer Phoebe is more miserable than ever.

'I'm an A-star student, for God's sake,' she whispers to Laura as they stand at the brochure carousel, listlessly thumbing through the various subjects.

'All the more reason for you to do something you really want to do.' Laura notices the dark circles beneath Phoebe's eyes; she looks as if she hasn't slept for a week. 'Come on, we're both getting ratty – let's go and get something in the canteen.'

They queue at the counter, where Laura picks up a Danish pastry and a pot of tea, while Phoebe orders fish and chips. She glances guiltily at Laura. 'I'm starving,' she says.

'Well, it *is* nearly lunchtime. Do you want a tea too?'

Phoebe wrinkles her nose. 'No – I've gone off tea lately. I'll get a Coke.'

Laura's breath catches in her chest as she recalls the fierce aversion for tea and coffee that she herself had developed with each of her pregnancies. And the deep fatigue; the dark half-moons that had appeared underneath her eyes. She slides her tray along the counter behind Phoebe, taking in the almost imperceptible swell of Phoebe's hips, the subtle plumping of her skin. At a guess, she must be three months gone.

'You sit down,' she says. 'I'll pay.'

With her own longed-for babies Laura had never got beyond eleven or twelve weeks, never stepped into that blossoming realm of ripening serenity promised by the mother-and-baby magazines she kept hidden in the bedside cabinet. After the first miscarriage with Doug, she'd held her subsequent pregnancies close, desperate to reveal them to the world at the turn of twelve weeks, only to have them slip from her too soon, like an empty promise.

She joins Phoebe at a table beside the window, looking out across the courtyard. Drizzly mist hangs over the benches and flower borders beyond the glass, painting it dreary, depressing. Laura sugars her tea and unravels her pastry; Phoebe concentrates on her plate, vanishing her fish and chips at speed. Only when she's mopping up the ketchup with her final chip does she look up.

'Wow, you *were* hungry,' Laura says.

Phoebe looks a little embarrassed. 'I didn't eat much for breakfast.'

'Do you want to get yourself a dessert?' Laura's anxious to let Phoebe see she's not judging her. 'They've got some nice cakes up there. And trifle – your favourite.'

She appears to think about it, before sliding her tray away and opening up the college prospectus. 'Nah, I'm fine. Don't want to get fat, do I?' She gives Laura a cheeky smile to show there are no hard feelings.

'So,' Laura says, spinning the brochure to face her, and flicking through its pages, 'is there anything here that takes your fancy?'

Phoebe shakes her head, despondent.

'Nothing? Well, let's look at it another way. What do think you want to do with your life – what really interests you? Something you can imagine doing as a job, not just a hobby.'

A gardener passes the window, pushing a wheelbarrow of cuttings. Phoebe's eyes travel with him, as he carries on along the path and stops beside the flower borders.

'I wouldn't mind being a gardener. Or someone who designs gardens. Something outdoorsy would be nice. I can't bear the idea of being stuck behind a desk.'

'Your mum liked gardening,' Laura is surprised to hear herself say.

Phoebe's eyes widen slightly. 'Really? I thought she was just a teacher.'

Laura laughs. '*Just* a teacher, eh? Well, yes, she was a teacher, but she had other interests too. Once she and your father moved to the house we're in now, she became a really keen gardener. The garden was always beautiful in springtime. It smelt of honeysuckle and jasmine, and wild roses. It was idyllic.'

'It doesn't look like that now. It's really boring.'

'That's because your mum's not there to keep it looking beautiful.'

Their eyes meet across the table. Laura reaches for her teapot.

'I don't mind talking about her, you know,' Phoebe says, breaking the tension. 'It's not like I'm able to miss her, is it? I only know her through photos. You're the one who brought me up, Laura, not her.'

'I know that. But it still feels strange talking about her, as though she's dead or something.' She stops, appalled by her own lack of tact. 'I don't mean that – I know she's not. I suppose I still miss her. She was my best friend, after all.'

'I don't know why you and Dad are so – so nice about her. After what she did. I mean, what kind of a mother just walks out?'

Laura shakes her head. 'It's hard to explain, Phoebs. You should talk to your dad about it some time. It would probably do him some good to talk it through with you.'

Phoebe takes a packet of sugar cubes from the bowl, unwraps it and pops one in her mouth. She turns to gaze out of the window, to where the gardener is digging out weeds with his hand fork. 'I think we should ask at reception about gardening courses. I think that's what I'd like to do.'

Back at the car with a clutch of new leaflets, they embrace, neither wanting to let go.

'I'm proud of you, Phoebe,' says Laura, 'whatever you end up doing – however life turns out. And I know your mum would be too.'

Although they never admitted as much, Laura is certain that Wren and Rob first got together after that horrible night she had spent in the student bar with Jack in their final year.

She didn't remember much about arriving home – barely a thing, in fact – except that she woke bathed in sweat in the early hours, thankful for the miraculously placed bucket by her bedside. She felt weak with dread, subdued by that unique thread of paranoia which comes after a night of alcohol-fuelled self-annihilation, her head throbbing like a fractured limb, every tiny movement vibrating throughout her trembling body. *I'm poisoned*, she thought as she fought the urge to retch again, and she tried to gather the stamina required to cross her bedroom to fetch her dressing gown from the back of the door.

After several failed attempts she was up, into her gown and out in the living room, gingerly making her way to the kitchen, where she would attempt to drink a glass of water without throwing up. She rested at the sink, gripping the units with white knuckles, a fresh film of perspiration beading up through her pale skin. She groaned through a long breath and reached into the cupboard for a glass – filled it swiftly and banged it down on the side with a slop of overspill, rushing to the medicine box to search for paracetamol before the nausea caught up with her again. '*Pills, pills, pills,*' she chanted in a whisper, until eventually she found them, picked up the water and retreated to the living room to perch on the edge of the sofa with her head on her knees. She stayed there for an age, long enough to actually drift into a light sleep, for her neck to seize up and complain as she finally raised her head to drink from the glass. Every movement had to be slow-motion, to trick her body into thinking it wasn't moving at all. She popped out the tablets into her hand and stared at them for a while, slowly reaching out for the glass, thinking too much about the journey they had to take, via her lips, her mouth, her gullet. She noticed the stillness of the flat at this hour, and wondered for a brief moment if she was there all alone.

That was when she noticed it.

The door to Rob's bedroom stood uncharacteristically ajar. Rob never slept with the door open; he needed complete darkness to sleep. Laura sat and stared at the foot-wide gap in the doorway, fighting back a tangle of images from the night before, each scrambling across the other to dominate her mind's eye. Jack in the toilet cubicle with that girl, her ivory leg hooked around his, the soft brown ghost of a bruise snaking up the bone of her shin, the metallic chink of his belt buckle swinging loose at his thigh. The girl's indignant expression; his dead-eyed shrug of indifference as he glanced over his shoulder then pushed the cubicle door between them, slotted the bolt into place. Mum and Dad framed in the window of their joyless kitchen; married for better or worse. His disappointment; hers.

On shaky legs, Laura trod softly across the ghastly carpet and peered through the gap, into Rob's bedroom. She pushed the door back a little, a little more, until it was quite, quite clear that Rob wasn't there – that his bed was empty. And that was when she heard it: the soft murmur of two voices joined as one, drifting through the plasterboard walls of Rob's room.

Unable to stop herself, Laura followed the sounds, laying her ear against the wall, her palms pressed flat either side of her head.

'I love you,' she heard Rob say, as clearly as if he were in the room beside her.

She closed her eyes, straining to hear Wren's response, paralysed by the sudden shock of jealousy at the thought of Wren in there with Robert, her Robert. She prayed for Wren to say nothing, but her words came through as clear as Rob's. 'I know,' she said. 'I wouldn't be *here* if I didn't believe that.'

Laura backed away, disgusted at herself, at her furtive eavesdropping, at the life she led, and retreated to the sanctuary of her sickbed, where she wept between retches and vowed to embrace her friends' union, to be the best friend that she could be.

A letter arrives for Robert on Wednesday morning, while Laura and Phoebe are completing application forms for the college. The light blue envelope is handwritten, with an unreadable postcode, and its arrival unsettles Laura for the rest of the day. In the afternoon, after Phoebe goes out, Laura turns it over in her hands a few times, even lifting it to her nose to inhale its papery scent, before placing it on the dresser with Robert's other mail of statements and circulars. *It's not Wren's handwriting*, is her first thought, but she can't shake the overwhelming feeling of its being somehow connected to her, to the recent resurrection of her ghost in the house.

By the time she hears Robert's car returning at seven, Laura is so deeply unsettled that she leaps up from the kitchen table where she's paring beans, and slides the envelope underneath the tea towels in the top drawer. Next morning, however, after a restless sleep, she forces herself to hand him the letter at the front door, as she helps him into his winter coat. Just as she had done, he turns the envelope over a few times and tries to make out the smudged postcode. 'You don't get many handwritten letters these days,' he says, kissing her on the lips and picking up his briefcase. 'Perhaps it's a long-lost inheritance cheque. You never know.' Smiling and waving it between them, he leaves the house for work.

Laura is astounded by his unruffled response; has he completely forgotten the journalist searching for Wren? Perhaps it's just she who has become paranoid, on the lookout for every little signal, every tiny sign of her? From the quiet of the hallway she tunes in to the sounds of his feet crunching over the drive, the bleep of the car unlocking, the soft thud of the car door as he closes it behind him. She stares at the coat rack, her mind racing, until, after a few minutes like this, it strikes her – his car hasn't left the drive. Moving into the living room, she looks out through the netted front windows. He's sitting in the driver's seat, the opened letter in one hand, his lower lip pinched between the forefinger and thumb of the other. Slowly he drops his hand, and raises his face to stare ahead through the windscreen to the street beyond, his body a silhouette against the salmon glow of morning. Laura wants to rush out to him, to prise open the door and ask him, *What is it? Who is it?* But she can't. Her feet are sunk into the plush champagne carpet of their living room, and all she can do is watch as he wearily fixes his seatbelt and disappears through the gate, his face a picture of alarm.

Throughout the day, Laura's thoughts return to Wren and Robert, to the early years they shared together, Laura ever-present as the couple graduated from lovers to partners to husband and wife. She thinks of their wedding day, a strangely subdued affair, overshadowed by the spectre of Wren's mother, by the weight of her absence. It took place in Weybridge register office, with a small gathering of friends and family, and a few of Rob's old schoolfriends thrown in for good measure. Wren had been adamant that she didn't want any of her work friends to attend; it was a private affair, she'd insisted, though she was fine with Rob's guests. Her mother had been in Austria in the run-up to the wedding, helping Siegfried host a conference on corporate efficiency; but *of course*, she told Wren, *yes, darling, I'll do everything in my power to attend*. Laura knew how much Wren was looking forward to seeing her; it had been two years since she had last met up with her, in Rome, and naturally her mother's presence on this special day was important to her. Laura was in charge of making the hotel reservations needed for their few far-flung guests, and she had phoned Wren's mother just two days earlier to pass on the details. It was the first time they had ever spoken, and she was effusive and charming. *She's very posh*, Laura had told Rob afterwards. *She's got a voice like Joan Collins*. Rob had replied that of course she thought she was posh, because Laura was a great big leftie and an inverted snob to boot.

In her characteristically distant fashion, Eliza Adler kept them all thinking she'd be there right up until the day itself, when in her place she sent a telegram, wishing the newlyweds good health and happiness for the years ahead.

'What does Wren have to do, for Christ's sake?' Laura hissed to Rob when she conveyed the news to him as they waited in the antechamber, moments before the ceremony. Dreary daylight filtered in through the high windows, and with the rising heat of the waiting guests the room was growing uncomfortable. 'Man, missing her graduation's bad enough – but her wedding? I've never met the woman, but she sounds like a selfish bitch to me.'

Rob rubbed his chin anxiously, before seeking out Wren to steer her into a quiet corner and deliver the news. Laura stood at a distance, watched Wren's calm façade shift momentarily, the involuntary grasp of her fingers, the fleeting darkness that passed over her face like a shadow. Rob laid a hand on Wren's shoulder; she shook her head, brought her expression back into repose and leant in to kiss him on the lips.

'*Sorry*,' Laura mouthed to her as Wren turned and met her gaze. She opened her arms and Wren abandoned Rob to rush into them, the hem of her simple lace dress bunched up in one hand, a posy of daffodils in the other.

'I'm fine,' she whispered into Laura's neck, her voice low.

Laura stepped back and took her face in her hands, careful not to smudge her wedding make-up. 'Sure?'

'I'm fine. At least your folks are here – and Rob's.'

'Some consolation.' Laura laughed. 'His are boring and mine are nuts. I'll be spending the next few hours worrying about the many ways they might embarrass me before the day's out. I already caught Dad boasting to the registrar that he's Father-of-the-Maid-of-Honour. I think he was angling for a front-row seat.'

Wren accepted Laura's fresh tissue and dabbed the corner of her eye as she scanned the room, deliberately looking past Rob who was standing at the opposite window talking with his parents. They were all pretending not to, but it was obvious they were talking about Wren's absent mother, as their sympathetic eyes moved from each other to her. 'Well, you can tell your dad there's a spare seat going if he wants it.'

'That's the spirit. Now, then – ' Laura lifted her floor-length gown to reveal her Doc Marten boots, tied for the special occasion with daffodil-yellow laces ' – what do you think of these?'

'I think they're perfect,' Wren replied, with a small, sad smile. 'Are you sure I can't marry *you*, Laur?'

They embraced, and Wren clung to her, the pads of her fingers pressed into the curves of Laura's shoulderblades. It was only when the registrar entered the room and announced their ceremony that she finally broke away.

'Love you, Wrenny,' Laura whispered, and she let her go.

After work Rob is evasive about the letter, his mood too light, too jovial. 'It was nothing, Laura, honestly – an old college friend hoping to meet up some time.'

'Which college friend?' she asks as she slices carrots, eyeing him with suspicion.

'Oh, Dominic – he was on my course, so you may not remember him.'

'So are you going to meet him?'

Rob turns away and starts sorting through a bowl of keys on the sideboard, making a pantomime of appearing busy. 'Oh, no. No, we weren't actually that close, so I don't think – '

'I'd love to see it.' Laura carefully lays down the knife, and grips the edge of the counter to steady the tremor that has been building up inside her throughout the day. 'The letter.'

He looks up, startled. 'Oh, sorry. I threw it away when I got to work. The bin men will have taken it by now.'

He's lying. She knows it; he knows she knows it. That evening, they eat a wordless supper beneath the glare of the kitchen light, and later, side by side in their shared bed, they lie motionless, each listening to the other's breath and wondering what on earth to do next. Thoughts of Phoebe and Wren muddle together in Laura's drifting state, digging deep into her anxious sleep, unearthing feelings and memories of an age ago.

They waited so long before starting a family – eight years – that Laura wondered if Rob and Wren would ever get on with it at all. It seemed there was never a good time, when you were constantly studying as Rob was, feathering your nest, securing your future. Saving up for a rainy day. Eventually, however, practicality won out, when Wren convinced him it was a good idea to start trying, in case it turned out that he had a low sperm count or something similar. Laura howled with laughter when Wren recounted the conversation over a pub lunch the next day, explaining in great visual detail the look of terror that had crossed Rob's face at the suggestion.

'He virtually ravished me on the spot,' she said, reaching across the table to pinch one of Laura's chips. 'So now we'll just have to wait and see if we can make it happen!'

Twelve months later, Phoebe was born, and Laura loved her instantly. When Rob phoned to tell her that the baby was on its way, Laura hurriedly packed her overnight bag and drove straight down, to fuss around in their big, comfy house, cleaning sinks and hobs late into the night while anxiously waiting for news from the hospital.

At just after six the following morning, Rob called. 'It's a girl!' he told her, the joy in his voice streaming through the telephone line and into Laura. 'She's beautiful, Laur. You've got to come straight away – Wren's asking for you.'

In the hospital, Wren had been taken off the main ward, as the birth, a ventouse, had been long and protracted, leaving her bruised and exhausted. The intervention had terrified them both, and for a short while, before she'd appeared, safe and sound, there had been fears that the infant was in distress. 'We're quiet at the moment,' the midwife had told Robert as they wheeled Wren's bed into the private room. 'We'll have to move her out if we get any high-priority cases in the night – but fingers crossed she'll get a good night's sleep in here.'

As soon as visiting hours permitted, Laura burst through the doors with grapes, chocolates, magazines and flowers. 'Where is she, then?' she asked Wren, as she threw her arms around Robert. 'Where's my honorary niece? I take it I'm to be Auntie Laura?' She released Robert and bounced on the edge of the bed, clutching Wren's hand.

A pale Wren, shrouded in white sheets and gown, weakly pointed to a Perspex crib at the foot of the bed, and Laura gasped, bringing her hand to cover her mouth. 'I'm sorry, little one! I didn't even see you there. Noisy Auntie Laura, coming in here and making all this fuss!' She brushed her fingertips across the baby's smooth crown, marvelling at the soft wrinkling of her stirring brow. She turned to Robert and Wren, almost mute with wonder. 'Aren't you just *completely* in love with her?' she asked.

'Completely,' they replied, as one voice.

By Friday morning they've barely exchanged a word. Rob has retreated so far into himself that he can't seem to climb out, and Laura has become increasingly preoccupied by Phoebe. She continues to behave as if everything's just fine, chatting about her college plans and making lists of the things she'll need before she starts her taster course in April. By April it will all be too late, Laura thinks, watching her goddaughter stretch and yawn in the kitchen doorway, her pyjama top lifting just enough to reveal the soft alteration in her waistline. Phoebe catches her looking and tugs at her top, stooping to kiss her dad on the cheek. Lazily she slides the phone handset on to the counter beside Laura, having just hung up from one of her friends.

'Hannah,' she says. 'She hates her uni course too. She's thinking of switching.'

Laura holds up a slice of bread. 'Toast?'

'OK,' Phoebe replies, and she drops into a seat at the table and rests her head on her folded arms. 'God, I'm knackered.'

Rob ruffles her hair. 'It'll be all that hard work you've been doing, Phoebs. You know, lying around on your bed, listening to Radio One. You must be shattered.' He throws a smile at Laura, momentarily forgetting their stand-off.

Beside her, the phone rings and Laura nearly shrieks with the shock of it, her hand shooting out to grab the handset on the second ring. She lifts it to her ear, her eyes never leaving Robert's, and somehow they both know it's a call of significance.

'Hello?' she murmurs into the mouthpiece.

The sounds on the other end of the phone are those of a roadside, somewhere like a motorway service station; after a brief delay, the caller speaks. 'Hello? Laura? It's Mike Woods here – from the newspaper.'

Laura? 'How did you get my name?' she asks, his brazen overfamiliarity stoking anger in her.

'Oh, the electoral roll. But that's not important – listen, Laura, I've got some news for you – well, more for Mr Irving, I suppose. Is he there?'

Laura taps her fingernail on the worktop, glancing up to see Rob and Phoebe studying her intensely. '*Who is it?*' Rob mouths at her.

'No, so you'll have to tell me.'

'OK – well, I'm not sure how you're going to feel about this – but we've found her.'

Laura can feel her blood pressure plummeting, the heat rushing out through her fingertips. She feels the expectant energy coursing off Rob and Phoebe as they stare at her still, their expressions demanding further explanation. 'I don't think I want to – '

'We've found *Wren*, Laura – we've found Wren Irving, and if you stay on the line, please, I've got an address that I'm happy to pass on to you. Have you got a pen handy?'

Outside, the rain starts to fall, hammering against the French doors in a harsh gust of wind. Laura's hand scrabbles along the sides of the dresser for an old envelope; it's carelessly torn open at the top, and with an irrational lurch Laura regrets that such a tatty scrap will be used for this purpose. *Wren deserves better*, she thinks, and she reaches for a pen, turning away from Rob and Phoebe, so that she's leaning on the counter beside the sink. 'Go on, then,' she says, and she begins to write down the address, one line after another. She stares at the letters she has just set down, for a moment forgetting the caller at the other end of the phone.

'So perhaps I could ask you for a statement, Laura?' Mike Woods' voice interrupts her thoughts. 'How do you feel now that you know Wren Irving's whereabouts? Do you think your long-term partner will be looking to claim half of his wife's Lottery fortune? It was only just over half a million, but still, if there's anything left of it he'll have a legitimate claim, particularly having brought up their child on his own.'

Laura slams the phone down on the counter with a hard plastic clatter. *They've found her; they've found Wren.* Envelope clutched in her hand, she presses her fist into her chest, feeling her ribcage rise and fall. She knows she has to turn back to face Rob and Phoebe, to give them some kind of account of what's just happened, of what's been said.

With a deep breath, she turns, her eyes darting from one to the other, alarm flooding her veins.

'Laura?'

She can't tell Phoebe yet – or Rob for that matter; she can't alert them to Wren's resurfacing until she's spoken to her first. If Wren chose to disappear so completely all those years ago, there's no way they can turn up mob-handed now, expecting to be welcomed back in. Wren might simply run again. Laura knows she has to do this quietly, alone. Decided, she finds her voice.

'I've got to go away for a few days,' she says.

Rob opens his mouth to speak, but she cuts him off.

'Please don't ask me where I'm going, Rob. I'll call you, I promise – I'll explain everything. But, for now, I just have to do this on my own.'

WREN

Wren turns the collar of her coat up against the chill morning as she takes in the newspaper headline, an anxious knot forming in the well of her stomach. On her daily walks she rarely looks at the news-stand – makes a point of avoiding it, averting her eyes from the misery and despair that goes on out there, beyond the bay, the world beyond her world. There's rarely peace to be found in those headlines. Yet, today, the letters jump out at her, and without realising it she is looking, absorbing the words like ink on a blotter before she has the sense to turn away.

NATIONAL LOTTERY CELEBRATES TWENTY YEARS

Two decades. A lifetime, for some. She stares at the stand a while longer, as Arthur prepares her coffee and rummages in the rusty cashbox for change. In one swift movement she snatches up a copy of the newspaper and tucks it under her arm. 'I'll take one of these, too,' she says curtly, feeling the flush rise from her neck as she runs a hand through her cropped hair and tries to avoid Arthur's searching gaze.

Arthur recalculates her change and presses it into her knitted palm. 'That's a first,' he says, folding his arms and leaning into the counter of the kiosk. 'Thought you didn't care for the news?'

Wren shakes her head impatiently as she pockets her change, and heads off towards the bay with Willow and

Badger bounding close behind, her red mussel bucket swinging from one hand.

'Have a good walk!' Arthur calls after her, and she looks back to see him leaning out across the news-stand, his fleece-clad arm held high in the biting November air. His smile spreads across his face in a map of weather-worn creases. 'Stay warm!'

Once on the beach the dogs run ahead, arcing across the vast expanse of virgin sand, their tiny dachshund legs working double-time as they yap and bound in the shallow waters. They know the routine and lead the way, stopping every once in a while to turn and check, to make sure their pack leader is still in sight. Wren's eyes move steadily across the sun-dappled waters of the bay, glancing back in the direction of the youth hostel and Arthur's hut, where a cluster of disappointed surfers stands at the beachside, clutching their boards as they survey the flat tide. Badger comes to a stop at her feet, raising one paw and patting the scuffed toes of her walking boots. She feels around in her coat pocket and brings out a morsel of chicken to pop in his soft chocolate muzzle, holding up another piece for Willow to see. In a dappled blur the dog races to join them, kicking up fans of wet sand and spray in her rush for the reward. 'Good dogs,' Wren says, stooping to scratch each under the chin. She pats their rears and sends them crazing off along the beach ahead of her.

At the rocks, Wren clambers up to the highest pool and sits cross-legged at its edge peering into the deep waters, running her fingertips along the dense covering of mussels that cling to the sides. She slides the newspaper beneath her as an extra layer against the cold, damp stone, feeling angry at herself for having bought it in the first place. Perhaps she'll just drop it in Arthur's bin on the way back up from the beach, save her taking it home at all. From up here, she has a good view of the horizon, where she sees a small red yacht moving through the water, heading out of sight towards Constantine Bay or Padstow. If she were to stand tall and look back beyond the sandblown path she walked in on, she would just about make out the faded blue eaves of her own cottage, beyond the rough meadow where the skylarks and swallows fly in springtime. Today, she longs for the gentle warmth of the spring, for the optimistic green shoots of April, the unfurling blooms of May. Up here on the rocks she is cold to her core, restless and afraid; it's an unwelcome shift in mood, provoked by that headline, she knows, and she curses herself for being taken in by it, for allowing its destructive force access to her placid inner world.

She takes out her bird glasses and brings them into focus, scanning the line of the sea from right to left. Further out, a lone bird makes its way inland. It flies with rapid, shallow wing-beats, skimming and turning like an overgrown swallow before it plunge-dives into the water, returning to the air moments later. Reaching inside her parka, Wren brings out a notebook and stub of pencil. *Balearic shearwater*, she writes on a fresh page, the letters of her brisk scrawl running together. *19 November 1994*. She studies the page, her heart contracting as she realises her mistake, and she fumbles with the little pencil, angrily crossing out the year and replacing it with *2014. Fool*, she thinks. She pushes the notebook and pencil back inside her jacket as Badger and Willow scrabble up the rocks to join her. They nose in beneath the warmth of her elbows, one on either side, resting their paws on the V of her thighs. Wren scoops them closer and swipes away the worthless tears that have leaked on to her face. *Fool*.

She stares out across the bay, focusing hard enough to hold herself down in the here and now, where the past is nothing more than a faded dream.

When she'd first seen the cottage twenty years earlier, Wren had known she'd found her place. They'd waded through the waist-high grasses at the rear of the property, pushing aside brambles and easing open the broken wooden gate, the estate agent apologising even as she slotted the key into the door and warned Wren to watch the step. *Tegh*, the house name read, etched into an ancient slab of slate and set into its flinty exterior.

The cottage was small, and seemingly un-lived-in for years; as they passed through its low-ceilinged rooms, dust motes billowed and fell, illuminated like ghosts by the slices of white November sun that coursed in through the flaking panelled windows. There was nothing remarkable about the cottage itself, and it was clear to see that it was run-down and lacked any homely comforts. But something in its smallness spoke to Wren, and her heart soared.

'God, I'm so sorry about this – I don't think anyone's been here for months.' Jenny, the estate agent, held the key fob gingerly between finger and thumb, her little nose wrinkled in regret. 'It's not even one of my properties. But we've had a few issues at the office – anyway, here we are!'

Wren's gaze moved about the place, slowly taking in its foundations: every crack, every plaster bubble, every creaking floorboard. It was imperfect, yet the floor beneath her boots felt stable, rooted to the landscape, anchored in time. She could make it work. She had money, more than enough to buy this place, to make it habitable – more than enough to secure its walls and fold herself within. The Lottery win hadn't been large enough to live like a queen, but already she had seen an accountant and calculated that she could make it last if she was careful – if she lived a simple life, with little expense. The solicitor she'd met a few days earlier had set the first formal alterations of her life into motion: a new surname and bank accounts, and an official letter to Robert, informing him that she wouldn't be returning home. Wren had at first rejected that idea, thinking that a communication so final was somehow cruel, but Mr Jarvis had been adamant. 'The last thing you want is your husband filing a missing person's report, Mrs Irving – it could mean a police investigation. Your best option is a letter from me on your behalf, via a central London postal address, simply stating your desire to remain undisturbed and relinquishing any financial claims on your marital estate. It really is the safest option if you're planning to make a fresh start like this.'

A fresh start.

Wren ran her hand along a dark, fractured beam, scoring its lines with the square nail of her forefinger, pressing her brow to the wood, and inhaling its salty history. The sharp tang of age was bloodlike, primal and raw; like the sun-drenched barns of her childhood, like the solitary sphere of childbirth. She exhaled, long and slow, paralysed in the past.

Jenny cleared her throat and waggled the key, awkward in her youth. 'So! Any questions? There's not much to show you, really, with it being so small. But, as you can see, this is the living room-slash-dining-room, and this – ' she turned the handle of a door that Wren supposed led to a cupboard ' – must be the bedroom.' It was big enough for a bed, a double at a push, and perhaps a chest of drawers, but not much more. 'Is it just you?' Jenny asked, hopefully. 'No family? I mean, you couldn't fit a family in here! Not without an extension – which might be possible…'

Wren found she couldn't answer; found herself gazing at Jenny, her eyes fixed on the girl's finely pencilled brows, wondering what her story was, what the future held in store for her. She was only a few years younger than Wren, yet the differences between them were endless.

Jenny grimaced a further apology. 'I'm sure this isn't what you're looking for,' she said, though it sounded like a question. She turned the property papers over in her hands. 'Of course there *is* still the garden – I haven't shown you the garden yet! It's quite a selling point, so the details say. Shall we…?'

She led the way through to a simple kitchen at the rear, the tap of her heels echoing harshly within the walls of the gentle cottage. Wren followed as Jenny drew the bolt and eased open the swollen back door, peeling away the salt-dried ivy that had crept over the lintel and up through the hinges. She stepped out, stood aside and allowed Wren to pass through the door and into the jagged, bright light of outdoors.

The land to the rear of the cottage was no more than pasture, gnarly and overgrown, running downhill a few hundred yards to meet the thick gorse bush that surrounded the property, pinning it in, holding it fast against this secluded stretch of coastal path. The garden was perfect, or at least it could be with some attention and time. But it was the view that stopped Wren's breath. Beyond the grassy decline of her lawn the landscape opened out into a panorama of vast sky, rocky headland and undulating tide, and she halted, giddy, wondering if this might be a dream, she felt so strongly that she'd been here some other time, in some other life.

Wren

As a soaring line of migrating birds shadowed the sky overhead, Wren knew she had found her place.

Storm clouds have gathered over the bay, and Wren makes her way back home with Badger and Willow, pulling her raincoat closer still against the rising wind. She jogs across the meadow, following the flattened footpath that she and the dogs have carved out over the years. The long grasses swirl and sway like a tide, one moment rippling high and light, the next lying flat and beaten against the salted earth. The dogs love this weather and run ahead with ears trailing, weaving in and out of the path to chase and snap at the surging meadow. At this time of year Wren has the place to herself, during those precious few months between the summer and Christmas, when the holiday-homers cease to congregate in their comfortable cottages that overlook the coastline and bays of North Cornwall. They come, they go. For a while, they pretend to live real lives in London or wherever they belong, before flocking to the coast to do the same here. Like migrating birds, hard-wired to seek a warmer, safer clime. *Do they ever find it?* she wonders. Wren lives for the silences, for the absence of voice, and has unconsciously constructed a life of few words, of few sounds other than those created by nature.

As the dogs near the edge of the meadow she reaches into her pocket and pulls out her whistle, blowing it silently into the turbulent air. They stop, alert, their little heads raised to attention, and they wait for her beside the stile, until she reaches them and rewards them with another treat.

The meadow adjoins the garden, which these days is given over to a large vegetable patch on one side, bird-feeders and shade on the other. The ground is freshly dug over, the job completed just last week as Wren began her preparations for the seasons ahead. She had hoped to spend more time preparing the ground today, thinking about the turn of the weather and the crops she hopes to grow, but she finds she is distracted, thrown off course. She unlocks the back door, holding it open to let the dogs enter. Flinging the newspaper at the kitchen table, she pushes the door shut with the heel of her hand and empties the contents of the mussel bucket into the sink for cleaning. 'Damn newspaper,' she murmurs, furious at herself.

Badger and Willow pad back across the room to stand at her feet and gaze up expectantly, their stem-thin tails swishing against the tiles. They know that she saves her few words for mealtimes and walks and so they think something good is about to happen. Their limpid eyes prick her with guilt, and, despite its being several hours until their supper is due, she reaches into the cupboard for their bowls. 'Hungry?' she whispers, and the dogs whine happily, dropping to a lying position as she puts down a fresh bowl of water and spoons out an unexpected lunch.

The next morning, Wren rises early after a troubled sleep and sets off with the dogs at dawn, walking down to the shore as daylight gradually fills the sky. Her mind hovers around the dreams of the night before – not so much dreams as sensations, anxieties breaking through her slumber, playing tricks in the moonlight. She dreamt there was a newborn in the bed beside her, nestled naked and warm against the heat of her curled body. She'd known it was there even before she woke, the soft rise and fall of the baby's breath moving in time with her own; she couldn't remember the birth, or how she had come to be pregnant, but she knew the child was hers and that she must keep her close, protect her at all costs. Time must have passed – how much, it was impossible to tell – when she was woken by the sound of the child hitting the floorboards with a dense thud. Wren had gasped – leapt from the bed, sweat-soaked, to retrieve the baby, panic coursing through her veins. Flailing around in the darkness, her hands had fallen upon the baby – not a baby at all, but Badger, sleeping on his pile of blankets at her bedside. Distraught, Wren had turned on the lights of the bedroom and rushed from room to room switching on every overhead light, every lamp, pulling closed any curtains that stood open. She'd sat at the kitchen table and sobbed herself dry. When Willow trotted in, her ears cocked in question, Wren got up and wiped her face, stooping to fetch the small dog into her arms. Eventually they'd settled on the sofa, the bedroom now inhabited by the phantom of her dreams, and dozed in each other's warmth until sunrise.

It's mild for November and the pink horizon shimmers beyond the barnacled rocks and pools of the bay, the peace only broken by the cries of gulls feeding some way out. Waders cast shadows along the wet shoreline, a colony of industrious migrants, digging deep for lugworms and rag. Wren doesn't wear a watch, having never replaced the dead battery in her old one. That, along with countless other personal effects from her life before, now languishes at the bottom of an old wooden trunk she stores in the back room alongside welly boots and garden spades and industrial bags of bird feed. The watch had cost Robert a small fortune, a gift for their first wedding anniversary; Wren is sure he would be sad to see it cast aside like a cheap trinket. She pauses to rest against a rock, vertigo rising through her limbs as she allows herself to think his name for the first time in years.

The dogs stop on the sand ahead, waiting for her indication that they can run on. They tilt their heads in opposite directions like small mirror images, their sturdy little bodies casting long, thin shadows along the beach, their tails standing stiff like car aerials. Wren closes her eyes and takes purposeful breaths, in, out, in, out, until her pulse rate decreases and she has the strength to carry on. Damned newspaper, damned Lottery. *Damned newspaper, damned Lottery.* She incants the phrase in her mind, the rhythm of it helping her along, helping her to regain her pace, her stability. By the time they reach the entrance to the car park, the beach community is starting to arrive in board-strapped camper vans and pick-ups, and Arthur's kiosk is open for business. The dogs bound ahead for their daily visit, arriving at his side just as he reaches below his counter for the dog biscuits he stores there. He leans across the newspapers, feeding a biscuit into each eager muzzle, simultaneously picking up a cardboard cup for Wren's coffee.

'Red sky in the morning – what d'you think? Shepherds' warning? Are we in for some rain?'

Wren feels around in her pocket for coffee money, surveying the skyline, her anxiety slowly subsiding in Arthur's warm presence, melting down through her boots and out across the sand. She counts coins into her gloved hand, handing Arthur the right change as he pours milk into the cardboard cup and snaps on a plastic lid. 'Could be.'

He drops the cash into his money tin. 'No newspaper today, Wren?'

Wren starts to walk away. 'One's enough, thank you. None of it's good news, from what I can see.'

'Too true, too true.' Arthur laughs. 'But you might want to look at last Sunday's, love.'

Wren stops on the path, turning back to face him. He stands behind his counter, wrapped in his coat and hat and scarf, a newspaper held aloft in his fingerless-gloved hand.

'Why's that?' Wren asks, barely a whisper.

Arthur smiles, kindly, his words hesitant. 'Well, I might be wrong. But it's an unusual name – Wren – isn't it?' He drops the tabloid newspaper to the counter and flicks through the pages, stopping on page five, which is dominated by a series of photographs, of seven faces. His finger comes down on the last one. 'Only saw this last night, when I was sorting the recycling. There we go. *Wren Irving*. Now I know your name's not Irving, but – well, if push came to shove, I'd say that one looks more than a bit like you.'

Gingerly, Wren takes a step forward to look at the picture. There's no doubt about it. It's her.

The moment her numbers came up, Wren knew she would tell no one. She had no way of guessing how much her fortune might be, or whether it would be enough. For almost an hour she sat motionless on the sofa, the baby slumbering in her arms, post-feed. Her imagination travelled over the possibilities, stumbling across the fog of her mind, a strange, shameful excitement growing in the pit of her stomach. Somehow the sounds of the house had grown magnified: the click of the boiler, the distant narrative of the kitchen radio, Robert's footsteps treading softly, barefoot between bedroom and bathroom overhead. He'd be going out soon, for his Saturday night pint at the Fleece. He'd be gone just for one hour, long enough for Wren to put the little one to bed, to make that phone call and claim her prize. Would they protect her identity? She was sure they would, certain there must be rules about anonymity if it was requested, if people didn't want their friends, neighbours – husbands – to know. Pushing it down, inwardly shaking with the repressed energy of her secret, she remained on the sofa, motionless, until Robert returned from his shower, fresh and revived.

'I won't be long,' he said, kissing Wren on the top of her head as he slid his arms into his heavy woollen coat. 'We can watch that film later, if you're still awake?'

Wren lingered in that position long after Robert had closed the front door, long after she'd heard his footsteps crunching over the gravel, listened to the squeak and clang of the low iron gate as he pulled it closed behind him. The baby didn't stir; nor did Wren. Despite her frozen exterior she could feel herself unfurling, as new thoughts and possibilities presented themselves, eclipsing the uselessness and apathy that invaded her every waking moment, chasing into the recesses of her mind her puzzled detachment, the sense of nothing being real. Her subconscious was awakening, planning, plotting another way, and the greater the anticipation, the calmer her exterior grew. And, when Robert returned from the pub, there they were, his beloved wife and child, sitting in the living room exactly where he had left them. Robert carried the baby to her crib and Wren slotted a film into the video player, pouring her husband a glass of red wine and returning to the warm spot on the sofa where she had been sitting all evening. *Tomorrow*, she thought. *Tomorrow I'll make the call*.

Back in the safety of her small kitchen, Wren spreads the newspaper across the table. She pulls out a chair and sits, turning the pages until she stops on one headed '*Where Are They Now? Britain's First Lottery Winners*'. There's an introduction saying that this coming week sees the twentieth anniversary of the first National Lottery, and then a small paragraph of detail given for each of the seven jackpot winners, along with two rows of photographs, the top ones taken around the time of the win in 1994, the bottom ones showing a more recent update. Under Wren's section there's only one picture, a tiny cropped image taken from one of her wedding photographs – and, below it, a blank silhouette with a question mark for a face.

She's not the only one who hasn't been found – in fact there are two others – but that doesn't reassure her in any way. She shouldn't be there in the first place, having asserted her anonymity from the outset, having protected herself so entirely from this type of exposure. Bringing her hand to her mouth, she braces herself to read the column beneath her image, the fear in her swelling and surging at the reality of her situation.

Wren Irving, now aged 50, is believed to be the seventh of the original Lottery winners. At the time of her win she was living in south London with her husband Robert Irving, a history teacher, and their six-month-old daughter. A National Lottery insider gives us reason to believe that after claiming her jackpot prize Mrs Irving elected to keep her identity a secret before vacating the family home, leaving no forwarding address. Though estranged, the couple are still married; however, Mr Irving was unavailable to comment on his wife's good fortune. If anyone has information regarding Mrs Irving's current whereabouts, we'd like to hear from you.

An insider. A secretary, an administrator, an employee with an axe to grind? Could have been anyone, it's not even important; the fact is, it's out there now. Wren's blood runs cold as she wonders where the photograph came from. Did Robert provide it, or her mother, or Laura perhaps? Wren's eyes fall on the line appealing for information and her breath catches in her throat, as she realises these people must have been in contact with the family, digging around for information. It's an idea she can hardly bear to contemplate.

She pushes her chair back from the table, fills the kettle at the sink, and gazes from the window across the lawn. Far out beyond the meadow, out, out on to the horizon, the waves are now tumbling, broiling and casting the tiny figures of surfers up and over the sea's surface. Memories flood her thoughts, words and images of a distant land, alarming in their precision, crushing in their impact.

It was Laura she saw first, holding up the lunch queue in the college refectory, standing alongside a straight-backed young man who was trying to hurry her along. Laura's dark red hair hung loose in thick, rich tendrils reaching the small of her back, where her black vest was tucked into baggy army surplus shorts, nipped in by a thick leather belt. She was tiny; a perfectly formed little woman, with lean, tanned legs ending in battered Doc Marten boots, a tatty friendship bracelet snaking around her wrist as her hand dithered between dishes. The young man beside her was Robert; he turned to her as she slid her tray along the counter to join the queue, mouthing a *sorry* and making *hurry up* eyes at his friend. Wren assumed they were an item – or perhaps even siblings – judging from the way he pressed his soft fist against her upper arm, urging her along, laughing at her indecision, whispering joke insults to the back of her head.

'The curry's quite good,' Wren offered, leaning around Robert to meet Laura's green eyes.

Laura returned a wide, surprised nod and her smooth face crinkled into a smile. 'Then I'll have the curry,' she told the canteen lady, and the queue moved on as the pair made their way to the till, leaving Wren at the counter, ordering the same.

Wren paid, picked up her own tray and surveyed the room, searching for a quiet seat where she might eat alone. She'd only moved into halls a few days earlier, so she knew no one and struggled with the self-conscious ritual of lone dining, the toe-curling ceremony of lifting fork to mouth while avoiding eye contact with all the other awkward diners. A window seat was always a good option, she had found, and a book. But then, as she scanned the tables that looked out on to the courtyard, Laura and Robert raised their hands, beckoning her over like an old friend. She hesitated, uncertain if it was her they meant. Laura pointed to the seat opposite.

'We don't know *anyone*,' the red-haired girl confided as Wren placed her tray on the table, sweeping the crumbs of a previous diner from her seat. Her eyes sparkled with mischief. 'Will you be in our gang?'

Robert's hand shot across the table, to shake Wren's enthusiastically. He wore a chambray shirt of the type her father favoured, and neatly ironed pale blue jeans, and his gentle charm was infectious. 'Ignore her.' He smiled. 'She's still overexcited about leaving home. You'd think Kingston-on-Thames was the other side of the world from home, not thirty miles away. I'm Robert, by the way – did I say that? And this is Laura.'

Flight

Laura leant over the steaming plates of food to embrace Wren in a shoulder-hug. Casting a long-suffering glance at Robert, she coiled her locks into a single thick rope and threw it aside as she retook her seat. 'Actually, you should ignore *him*. He's an old man before his time. Thank God he's got me to lead him astray!'

He was such a good man. Wren's anxiety claws beneath her ribs as she paces the tiny cottage, trying to organise the jumble of words and memories that in such a short space of time have infiltrated her peaceful world. Badger and Willow are unnerved too; they move from sofa to armchair, from kitchen to bedroom, keeping Wren within their sights, a little whimper escaping Badger every time she moves out of view. It's gone midnight and nothing is done; the house stands still. Wren has spent years cultivating a soothing routine that works for her, one that fits with the rhythms of the seasons, for the motions of her mind. But now this – this hideous intrusion, this rupture that threatens to break her peace apart... On this clear, cold night Wren can see far out across the water, out to where the night fishing boats bob and blink, to where the seals bask, as dolphins slice through the icy waters. This is her whole world, and today it has been blown asunder. For the first time in all these years, Wren pulls the blinds to the kitchen windows, and shuts out the sea.

During her afternoon walk, Wren is met on the coastal path by a young man wearing ridiculous shoes. His pointed toes shine brightly in the autumn light, below too-narrow trousers and a cliché of a business coat. He must be all of twenty-two, a polished boy in the guise of a man.

'Wren Irving?' he asks, as he approaches. He smiles broadly, displaying straight white teeth and a trusting face.

Wren gives Badger's lead a little tug, a signal for him to growl at the stranger. 'No,' she replies, and she continues walking, with Badger casting warning snarls back along the path. She studies the light of the sky – it must be an hour later than her usual time. How could anyone know she's here? It's been so long, and she covered her trail so well; *no one* could know she was here.

'Mrs Irving? Listen, I know you didn't want your Lottery win advertised, but now it's out there – you might as well share your side of the story. You're one of the original seven – it's something to be celebrated!'

She halts, her back resolutely against him. 'Who are you?' she shouts into the breeze, her voice emerging harsh, and older than she remembers.

'Mike Woods, freelance journalist.' Wren looks back to see him reach inside his jacket pocket and wave a business card in the air, as if that solves everything. 'I'm just interested in giving your version of events – there's bound to be public interest.'

Wren lowers her head and walks on, her heart pounding, willing the journalist to vanish with every watched step she takes. At the car park, Arthur's wave turns into a beckoning motion as she sets course to bypass him, and he calls her over, whistling for the dogs, not taking the cue from her studied stance of avoidance. Badger and Willow decide for her, bounding ahead, and with heavy feet she turns about, following in the kicked-up trail of the dogs to join them at the kiosk.

'You look terrible,' he says, as he pours her a tea. The dogs paw at the side of Arthur's counter, demanding their treats.

'I didn't sleep too well.'

Arthur snaps a lid on the cardboard cup and hands it to her. 'So what did the city boy want?' He tips his head towards the journalist, who now stands watching from the brow of the path, his ugly shoes obscured by billowing sea grass.

Wren sighs, feeling her breath shudder as she exhales. 'My *story*.'

'And is that something you want to tell?' Arthur hugs himself, patting his upper arms with gloved hands, his breath white in the crisp air.

She pulls her collar up around her neck, tugs her hat lower, and looks out across the water to where the gulls dip and dive. The tears spring to her eyes before she can stop them, and she holds her gaze on the shore, clicking her fingers for the dogs to come. 'I can't, Arthur. It's not my story to give. The picture of me in the paper yesterday – I don't even know that woman any more.'

Wren was always the sensible one, level-headed in a crisis, reliable and focused where others around her would crumble. From the very first time they met, Laura's fierce feminism enlivened her, as she'd sit and listen to her peppering the air with a whole new language, waving her cigarette smoke in theatrical whirls and challenging Wren's adolescent viewpoint with her own developing ideologies. At home, Wren had never had to fight her corner when it came to being or becoming a young woman; her father had been curiously brusque on the issue of women's careers and education. 'You've got a brain,' he'd told her when, at twelve, she first expressed an interest in teaching. 'Why not? Your mother – she could've done anything she wanted with a brilliant mind like that. She was top of her class at university when we met – a far better scholar than me.'

'But she doesn't do anything now,' Wren had replied, the enormity of the future rising up around her. 'She just looks after us. And the house.'

'And very nobly she does so. The point is, she *could* have done anything. She had *choices*. The world is out there for you to explore, Little Wren. I hope you'll exercise your choices sufficiently.'

At times like these, from the youngest age, the idea of the future crashed in on Wren, so that she felt the way she did in those dreams where she was running and arriving nowhere. She would observe her parents and their friends, listening in on their dinner party chatter from the top step of the stairs or dawdling in the hallway beyond the dining room. Between the clink and scrape of cutlery on china, the earnest talk and jovial laughter could set her ill at ease for days: talk of joblessness, the starving millions, poor Sophie Hopkins who'd lost another child. *How do you lose a child?* she would fretfully wonder. *Are the people starving because there are no jobs?* Low voices and concern over Jill and Tom Springfield, who were absent tonight – *going through a divorce* – and Wendy-Anne Charlton from her class, recently removed from school because of *concerns at home*. Met Office fears for the rise in the tide table – the plight of the dolphins – the fence at the back of the house that was *sure to blow straight through the patio doors if we get another storm like the one last week*. Each of these things, filtering into Wren's young consciousness, were in themselves manageable, if somewhat bleak. But it was the creeping accumulation of her fears which could, at times of uncertainty and fatigue, reach out to grab at her ankles and send her scurrying to her room in a fog of terror. There she would fashion her pillows and blankets to form a small, dark cave, into which she'd crawl, surrounding herself with the reassuring company of her careworn bears and Raggedy Ann. At best she would slip into fitful sleep, before Dad stopped by to kiss her goodnight and straighten her bed sheets; at worst, she would remain there awake for hours, wishing herself rather dead than alive and responsible in some way for the ever-shifting state of the world.

She spoke once of these terrors with Laura, many years after they had first manifested themselves at the age of nine, on a night in January when a gin-loaded pal of her parents' crashed his car on the way out of the drive. Wren had seen the whole thing from the landing window, where, fuelled by the disquieting stories the grown-ups had been sharing over dessert, she had gradually convinced herself that according to the law of averages at least one of her parents was likely to die prematurely. The friend was fine, no more than a small bump and a bruised ego, but that made no difference to Wren: it could have been a lot worse.

'Does the future frighten you?' she asked Laura, who was sitting, her legs stretched out across Wren's, at the other end of their futon in Victoria Terrace, the student digs they had moved into at the start of their second year.

Laura leant out, her hand feeling around the carpet for her cigarette packet. She passed one to Wren and flipped open her lighter, drawing deep to ignite her own cigarette before passing it along. 'In what way?'

'I don't know – jobs, children, nuclear war. Breast cancer. Loneliness – anything.'

Laura rubbed the thumb of her cigarette hand along her jawline. 'Hmm. Yes and no, I guess. I mean, the world's pretty much one great shitty melting pot of evil and disaster, but I can't say it keeps me awake at night.'

'But when you think about all those world disasters – people starving in Cambodia or animal testing or all those poor men burnt to death in the Falklands – doesn't it scare you, that you can't do anything about it? That it'll all be a hundred times worse when our kids are our age?'

Laura drew deeply on her cigarette, blowing three perfect smoke rings into the space between them. 'Well, I've already decided I'm not getting married or having kids, so that's one less thing to worry about, I suppose. *Of course* that stuff bothers me. But why get all angsty about these things, that's what I say. If you care enough about something, you should *do* something about it. It's mad to give yourself a coronary worrying about things you have no influence over.'

'Yes, but how *do* you "do something about it"? When you're just nobody from nowhere, with no voice.'

'Everyone's got a voice, Wren,' Laura said, with a face that told her she was shocked by Wren's naivety. She ground her cigarette into the ashtray on the floor and pulled her chin in. 'You do believe that, don't you? *Everyone's* got a voice.'

The sky is already growing dark when Wren arrives back at Tegh Cottage. She stands for a moment in the dimming light, looking back along the meadow path, down towards the beach and the caves beyond. The dogs run on, to wait patiently at the threshold of the house until Wren crosses the garden and lets them in. Inside, she drops her keys on the side and enters the back room to ease off her boots and hang up her coat. The wooden trunk sits under the coat rack, almost entirely hidden by buckets and trowels, and sacks of birdfeed. Grasping a metal handle at one end, she drags it out, pushing the various obstacles aside and lowering herself to the stone floor as she unlatches the catch to ease open the heavy pine lid. Willow and Badger stand in the doorway, looking concerned; by this point she'd normally have reached the kitchen to hand them their treats.

'*Shoo*,' she whispers, and they turn, dejected, and trot over to their blankets on the sofa.

Inside the wooden box are many of the things she brought with her when she first arrived at the cottage, things she'd thought she'd need, but then found she could do without. A large leather handbag containing the trivia of a past age: a cosmetic bag stuffed with expensive make-up; a red leather Filofax; a dried-up packet of baby wipes; a Clarins hand cream and a pair of tweezers. Wren flings the bag to one side, planning to dispose of it later. One whole side of the trunk is taken up with clothes she had brought away with her, and she lifts them out now, one by one, marvelling at the stark contrast between them and the small capsule wardrobe of earthy garments she wears today. She's no heavier now than she was twenty years ago, but she could no more wear these clothes in this life than run on the beach naked at low tide. The materials are exquisite – silks, cashmeres, angoras – and the fit of each is feminine and sensual. She holds up a burnt orange blouse, shimmering and sheer, with a draping neck tie at the chest, and without a pause she recalls the day she bought it. It was a bright Saturday afternoon, and Robert was back at home working on his PhD proposal, some months before they would discover the news that they were expecting a child. Wren had phoned Laura to see if she could meet up, but, as had become increasingly the case, Laura was elsewhere, doing other things, and so Wren had headed up west alone. From across the road in New Bond Street she'd spotted the orange shirt in the window of Fenwick's, at the heart of an autumn display ablaze with colour and hope. In what seemed like moments later she was at the counter of the ladies' department, handing over her credit card and running her thumb over the thick handle of a green carrier bag. Now, Wren holds the blouse up, smoothing the silk fabric against her torso, wondering if she might wear it some time again, perhaps in the spring?

'Ha!' she scoffs, embarrassed by her folly, and slings the orange shirt on top of the handbag and the growing junk pile. Standing abruptly, she slams shut the lid of the wooden trunk and sets off to the kitchen to fix the dogs their supper.

Rob was by nature awkward around girls – *overly courteous*, Wren and Laura would often tell him. If he liked someone, he found it almost impossible to let them know, being inclined to avert his gaze almost entirely, snatching furtive glances only when he thought their attention was diverted. Wren knew this to be the case; she was for the most part the object of his glances, and she did her best to hide her awareness of this fact. By the time they had been living together in Victoria Terrace for several months Laura had already tried and failed countless times to set him up with college friends of hers, and she and Wren had been all but ready to give up on the mission and leave him to work it out for himself.

In June, as the second year at college came to an end, Laura talked Wren and Rob into travelling with her to Stonehenge for the midsummer festival, promising them it would be a trip to remember. 'Be there or be square,' she warned Rob, prodding the two fingertips of her peace sign against his chest. 'Hippy,' Rob replied, but he agreed all the same and spent several days in the run-up fretting about what to wear so as to not stand out. A preppy polo shirt definitely wouldn't cut it, and ironed jeans were a definite no-no. 'Think chilling out – think dressing down.' Rob seemed none the wiser.

Laura and Wren managed to borrow a family tent from one of their lecturers – mildewed and unused for years – and a set of portable trolley wheels with which to cart it, along with a carrier bag of provisions, to the train station at Kingston where they had arranged to meet Rob after his last tutorial. They planned to take the train as far as Longcross, before getting off and taking their chances hitching the rest of the way from the side of the M3. When Wren and Laura arrived at the train station after a wobbly and exhausting walk with the tent trolley from Victoria Terrace, Rob was already there in starched beige shorts and a new black T-shirt… and he had a girl with him.

Laura halted the trolley at a distance, and stooped to adjust the bungee cords that held the tent in place. 'Who's he with?' she hissed at Wren.

Wren leant in and pretended to help, taking a brief peek in Rob's direction, summing up his body language, and hers, trying to establish if she recognised the girl or not. She was petite, carefully dressed in neat yellow shorts and a pink tie-waist top, and her ash-coloured hair was long and poker-straight. 'She's kind of familiar, but I don't know her – perhaps she's on his course?'

Laura stood upright and hoisted her rucksack higher up her shoulders, taking hold of the trolley handle to continue along the path. 'Look at him!' She brought her hand to her face and pretended to scratch her nose, obscuring her mouth as she spoke. 'He's got his hand round her waist!'

Wren noticed the floral beach bag at the girl's feet and, as the girl smiled up at Rob, irritation rippled in the shadows of Wren's mind. 'That's a big bag,' she muttered to Laura. 'Is she coming with us?'

'Fuck it, I hope not.' As she reached Rob and the girl, Laura threw her arms around him and planted a noisy kiss on his lips. 'Rob!' she sang, grinning back at Wren as she released the rucksack from her shoulders, dropping it to the pavement with a thud.

'Hi,' Wren said, raising an awkward little wave. As ever, her manners kicked in, uneasy as she was at the girl's discomfort. 'I'm Wren – this is Laura.'

The girl looked relieved. 'Lisa,' she said, and her hand quietly reached for Rob's, their fingers lacing in the narrow gap between their bodies. Wren didn't know how to feel about this, having never seen Rob with a girlfriend before. There was something unsettling about seeing those two hands intertwined, when the owners seemed little more than strangers.

'*Rob?*' Laura asked, nodding her head at Lisa. *You dirty beggar*, her face said. 'Anything you want to tell us?'

Rob flushed a deep shade of pink, and Wren realised he was avoiding eye contact with her, addressing Laura and Lisa, but managing to blank her out altogether. 'Um, so – this is Lisa. She's – well, she's kind of – coming with us to Stonehenge.' His eyes met Laura's, mutely begging her to be nice.

'Really?' Laura said, and Wren could sense her assessing Lisa's attire, her clean hair and fresh skin. 'Have you been to Stonehenge before, Lisa?'

Lisa tugged at Rob's hand. 'No. But I'm really looking forward to it – it should be fun.'

'Fun. Yup. Should be fun.' Laura stuck an unlit cigarette in the corner of her mouth and wrestled herself back into her rucksack. She passed the trolley handle to Rob. 'You can take this now you're here. It's a bloody liability – the wheels keep jamming and it weighs a ton. It'll give you a chance to show Lisa your man-muscles.'

After the first leg of their trip, they were lucky enough to get picked up by a minibus driver who was heading for Salisbury. Once she had settled in to the journey, it turned out Lisa was a chatterbox, filling every silence with stories of her work behind the counter in the student union bar, grasping Rob's thigh every time she laughed or told a joke. Laura sat up front, making faces over the headrest and chatting to the driver, who eventually took pity on them and went out of his way to drop them close to Stonehenge, where they could walk the last stretch to the festival site. They took it in turns to wheel and drag the cumbersome tent trolley, although Rob wouldn't let Lisa anywhere near it, instead taking her turns for her. The road was lined with slow-moving camper vans and flag-draped rusting buses, while hundreds of dusty ramblers took the same route on foot, entering what appeared to be an entire village dedicated to the celebration of midsummer. In the distance, the strangely unimposing stones stood to one side of the road, against a landscape of tents and tepees to the other. In the queue to the site, one woman reclined on the truck bed of an old Austin van, her long skirt pulled high as she sunned her legs in the bright Salisbury light. A dehydrated-looking greyhound lay panting at her feet. From her horizontal position she was reading poetry aloud, accepting the applause from the stationary vehicles to either side. It was uncomfortable to be there alongside Lisa: she looked like an overprivileged child in her pastel outfit and scrubbed skin, gaping in alarm at the noisy hordes of unwashed explorers who hung from their van windows smoking roll-ups and laughing with fellow travellers.

'Hashish?' This was the first word uttered to Lisa as they passed into the tent field, spoken by a loose-eyed stranger, topless and nut-brown. His ribcage corseted his body in deep grooves as he lunged towards Lisa, flapping a sinewy arm after her. 'Hey, angel? Brownies?'

A huge dog squatted to crap in the middle of the path, fixing his blood-strained eyes on Lisa as she approached. She shrieked. Laura and Wren, walking behind, clapped their hands over their mouths to control their laughter and Rob looked back and scowled. 'You're like a pair of bloody kids.' He sighed, trying hard to deflect their idiocy. 'So, where do you want to camp?' When Laura shrugged and smirked in reply, Rob looked furious and he stomped ahead with a startled Lisa trailing from his hand like a pretty flutter of streamers. 'We're off to find the toilets,' he called back to them. He pointed to a large striped music tent, from which the whine and screech of a sound-check filled the air. 'Wait for us here. Don't move!'

Twenty minutes later, Lisa and Rob returned to announce they were leaving. Lisa looked traumatised.

'What?' Wren looked at Laura, confused, wondering guiltily if perhaps they'd pushed them a bit far.

'The loos are *disgusting*!' Lisa gasped. 'They're insanitary! There isn't even a separate ladies'. It's like a concentration camp!'

Laura covered her mouth again and Wren tried not to join in, instead focusing hard on the toes of her dusty boots.

'Well?' Rob asked impatiently, finally managing to look at Wren too. 'Are you coming or staying?'

Wren and Laura silently consulted each other and nodded, resigned to the idea. 'Alright,' said Wren softly. 'Come on, why don't we look for somewhere else to camp nearby?'

'Oh, yes – that way we can still visit the stones, but without having to use the death camp facilities.' Laura threw Lisa a patronising smile. 'Perhaps we'll find a Caravan Club site along the way.'

Poor Rob; the relationship was doomed from the outset. When it fizzled out after just two or three weeks, Wren was relieved. 'She's not right for him,' she told Laura after an evening dissecting the ins and outs of his brief love life.

'Agreed,' Laura replied. 'He doesn't know how lucky he is to have us looking out for him.'

Wren wakes early and returns to her task of clearing out the wooden trunk. She fills a large garden bag with the clothes and oddments she sorted through yesterday, and settles on the floor to tackle the rest of the box. She had another fitful sleep last night, dreaming of the journalist turning up on her doorstep in the black of night, bringing Robert with him. Robert had been young, the Robert she'd known in college, only he'd looked broken and pale. *I'm sorry*, she'd said, not letting either man cross the threshold of Tegh Cottage. She recalls the rhythmic sigh of the waves clawing against the shore below, the chill of the midnight air as she stood in the doorway, barring their entry with her hostility. *I forgive you*, Robert had replied, his eyes growing darker, older. *You wouldn't*, Wren had answered, closing the door on them. *Not if you knew the truth of it.* Sweating and breathless, she'd forced herself up from the dream and left her bed, to check the locks were secure on the front and back doors before returning to sleep.

Now, in the back room, she lifts a shoe box from the trunk and places it on the stone floor in front of her. The box itself is pristine, containing a pair of gold Italian sandals, expensive and strappy with a kitten heel – a gift from Robert after the birth of Phoebe. A cold flush floods through Wren's veins, as she allows herself to conjure up her child's name, her daughter's name for the first time in twenty years. *Phoebe*: bright and pure; god of light; a flycatcher in springtime. Phoebe was the name Wren had always had in mind for a girl, though they still spent hours poring over the baby name books. Try as they might, there was nothing that they could agree upon for a boy, and when their baby arrived and was a girl it was a relief to find the name suited her instantly. 'God knows what we would've done if we'd had a boy,' Robert joked. 'We'd have had to call him Eric, after the anaesthetist.'

Wren lifts one of the shoes from its pink tissue paper, and turns it over in her hands. In her old life she would have regarded it as a thing of beauty, with its shimmering straps and dainty curves. But now the sight of it disgusts her; its frivolity reminds her of the Victorian butterfly display in the Natural History Museum – beautiful, selfish, cruel. Carefully, she places it back beneath the tissue and adds the box to the rubbish pile.

From their earliest days together, Wren suspected that Rob's feelings towards her were more than those of simple friendship. His furtive glances, the way he became tongue-tied whenever Laura left the room, how after a few drinks he lost all his inhibitions, allowing his glances to linger and smoulder. And she loved him too. She loved his gentle nature, his naïve charm – she loved his love for Laura and all her craziness.

Their first night together came as a surprise to both of them, following an evening tending to Laura after she'd arrived home in a distressed state after a doomed night out. Laura had a weakness for musicians – the more black-eyed and dysfunctional the better – and they went for her in a big way too. In the previous year alone she'd been out with all four members of a post-punk student band called Smack Jack; in quick succession she'd slept with all four – three had fallen into deep unrequited infatuation with her, and the fourth, Jack, had reversed the roles entirely. Jack was the lead singer, a nineteen-year-old Bristol boy who modelled himself on the Dead Kennedys' Jello Biafra. Laura was smitten, and over a three-month period she embarked on a stormy affair which was to leave her broken-hearted and filled with self-loathing. On this particular night, Laura had been at a Smack Jack gig in the college bar, and, knowing she was hoping for a romantic reconciliation with Jack, Wren and Robert had decided to give her some space and let her go alone. They rented a film from the video shop down the road, and stayed in watching *Tootsie* with the lights low, eating vegetable lasagne side by side on their scarf-draped futon. There was no romantic tension; they both understood the unspoken boundaries of their friendship, and so the evening progressed amiably as they passed Wren's chocolate orange back and forth, bickering over who would eat the core nugget in the middle.

When Laura fell through the door soon after midnight, she was barely coherent. Her usually flawless skin was streaked with dark trails of mascara, and her breath reeked of Jack Daniels, Jack's tipple of choice. She shrieked with laughter at the sight of Wren and Robert cross-legged on the sofa and she flopped into the armchair opposite, throwing her velvet rucksack on the coffee table between them. She appeared possessed, her inebriated eyes roaming the room, as her mouth moved silently in an attempt to form words.

'FUCK HIM!' she eventually managed, both hands flying up in rage, and she wailed, breaking down in groans of profound grief.

Wren and Robert moved towards her.

'Are you hurt?' Wren asked, as she came to one side of the armchair, taking Laura's hand in hers.

Laura let her neck go soft, shaking her head like a child.

Robert was at the other arm, his hand on her shoulder. 'What happened, Laur?'

She sobbed some more, retching and appalled. 'He screwed me! Like he always does – after the first set, he came off stage and screwed me in the toilets and then, and then, when we were meant to be going home together at the end, I found him in there again – with *someone else*!'

Wren helped her friend to the bathroom, holding her luscious hair back while she threw up all the hate and bile she'd absorbed, until there was nothing more to expel and she slumped against the sink like a rag doll. Steering Laura into her bedroom, she undressed her, rolled her on to her side and stroked her furrowed brow. In the half-light from the hallway she remained sitting on the edge of Laura's bed for some time, watching closely for the motion of her breathing, marvelling at the beauty of her porcelain skin, remarkable even now in this undone state. Robert appeared beside her, a bucket in one hand, a pint of water in the other. He placed them at Laura's bedside, kissed her on the forehead and took Wren by the hand, leading her to the doorway, where they stood together like concerned parents, their fingers linked.

'I can't bear what she's doing to herself,' Wren whispered.

Robert inclined his head, so that his face rested on hers. Wren could feel the pressure of his fingertips on the back of her hand, the warmth of his skin against hers, and it felt honest and welcoming.

'We'll look after her,' he breathed into her hair, and in a single natural movement he turned his body into hers, their lips finding one other's like a reflex as he spun her into the next room – her bedroom. And that was the moment when the future shifted and changed shape altogether: the start of their new life as Robert-and-Wren.

Out on the beach car park Arthur is serving a group of surfers, five young men in wetsuits, their beach-blond hair stereotypically tousled and free. Wren enjoys seeing the youngsters who come and go. Over the years, she's spent hours at a time following their hypnotic movements through the lenses of her binoculars, as they dive and glide across the water's shimmering surface.

Willow and Badger barge in among the group, rounding them up, causing the lads to become small boys again.

'Sausage dogs!' one cries out, laughing at Willow's waving tail. He takes his hot drink from Arthur and runs a hand along the dog's long back. 'I love these dogs,' he says as the group moves away. '*Wieners*.'

His friends laugh, and they disappear from view as Wren reaches the kiosk.

'Seem like nice lads.' She smiles at Arthur.

'Townies,' he replies. 'They liked these two.' He holds out a treat in each hand; the dogs balance on rear legs to hoover them up. 'So, any more bother from that journalist?'

Wren shrugs, doesn't know how to talk to Arthur like this. Their relationship has always been based on small talk, on coffee, on dogs, on 'looks-like-a-nice-day'. Now, he knows more about her than she knows about him, and she feels sick with the anxiety of it.

'Tell me to butt out if I'm interfering, Wren. I'm not digging for dirt. I'm just worried about you.'

'No need,' she replies, pushing her hands into her pockets, turning impatiently towards the sea. She's been busy all day and now she's only got a good hour of daylight left to walk the dogs; she hates this time of year, resents the meanness of these short winter days.

Arthur holds up his palms. 'OK, OK. But, just so you know, that fella was back looking for you this morning – asking for directions to the cottage – and I sent him packing.'

Wren spins round to face him, defensive. 'Really? What did you say to him?'

'I said I know people round here, people who could break his legs in a heartbeat.'

Wren stares at Arthur's pleased face, dumbstruck.

'I told him to – excuse my language – piss off back to wherever he came from and look for a real story instead of poking around in ordinary folk's lives. And I showed him this.' Arthur reaches under his counter and pulls out a large rusty blade.

'You're kidding me?'

Arthur smirks. 'It's only my old whelk knife – couldn't cut butter. But he doesn't know that, does he?'

Wren laughs, counts out her tea money and offers it to Arthur.

'Not today, love. This one's on me.'

With a small nod, Wren takes the tea and whistles for the dogs, to head off towards the shore.

'Don't go expecting a freebie every day!' he calls after her. 'I'm not made of money, you know!'

She raises a gloved hand and drops down on to the beach, with Willow and Badger in tow.

Up on the rock, Wren surveys the horizon through her bird glasses, picking out the various species as they come into view. The dogs are nuzzled into her lap as usual, their ears protected from the biting wind, their bodies soaking up the November sunlight. A swell is building further out at sea, and Wren zooms in on the distant surfers as they drop to their bellies and head out, chasing the waves, swimming against the tide. Further inland, a kestrel glides into view; she swiftly adjusts her focus, moving it back and forth until she brings the bird into full clarity, the image so sharp that she is able to make out the detail of its vibrant yellow bill and claws, the dappled plumage of its wingspan. It rests on the current, its black tail tips flexing and retracting as the wind pummels its resolute form. Overhead the sky is clear and blue, and Wren allows herself to wonder if this is the end of it, if life will return to normal now that the journalist has gone away. Just her, the sea, and the dogs.

She lowers her binoculars and breathes deeply, momentarily closing her eyes as she rests her hands on the dozing heat of her two companions. Their bodies rise and fall in harmony; her own pulse slows, relaxes, steadies, and she opens her eyes and soaks in the calming panorama of the gathering tide. Down on the beach, a lone woman walks parallel to the water's edge, following the path Wren took herself. Wren watches her as she walks across the sand, her pace determined, her posture straight. A memory stirs within Wren and she raises her spyglass, to focus in on the woman, who, it is now clear, is heading straight towards the rock, straight towards her. A small cry escapes Wren's lips as her world stands still. The woman, made tiny through the viewing lens, is small and beautiful, with flowing locks of the richest red. It's Laura.

ROB

As Laura drives away in her car, Rob and Phoebe stand side by side in the kitchen for several silence-filled minutes, neither of them able to articulate the fear and confusion that fills the space she has just created.

'I'll make a cup of tea,' Rob says, blinking hard as he tries to retain his composure for Phoebe's sake. 'Want one?'

Phoebe pushes away her half-eaten toast and makes to leave the room, hesitating in the doorway as she runs the heel of her hand over her brow. She looks as if she hasn't slept for days. 'I'm meeting Hannah,' she replies, and she leaves, leaving Rob to face his anxieties alone.

When the initial shock subsides, Rob tries phoning Laura repeatedly, reaching her voicemail every time. She left in such a hurry, telling him only that she needed to sort something out, that she would be in touch when she knew more.

'Know more about what?' he had demanded, watching her helplessly as she threw together an overnight bag and headed down the stairs.

'I'll phone you!' was her final reply, and she kissed him – a brisk peck on the lips – and she pulled the front door shut between them.

She's driving, he tries to reassure himself now – *of course she's not picking up*.

By half-eight he's sitting on the bottom step of the stairs, phone in hand, calling in sick for only the second time in his fifteen years as head teacher. 'I think it's some kind of stomach flu,' he tells Anita in the office. He can hear the shake in his own voice, and hopes she will put it down to his illness. 'I'm going back to bed,' he lies, the unaccustomed guilt of deception adding to his galloping sense of disquiet.

He spends the next couple of hours pacing the house, clearing the dishes and refolding the laundry, questioning himself endlessly as he tries to make sense of the strange phone call and Laura's startling exit. He suspects that this is all connected with the journalist who phoned a week ago, and, after much deliberation and a fruitless rummage through Laura's paperwork tray for clues, he switches on his PC and fritters away an hour reading his emails, looking up the weather, checking on the status of his various savings plans. Anything to still his jittery mind, stop it drawing unwanted conclusions. There's nothing distracting enough: *twenty per cent off in the Gap autumn sale*; *south London cloudy with a chance of showers*; *gross interest added this month £22.54*. *Wren Irving*, he types into the Google bar – only to delete it again before hitting the Search button. He's at a loss – anxiously afloat, rudderless without Laura to steer the way.

Now, in the rising light of late morning, he sits alone at the foot of his bed gazing out over the front drive, out across the neat neighbouring hedges and rooftops towards the buttermilk skyline. The rain has slowed, but the wind continues to batter at the windows, sending rattles through the wooden frames, and causing the tall, thin birches of the tree-lined street to wave and willow like a flower bed. Acid waves of uncertainty claw at the spectre of an old stomach ulcer, as his mind roams across the possible causes of Laura's sudden shocked-faced departure. It's not the leaving that unsettles him so deeply, it's the total exclusion – the *secrecy*.

Rob

How could she just up and go like this – how could she not think of the impact her leaving would have on him? He reminds himself of his own secret – of the letter, of his lie – and is at once pricked with shame at his rambling, critical thoughts. He should have shown her the letter. They share everything, don't they? Why not this? Perhaps this is why Laura has gone; perhaps she knows what is in it already or is deeply hurt by his shutting her out.

Exhausted, he allows his body to fall back against the bedspread, the pads of his fingers pressing into the spongy texture of patchwork quilting. The family home hums with silence. In an attempt to slow down his chaotic thoughts, Robert breathes deeply – in one, two, three, four, five – out one, two, three, four, five – all the while fighting the urge to get up from the bed to pour himself a drink, something to calm the tremor that's building up inside. He never drinks during the day – not since college. He wonders about Phoebe, whether she'll be home tonight, or whether he might make real his fantasy of descent into a scotch-soaked afternoon in gentle suburbia.

If there was really such a thing as love at first sight, Rob felt it when he first laid eyes on Wren. There was something so unusual, so utterly contained about her, that from their earliest meeting in the college canteen she was never out of his mind. Of course, Rob barely spoke to her that day – Laura could talk enough for the pair of them – but to be in her presence for that brief first meeting was sufficient to lodge a part of her within him, and he loved her from that day forward, without pause. If he were to be pressed on the subject, even after all these years of absence, and despite everything, he would have to say that he loved her still. She has left her mark on him, an indelible mark.

On a bright June morning at the end of their first year, Laura suggested a day trip for the three of them to Camden Market, to eat and shop and 'soak up the vibe'. Rob and Wren were not yet an item, though he yearned for that to change. Wren was steadfast in her position as best friend, confidante, guide; if ever he teetered too close to a shift in gear, perhaps poised to lean in for that first longed-for kiss, she would effortlessly sidestep him with a cheery hug or a peck on the cheek, telling him how lucky she was to have two best friends she could rely on *so entirely*. For a whole year, he loved her from this painfully close proximity, and while it was clear Laura knew – could read his mind almost – it was never discussed between them, lest the genie be released from the bottle.

They took the overground train to Camden Road station, stepping off the platform into the vivid light of midday, heading out across the traffic and noise of the main streets towards the brightly coloured shop fronts and canopies of the markets beyond. Laura clapped her hands like a delighted child, before linking arms with Rob and Wren to charge down the road towards the watery horizon of the lockside, heedless of the obstruction they caused in their three-abreast tangle.

'Brunch first – there's a greasy spoon down by the canal – best cooked breakfast for miles. Then, I thought we could wander along to the flea market – it's brilliant for vintage stuff and army surplus – ' she moves to help Wren avoid stumbling over a tired-looking homeless man sitting on the steps to a travel agent's ' – and then, I thought we could hunt out this jazz bar Charlie Lyons told me about. It's somewhere along the waterfront too, and apparently they do *the* best margaritas in London.'

'Do you think we should've given him some money? That homeless guy?' Wren is looking back over her shoulder to where the young man is now talking to an older woman in a smart trouser suit. 'We just stepped over him, like he was nothing.'

Laura gave her arm a yank and kissed her on the cheek. 'There are a lot of homeless people around, you know, Wrenny? You can't go giving yourself a hard time about it – it's not your fault.'

'She's got a point, though,' Rob said. 'I never know what to do in those situations. Should you give them money? I don't know. It always makes me feel bad.' He steered Laura aside as two dreadlocked musicians carrying guitars and bongos rushed past them in a fume of patchouli oil. The sole of the bongo player's leather boot flapped at the heel, snapping in rhythm with his stride, opening and closing like a lazy mouth.

Laura paused outside a shop to browse the jewel-coloured silk scarves draped from its canopy. They shimmered and rippled with the movement of her fingers, revealing glimpses of the young shopkeeper who sat beyond the display. She carried on along the pavement ahead of them, dancing on and off the kerb to avoid oncoming pedestrians, calling back over her shoulder. 'It's possible he's not even homeless – I've heard there's a lot of that going on in London – people pretending to be homeless when they're not. It makes a mockery of the poor beggars who really are.'

Robert laughed. Laura never failed to amaze him with her constant snippets of 'fact'. 'For a raging leftie, Laur, you're certainly sounding pretty middle-class right now.'

She stopped dead, her jaw dropping wide in offence; Rob knew this was a surefire way to wind her up. 'Joke,' he said as he ducked the ring-laden fingers of her swiping hand.

Wren turned away to take a last look at the homeless man, before they crossed the road beyond the high street and he was obscured behind a bank of tourists and sightseers. 'Maybe he just wants enough for the train fare. Maybe he's lost, and he just wants to go home.'

By mid-afternoon, Rob has got through several whiskies and is now considering starting on an unopened bottle of Rioja. He's hungry, he realises, and he turns off the television and heads to the kitchen to search out some food. *There's no need to let it all go to hell.* That was what Laura told him in those first few days after Wren had gone, when, after his third night of heavy drinking, she'd made the grand gesture of pouring all his alcohol down the sink while he watched. 'You've got to eat, you've got to wash, and you've got to care for a baby. You can't let it all go to hell,' she said. 'You simply don't have the time.'

Laura. What if this is the same as before? What if she just disappears, cuts off all contact, leaves him hanging? He couldn't take it; not again. Rob checks his phone for missed calls. When he sees there is none, he switches the device off and removes the battery, vigorously polishing it on the hem of his shirt, turning it up to the light to inspect it for signs of damage. He clicks the battery back into place and switches it on; after five minutes of interminable loading, his phone comes back to life. Still there is nothing: no voicemail, no text messages, no missed calls. He grasps at the idea that it's a problem at her end, and keys in another text to her, repeating much of what he's already said in earlier messages – *Where are you? Are you OK? We're worried. Call me, Laura. PLEASE.*

After several more minutes staring into the blank screen of his phone, Rob loads up a tray with wine, bread and cheese, and carries it upstairs to his study, with the intention of running a search for that journalist who called. He switches on his desk lamp, opens up his laptop and pours himself a glass of wine. He'll check his emails again while he's at it, make sure he hasn't missed any news of Laura that way. As the screensaver image of Phoebe and Laura fills his view, Rob's thoughts are drawn back to the letter in his bag and he is hit with a sudden burst of courage and resolve. He's suddenly disgusted at his cowardly reaction so far, his evasion, and in a flash of inspiration he realises this could be the key to making it right again with Laura – he must act *now*, sort it all out and come clean to Laura when she comes home, tell her everything – no more secrets, no more lies. Reaching into the bottom of his work bag, his fingers scrabble in fleeting panic before they land on the envelope – still there, thank God, the letter inside deeply scored from the folding and unfolding of countless views. He smoothes it out across the surface of the desk, his lips moving in sync as he reads it through for yet another time. Pressing his shoulders against the back of his office chair, he lets his fingers drift over the keyboard of his laptop, poised for action as he considers his next move.

Taking another slug of wine, he opens his mailbox and enters the email address she gave at the bottom of her letter. What to write? He starts typing, and after a few false starts his words begin to flow more easily, his questions growing clear.

Flight

Dear Ava

I'm sorry it's taken me so long to answer your letter. When I first received it, I just didn't know how to respond, though that's no excuse, I know. But the truth is, it was a complete shock to me. That sounds terrible, I apologise – a surprise, I mean. It was a surprise. Of course I have a thousand things to ask you, as I'm sure you have me.

Please let me know if you are happy to correspond via email in this way?

Robert Irving

He reads and re-reads the message, his cursor hovering uncertainly over the Send key, before he slams his forefinger into the mouse and propels it out into the ether, to Ava. His mind lights guiltily on thoughts of Laura – of Wren – and he flips shut his laptop and staggers along the hall with the weight of his conscience upon him.

Before Wren, Rob had experienced only the briefest of relationships – a few girlfriends here and there, never lasting more than weeks, a couple of months if he was lucky – and fewer sexual partners than he could count on one hand. On half a hand, if he was completely honest. As a youngster he had been tongue-tied around girls, and he hid behind the bravado of Laura, happy for his college mates to assume they were an item if it gave him a quiet life.

There was one girl, Lisa, a wispy little thing from Berkshire who he met in the student union bar at the end-of-term history department bash. She was working behind the bar – 'for shoe money!' – and she talked enough for the pair of them, glossing over his bashfulness and putting him at ease. By the end of the night, to his surprise, he had invited her to join him on a festival trip to Stonehenge, an excursion organised by Laura and one which he'd been increasingly dreading as the day grew nearer. But now he had Lisa to take, and it would be fantastic! He had visions of basking in the sunshine beside the stones, her long blonde hair fanning out across the grass; of huddling under blankets beside a camp fire, toasting marshmallows and sharing a sleeping bag beneath the cool canopy of a tent, nestling close to ward off the cold.

As it was, the trip was a disaster. Laura hated Lisa on sight, sniggering and pulling faces throughout the journey there, and trying to draw Wren into her menace with nudges and barbed comments. To make matters infinitely worse, Lisa couldn't bring herself to camp on the festival site, and they ended up a couple of miles down the road, pitching the tent in a secluded field beside a stream. They failed to get the campfire going, and ended up eating white sliced bread and cold baked beans washed down with lager; and Lisa was almost eaten alive by mosquitoes on a visit to the water's edge to take a pee.

They did, however, share a sleeping bag; Lisa was insistent. The tent was large, so they organised themselves with Wren and Laura at one end and Rob and Lisa at the other, with a large expanse of pitch-black canvas between them. But, just as things were looking up for Rob, as Lisa gently moved in to kiss him, to run her fingers along the arc of his hip and send thrills of pleasure through his ribs, Laura and Wren corpsed into peals of laughter. They snorted and hooted and spluttered until it seemed they might both be on their final breath, and Lisa, tired of it all, turned her back to him and went to sleep.

'Night, you two,' Rob groaned out into the darkness, and he closed his eyes and slept too, imagining it was Wren with him there in the sleeping bag, Wren whose warmth he felt mingling with his.

Rob is woken by the sound of the telephone ringing on the bedside table. It's dark; 6.55pm, the digital clock reads, and he's lying flat out on the bedspread, pins and needles coursing through his legs where they hang over the edge like dead weights.

He grabs for the telephone receiver, his stomach lurching as he thinks of Laura. As he thinks of Ava. 'Hello? Hello?'

'Dad?'

It's Phoebe, his mind registers, disappointment jarring against the rush of alarm that woke him. *It's just Phoebe.*

'Dad? Are you there?'

Rob clears his throat, moves sluggishly over to the bedroom window to look on to the quiet street below. 'Sorry, love. You caught me napping. I'm a bit fuzzy. Everything OK?'

'Have you spoken to Laura yet?' Phoebe sounds frosty, sharp.

'I've been trying. She seems to have her phone switched off.' Phoebe doesn't reply. 'Have you?'

'No. I've sent her a few texts – I figured if she was driving she'd pick them up when she got to wherever she's going. But I haven't heard a thing.'

Rob's helplessness is overwhelming. What to say? What to do?

'Dad?' Phoebe sounds lost too. 'What's going on? All this weirdness between the pair of you – I don't get it. Are you two OK?'

A dog-walker passes the gate to the house, moving along the pavement in the darkness, disappearing beneath the drizzly glow of the street lamps and into the shadows beyond.

'We're OK, love. There's nothing to worry about – *really*.'

'Well, I don't think Laura sees it that way. She told me about this letter you received, and I'm pretty sure that's got something to do with all of this.'

Rob's pulse quickens. 'Letter?'

'She said you got a letter recently, and that you wouldn't show it to her – you said you'd thrown it away at work.'

'Oh. Yes, it was from an old college friend.'

'That's what she said you said. But she said you were "shady" about it.' A pause. 'So? Are you having an affair or something? I can't think what else you could be hiding. Is that why she's gone, Dad?'

Rob is so shocked by the question that he struggles to answer. He listens to Phoebe's expectant silence, hears it echoing like hollow space along the telephone line. '*No*.' It's barely a whisper.

'*Is that it?*' she asks, lowering her voice. A click of a door latch and change of background noise suggests she's stepped outside. 'Dad? You know what, Laura just going off like this got me thinking – maybe that's why my mum left, too. Maybe you did the same to her? Why else would a mother walk out like that? Why else – *how else* could a mother bring themselves to abandon a baby like she did?'

She's angry now, and Rob can't find words adequate to deny her accusations, to soothe her rising fury. 'I'm sorry,

Phoebs, really I am – I don't know what else to say to you. I'm struggling to work all this out myself at the moment. Can we talk later? When you get home?'

She sighs heavily. 'No. I'm going to stay at Hannah's – and you could probably do with some time on your own right now. To *work it all out*. I just hope you can work it out quickly enough to save what you've got with Laura, because from what I can see you're fucking it all up, Dad. Left, right and centre. I'll give you a ring tomorrow.'

The line cuts off, and Rob returns the phone to its base on the bedside table, breathing rapidly into the darkness as the dots of the digital clock blink red and the seconds tick by. The beginning of a hangover starts to pulse in the nape of his neck, and he presses his temples between his knuckles as a fresh dread memory of his message to Ava presses to the front of his thoughts.

'Ava,' he says aloud, trying it out in the gloom of the bedroom. '*Ava*.'

On weary legs, Rob returns to his study to check his emails.

There was an August bank holiday weekend, not long before they started back into the second year of college, when Wren caught the train to Surrey to spend a few days with Rob and Laura in Gatebridge. Her mother was away on another European tour with Siegfried, and Wren had spent most of the summer at her family home alone, dividing her time between coursebook reading and working in a family friend's ghastly fashion boutique. In Gatebridge, she'd stayed with Laura, and on the Sunday they were all invited to join in the family lunch.

Rob

'*Robbie*,' Laura's father greeted Rob when he arrived on the doorstep at midday sharp.

Rob took his hand, allowing Mr Self to show him what a man he was, by way of his vice-like grip. It was the usual routine, one which Rob had gradually come to anticipate with neither awkwardness nor offence.

'Cor, you wanna work on that handshake, lad! It's a bit on the limp side – a bit lettuce-like! A bit Kenneth Williams!' With a gravelly laugh he slapped Rob on the shoulder, and jerked his head towards the kitchen to tell him to go on through, as he returned to his balding flocked chair and his weekend sports pages.

Laura and Wren were out in the small box garden, sitting on deckchairs with their skirts pulled high enough to show a glimpse of their knickers. Their feet were propped on upturned flowerpots, and Laura lifted a leg to wiggle her toes at him as he appeared through the kitchen door. Rob crossed his arms above his eyes and pretended to be startled by the white of their legs, though in reality it was the white of Wren's underwear that caused him to blush under the fierce sky.

'Robbie!' Laura flapped a hand towards the fence, where another deckchair was leaning. 'Look at you in your jeans, man! Aren't you roasting? You should get your legs out, get a bit of a tan, like me and Wren.'

He dragged the seat over and wrestled with it a while, making the girls laugh at his ineptitude until finally Wren had to take it from him and set it up.

'Tans are overrated, if you ask me,' he replied, easing off his deck shoes and rolling back his sleeves. 'They're short-lived – and they give you cancer. There's not much going for them really.'

'Yeah, but *everyone* looks better with a tan,' Laura said. 'Healthier. Better-looking.'

'*Sexier*,' Wren agreed, with a provocative smile. She squinted one eye shut, tilting her head to one side to laugh at Robert's reaction. 'It's true!'

Rob wanted to reach out and touch the skin on her thigh, imagined her letting him, her wanting him to. 'I suppose there is that.' He smiled back, then closed his eyes and allowed the sun to break through his skin and thoughts, as they sat side by side in their stripy old deckchairs, three wise monkeys, waiting for lunch.

Over Sunday roast, Mr Self insisted on making Rob drink bottles of brown ale with him, so that by the time they were finishing pudding – a bread and butter pudding, as he remembers it – he was handing a fiver to Laura and Wren and telling them to pop down to the Spar shop and ask Trevor for a few more bottles. 'Go round the back door if he's shut,' he added, winking at Rob to show him he was a man in the know. 'He's an old mate. Tell him it's for George.'

Rob wanted to go with them, but Laura's dad wouldn't hear of it, laying a firm hand on his shoulder as he tried to leave. 'Let the girls do it, son. Makes 'em happy, running around after us men – doesn't it, Laura, love?'

He was in larky spirits, and Laura raised a flat palm to block him out as she and Wren left them sitting in the small parlour room and set off down the road. Mrs Self smiled sympathetically as she got up and cleared the table.

Laura's dad reached into his shirt pocket and produced a packet of cigarettes, lighting one as he spoke from the side of his mouth. 'Want one?'

Rob shook his head. 'I don't smoke.'

'Figures.' Mr Self coughed into the back of his hand and got up to fetch two more brown ales from the sideboard cupboard. 'Forgot about these,' he grinned, as if Robert were in on the ruse. 'Still, it's always good to get a bit of peace and quiet away from the females, eh?'

Robert never knew quite how to reply to Mr Self's particular brand of sexism. He found it almost impossible to work out whether he was joking or not. 'Ha,' he responded with a non-committal jerk of his chin.

Mr Self eased the crimped lids off with the end of his lighter, sliding a bottle over to Rob. Rob was actually feeling queasy at the thought of a third beer; he could visualise it floating like oil on top of the Sunday roast and stodgy pudding. But he couldn't say no to Mr Self – it seemed no one could.

'Shouldn't I help Mrs Self with the washing-up?' Rob asked, suddenly lighting on an escape route.

'No! She's fine – she likes it in there on her own. Now, son, how long've I known you? Since you were so high, eh? Forever it seems. I remember you calling round here in your Cub Scout uniform every Tuesday – knees like tiny white spuds, you had! And that daft haircut you got the year Argentina won the World Cup.'

Rob laughed, amazed that he should remember such a small detail, and wondered if he should have shared a cigarette with Mr Self after all.

'And it's fair to say that, over the years, I've been pretty unwavering in my opinion that you're – and don't be offended, son – a bit soft. Get what I mean? I'm not calling you a woofter, but you're not exactly a *man's* man either, are you? Can't imagine you getting down the pub for a pint and a game of darts.'

'O-*kay* – ' Rob wished Laura could be there to hear this. She would have burst her bladder laughing.

Mr Self pointed at Rob's bottle, encouraging him to drink it.

'Anyway, that's all beside the point. Because what I want to say to you now, man to man, is this. That Wren girl? I can see how much you like her. I wondered if you and my Laura would ever – well, I realise now that you'll never be anything more than friends – but that Wren, you're mad on her. My advice – and I'll only give you this once – do something about it before she gets away.' He eyed the open door meaningfully, and lowered his voice. 'See my missus? Love her to bits. Couldn't be without her. But, between you and me, she wasn't *the one*. That one got away because I was a fool. Don't make my mistake, son.'

Rob stared at him, wide-eyed, stripped bare.

Mr Self ground his cigarette into the ashtray and reached over to take Rob's unfinished beer. 'Now you can go and help with the washing-up. The missus could probably do with a hand.'

Back at his desk, Rob takes a bite of stale bread and cheese, chewing it laboriously, his mouth dry. He refills his wine glass as he waits for his laptop to come to life. It's so slow, so laboured; perhaps it's time for an upgrade. *God, it's slow*. He takes another mouthful of cheese. A top-up of wine.

Eventually, he's in, refreshing his Outlook, watching the stream of useless emails that fill his inbox. How do these fuckers get his email address? *Saga*; *LosingPounds.com*; *Dental King*; *Chelsea FC*; *PPI Hunters*; *Accident Claims Inc.*; *Funeral Insurance Planners 4U* – an endless stream of crap and bollocks he's never subscribed to. Tossers. Rob knows he's drunk; it's the only time he feels really at ease swearing, even if it's only in his head. Still the inbox fills with backed-up junk as he leans in to search the scrolling messages for Ava's name and his stress levels soar. The final email loads and he scans them again, hoping to locate her name.

Now, growing increasingly neurotic, he opens his sent mail to study the message he sent to her, and just as he starts to read it through for a third time he is alerted to a new message, sounding a startling *bong* as it lands. With rigid fingers he clicks over to the inbox and there it is. A response from Ava.

'Shit, shit, shit, shit,' he chants, shaking his head as he tries to sober up, to clear his thoughts. He pushes the almost empty bottle to the back of the desk, manically running his hands over his face before his nerves kick in, and he opens the message to read her reply.

Hi, Robert

Thank you for your email – I wasn't sure if you would answer at all, so I'm feeling a bit surprised too! This whole thing seems a bit surreal to me, so I totally understand. I'm not really sure what you're meant to do in these circumstances. Arrange to meet up? Talk on the phone? What do you think? Sorry if I sound overexcited – but I am! Here is my mobile phone number just so you've got it.

Ava Huxley

Robert blinks at her message, stunned, and taps out a brief response.

If you're happy with email to start with? I have so many questions – I'm sure you do too. To start – how long have you known about me, and what do you know about your mother? Your natural mother, I mean (is that the right term?) You said in your letter that her name was Anne, but I've never heard of her.

Ava's next reply takes a little longer, but within ten minutes it arrives.

We hardly know anything about her at all. When my adoptive mum died earlier this year we discovered in her things a letter from my birth mother together with the official adoption records. The letter names you, but the records say that when I was abandoned the hospital came to the conclusion that Anne White was a false name. So I guess it's no surprise you've never heard of her!

Robert replies immediately:

But if she named me as the father, why didn't the adoption agency contact me when you were brought in? I'm not doubting you, just anxious to know more.

He stares at the words he's just sent, realising how bullish he sounds. He didn't even say he was sorry about the death of her mother. Idiot. God knows what she must think of him now. He waits, and waits, staring at the screen, willing her answer to arrive, dreading it all the same. Before too long, a new message pops up:

Rob

It's complicated – but I'll try to explain! The letter says my father was a man called Robert L. Wing and that he was a history teacher at a school in south London, but according to the records they found no one matching those details at all. I thought we'd hit a brick wall, until this Monday I was sitting in the dentist's waiting room, reading an article in a weekend paper about the National Lottery of all things, and one of the names jumped out at me – Robert Irving, a history teacher living in south London. I suddenly thought, what if we've got the name wrong? As soon as I got home I took another look at the letter – it was written on a paper napkin – and I just knew I was right! The name they had transcribed as Robert L. Wing was actually Robert Irving. I hired a family tracing agent, and after just a few phone calls, following up with schools and so on, the trail led straight to you.

So what happens now?

A simple error; a slip of the pen. Robert feels himself reeling at the speed of this exchange. Could Ava's detective have got it wrong? He struggles to recall the cluster of wretched encounters during those months following Wren's departure, a blur of hazy, distant coitus shared with hazy, distant bodies. Sarah from the PTA; Ruth from the office… one-off mistakes, never to be repeated. The string of unhappy women and strange beds he ended up in on Friday nights out while baby Phoebe went to his parents, while he staggered through his fog of grief and came to terms with his life alone. God, he could hardly remember the names – or faces – of these strangers, let alone imagine that together they might have created a new life. And what about this newspaper? Laura said the journalist who phoned talked about Wren winning a Lottery prize – but why were they mentioning him in their article? That Ava should stumble across the story in the national press is too much to take in.

Rob re-reads the email, feeling the cold, damp fingers of nausea travelling up his neck and behind his ears; he should never have drunk so much. Staggering out into the hallway, he makes it to the bathroom just in time to vomit into the toilet bowl, heaving from the pit of his stomach until there's nothing left to expel. 'Jesus,' he mutters at his reflection in the mirror, running a wet cloth across his face and pushing the front of his short greying hair up into spikes. There's a fallen quality to his skin that wasn't there even a fortnight ago, giving him a translucent appearance, as if he's missing a part of himself, as if he isn't entirely there. He thinks of Phoebe, imagines her worrying that Laura has left for good – Laura who has loved her, mothered her, gathered her up in her arms when a hug was the only thing she needed. Leaning against the rim of the washbasin, he studies his eyes, so like Laura's that it brings thoughts of her to the front of his mind, sending him sprinting down the stairs in search of his phone, to check again if she's tried to make contact.

Soon after Wren's father died, she was sent off to St Frederick's girls' boarding school, to complete her last few years of education. Wren told Rob she had been glad to be a boarder, as her mother's social calendar left little time for the domestic niceties of home life, and at least at school there was company when she wanted it.

'Did you miss your mum when you were away at school?' He was yet to meet Eliza Adler, yet to experience her particular style of parenting and charm.

Wren pulled her legs up on to the futon, hugging a cushion to her chest. 'I missed the idea of a mother, but not her specifically. I often used to wonder what she was up to – where she was in the world. She travels quite a lot – especially since she got together with Siegfried. And she wasn't all that good at keeping in touch. Still isn't, as it goes.'

Rob couldn't conceal his surprise. His own mother was a wonderful woman, devoted, kind, always simply there.

'Don't get me wrong,' Wren said, in response to his shocked expression. 'She's not a bad woman. She's just very selfish. Self-centred. It was fine when Dad was around; he sort of balanced that out in her. He could be so funny – he never let her get away with too much. He'd say, *Ellie, you're being a brat!* But, once he was gone, she didn't know how to be any other way. She's not an unkind woman.'

'That sounds pretty unkind to me,' Rob replied, instantly fearing he'd said too much. They had only recently moved into Victoria Terrace with Laura, and were still getting to know the boundaries of their friendship, the margins of conversation.

'Not unkind,' she repeated. 'Singular. She's a singular kind of gal. She likes her own space – *grown-up space*, she'd say. I guess some women aren't made of maternal stuff – Ellie Adler just happens to be one of them.'

He knew she was trying to make a joke of it, but it upset him, seemingly far more than it upset her. 'Is she affectionate? Does she ever hug you?'

Wren laughed, before her face fell into serious repose. She turned away, picked up the remote control and changed the TV channel. 'Only in public,' she replied, and Rob knew from the barbed hurt in her voice that, for now, the conversation was at an end.

When he wakes in the early hours of Saturday, Rob finds he is slumped into the corner of the sofa, desperately cold and fully dressed. He reaches out to retrieve his phone from the floor, and a shooting pain makes itself known along the tendons in his neck. As soon as he registers that there are no messages from Laura, he thinks of Ava, and on heavy legs he trudges upstairs to his office, flinching at the bright glare of the first-floor landing, where the overhead light has been left on. He had meant to return to his desk last night, to reply to the last message – but what? He can't remember anything after he sat down in the living room to look at his phone.

In his inbox, he finds nothing new. The top email is Ava's last message, with her expectant sign-off, *So what happens now?* Rob takes a deep breath, and tries to feel something, anything other than the dread that Ava's sudden materialisation has provoked in him. What were you meant to do in this situation? Was there an approved protocol for dealing with long-lost and unexpected children? Did you *have* to do anything? He scans her last message one more time, before hitting the reply button and starting to type.

Dear Ava,

I'm sorry about last night – I fell asleep before I managed to send you a reply. It's been a bit of a week for me this end, but I won't bore you with that. Listen, I don't know how to ask you this without sounding like a complete waste of space – but are there ANY clues about your mother? What is your date of birth? Back then I had a bad few months after my wife left me, and – well, I had a number of relationships during that time, some meaningful, others rather less so. Please don't judge me, Ava. I really am pleased to hear from you – and I'm so sorry to hear about your adoptive mother. I should have said that earlier.

Warmest wishes, Robert

Surely he should feel something more generous than fear at the discovery of this hidden daughter; a better man would embrace the news, welcome her into the bosom of his family, not hide her existence like a shameful secret. But he does feel ashamed. There's nothing about that period of time after Wren left that makes him feel good about himself; over the years it's something he's managed to sublimate into insignificance, a mere smudge in his otherwise honourable copybook. Even now he tries to push away the reminders of his bad character – even now, with the living, breathing evidence of his actions rising up to incriminate him. Feeling miserable with shame, he sends the message and checks the time – 6.05am – before stripping out of his musty clothes and running a shower. In the rising steam, he stands before the bathroom's full-length mirror and considers his naked form. He's still in relatively good shape, at least compared with many of his colleagues who have run to fat. The grey in his hair is fine, distinguished even – but his face... his face looks shot to hell. It's the hangover, he tells himself, making him ugly, but still, he doesn't like what he sees. Where's the Rob of his youth, the lean-faced eager beaver of days long gone? Robert steps into the shower and attempts to wash away his grubby sense of worthlessness, his fear of what's to come. *Has Laura found her?* he wonders, holding his face up to the hot blast from the shower head. *Has Laura found Wren?*

The night he and Wren got together is stored in Rob's memory as one of the purest moments of happiness in his entire life. He recalls the tremor of Wren's hand linked in his, as they stood in Laura's doorway, looking on like anxious parents, their shared protection and concern entwining like some strange alchemy. Rob had imagined some such scenario more times than he could recall, and yet in that moment he needed no Dutch courage, no gearing up to make his move, no internal struggle or fear of rejection: they simply kissed. He kissed her, and she kissed him – and the rest simply followed.

The next morning he told her he loved her.

'I know,' she said. 'I wouldn't be *here* if I didn't believe that.' She lay on her side, stretched out in the dawn light like a shadowy cat, circling her hands around his neck.

'Have you ever done this with someone who didn't love you?' he asked in newfound boldness, as a sudden jealousy of men gone by reared up.

'A few times,' she replied, 'more fool me.' And she held his gaze in such a way that he knew there was no more to be said on the subject.

It took them four weeks of furtive lovemaking and subterfuge before they were able to break the news to Laura, who crumpled into tears of joy, grabbing them one in each fist to pull them to her, to roll about in a knot of limbs and tears while she yowled and laughed and kissed their cheeks till they were wet.

After his shower, Robert tries phoning Laura again without success. Knowing it's too soon to expect one, he checks his inbox for a new message from Ava, before sending a text to Phoebe, asking her what time she might be home. There's nothing to be done in the house; apart from the single glass and plate he used last night, it's still spotless from his manic cleaning efforts of yesterday morning, and he now stands staring at the fridge, pointlessly pushing around alphabet magnets. The plastic letters have been up on the fridge for years, gradually dwindling in number, as pieces were lost beneath units and sucked up inside various vacuum cleaners. The pieces for W-R-E-N still exist. He can do R-O-B too, and he can spell out half of Laura – L-A-U. The P, H and O for Phoebe can't be found; she used to get them down so often that they disappeared long ago. With the remaining pieces, if he steals the A from L-A-U, he finds he can make A-V-A, which he finds strangely reassuring. He stands back and looks at the words, in a soft-focused haze of fatigue – and reaches for his car keys. He can't stand around here all day, just waiting for something to happen. Rob checks all the doors and windows are locked, and leaves the house; he's going for a drive.

Sitting in his car outside No. 3 Victoria Terrace, Rob realises that very little has changed at all. The tatty curtains and flaking paintwork suggest that most of the flats are still student lets; there's even a purloined traffic cone on the inside windowsill of one ground-floor flat, a university sticker on the inside of the glass. No longer a college, he notes; everywhere's a university these days. He gets out of the car as a young couple comes out through the communal entrance, looking so like the students of his own day that for a moment he feels as if he's stepped back in time, as if he could simply walk across the road and through the door himself, up to Flat B. The strangest thing is, that's exactly what he does.

Up on the landing, he faces the closed door of Flat B, wondering who and what he will find beyond. Will he recognise it? Will it feel like home? The smell of the place has hardly changed at all, the mustard colour of the stairwell walls just as it was all those years ago. He knocks, and, as the door opens, he is met by the sight of a young man in low-slung pyjama bottoms walking away from him across the living room, spooning cereal into his mouth from a bowl.

'Er, hello?' Rob calls after him. He steps over the threshold, taking in the sparsely furnished lounge in one sweeping gaze, as the surprised student turns, cradling the bowl in one hand and scratching at his goatee beard with the handle end of his spoon. The hint of geranium and damp wood still hangs in the air, though absent is the aroma of Laura's ghastly tuna-pasta bake with a sprinkling of Paxo.

'Shit – sorry, mate – I was expecting someone else.' He puts his bowl down on the magazine-strewn coffee table, tugging at the baggy waistband of his pyjamas. 'Who – ?'

Rob takes another step forward, thrusting out his hand. 'I'm Rob.'

'Ben,' the lad replies, looking bemused but shaking his hand all the same.

'Look, I'm really sorry to intrude like this. I know it's early. It's just... well, I used to live here.' Rob feels ridiculous, *old*, in his conservative grown-up clothes and neat haircut. 'Nearly thirty years ago, I shared the flat with a couple of friends when I was at college.'

'No kidding? *Wow*.' The lad looks a little dazed by the notion.

'I was wondering, if you didn't mind – if I could have a quick look at the place? For old times' sake?'

At that moment another young man appears through the open front door and Ben is distracted as he and his friend exchange a series of complicated handshakes and fist bumps.

'Bloody hell, my head hurts,' the new lad announces, shoving his hands deep into his skinny jeans pockets. 'What happened last night?'

'Thought you might be able to tell me,' Ben replies, and they laugh, shaking their messy heads and simultaneously turning to Rob as if he might be able to shed some light on the mystery.

Rob tugs at the top button of his shirt, which suddenly feels too tight. 'So, do you think that might be OK? To have a quick look around?'

'Sorry, mate!' Ben says brushing his forehead with the heel of his hand. 'Course you can – help yourself. The other two are out at the moment, but I'm pretty sure they won't mind.' And he turns back towards the kitchen where he and his friend huddle beside the kettle waiting for it to boil.

With a lurch of energy Rob heads straight for Wren's old bedroom, smiling back over at Ben and his friend, trying to appear casual, though they're not even looking in his direction. The double bed has gone, replaced by a single – in fact, all that remains of the room as he remembers it is the sliding built-in wardrobe, where Laura was apt to hide after a few late-night drinks, poised to leap out on Rob or Wren when they were least expecting it. The carpet is different: gone is the geometric hangover from the 1970s, in favour of a nondescript oatmeal from a decade or two later. On balance, he thinks, at least the ugly Seventies flooring had character. Taking a glance back into the main flat, he sees the lads are still in the kitchen, safely occupied in the mechanics of tea-making, and he runs a hand over the plywood door of the built-in cupboard, slipping his fingers into the concave hand groove, giving it a little push to test the runners. A flash of memory hits him hard: of Laura embedding their photograph beneath a loose floor panel in the back of the cupboard, Wren and Robert standing over her, watching her actions in a mood of happy-sadness at the ending of an era. It had been their last day – the night before they'd all moved out.

'Cup of tea, mate?' Ben asks from the doorway.

Rob retracts his hand from the wardrobe door as if burnt. 'That'd be great,' he replies. The moment Ben walks away Rob is on his hands and knees in the cupboard, pulse racing, feeling along the floor for the finger slot Wren had described to Laura as she hunted for the secret opening. There! In a moment he has the board up with one hand, as the fingers of the other claw around in the cobwebs and dust balls. Just as he thinks there's nothing to be found, a square corner catches his thumbnail.

Lifting the photograph out of its hiding place, he takes it over to the light of the window, where he blows away the dust and dirt of nearly thirty years. As he leans against the low ledge of the windowsill, Rob is barely able to believe that their totem has survived, buried in this place for all these years. It's a black and white passport photo, showing Wren in the middle, with Rob and Laura on either side – an exact match for the one he carries in his wallet to this day. Wren's direct smile is like the Mona Lisa's; Rob's eyes are on Wren; and Laura looks like an advert for the loony bin, her tongue lolling to one side, her eyeballs crossed. The picture was one of a strip of four taken on their day trip to Camden Lock, soon after they'd sampled Charlie Lyons' recommended margaritas – and it had lived on their fridge, intact, for the remaining two years of college, before they'd had to pack up their belongings and move on. That final sultry June evening, they'd eaten salmon and eggs in the dappled sunlight of the living room, drinking French beers and gin as they sang along to 'The Love Cats' and 'Johnny Come Home' and 'Nellie the Elephant', laughing and commemorating their last few hours in Victoria Terrace. At midnight, damp with the sweat of dancing, Laura pirouetted to the kitchen, where she took down the strip of photographs and carefully separated the four identical images with a pair of nail scissors. She handed the pictures out, one each, with one to spare.

'Swear you'll carry our photograph with you wherever you go – *whatever you do.*'

'Swear,' Rob and Wren replied, exchanging a smile at Laura's expense.

She slapped Rob on the arm. 'I'm serious. So what shall we do with the spare one? We should do something symbolic – like burn it!'

'You can't burn it,' Wren said, scowling at the suggestion. 'You'll curse us forever, you witch!'

'Float it down the Thames?' Rob suggested.

'Or bury it in the garden?'

Eventually they came up with the idea of hiding it somewhere in the flat, the backdrop to their recent years of life and love and pleasure and pain. Wren told them about the hideyhole where she kept her rent money, thick envelopes of cash her mother would hand her on the rare occasions they managed to meet up. So it was agreed: the photograph was entombed within the floor of the cupboard of Wren's bedroom of Flat B, 3 Victoria Terrace.

'And here it will stay, until they pull the place down,' Laura announced in solemn tones.

'Amen,' said Robert and Wren.

Now, Ben reappears with his cup of tea, and nods at the photograph in Rob's hand. 'What've you got there?' he asks.

Rob holds up the picture for Ben to see.

'God, I love those old-fashioned photos,' he says. '*Retro*.'

Rob laughs, tucking the photograph into his wallet next to its twin. 'Actually, Ben, I'll skip that tea after all. I've got to dash. But thanks for letting me see the old place.'

Ben offers Rob a fist bump and walks him to the door. 'No sweat, mate,' he says. 'Be lucky.'

Laura was always so vibrant and confident, it was easy to think that she really didn't have a care in the world, that she had never suffered fear and loss and uncertainty of any kind, unless you knew her the way Rob did. In contrast to Laura's exuberance, Wren was wise and steady; between them they represented everything that Robert valued in a person. Sometimes, when she wasn't aware, Rob would watch Wren, study the way in which her eyes followed people, resting a while as she processed her thoughts. There was a depth and colour to her that he found lacking in others, an intangible something she held within. But, despite this bright flame within her, when Laura was not around Wren's light would flicker like a fading bulb, growing faint with her absence. Rob came to know this by way of a slow, stealthy understanding, and there formed a silent agreement that the circle could never be broken, at least not in any permanent way.

After moving out of Victoria Terrace at the end of college the trio remained inseparable, although they deeply missed living together and spent most of their spare time hopping between Rob and Wren's place in New Malden and Laura's bedsit a short bus ride away in Surbiton. Life took on a new, more adult shape, as they completed their teacher training and Laura continued to date a string of new lovers while Rob and Wren made more sturdy plans for their wedding. When the wedding itself had come and gone, they flew off to Oregon on their honeymoon trip of a lifetime, and Laura went too. Friends and family frowned in surprise when they heard of the arrangement, but Rob and Wren laughed it off, replying that they would have far more fun with their best friend there than without.

'You know your mother thinks we're in a *ménage à trois*, Rob,' Wren joked as they fastened their seatbelts and sipped champagne aboard the BA flight to Portland.

Rob, sitting in the centre seat, made a retching noise and told Wren his mother wasn't capable of such warped notions. 'She knows I'm a good boy,' he said and he waggled his eyebrows, turning first left then right to kiss them each in turn. '*My lovely wifeys.*'

'Urgh, don't even suggest it!' Laura shuddered, leaning past him to make faces at Wren. 'At least she doesn't think you're a "raging woofter", like my old man does.'

Wren spluttered into her glass, catching her tiny bottle before it fell from her tray. 'Yes,' she agreed, bringing her face into sober repose, 'but he's *my* raging woofter.'

Laura raised her hand and pushed the steward button to requisition more champagne.

In Oregon, their hotel was exquisite, a haven on the rural west coast, with panoramic views looking out over acres and acres of deep red clover, a strange and beautiful foreground to the distant misty mountains beyond. They had booked two rooms with a connecting door, but Laura insisted she would only use it when Rob and Wren left it unlocked and clearly ajar. 'You are honeymooners, after all,' she said, giving Rob a light punch on the arm, as the three of them stood at the vast windows of the bridal suite, gazing out across the rolling fields of red. 'I'd hate to barge in on you consummating your vows. Really, I'd have to punch out my eyes to obliterate the memory.'

Wren held open her arms and Laura stepped into her embrace, a gesture so natural as to be that of mother and child.

'Love you,' Laura sighed, reaching back a hand for Rob.

Rob looked on as Wren pulled her tighter, deeply breathing in the scent of her hair.

A new email from Ava is waiting in Robert's inbox when he arrives home from Victoria Terrace. It's getting dark outside, and he draws shut the curtains to his study and sits behind his desk for half an hour or so before he can bring himself to open the message.

Hi, me again! My birth date is 1 August 1995 – but because my mother gave false details they couldn't know if I was born early or late or exactly on time. My adoptive parents chose to keep the name she gave me in her letter – and the letter also mentions a photograph, but I've yet to find that in Mum's things.

I'd really like to meet up, or maybe talk on the phone first? What do you think? You've got my number, haven't you? Here it is again just in case.

Ava x

August. Rob counts the months back on his fingers. If the date was uncertain, give or a take a week or two, any one of those early encounters could fit the bill. He leans on the desk, pushing his brow hard against his fingertips, concentrating, focusing, as he tries to narrow it down to that first month on his own, his first month after Laura, like Wren, disappeared from his life...

Rob's world splits in two as his thoughts are propelled back to that icy December morning, so soon after Wren left, standing on the threshold to the spare room, Phoebe in his arms, watching Laura as she hastily grabs clothes and stuffs them into her rucksack. He sees the tears that stream down her face, bouncing off her hands as she swipes them away, averting her eyes as he begs her *please Laura please Laura please don't go...* Powerless, he remains planted in the doorway of the bedroom that they woke in just moments earlier, and his heart weeps for everything they've lost, while Laura, looking broken with the shame of their betrayal, picks up her bag without a word or a glance, and leaves.

As his mind shifts back to the present, Rob becomes aware of the tears that moisten his cheeks and wipes them away. He thinks of the year after Laura had gone, during which he heard nothing from her – not a phone call or postcard, no news, nothing. Until she arrived on his doorstep the following Christmas with tales of travel and adventure – and not a single photograph to show for them.

By the time Phoebe arrives home on Sunday morning, Robert has been up and about for over an hour, filling the time by wiping down the kitchen, and synchronising his phone so he can pick up his emails without constantly checking his PC. Laura's been on at him to sort it out for months; she'll be pleased when he tells her he's got it figured out. His mind hurdles over the unspeakable questions, forcing him into the banal, the domestic thoughts of everyday life, where everything is as it should be. *She'll be back today*, he tells himself; *it's Sunday. Laura will be back from her weekend away, and we'll be fine.*

As Phoebe enters the kitchen, she drops her overnight bag with a thump and scowls at him, waiting for her dad to say hello first. He doesn't; instead he smiles nervously and turns over the phone's user manual in his hand.

'You're home early,' he says, looking at his wristwatch. 'It's barely eight.'

Phoebe slides her phone from her jacket pocket and scrolls through her messages before holding it out to him. 'Laura's been in touch – she must have sent this late last night. I've been trying to phone her back since seven, but she must still have it switched off.'

Rob clicks on Laura's message, reading its contents several times, relief flooding his veins at the news that she's back in contact. It ends, *Tell your dad I love him x*.

Laura hasn't gone, thank God. She's still here; she's still with them.

'She's found your mum?' he asks, looking up at Phoebe who stands at the centre of kitchen, her arms crossed over her chest, her expression a blend of apprehension and anger. 'She's found her?'

Phoebe blinks at Rob impatiently. 'Did you read it, Dad? She's given me the address – *Wren's address*. It's about five hours away and I reckon we could be there by early afternoon if we get a move on. Dad?'

Rob knows he must prepare himself for the possibility of seeing Wren again, of prising open the past. But this other thing, these questions he must ask Laura – the secret of Ava, the issue of her birth – all these things crowd in on one another, until he hardly knows which matters more, who matters more. He's distracted with guilt about not replying to Ava's email last night asking to arrange a meeting, but he just can't focus on that right now; he has to get to Laura, to speak with her, to hear what she has to say first. He runs his finger along the edge of the breadboard, pausing to press his fingernail into a knife groove.

'Dad? Snap out of it! Do you realise how huge this is? *Laura has found my mother*. Go and stick some things in a bag, will you? You can't just stand there waiting for life to happen, you know. If we don't go now, I might miss my one and only chance to speak to her, to meet her – and I'll forgive you a lot of things, but I won't forgive you that. Do you get it?'

She's so strong, so unshakeable, and his love for her swells in his chest like a pain, as it did when he first held her in his arms two decades ago. He takes her face in his hands and kisses her temple. 'Sweetheart, sometimes you're so like Laura, it scares me.' He kisses her a second time, before releasing her cheeks and heading purposefully for the hall. 'Give me two minutes, OK? You grab some drinks and snacks for the journey while I get my stuff together – I'll be a matter of minutes.'

Phoebe flips several pieces of bread out on to the counter and starts to make sandwiches. 'You've got exactly two minutes!' she shouts after him. 'Two minutes!'

WREN

When Wren thinks back to those early months in Tegh Cottage, her clear-headed activity seems akin to the natural rhythms of nesting she observes from her window view each springtime, the focused industry of securing a habitat, a nest sturdy enough to endure new seasons, new life.

When she first arrived, the cottage was solid with age, but work was needed to replace the rotted window frames and shore up a section of loose tiles on the north side of the roof. She needed new locks on the doors and windows and someone to check out the chimney to ensure she'd be able to run a fire throughout the cold months. When the foundations were secured, she spent days on end whitewashing every room, unscrewing the damp-spotted bathroom mirrors and putting them out with the rubbish, creating a blank canvas of the walls, erasing the past. With startling ease she relinquished all thoughts of those she had left behind, as she fortified her new home and stocked up for the dark days ahead. In the local village, the shopkeeper arranged a delivery of long-life supplies – cans of fruit, beans and soup, toilet rolls, soap, porridge oats, salt – delighted with the large and unexpected order during his out-of-season sales trough. She established a firm monthly routine, visiting Constantine for any provisions she couldn't stock long-term, and using the cashpoint there to draw out enough cash to cover her everyday expenditures like paying Arthur for coffee and eggs.

Flight

Early on, after a chance meeting on the beach path, Arthur became her first port of call for all things practical: *where can I buy my log supply? How often does the bus run into town? Do you know a good locksmith? A carpenter? Where can I buy a chest freezer?* He never asked questions, never accepted her clumsily offered twenties for dropping off the sacks of bird seed and garden manure that she'd paid for at the garden centre she'd visited on foot but had no way of transporting home. Once her vegetable garden was thriving, Wren was able to repay him in some way, delivering small bundles of earthy goods to his kiosk on the beach and listening to him talk about the ways his wife had cooked the last batch. The rhubarb was the sweetest he'd tasted, the lettuce the most crisp. These exchanges were simple and good; he knew no more about her than she knew about him, and there was a peace in that.

Laura is sitting at the kitchen table, clicking and unclicking the catch on her leather satchel. Beyond the windows the light across the bay is dimming rapidly, as the tide broils up and heavy clouds blow in. Wren wishes she could sit and watch the storm tide alone, just she and the dogs, but she has retained enough social awareness to know she can't, not with this unexpected guest in the house.

Out on the beach, when she'd recognised her as Laura, Wren had packed up her binoculars and climbed down the rocks with Willow and Badger, her first instinct that of flight. But, as she reached the tide-soft sand at the foot of the rocks, Laura was already there, waiting at the water's edge like a girl at a bus stop, hands in pockets, feet planted wide. She looked older and yet still so young, Wren thought, a strange recognition washing over her as she took in Laura's fur-lined parka, the scuffed Doc Marten boots, her unruly waves of red hair. Different, and yet so very much the same.

'What must I look like?' was the first thing Wren could think to say, and she hated herself for it. God, she hadn't given a thought to her appearance in over twenty years, and here she was now, apologising for it.

'You look just fine,' was Laura's reply, and they'd walked together in silence, along the beach path, up across the wind-beaten meadow and in through Wren's back door.

Now, Wren makes herself busy, filling the kettle, wiping out clean mugs and running a cloth over the scarred wooden work surface. She has already built a fire up in the lounge, lingering over the task too long, trying to delay the moment when she would have to return to the kitchen and face Laura. The fire took immediately, the rising wind drawing ravenous flames over the kindling to send orange sparks skittering up the blackened chimney. Every now and then she risks a sideways glance at Laura, who sits on the one kitchen chair fiddling with the strap of her bag, her mouth slightly open as if she's constantly on the verge of speaking. Outside, the male blackbird has found this morning's breadcrumbs and stands alert, his handsome orange beak thrust resolutely against the darkening clouds as he calls to his mate.

Wren clears her throat, pats the side of the kettle to check it's working.

'Do you get many visitors?' Laura asks, just as Wren has fixed on leaving the room in search of another chair.

She pauses in the doorway, one hand on its painted frame, trying to form an answer. Laura's expression is nervous, and Wren realises it's because she's scowling hard at her, as her mind races to process the rhythms of conversation, a skill she's long forgotten. 'No,' she replies simply, and she heads for the back room to locate an old wooden stool she found there when she first moved in.

The cool of the room is instantly comforting and she quietly pushes the door closed and stands quite still in the muted light. She inhales the earthy scent of garden manure and bird seed, her eyes darting over the pile of throw-outs she was sorting through just this morning, and the storage trunk with its few totems of the past contained within. A surge of shame engulfs her: what if Laura were to enter now, to see these things from a forgotten time – the blouse, the shoes, the handbag – useless, meaningless things that somehow link them to a shared past, a past that might be forgotten entirely if the things could be vanished away? Perhaps Wren will just open up the lid of the wooden chest and curl inside, drawing herself into its reassuring darkness and shutting the room and the world out… shutting Laura out.

Willow scratches at the door, whining softly to be let in, shaking Wren from her thoughts.

'I'm coming,' she says to the little dog, and lifts the three-legged stool out into the living room, shutting the door and its contents from view. She looks at the stool in her hands. 'Three is the Magic Number' – it springs to mind instantly, the lyric from the De La Soul track Laura would sometimes put on when she came to stay with them in Peynton Gardens at weekends during the year or two after Wren and Rob were married. With the edge of her sleeve Wren wipes the dust from the seat, turning with a start to find Laura standing behind her, holding two steaming mugs.

'Hope you don't mind – I went ahead and made the tea.' She holds one out to Wren.

Wren nods, feeling as if Laura has heard it all, eaves-dropped on every lurching recollection that's just tumbled through her mind. She takes the mug, noticing for the first time the dark, earth-stained colour of her own hands, starkly contrasting against Laura's smooth white fingers and neat, square fingernails. They face each other across the lounge: Wren with the mug in one hand, the stool in the other, Laura, standing firm, silently urging Wren to say something, to say anything.

'You can't stay here,' is what comes out, harsh in tone, in a voice Wren doesn't recognise as her own. Outside, the howl of the wind is directly above them, whistling down the chimney and sucking at the swelling flames in the grate.

Laura's eyes expand, wounded. She looks around the room, at its small sofa and throw-draped armchair, at the untidy stack of books that render the mantelpiece unbalanced, the rag rug beside the fireplace – a craft project Wren had set herself soon after her arrival at Tegh Cottage, something to occupy her hands in the cold, quiet evenings. Wren watches Laura's eyes as she takes it all in, the room's lack of frill or pretension, the absence of a television or a telephone or radio. 'Have you been here – ' Laura tries to ask, only to be sharply cut off.

'There's only one bedroom,' Wren says firmly, and she brushes past Laura to set the stool down beside the kitchen table.

Laura follows her in, pulling out her chair roughly. 'Can we sit down, Wren? *Please*. You've hardly even looked at me since I got here.'

Wren lowers herself on to the stool, focusing on the cup of tea in her hand, still unable to meet Laura's gaze full on. She must appear like a petulant schoolgirl, she knows.

She must snap out of it, remember how to behave, face up to what's going on here. Be a grown-up. 'There's only one bedroom,' she repeats.

'Then I'll sleep on the sofa.'

Laura's not taking no for an answer, and Wren's slipping control is a slice of terror. 'I don't have any bedding. I told you, I don't have visitors.'

From across the table, Laura leans in and chucks her under the chin as she used to do when she wanted her attention. The intimacy of it takes Wren's breath away, and she's forced to meet Laura's full gaze, to stare into those eyes she knows so well, those eyes so like Robert's that it's like having him in the room. 'I've got a blanket in the car,' Laura says. 'I'll be fine. But, Wren – '

Wren can't look away, can't speak. She feels as powerless as she did as a child, sitting at the dining table with neatly folded hands, listening to her mother's opinions; fearing she had no voice of her own.

'Wren, I'm not going anywhere. I'm staying until we've sorted things out.'

The first time she took Robert home, Wren's mother phoned the flat ahead of time so that she could interrogate her to find out a) what he liked to eat (in order to impress him with her cooking), b) what his parents did for a living (so she could make relevant conversation), and c) his political and religious persuasions (so as to avoid difficult subjects over the dinner table). She had always been nothing if not precise in all things convivial, so it had seemed only natural when she had taken up with Siegfried soon after Wren's father's death, by way of filling the social gap that opened up like a crater when a beloved couple of friends became a bereaved single. Siegfried was also widowed, some years before, and so their union was equal, both in terms of marital situation and of independent finance. Their separate circles embraced each newcomer, and Eliza Adler's life began anew.

Once Eliza had Siegfried, Wren had realised with relief that she wouldn't need to worry about her mum when she went off to college a few years later. And Eliza Adler hadn't needed to worry about the cost of Wren's expensive boarding school education, as their financial future was secure. 'Life goes on,' she'd said, smiling, as she'd delivered the news of her and Siegfried's impending wedding. Just like that, her mother had transformed from grieving widow to blushing bride. 'It all works out in the end,' she'd said, reaching across the coffee table for the large onyx cigarette lighter that Dad had brought back from Tunisia, clearly relieved to have got it off her chest.

As for the first supper with Robert, her mother was charisma personified, serving up steak and potato *gratin*, and asking carefully rehearsed questions about his life as the son of a grocer. 'I suppose your mother never got caught wanting for a pint of milk!' she joked as she passed him the salad. After dinner, Rob told Wren that he thought her mother was adorable. And after he'd gone home, Eliza told Wren that she thought she could do better.

At first light, Wren slips from the house, noiselessly steering Willow and Badger through the back door while Laura sleeps. The high winds of the night before have torn through the sea-whipped garden, knocking out bamboo canes and plant pots and tossing up the pile of dead leaves she recently raked back against the yew hedge. She'll have to leave the clearing-up till later, she decides, as she makes her way through the meadow and out on to the coastal path; later, when Laura has gone.

Last night, after Laura had returned from the car with her overnight bag and blanket, they'd spent an uncomfortable hour or so skirting around the strangeness of their reunion, avoiding both questions and explanations, with Laura haltingly providing most of the small talk. Wren had made it clear she wasn't ready to talk at any length, or depth, instead busying herself with the task of making omelettes, using Arthur's eggs and home-grown beans from her large stock in the freezer.

'Lovely orange yolks,' Laura had said as Wren cracked an egg into the jug.

'I buy them from the man on the beach,' she'd replied.

'Arthur?' Laura asked, and Wren returned a curt nod, feeling curiously aggrieved that Laura had managed to establish his name after just one brief conversation. They'd eaten a silent supper, and not long after eight o'clock Wren had announced that she and the dogs were going to bed. Leaving Laura sitting alone on the sofa in the tan light of the bellowing fire, she had secured herself behind the barrier of her closed door, feeling sick with anxiety at the presence of another person sleeping under her roof. She'd pulled the covers over her head, drawing the dogs close, and tuned in to the moan and keen of the storm as it passed overhead, thrashing at the roof tiles and bulldozing flat the grass of her tidal meadow. On nights like this, the wind was a friend.

Wren is thankful that it's too early for Arthur to be out yet, and she walks directly down to the shoreline, where dense, dark tangles of sea lace and thongweed coil along the water's edge, their spidery ends trailing back and forth with the flow of the tide. Badger bounds ahead to attack an empty milk carton which sails in and out on the wave, resting long enough for him to circle it once before the water tugs it back out again. He barks furiously, raising his hackles as the hollow container courses towards him again on the incoming surge, while Willow sticks to Wren's side, one ear inclined as she watches her brother's display of bravado.

Today, rather than walking to her usual viewing point, Wren heads for the caves. Laura's arrival has stirred up so many memories in her, and now thoughts of her parents rise up as she imagines this coastline seen through their eyes. They had honeymooned in the area, somewhere around St Ives, and shortly before his death Dad had been planning a family visit for that coming summer, to introduce Wren to the sights, to tour along the north coast, from Tintagel to Land's End and back home along the south coast via Lizard Point and Looe. He had painted a romantic picture of golden sands, luminous blue skies and storm-hollowed caves, and Wren had been sleepless with anticipation of the holiday to come. Already she was in love with the sounds of the places, the roll of their shapes on her tongue, and she'd begun writing a packing list in anticipation of their great adventure. But after the accident the trip was never mentioned again. On the morning of the funeral, her mother handed Wren a Rupert Bear annual, one Dad had found in a second-hand book store off the King's Road just hours before his accident, and which had subsequently lain undiscovered in the fog of the week that followed. Despite being almost fourteen, Wren had spent hours alone poring over the pages of her new book, losing herself in the reassuring tempo of its rhyming couplets, in its tales of enchanted crystal kingdoms and golden gnomes, of dark, barnacled rock pools and stalactite-festooned caves, of magical seaweed and secret passages. She'd imagined Cornwall this way, and in her grief she had almost allowed herself to believe the book was some kind of message from Dad, from beyond the grave. Silently, she had vowed that some day she would see Cornwall for herself.

Now, as she enters the largest cave, Wren switches on her pocket torch to find her way to the deepest of the pools at the rear of the cave, and for the first time since she left her old life she yearns for news of her mother. Her mind worries away at memories of her father's death and the weeks that followed, as she'd teetered on the edge of the vast hole he had left in the material of her life.

Rotten bad luck, was how Eliza Adler had described the car accident to friends and family, speaking on the telephone that seemed to ring day and night as news of Dad's death reached out into the world. From the shadows of the landing, Wren had watched her mother in the entrance hall below, checking her polished reflection in the hall mirror as she spoke into the phone, conveying reassuring responses to well-wishers near and far: *stiff upper lip, these things can't be helped, onwards and upwards*. But *they* couldn't hear her soft murmurs at night-time as Wren could, the low groans of grief penetrating the solid walls of No.6 Highleigh Gardens, the sorrow of a loved one left much too soon.

Wren shines her light into the deepest pool, illuminating a Bloody Henry starfish, crookedly clinging to the criss-crossed walls of the pond, two of its limbs nestling neatly within an age-smoothed fissure. Tiny goby fish dart in and out of weed cover as she moves the light beam across the water, disturbing their peaceful slumber. She pulls back her sleeve and eases her hand beneath the water, to gently run a forefinger over the bumpy-smooth surface of the starfish. It shrinks back, and she gingerly removes her hand to watch its slow journey across the rock, the body trying to follow its probing legs into the narrow vertical crevice. Behind her, Willow and Badger stand in the pool of light at the entrance to the cave. Willow whines, lifting a paw in question, sensing the change in Wren, the shift in their world.

Wren switches off her torch and slides it back inside her jacket pocket. The dogs edge closer, still not venturing all the way, eventually finding a position between her and the opening to the beach, a spot where they lower themselves to settle on the damp morning sand, alert and anxious, guarding their leader as she slumps against the dripping walls of the cave and weeps.

They married on an overcast afternoon in 1986. They had all graduated from teacher training just weeks earlier, and the spirit of change and possibility was ripe in the air; the world was shifting, and it seemed anything was possible. To everyone's surprise, in place of the traditional honeymoon Robert and Wren shared plans to spend the summer with Laura, travelling to Oregon together, before they eventually had to fall into the conventional rhythms of careers and marriage. Wren was twenty-two, Robert not even a year older. Laura, naturally, was maid-of-honour, and she performed the task with style, dragging Wren up west for her hen night, where they wined and dined at Ronnie Scott's all evening, just the two of them, talking and laughing and drinking champagne. Robert was away for the night too, having taken the train back to Surrey for an evening at the local pub with his father and uncle and a few old schoolmates. He'd complained as he left the flat they shared, standing in the doorway of Laura's bedroom, watching as they pencilled on their make-up and adjusted the shoulder straps of their new posh frocks.

'How can I enjoy a good stag night, when my best friends won't be with me?' he'd asked.

In reply, Laura had blown him a kiss and ushered him out with a dismissive hand. 'We'll raise a glass to you,' she'd said, and she chased him out of the door before he could dither any longer. At the end of the evening, the girls dashed out into the night to escape would-be suitors from the table next to theirs, and tumbled into the back of a black cab to reach the comfort of the flat before they turned into pumpkins. That night they slept where they fell, sharing Laura's bed, Wren's drink-fuzzed head slumbering peacefully on her shoulder, as she drifted into dreamless sleep. A few days later, on the morning of her wedding, she had faced her own polished reflection in the mirror of her dressing table and wished that that evening, with just the two of them, could have gone on forever.

On her return to the cottage, Wren finds Laura in the kitchen, cutting sandwiches into crustless triangles with a bread knife she will have searched through the drawers for. She smiles brightly as Wren hangs the dog leads on the back of the pantry door, as if everything is just fine; as if no time has passed at all.

'I'm taking you out,' Laura says resolutely, easing the sandwiches into a clear food bag. She must have driven out to Constantine for supplies: the table is spread with items Wren doesn't keep in the house. 'I've made us a picnic – look, smoked salmon and cream cheese – your favourite. There's plenty of fruit and some of those little cheddar biscuits you like. And I thought we could stop for a cream tea later on, if we fancy it.'

Wren stares at the scattered industry of the kitchen table, struggling to adjust to Laura's buoyant presence under her roof. 'What?'

'We're going out,' Laura repeats. Just like that. *We're going out.*

'Where?'

'Well, I've always wanted to go to St Ives, so I thought you could show me around. I'm dying to visit the Tate gallery – and it looks like it's going to be a lovely day after that storm last night. The sun's breaking through.'

Wren runs a rough hand through her cropped hair. 'No. Sorry – you'll have to go on your own. I have things to do here.'

Sliding the sandwiches to one side, Laura casually sweeps the crumbs into the palm of her hand, depositing them into the bin in a single brisk motion. 'Wren, I haven't come all the way to Cornwall just to wander about on my own. I'm not exactly passing through. You do realise I came here specifically to see you?'

'I didn't ask you to,' Wren replies, hating herself as she says it.

'Well if I'd waited for an invitation – ' Laura picks up a bread crust and lobs it at Wren's shoulder.

It's all moving too fast. Gone is the reserve and formality of yesterday's first meeting; Laura is slipping back into her old, playful mode at terrifying speed, and it feels like vertigo to Wren, disorientating and unwelcome. This Wren doesn't know how to respond, how to react to that Laura. 'I've nothing to wear,' she says, her voice monotone.

'Go as you are! It's not like we're going out on the razz, is it? Look, if we leave now we'll be there in time for lunch – your friend Arthur said it should take us an hour to drive to Lelant Sands, then ten minutes or so on the coastal train to St Ives. He said it'll be easier than parking in the town.'

'Arthur.' Wren shakes her head.

Laura stuffs food parcels into her rucksack and flaps her hands to hurry Wren along. 'You mustn't be cross with him,' she says. '*Arthur*. I told him I was your sister, that you were expecting me, so you can't blame him. He said you'd had a bit of bother with a journalist recently. Probably the same little twat who told me where to find you.'

Wren is horrified to think of Mike Woods phoning around all her old contacts. Who else did he call? Robert? Her mother? 'The dogs haven't eaten,' she blurts out, and she strides across the room towards the fridge, unbuttoning her coat.

Laura stops her with a firm hand, tugging the collar of her jacket back on to her shoulder. 'Then feed them! Hurry up, Wren – there'll be nothing left of the day if you dawdle forever. I'll get the car running – see you out there.'

Wren says very little on the journey to Lelant, glad of the third voice in the car with them, the softly lilting Irish narrator of the satellite navigation system. She's never seen such a thing before, and she fights back the desire to ask about it, to enquire what it is, *how* it can possibly know which direction to send them in. Laura makes polite enquiries about the area, about the weather, about the cottage, and Wren replies with economy, dwelling only where the answers don't challenge her in any personal way.

'Where did you get the dogs?' Laura asks, her focus on the road ahead. She hadn't been able to drive last time Wren had seen her, having failed her test several times in the years since college. She used to take the train everywhere, and Wren was constantly picking her up and dropping her off at the station in her old green Mini. She wonders how long Laura has had a licence – whether she's a safe driver or not.

'Arthur,' she replies. 'His neighbour had a litter, and Kelly had just died.'

'Kelly?'

'My first dog. She was a stray.'

'Sounds like Arthur's a good friend to you.'

Wren turns away to watch the fields and coastal paths rushing by. She hasn't been a passenger in a car for years. Through the fog of time she recalls another journey, almost two decades ago. Even now, she can conjure up the salty vinyl tang of Arthur's old van, as he helped her into the back seat and tried to calm her through the delirium of a fever, insistent that she must see a doctor.

'We're just acquaintances, really.'

'Still, he seems like a nice old boy.'

The drive continues without conversation for the next twenty minutes, as Wren tries hard to think of her own questions for the sake of good manners, not knowing where to begin. 'How does it work?' she finally asks, breaking the silence and indicating towards the little screen perched on the dashboard.

'The TomTom? God knows. But I tell you what, I couldn't manage without it. You know what my sense of direction's like, Wrenny. *Non-existent.*'

Wren smiles, despite herself. Laura catches it, latches on to it in a heartbeat. 'Remember when you and Rob had to come and fetch me from the other side of campus in our first year? Because I'd lost my way following someone I fancied in the science department. I had to call the flat from a public phone box! You two took the piss out of me for weeks afterwards.'

'Rob called you the Surrey Stalker.'

'Ha! Yes!' Laura's laughter is full and uninhibited, the familiarity of it plucking deep into Wren's memory, making her want to curl inside its warmth. 'The Surrey Stalker. Bastard!' She turns to look at Wren again, her hand leaving the wheel momentarily to brush against her folded arm. 'We did have good times together, didn't we, Wren? They *were* happy times.'

Wren returns her gaze to the passenger window, to avoid Laura's shining eyes. 'Yes,' she replies, and the remainder of the journey passes without another word.

Rob wasn't her first lover, although Wren could never exactly describe herself as experienced with the opposite sex. She'd gone out with John Shelbourne on and off for a whole four months, when she was fifteen, and she had liked him well enough, but she felt nothing for him that even bordered on desire. He was a friend of a friend, a boy from the next town along whose parents, a policeman and a housewife, were kind and dull, and whose siblings were rowdy and many. He was the middle child of five, mousy and invisible for the most part, and his gratitude to Wren for accepting his invitation to watch *Moonraker* at the Guildford Odeon in the Easter holidays was charm itself. At the intermission he bought her ice cream and told her with affection that she ate like a mouse, as she carefully balanced slivers of raspberry ripple on a fiddly flat spatula, desperate not to spill it on her new white skirt. During the second half, John wriggled his hand into hers, and after the film they kissed against the wall of the electricity works, Wren furtively recoiling at the monstrous intrusion of his tongue on hers. They went on in this way for several months, whenever she was home from school for the weekend or half-term, he edging ever closer in his amorous manoeuvres – a hand over the jumper, a brazen attempt at a love bite, a cautious fumble at the clasp of her bra strap against the pushed-back seats of his mum's Reliant Scimitar – while Wren expended equal energies in keeping him safely at arm's length. One sweltering night in late August, on the antique chaise-longue of her empty house (Mum was out dancing with her new husband, Siegfried), John, panting with pubescent verve, slid his hand up her skirt and collided ineptly with her sturdy underpants. She knew it was time to put him out of his misery. 'I've got a headache,' she claimed, and she sent him and his sweaty upper lip home, phoning him from a call box the next day to finish it once and for all.

At sixteen, Wren insisted on leaving boarding school to attend the local sixth form college, where in her second year she met the youthful Mr Reece, head of English, an Adonis of a man with shoulders like Bodie and lips like Doyle. It was like a switch going off in the deepest part of her. Never before had she known such longing, such emotional obsession and physical yearning. On Valentine's Day, just after she had turned eighteen, she threw all usual caution to the wind and slipped a card, signed with a kiss, between the sheets of her essay on Chaucer and added it to the homework pile at the edge of his desk as she exited his classroom. The following Monday she took her seat in class, her heart pounding with fear and exhilaration as she waited for some kind of acknowledgement. He ignored her for the entire lesson, avoiding eye contact throughout and holding back all marked homework until the moment the bell went. As he stood at the desk, handing papers to his homeward-bound students, Wren was rigid with the terror of rejection and disapproval. She had made a fool of herself; she could feel the heat of shame rising up over her chest and neck, and all she wanted was to grab her marked paper and run. The last piece of homework was handed to the final departing student, and then there was just Wren left standing alone. Mr Reece, tall and handsome, framed in exquisite relief against the vast wall of his blackboard, turned the full light of his attention upon her, his empty palms turned heavenwards, like those of Aunt Veronica's religious saints.

'Ah, Wren. I don't seem to have yours,' he said, his expression earnest, scholarly.

Her mouth dropped slightly, her fingers rising to the blush at the dip of her throat.

'Go and check on the shelf in my cupboard, will you? I've probably left it in the top tray with the term papers.'

Wren placed her bag on the floor beside his desk and did as she was instructed, her pulse racing as she entered the dark space, flipping on the dull overhead bulb and stepping up on to the step stool to feel along the top shelf for her marked homework. Mr Reece closed the door behind him, kicking the wooden stop into place with a sharp, fluid movement before stripping her of her cotton knickers and taking her against the metal filing cabinet. The lift and fall of chalk dust in the forty-watt glow, the scent of his suntanned skin in her nostrils, the hollow rattle of academic files shifting in rhythm with their movements… it was, and would remain, the single most erotic experience of her entire life. Afterwards, he straightened his tie and handed her her underwear, before easing her aside to open the top drawer of the filing cabinet, where her marked homework had been concealed.

'An excellent essay,' he said, thumbing through to the last page. 'I gave you an A.'

'Really?' Wren asked, delighted, as she scanned his red-penned commentary. *Intelligent. Astute.*

'*Really*. Absolutely on merit.' He smiled, a sexy, lopsided curl of the lips, and leant in to kiss her in the crook of her neck, sending a thrill of excitement down the bumps of her spine. 'You're a bright girl, Wren.'

They kept up the affair for the rest of the spring term and most of the summer one, meeting for hurried sex and small talk twice a week, Wren ever hopeful that he might fall for her completely, that one day they might graduate to love outside the stationery cupboard, might embrace beneath the honest glare of open daylight. Eventually, however, after her A-levels were done with, Wren discovered she had been replaced by Karen Taylor in Lower Sixth, and she thought her crippled heart would never recover.

The short coastal train journey to St Ives is nothing short of awe-inspiring. Having lived all this time so close to the water's edge, having grown so accustomed to the relentless and brutal nature of the sea, of *her* sea, Wren had all but forgotten this serene version of the Atlantic Ocean when viewed at a distance. As the rail path sweeps them along the coastline, alongside golden sands and dramatic rock formations, the sunlight casts a startling hue across the horizon. For a brief moment Wren forgets she is with Laura, so captivated is she by the panorama. She gasps at the sight of guillemots, more numerous than she has ever seen at the bay, their white underbellies flashing in the sunlight as they plummet towards the surface of the water.

'Aren't they wonderful?' Laura says in response, splitting Wren's thoughts in two.

'The guillemots? They're beautiful,' she replies.

'You're so lucky to live here. To have somewhere like St Ives almost on your doorstep.'

'Perhaps,' Wren says. 'Although I've never been before.'

Laura's expression is of disbelief and Wren suddenly feels the need to explain, to tell her more. 'I don't have a car,' she says. 'I stopped driving soon after I arrived at Tegh Cottage. I don't go far. I don't need to – and if I do need anything more than groceries there's a bus to Padstow. I like not having a car to worry about.'

'That's better.' Laura smiles warmly. 'We're talking.'

Wren hates to admit it to herself, but it feels good. Something feels good about leaving the cottage for a while; her movements are lighter, as if she'd shed a layer when she stepped on to the coastal train, and left that version of herself behind.

The train eases to a halt at St Ives station and, along with most of the other passengers, Laura and Wren disembark and head up through the winding criss-cross of streets and alleyways, stopping at the tourist centre to pick up a map of the town before searching for somewhere to eat their picnic. They eventually decide on a bench on the wharf, where they can look out over the harbour at the fishing boats that shimmy and jangle in the breeze.

'It's warm, for November,' Wren says, taking a sandwich from Laura. The taste of salmon and cream cheese floods her senses, and she wonders if she's tasted anything quite as good in the last twenty years. 'Rob loved these,' she says, closing her eyes to savour the sunlight that penetrates her skin. 'They were three times as expensive as the other sandwiches, but he wouldn't have anything else.'

'I remember. One time, at college, he gave me money to fetch his sandwich from M&S while I was getting mine. He told me what he wanted, but I used my initiative and got him tuna and sweetcorn instead, and spent the rest on a bag of salt and vinegar twists. I thought he'd be chuffed with the crisps – but he sulked all afternoon. He said the tuna looked like something a baby had spat out, and he dropped it in the bin without even opening it.'

Wren smiles. 'You two were always having little spats like that. Like brother and sister.'

'Some things don't change,' Laura says, and her body stiffens, as if she hadn't meant to let it out so soon, hadn't meant to let Wren know the extent of their contact.

'So – so, you still see each other?' Wren asks, glancing at Laura as she does so – Laura who looks at once pale and caught out. She takes another sandwich. 'Of course you do. Why wouldn't you? I don't mind,' she adds, her eyes following a motorboat as it heads out across the harbour between rows of undulating red buoys. 'In fact I'm relieved; it's what I'd hoped for. Life goes on. Isn't that the expression?'

Laura picks up the last sandwich with a heavy sigh. 'Yup. Life goes on.'

As they step into the foyer of the Tate, Wren is soothed by the peace of the place.

'This is your map.' The receptionist smiles, handing Laura a leaflet. She's wearing a vibrant floral dress, with a slash neck and three-quarter-length sleeves. The woman looks astonishing, flawlessly stylish, radiantly confident. Wren stares for a moment too long, and a little pucker appears between the woman's eyebrows. 'Oh – and don't forget to see the view from the first floor – it's the most stunning horizon on a clear day like today. You can see why artists have been coming to St Ives for decades!'

Wren returns her smile and it lights her up inside, the warmth of reciprocation.

She and Laura tour the gallery, taking in the permanent collection first, then moving on to the current exhibition. In the echoing silence of the main studio Laura points out an elderly American couple standing at the centre of the room, pinching their chins and nodding sagely at a large nude. They're both tall and thin as scaffold poles, he wearing cherry-red trousers and a tight biker jacket, she in suede leggings and a silver fur gilet. A little way behind them Laura apes their wide-legged pose, pinching her chin and pouting in exaggeration. She reaches into her pocket and brings out her sunglasses, placing them on the end of her nose for effect, puckering her lips as she does so. When Red Trousers turns irritably to locate the source of the disturbance, Wren's laugh comes full volume, hurtling out into the white space like a dog's bark. With a startled expression Laura tugs her by the sleeve and they beat a hasty retreat, picking up pace as they take the steps two at a time, to give up on the rest of the gallery and burst out into the bright blue light of the St Ives shoreline.

The tide is out, and they walk down on to the sand, to stand at the water's edge where the tide laps gently at their toes. 'That's blown my plans for cream tea in the gallery café,' Laura says, digging a hole in the slushy sand with the toe of her boot, watching it fill as the tide returns.

'I haven't done that in twenty years,' Wren says, her heart still pounding with exhilaration.

'Visited a gallery?'

'No. Laughed.'

Laura turns to look at her. 'Don't be daft. Of course you have.'

Wren shakes her head.

'For twenty years? You're lying. Laughter's one of life's few free pleasures. Wren, I don't believe you haven't laughed for twenty years.' She smirks, challenging Wren to own up.

But Wren shakes her head again and starts along the tide line. 'I haven't,' she says.

'Why not?' Laura falls into step, reaching for Wren's fingers, slowing her down. 'Wren?'

'Some people don't deserve laughter, Laura. If you knew the truth of it, you wouldn't disagree.'

Married life felt like a distant land from the outset. While Wren and Robert moved into a small bungalow in south London to be near work, Laura gravitated towards the North Circular, meaning their free time together was gradually whittled down to weekends and holidays. Their lives were busy; Wren felt as though they did nothing but work and fulfil social obligations, and, with Laura preoccupied with her own new relationship, the gaps between visits had grown longer. They spoke regularly on the phone, comparing notes about the schools they were teaching in – Wren and Robert's being a well-funded grammar school near the river, Laura's a low-performing comprehensive in a tough urban community – and they found sport in competing over the mundanities of marriage versus the thrills of newfound lust. The couple had no money problems, since Wren's mother had placed a large deposit on the bungalow as a wedding gift, and with the pair of them both working full-time Wren enjoyed the newfound freedom of shopping with her monthly earnings. Robert, despite being the more sensible of the two, encouraged her sprees, enjoying the excitement she displayed as she unveiled her latest purchases, rushing off to try them on and parading up and down the kitchen for his approval. Shoes were her particular weakness – and his, he confessed – and before long she had amassed a collection of expensive and glamorous footwear she knew she might have neither the cause nor the courage to go out in. Robert employed a builder to split the spare bedroom in two, converting one side into a walk-in wardrobe, fitting the other with a single bed, leaving space for 'whatever the future may bring', as he liked to say more often than Wren liked to hear it.

Despite their phone calls, Wren missed Laura, missed her physical presence in their life, the sound of her laughter and tears in the room, the warmth of her embrace. A few weeks after they had moved into the bungalow, Wren prepared a supper of beef stew and potatoes, and as she leant across the table to pass Robert the salt she spilt gravy on the new linen tablecloth and broke down in tears.

Robert was at her side in an instant, cradling her head in his arms, smoothing the hair from her face. 'Is it work?' he asked. 'Is it me?'

She sobbed, unable to contain her grief. Part of her wanted to say, *Yes, it's work, it's you, it's this tiny bungalow, it's this street…* She wanted to ask him, *Is this it? Is this everything? Because I didn't see my future looking like this, feeling like this.* He hugged her tighter and she shook her head, wiped the streaks from her cheeks and laughed at her own stupidity.

'Of course not,' she said and she kissed his hand. 'I miss Laura sometimes. That's all.'

And he smiled, relief flooding across his smooth face as he pulled her back into his arms. 'So do I, sweetheart. So do I!'

It's dark when they arrive back at Tegh Cottage, and Badger and Willow start up their chorus as soon as the car draws alongside the back gate. On the doorstep are a dozen eggs. Arthur. Of course, Wren remembers, it's egg day, and he'll have noticed her absence when she didn't collect them from the kiosk this morning. There's no note, but they don't do notes, Arthur and Wren; it's one of the things she likes about him. His brevity, his lack of excess. Opening up the cottage, she pets each of the dogs and sends them out to scamper down through the shadowy garden to do their business and carry out their nightly perimeter patrol, sending gruff little barks ricocheting into the salted night sky.

'I could make us frittata,' Laura says, lowering a small box of shopping on to the kitchen table. 'I picked up some ham at that nice deli in St Ives, as well as a couple of these – ' She waves a bottle of merlot at Wren, her eyebrows rising wickedly. She's just as beautiful as she ever was, Wren thinks, turning to catch her own reflection in the black of the kitchen window. The vision momentarily shocks her; since Laura arrived yesterday, it's been too easy to forget they're both fifty. She tries to smooth down her hair, which sticks out madly at the sides if she lets it grow too long. It's about thirty per cent white now, with the lightest streaks congregating around her widow's peak and temples, almost as if she planned it that way. 'It's actually quite a funky look,'

Laura had told her earlier, and Wren was ashamed of how ridiculously pleased that made her feel.

Wren opens the kitchen door to let the dogs back in. 'I'm not much of a drinker these days,' she says.

Laura searches around in the cupboards for glasses. 'Clearly.' She frowns at two squat juice glasses she's found at the back of the shelf and rinses them under the tap, drying and plopping them on to the kitchen table with ceremony. 'You're not going to make me drink alone, Wren? That would be just *rude*.'

Wren stares at the glasses as Laura snaps open the screw top and pours the wine. There's something remarkable about the sight of those two glasses of wine. Two glasses, for two people. More than just one. But it's not just the number of glasses, it's the wine itself. She hasn't touched a drop since the day she left Rob.

Laura's mouth is moving, and Wren realises she hasn't heard a word she's said.

'Say again?' she asks.

'You and Rob were always much better at knowing when to stop. I never seemed to know my limits. God, I spent most of my college years throwing my guts up. It's a wonder I went on to pass any of my exams!'

Wren brings the glass to her nose, inhales the rich notes, instantly recalling a night in late spring when Laura and she had sat out on the flat roof under a full moon, polishing off a bottle of cheap plonk from the corner shop. Laura and Jack had broken up once and for all, and she was *over him*, over men FULL STOP, she kept saying, and she'd vowed that from now on it was friends all the way. She'd far rather marry Laura than any man she'd ever been with – any man in the whole world, she'd said, waving her arms around her head in a wide circling motion. 'Let's,' Wren had replied, pouring the last of the wine between their glasses and laughing as Laura fashioned a ring from her hair bobble and slid it on to Wren's wedding finger. 'What will we call our babies?' she'd asked as they made their precarious way back down from the roof and in through the living room window.

'Phoebe,' Laura had replied as she flopped against the futon mattress, slurring the 'e's so the name became long and childlike. 'Or Ava,' she said. 'They're bird names – like Wren,' and with that she'd slid off the sofa and passed out on the floor. She hadn't remembered a thing about it in the morning, but Wren had, and she'd stored her bobble wedding ring, and the memory, in her special box of treasures.

'So, why don't you drink any more?' Laura asks as she opens the second bottle. Unused to the lack of central heating, she's wearing fingerless mittens, with a heavy scarf wrapped around her neck.

The remains of supper lie strewn across the table, a strange sight to Wren, who normally uses no more than the one setting of plate and cutlery necessary for her mealtimes. The frittata sits on a dinner plate, half-eaten; crumbled pieces are scattered carelessly between the dish and the salad bowl, alongside hunks of French bread and a board of cheeses. There's a ring of red wine where Laura missed the glass on the third refill, and a small pile of orange peel and pith on the edge of her plate. It's a warm scene, a comforting scene.

'It's not as if you ever had a drink problem or anything,' Laura continues. 'I mean, that's the usual reason people stop drinking.' Her chin is propped up on her hands; she pushes a tendril of red hair behind her ear.

'You haven't changed a bit, Laura. You look exactly the same as I remember you.'

Laura laughs. 'I look ancient! See this – ' she lifts up her hair to reveal a small smattering of white ' – and these!' She gives Wren a lopsided wink, to demonstrate the crow's feet at the outer edges of her eyes. 'But thank you – you always did know how to make a girl feel good about herself.'

Wren lifts the glass to her mouth. She's already giddy, but the spirit is in her and she wants to carry on drinking all night and into the morning. 'I think of it as a sociable thing, drinking,' she says. 'And I don't socialise, so I don't drink.'

'But you must know plenty of people around here, after all this time? You must meet people, get invited to things?'

Wren shakes her head. 'Arthur's the only person I have any contact with, and that hardly counts. I buy a coffee from him each morning. He sells me eggs. We say hello, make small talk about the weather and the tourists, but that's it.'

Laura frowns, trying to make sense of her.

'I don't need anything – or anyone – except for Badger and Willow. I like it like that.'

'We *all* need someone, Wren, even you. And you're not being honest with yourself if you say you don't.'

Wren knocks back the last of her wine and stands, unsteadily crossing the kitchen to fetch her coat from the hook. Laura's eyes follow her, watching intently as she pulls on her jacket and starts to fumble with her walking boots, tying her laces with disobedient fingers. 'Off somewhere?' she asks, as Wren's laces fall away in an unsuccessful bow.

'Yup. I'm taking you to the beach. It's a full moon tonight. I want you to see my cave.'

She was a good teacher – 'a very fine teacher', the headmaster Mr Vernon told her at her first annual review. The kids loved her, and her results were impressive. But she never shared Robert's ambitions to rise through the ranks, to take on a department or a headship, or to lead others in education. And so, their lines were clear from the outset: Wren would teach; Robert would excel. Within the first year at Kingly High Robert was selected as a fast-track teacher, rising quickly to head of humanities, and within three years he was applying for a PhD in the study of social mobility and education. Mr Vernon held him up as a shining example, and Wren couldn't have been more proud of her clever, kind husband. His working hours grew longer, and, while they enjoyed a social life with colleagues and their spouses, Wren's independent world had shrunk, and she spent many an evening alone, cooking supper and waiting for Robert to come home and join her. 'It won't be forever,' he reassured her. 'Just while I get myself established.' And she was happy to support him in this, proud to phone home and tell her mother just what a successful marriage she'd made.

It was soon after their third wedding anniversary that Laura moved back into their lives for a brief spell, when she turned up unexpectedly, having briefly left her erratic boyfriend and their home in Hackney. It was a warm late evening in July, and Robert was still at school typing reports, catching up on paperwork for his forthcoming assessment. Laura arrived pale and clearly shaken, her startled eyes roaming the room restlessly while Wren took her coat and sat her down at the kitchen table. She served up the spaghetti bolognese she'd saved for Robert, pouring two glasses of red wine and taking a seat on the opposite side of the table, listening while Laura talked.

Laura ran trembling fingers through her wild mane, twirling it into her habitual coil, casting it over her shoulder.

'The thing is, Wren, *it's a squat*. No matter how nice we've made it look, how many coats of paint I've given it, how many throws and rugs we hurl at it – it's still a squat.' She glanced at Wren meaningfully, her eyes wide and waiting. 'I'm working all the hours just to pay for our food and whatnot, and Doug – well, you know, he's Doug. Still waiting for the big break. Forever "on the brink" of something exciting. He's never up before midday – and the speed! Do you know how much of that stuff he puts up his nose each week? It's *terrifying*.'

Wren reached across the table to still her hand. 'You want security – I can understand that, Laur. We're not students any more, are we?' Laura returns a blank stare, and Wren wonders if she's said the wrong thing. 'What does Doug say about it all?'

She drained her glass, and pushed it back towards Wren, indicating for more. 'He couldn't care less, Wren. Honestly. About me. About the house. About *it*.'

'About *it*?' Wren refilled the glasses, passing one back to Laura, who was now pushing her uneaten supper about the plate.

'About the baby,' Laura replied, still staring into her plate, her fork poised in one hand. She raised her head, and for the first time that evening looked steadily into Wren's eyes. 'I've just come from the clinic,' she said, the tears now spilling from her eyes.

'*You're having a baby*?' Wren whispered, a strange blend of hope and envy rising up in her chest.

'*Was*, Wrenny. I *was* having a baby – I was nearly three months gone – and this time, this time I really thought – ' She pressed her fingertips hard against her cheekbones as if to stem her tears.

'This time?' Wren asked, the news of being excluded from this part of Laura's life hitting her like a blow. 'Were there others?'

'Two others,' Laura replied, casting her eyes to the table, betraying her guilt at having kept it from Wren all this time. 'I wanted to tell you, Wrenny – but I was so uncertain about things, so unsure about Doug, and then – then, they never worked out anyway. This time, though, I thought, if I had *this* baby, I wouldn't need Doug any more. It would be just the push I needed to leave him, to make my own way, just me and – '

'But Lolly, tell me what happened? What did the clinic say?'

'I went along because I've been losing a little blood – it's not uncommon, my midwife said.' Laura looked suddenly aghast, as if the reality of her loss was only just dawning on her. 'So she checked my urine, just to be sure. But there was nothing there – no signs of pregnancy. And then she went off to get a second opinion from one of the GPs – I could hear them whispering in the hallway – and before I knew it I was rushing off to the hospital for an emergency scan. All the time I was just lying there, staring at the screen and willing them to find something, praying that it was just a horrible mistake!' Wretched, she looked up at Wren across the table, and finally broke down. 'But the screen was lifeless, Wren. There was no heartbeat.'

When Robert arrived home, they took Laura to the sofa and wrapped her in a blanket, where she rested her head on Wren's lap, her feet on Robert's, and fell asleep in the warmth of their friendship. 'Stay as long as you need to,' Robert said as they settled her in the spare bed, tucking the covers tight, kissing her forehead. Wren and Robert linked fingers as they left the room. In the room next door they made love, and for Wren life seemed full again – vibrant, hopeful, complete.

The tide is on its way out when they reach the shore, halfway down the beach, with the moon a perfect white globe high in the black sky. It's clear, but for a few wisps of cloud cover, and the wet sand appears slick as silver across the bay.

Wren slides her torch into her pocket and stoops to pick up a stick to throw ahead for the dogs. They race after it, their velvet ears alert and flowing, little silhouettes darting over the vast watery plain like mice across a ballroom floor. Laura doesn't speak, but Wren sees the awe in her expression – in her eyes as they scan the moon-bathed horizon, in her lips, parted in wonder. Out to sea, a smattering of lights blink and ripple as fishing boats toil and pass in the night. Wren breaks into a jog, beckoning Laura to join her, to run along the water's edge towards the rocky outcrop where water pools gather and caves pierce holes into the ancient coastline. A solitary woodcock takes to the sky, startled by these nocturnal humans chasing along its beach; it disappears inland, its long, tapering bill pointing homewards as it seeks the dense cover of the meadow beside Wren's cottage.

They pause at the entrance to the cave, gathering their breath as the dogs pick up Wren's whistle and sprint away from the lapping tide. The moonlight casts a teasing arc inside the grotto, lighting up the outer edges of the first raised rock pool, its glimmering surface a stark contrast against the endless black of the unlit cave. The dogs sit on the sand in the circle of light as Wren takes Laura by the coat-sleeve and leads the way by torch, venturing gradually further into the cave until they reach the furthest pool, a mussel-cloaked pond, still wet with the seaweed of high tide and sunk into a knee-height ledge of rock.

Wren pushes back her sleeve and lowers an arm into the icy water. 'Hold out your hand,' she tells Laura, and she gently lays a small cushion star in the centre of her palm.

Laura's eyes grow wide as she brings it closer to inspect the softly cushioned dome of its back, the tiny nubs of its five legs. 'Is it a baby?' she asks. 'It looks like a baby – it's so tiny and round.'

'No, it's fully grown. Put it back now – there, by the other one.'

Wren shows Laura everything she knows about the rock pool, lifting stones and separating weeds to reveal pipefish and velvet crabs and tompot blennies. Gobies and prawns dart between their fingers, dodging capture and sending cloudy billows to the surface as they disturb the sandy floor of the pool. Laura watches, rapt as a child. Wren dries her hands on the sleeves of her coat and sits on the ledge beside Laura, switching off the torch, plunging them into darkness.

'Have you ever experienced real darkness like this, Laura?' she asks. Her soft voice echoes out into the cave. 'In the real world, there's always something to keep the night away – street lights and cars, houses, people – the moon. But, inside a cave, there's nothing to distract from the night-time. Just silence and darkness.'

Laura bumps her knee against Wren's, and reaches out to take her hand. 'Do you often come here at night?'

'Only when there's good light from the moon. It's the contrast, you see. The beauty of the moonlit beach against the – the nothing of the cave.'

'Why would you want "nothing"? Don't you ever get

frightened, sitting here in the darkness, all alone?'

They sit in silence, until Wren eventually answers. 'It's not what's in the caves you have to be scared of. It's what's outside.'

'Outside? Wren, what have you got to be scared of outside?'

Wren sighs into the emptiness. 'I don't know. Nothing. *Everything.*' She pauses, trying to grasp the right words. 'I'm sorry, Laura. I'm not so good at talking these days.'

Laura doesn't answer immediately, and Wren can sense her resentment growing, flexing its fingers out into the blackness of the cave. Wren considers fleeing, taking flight, to rush home across the empty plane of sand and moonlight, to raise the drawbridge and block Laura out.

Laura speaks. 'Wren – I've been going easy on you these past couple of days – but you know, you can't avoid talking to me forever. At some point you have to face up to the world – talk a bit – answer questions. *Ask* questions. We've been together for more than twenty-four hours now, and you haven't asked me *a single thing.*'

Wren clamps her eyes shut; removes her hand from Laura's. She hears the impatient passage of breath beside her, feels the heat of Laura's disapproval.

'*For Christ's sake, Wren.* Aren't you even a little bit curious?'

'About what?' she whispers, her voice that of chastised child. Her mother springs to mind again – the way she could make her feel foolish and impotent.

'About what?' Laura releases a little cough of disbelief. 'About Rob. About me. About *your daughter*. Are you seriously telling me you're not interested? That you don't want to know how we all are – to hear what happened to us after you went?' Roughly, she snatches Wren's hand back, clenches it to her lap.

Wren flinches, trapped, her mouth trying to form words, failing.

'Do you want me to tell you about Phoebe? Because I can, Wren. There's so much to tell you – twenty years' worth. I could start telling you about her right now and carry on right through to morning if that's what you want? But where to start?'

In the darkness, every movement, every breath, every pause is felt. Wren's pain is palpable, like a third body in the cave beside them.

'I know this is hard for you, Wrenny. If it's any comfort, I never stopped being the best godmother in the world to her – remember how I promised I'd be there for her if anything ever happened to you? I know Phoebe and love her as well as if she were my own daughter. She's never been short of love.' She waits for Wren's response, but none comes. 'Wren? Do you want to hear this? *Wren!*' Laura's voice shouts out into the cave, its anger thrusting into the deepest corners in a violent wave of feeling.

'Are they happy?' Wren asks, her voice barely audible.

'Very happy,' Laura replies, and Wren hears the pleasure and pride in her voice. 'And Phoebe – she's beautiful, and clever, just like her mum.'

Wren's breath draws in and out, sharply ice cold. 'Just Phoebe?' she whispers.

'No, of course not *just* Phoebe. I know it's hard for you to ask about him, Wren. But Rob – he's a brilliant dad. If you could see him with her. She's the apple of his eye.'

'Just the two of them?'

Laura hesitates. 'And me. I – when it was clear you really

weren't coming back – I moved in. We stuck together, Wren. Not only for Phoebe – you understand? Without you there, we needed each other more than ever.'

'Yes, yes – I had hoped – ' Wren's mind scrabbles for reason, unable to articulate through her swelling panic. 'But no other children? You didn't – '

'No,' Laura replies. 'We didn't.'

A new grief rushes in at Wren, a missing piece, an absence as profound as death. In the cocoon of the cave, Wren can almost conjure up the clean scented heat of her newborn daughter's downy head, feel the invisibly soft chub of the back of her little hand, the flutter of sleepy eyelashes against the crook of her neck. What can she say? What is there to say?

'Does she still have dimples on her knuckles?'

Laura shifts on the ledge, turning to face Wren in the blackness, never releasing her hand. 'No, Wren, her fingers are long and slender, just like yours. She's not a baby any more. She's twenty, and God knows I hope Phoebe will forgive me for telling you this – but Wren – I think she's pregnant.'

LAURA

Soon after they rise on Sunday morning, Laura starts to regret her decision to tell Wren about Phoebe's pregnancy. Until then she had managed to bite her tongue, to hold back and resist the almost overwhelming urge to reach out and shake her friend, demand answers to all the questions she left floating in the empty space she created all those years ago, when she walked away from them. When she ran away. She has to tread more carefully, Laura reminds herself, if Wren is to trust her.

Wren has retreated within herself again, withdrawn to the aloof, unreachable place from which she greeted Laura when she first arrived at the cottage on Friday afternoon. It feels as though the returning warmth and friendship they shared yesterday – the comfort and honesty – as though none of that ever happened at all, and they're right back to where they started. Even the dogs can sense it; they pace from room to room at Wren's heels, Willow releasing a little whimper every time Wren closes a door on them.

Laura helps herself to toast, putting the kettle on and searching through the cupboards for jam or honey. 'Want one?' she calls out through the back door, where Wren is busy with a blunt screwdriver, cleaning the mud clods from the soles of her walking boots.

Wren maintains a fixed expression, continuing to dig into the tread of her boots.

'Want a cup of tea?'

157

After a brief hesitation, she jerks her head in assent, still refusing to meet Laura's eye. She looks furious.

Beyond her, the view out to the rocks is a clear one; it's going to be another fine day, icy and bright. Laura wonders if this is the last she'll see of Wren in this lifetime – if *this* will be their final time together. Anxiously she wonders if her message reached Phoebe – whether she's been trying to make contact since Laura switched off her phone last night and put it back in her bag.

'I bet it's beautiful here in the summer,' she calls out to Wren, the troubling ripples of her thoughts compelling her to speak. 'It's really quite idyllic.'

'Gets busy,' Wren replies. She drops her boots to the stone step with a clump and pushes her socked feet into them, rigidly tying the laces in double bows. 'Londoners.'

Laura smiles, handing Wren her tea. 'Like you, you mean?'

'Not like me at all.' She takes the cup and walks away, leaving a dark trail through the dewy grass of the sloping lawn, down to the old bench, where she brushes away dead leaves and sits facing out across the quiet bay. The dogs trot along in her wake, and Laura watches from the doorway as Wren stoops to lift them on to the bench beside her, one on either side. Badger eases his long snout beneath her arm, to rest on the warmth of her thigh, and Wren continues to gaze out over the horizon, one hand on her mug, the other absently stroking the neck of the little dog. Her white breath lifts and carries like mist and it strikes Laura that here, alone at Tegh Cottage, Wren really could be the last remaining person in the whole world.

The image is that of a still life, a moment captured in history – a study of solitude. Slowly, Wren turns to face

Laura, and the unflinching fix of her gaze tells her that she knows she's been watched all this time. She lifts a hand to beckon, shifting Badger on to her lap to make space on the bench. Laura follows the dew tracks and sits, wrapping her coat tighter against the frosty morning, letting her eyes fall across the waking bay as she waits for Wren to speak.

Minutes pass and they sit in silence, both focused on the ocean and the clearing sky beyond. Laura cannot stand the waiting, cannot stand Wren's lack of words. 'Do you regret it?' she asks. 'Do you regret leaving Phoebe?' She finds herself studying Wren's profile, the lean curve of her long neck, the strong, aquiline nose and the roughly cropped hair.

'You could never understand, Laura,' Wren replies. 'You've never had a child. I gave up more than just Phoebe, when I walked away. Do you think it was easy?'

Laura hates her for it. 'I know about loss,' she answers. 'And I know about giving things up.'

When she was sixteen, Laura decided she wanted to be a guitarist, to be in a rock band, and therefore she wanted to learn to play the guitar.

Her father was dead set against the idea. 'It's a waste of bloody money, if you ask me. If you'd wanted to play an instrument you'd have done it years ago. I'm not coughing up for a bloody fad.'

But Laura already had a Saturday job clearing dishes at the Maystream Hotel, so as far as she was concerned she was a woman of means – she would pay for her own lessons.

The school put her in touch with an ex-pupil, a young peripatetic music tutor who was happy to teach her popular chords rather than classical guitar, and who could fit her in on Saturday afternoons after she had finished her kitchen shift. His name was Declan – Dec – and from the outset he treated her like an adult, not just some dippy kid to be humoured. The hotel manager, Mr Adams, let them use a small corner of the function room, and there, in between short bursts of 'Smoke on the Water' and 'Brown Sugar' they talked about music, films and TV, discussed the historical significance of jazz versus punk, gossiped about the many failings of Mr Clitheroe, the headmaster at the primary school they found they'd both attended. They could talk without pause, sharing their ideas, debating their tastes, until the weightwatching ladies of Gatebridge arrived to bustle through the doors at 5.45, putting an end to the lesson. Through Dec, Laura learned the language of politics, and with it a rich new vocabulary was hers: of arms treaties and car bombs, milk increases and militants, missiles and miners, Thatcher and Reagan, Gandhi and the Ayatollah Khomeini. Her ideas and opinions took root and blossomed. Her passions were ignited.

The day she told Dec comes back to Laura with knife-sharp precision: the slump of his wide, angular shoulders and the way the light from his first-floor window lit up the unkempt fuzz of his golden tangle of hair, the shift in his face from cheery intrigue to ashen horror. The image of his tanned knee pressing against the tear in his age-worn jeans, the threads of material straining in soft webs of cotton. He put his face in his hands. Soon afterwards a decision was made, with the background help, she's sure, of his parents.

On the evening they returned from London, Dec parked his dad's BMW at the end of her street and turned off the engine.

'Are you OK?' he asked.

She nodded, still woozy from the procedure. For the entire journey she hadn't been able to stop weeping, and her eyes felt swollen and sore. *This is happening to someone else*, she repeated wordlessly, *and soon this will seem like a film I watched on TV, another person's memory, not mine.* Outside the car, the street lamps were already on; she hoped her parents weren't watching the clock. With any luck her dad would be absorbed in *A Question of Sport* or *The Krypton Factor*, too busy berating the knucklehead contestants to notice his only daughter returning home from an abortion clinic. She winced at the words inside her head.

'What will you tell your folks?'

Laura dabbed the corners of her eyes with a crumpled tissue. 'They think I've been on a shopping trip with friends. I'll tell them I've got a cold and go straight to bed.'

'Remember what the nurse said: plenty of bed rest and painkillers until you're feeling ready to get up and about.' He touched her wrist gently, talking to her for the first time as if she *was* just a kid, not the young woman she'd thought she'd become with him. 'Now, do you want me to drive up a bit nearer, so you don't have to walk?'

Laura shook her head and felt around for the door handle. The last thing she needed was her dad spotting Declan and quizzing her about where she'd really been. As she eased her legs from the car her abdomen cramped like crushing bone, and she felt the deep regret of reality as a rush of blood left her body to soak into the surgical padding supplied by the hospital. She leant in to retrieve her bag, catching the expression of fear on Dec's face as he bent low to see her off, one arm hooked over the steering wheel.

'Don't worry,' she said quietly, the bitterness seeping through. 'I won't tell anyone, Dec. You're off the hook.'

She'll never forget the look of relief on his face; the gratitude.

When Laura has finished talking, Wren leaves the bench and fetches a wide rake that's leaning against the side of the cottage. She hands it to Laura. 'You can rake up the leaves,' she says, 'while I dig the compost into the vegetable patch. The garlic wants putting in before November's out.'

Laura sets to work on the autumn debris that litters the garden, glad of the distraction. Every once in a while she glances over at Wren, noticing how differently she moves when she's labouring, how easily her limbs work with the elements, in the open. She wishes she could look inside her head, see what it is she's thinking, know what she's feeling. She wishes Wren would say something, *anything*.

'Do you think I should feel guilty about what I did?' she calls over, the rake gripped in her hand like a staff. She hears the challenge in her own voice. 'Getting rid of a baby like that?'

Wren continues to drive her fork into the earth, turning great clods of frost-hardened soil, breaking them up with a smash of the prongs. Why won't she speak, say something about the things *she* left behind, the baby *she* gave away?

'Because I do,' Laura presses on. 'There's not a day that passes when I don't.' She raises her voice against the gulls that screech and soar above them. 'But that's OK – I think we should accept responsibility for our actions, don't you? I miscarried four times in the years since that termination. *Four times*. So many times that in the end I couldn't bear the thought of having a baby at all, for fear that it might end up dying on me anyway. But the abortion was my decision; I should expect to feel something – for there to be repercussions. Why wouldn't there be?'

From the shift in Wren's posture Laura knows that she recognises this as a personal attack. It is. Laura wants a confrontation, for Wren to admit to her own failings, to explain why she left them all; why she left *her*, Laura, to fend for herself.

Instead, Wren strides casually towards her and takes the rake from her hand, exchanging it for the fork. Laura watches as Wren walks away and begins to gather the small leaf-piles into one large pyre over an already blackened patch of lawn. Her arrogance is staggering.

'How come I have to do all the talking?' Laura demands, driving the fork into the vegetable patch, ramming the prongs into the soil with the force of her boot. 'When do I get to hear what you've got to say? Because believe me, Wren, you've got all sorts of good reasons to judge me – but you're far from spotless yourself! At some point you're going to have to face up to things – you can't run away forever!' She's shouting now, so absorbed in her own anger and grief that she's taken aback to see Wren walking away, out through the garden gate with Badger and Willow at her heel, down through the meadow towards the coastal path.

'Wren!' she shouts after her, but Wren just keeps on walking.

Thinking back to their earliest days together, it was obvious that Rob fell for Wren on that very first day in the college refectory. He was tongue-tied, dopey with it, like a sparkly-eyed pup. He would knock things over, struggle to remember the simplest of words – unless he'd had a few drinks, when the words would spill out of him like a rushing tap. Initially, Laura put his mute adoration down to his inexperience with the opposite sex; after all, he had spent his entire childhood running around with her, Laura – chief tomboy of Gatebridge village – and she didn't exactly count as 'the opposite sex'. But who was Laura to disagree? Wren *was* captivating, different. She didn't seem to need people in the same way as everyone else, and she certainly didn't seek anyone's approval but her own. Laura loved her fierce independence, her quiet resilience; she took power from it when she herself was failing all over the place, needing too much, on her own solitary quest for approval. For Wren there was no anxious mum and dad phoning on Sunday nights, no one checking if she was eating well, how her exams were going, whether she'd paid this month's rent. No cosy trips home in the holidays for laundry services and home-cooked food. Wren had been by herself from the very beginning. And that was the strength of her – her ability to be entirely alone, entirely at peace. So unlike Laura, who needed everything, everyone. Looking back, Laura can see how wrong both states were for a young woman starting out in the world, and her gratitude for Rob rushes in at her like a wave of shock, reminding her of his existence. Rob was their balance, their well-adjusted prop-in-the-middle.

Now, Laura stands at the gate to the meadow, watching, watching, until finally Wren comes into view again, a small dot of a woman leaving prints in the wet sand as she heads towards her rocks, with two tiny dogs weaving a path behind her. What would Rob do now? In a rush of urgency, Laura returns to the house and locates her mobile phone in the deepest pocket of her overnight bag where she'd stashed it last night. She flips through the address book until she reaches the icon with Rob's face on it. *Call Rob*, she selects, and she brings the phone to her ear and listens as the line starts up, sending out a signal, reaching out to the man she's loved her entire life, the one man who's never let her down.

It rings, five times, six, seven, and then, just as Laura is starting to fear that he doesn't want to hear from her – that she's blown it, that she's blown the whole thing – Phoebe answers.

Phoebe possessed a sweet serenity from the day she was born. From the first moment she held her in Wren's hospital room, breathing in her warm, animal scent, Laura was smitten.

'If we were churchgoers you'd be officially made her godmother at the christening, of course,' Rob said, when she joined them for Sunday lunch a week after Wren and the baby had arrived home. 'But we're not, so instead we thought we should have a special toast for you today – and give you this.' He handed her a tissue-wrapped gift and started to unpeel the foil of a chilled bottle of champagne, a long-distance delivery from Wren's mother.

Laura opened the small parcel to reveal a silver frame, containing a black and white photograph of her holding Phoebe, taken in the afternoon light of the hospital window, the baby sleeping in her arms, a wide, delirious smile on Laura's face. On the back of the frame, was a label: *To Godmother Laura, with all our love, Rob and Wren x*

'I'll be the best godmother,' she cried out in a burst of good feeling, rushing to embrace Wren and Phoebe in one sweep, as the baby suckled at her mother's breast.

Rob handed her a flute of champagne. 'Wren?' he asked, 'Maybe just a small one?'

She shook her head, indicating towards Phoebe.

Laura grabbed the bottle from Rob and poured another half-glass. 'Oh, go on, Wren! A little can't hurt, can it? To toast the new godmother?' She placed the glass in front of Wren and returned to her seat, where she raised her own to mirror Rob's.

'To Godmother Laura,' Rob said, and she and Rob cheered as they clinked and took a drink.

Wren raised hers too, and she smiled and touched glasses, but she didn't drink. Not even a sip. When Laura pulled a daft face at her, Wren's face clouded over defensively. 'I'm not going to risk it, Laura. Not after keeping her safe all this time. I'm not going to subject her to a flush of toxins just because *I* fancy a drink.'

Laura nodded, resisting the urge to make a joke of it, to make fun of Wren's sensitivity.

'OK, I get it – sorry. It's all new to me, this baby stuff! Mind you, I'd better gen up on it all, now I've got an official role to fulfil. Because if you two fall off the edge of a cliff tomorrow it's Auntie Laura here who'll have to take over. Blimey. There's a responsibility.'

Rob laughed, reaching over for Wren's glass and pouring the contents into Laura's. 'Actually, that's the other bit. We want to put you down as guardian – you know, officially – should we fall off that cliff tomorrow. Obviously we'll be updating our wills now that Phoebe is here. We'd be honoured if you'd agree, Laur.'

Laura looked at Wren.

'Really, we wouldn't want the duty to go to anyone else,' Wren said. 'I couldn't bear her to go anywhere else.' Her eyes filled with tears.

'What about your mothers?' Laura asked.

'No,' Rob and Wren said at once, and they all laughed at the definitive tone of their answer.

'No,' Wren pressed. 'It has to be you, Laura. Promise me, if anything ever happens to me, you'll be there for her? You'll look after Phoebe?'

Laura put down her drink. She looked at her two friends, her only true friends, framed in their own perfect portrait of family bliss – a mother, a father and their infant at a table of plenty – and her heart broke a little more. 'You know I will. Not that you're going anywhere, you ninny. But yes, I promise, I'll be there for Phoebe.' She swiped a finger beneath her lashes and laughed away her own sentimentality. 'She's my goddaughter.'

'Laura?' Phoebe sounds cross. 'About bloody time! We've been calling and calling you.'

'Where are *you*?' she replies. 'Are you with your dad, Phoebs?' She can hear the low roar of motion in the background; they must be in the car.

'He's right here – he's driving. *Laura!* We've been out of our minds with worry!'

Of course you have, she thinks. How could she not have thought of that, of them?

'Where is she?' Laura can make out Rob's muffled voice above the noise of the engine. 'Is she still there?'

'Well?' Phoebe says. 'What have you got to say for yourself?'

'Can I speak to him?' she asks, trying to maintain a light tone in her voice.

'The trouble with you, Laura, is you just don't think of the impact you have on other people. It's plain *thoughtless*.'

In her pent-up nervousness, Laura almost laughs. When did Phoebe get to be so grown-up? 'You sound like my mum,' she says.

Silence.

'Listen, Phoebe – I need to talk to your dad.' She waits for her answer, strains to listen over the rustling of Phoebe's hand covering the receiver as she consults her dad. 'Phoebe? Tell him to pull over somewhere.'

'We're on the motorway, Laura,' Rob yells loud enough for her to hear. 'It's not that easy right now – we'll call you back when we're near Padstow!'

'Padstow?' she says, switching her phone to the other ear, as she remembers driving past signs to the nearby town. 'You're coming here?'

But Phoebe has already hung up. They're on their way.

The day Wren vanished, Laura was back in Surrey visiting her parents, for an excruciating weekend of half-truths and restraint. After seven years together, she and Doug were staggering towards the end of their relationship, and Laura had wanted to get out of the flat after he had returned from a three-day bender with one of his old bandmates who had turned up midweek. There was no argument between them; she simply left him to it, delaying the decision she knew she would have to make on her return. Their time together, which on some level Laura had always suspected was transitory, after nine holidays, seven Christmases, two changes of job and four heartbreaking miscarriages had simply run its course. The version she gave her parents was quite different, filtered to avoid their questions and disapproval. Doug was redecorating the flat, she said, and she couldn't stand the fumes – it was the perfect excuse to come home for the weekend.

'So he's not put a ring on your finger yet,' was her dad's observation.

Laura had long ago learnt that she'd never change her father, so deep-rooted was his dour chauvinism. Even so, she couldn't help but rise to his bait every time, picking her words carefully to stab at the angry man in the threadbare armchair.

'I think it's because I'm a terrible homemaker, Dad. I know, I know – you warned me. Honestly, I haven't ironed a single shirt of his throughout our whole relationship. It's no wonder he doesn't want to marry me.'

'So who does his shirts?' her father replied, genuinely bemused.

Laura laughed aloud. 'He does! Here, you don't think he's one of those nancy-boys you're always going on about, do you? I mean, sometimes he *even* washes the dishes. Hell, Dad, I'd better rethink this relationship.'

Mum laid a hand of caution on Laura's forearm, silently urging her to stop, making Laura feel bad. She always felt sorry after one of their barbed exchanges, not for him, but for her mother. It was Mum who would have to soak up his suppressed fury and dissatisfaction when she'd gone home, Mum who would bear the brunt of his miserable moods.

'Sorry, Dad,' she said. 'I'm only joking. You know what I'm like.'

He picked up the remote control and switched channels. 'A dozy mare, that's what you're like,' he said, and he allowed the glimmer of a smile to touch the crease of his eyes.

In the kitchen, Laura picked up a tea towel and helped her mum to clear the lunch dishes.

'How's your friend Wren getting on with her baby?' her mum asked.

'Good, I think. I haven't seen them for a month or so. I've been busy with this new job.'

The pause told Laura where the conversation was going, and she felt tiny knots clench along her jawline.

'It's lovely, isn't it, that they've started a family? She must be very happy.'

'Worn out, more like. She looked as if she'd aged ten years last time I visited.'

Her mother smiled affectionately. 'Well, it *is* exhausting, at the start. But that's not to say it's not the most joyful thing in the world too!'

Laura pulled out the under-cooker drawer with a clatter, and dropped in a handful of serving spoons.

'Oh, not those ones – ' her mum said, retrieving them carefully, her little fingers cocked as if trying to avoid making the spoons more dirty. She handed them back to Laura. 'They hang on the hooks under the cupboards over there. Wouldn't you like a family of your own soon, love? You're thirty, after all. In my day, you'd have been thought past it by now. I remember the woman down the road from us – Mrs Beatty – she was thirty-five when she had her boy, and everyone thought it was scandalous! Mind, things are different now, aren't they.'

Laura felt the swelling memory of own lost babies: so many lost, a hundred dreamed of. If she tried to explain this to her mother she'd never understand, would never comprehend why a young woman would choose to terminate her own infant, to wish it away, or how the implications of those thoughts and actions could haunt a person forever after.

In the living room, the phone rang. Her dad answered, and after a few words with the caller he yelled, 'It's that nancy from up the road! Robert!'

Laura dropped the towel on the side, rushing to the living room to snatch the receiver from her father before he could cause any more offence.

'Don't worry.' He smirked. 'I covered the mouthpiece.'

Laura turned her back to block him out. 'Rob? Sorry about that, he's still as obnoxious as ever. How'd you know I was here?' There was an empty silence at the other end. 'Rob?'

'Sorry to call you at your folks, Laur,' Rob eventually replied, his voice thick and slow. 'I just – I didn't know who else to call. It's Wren – she's not with you, is she?'

Behind her, her dad huffed and picked up his cigarettes, shuffling irritably from the room as if he'd been kicked out.

'Of course she's not here – what do you mean, Rob? Have you had a falling-out or something?'

'No, that's the thing – everything's been just fine. You saw her last time. She was looking great, wasn't she? She's been fine, especially since Phoebe started to sleep through the night.'

Laura could almost hear his mind ticking over. The last time she had seen Wren, she hadn't thought she looked either great or fine – but she'd been too wrapped up in her own problems to say anything to Rob, to do anything. And wasn't it better that way all round: to keep the tone as upbeat as possible, act as if everything was alright until eventually it really was? Wren would agree, Laura was sure. With a shudder, Laura realised it was her mother she was thinking of, not Wren. Her mother, drifting through life like a woman with a brain injury; smiling benignly to block out the monotony.

'There's no note, Laur – she never goes out without leaving a note – and when I got back from playing squash Fiona from next door came round with Phoebe, saying Wren had asked her to babysit for an hour.'

'Perhaps she just needed a bit of space. Maybe she's gone shopping?'

She heard the whistle of Robert blowing air through his pursed lips. 'She's taken stuff with her. Her coat, welly boots of all things. A bunch of clothes, I think.'

'Have you checked the bathroom for her toothbrush? She won't have left that behind if she's gone for a while.' Laura listened to the crash of the phone receiver at Robert's end, the sound of his shoes treading through the hallway before returning to the phone.

She waited for his words, but could hear only the slightest movement of his presence at the end of the line and the sound of tearing paper. 'Rob? What it is?'

'Hang on, Laur – let me just get this envelope open – '

'From Wren? What does it say?'

Rob sighs, long and low, his breath stuttering as he forms the words. '"*Dear Rob, I'm sorry but I have to go. Please don't worry and don't try to find me – I promise I will be in touch. Look after Phoebe and tell her I love her. Wren x.*"'

'She put a kiss at the end, Rob?'

'Yes.'

'That's got to be a positive sign, surely?'

After a pause, he speaks again. 'Will you come over, Laur? I don't think I can be on my own tonight.'

Laura stands high up on the coastal path and scans the beachscape, searching for Wren and the dogs. Memories and emotions overlap as she thinks back to that day at her parents' house twenty years ago, when Rob tracked her down in his search for Wren. He'd had no way of knowing she'd be there, no way of knowing that she had that very weekend been considering her plans to leave Doug, just as Wren had walked out on him. Was it meant to be? Were she and Rob always meant to be together? She wonders if the love one person felt for another could ever be entirely matched – if the depth of it, the height and the width of it could ever be equal. Surely one would inevitably love the other more infinitely, whether by a small or large margin? It was always clear to Laura, now as then, that Rob's love for Wren was the greater – and that Wren could never match his devotion as deeply, as endlessly. And, as much as Laura loved them, as individuals and as a pair, it broke her heart a little more every time she noticed the imbalance.

Her head throbs as she tries to work out what to do next. Rob and Phoebe must be nearly here by now – it's gone one-thirty, and still Wren hasn't returned to the cottage. That Rob and Phoebe will want to see Wren is not in doubt; it's why they're here. But Wren? Will she want to see them? Will she want to open herself up to them after all these years of seclusion – to their questions, to their demands?

A small figure comes into view at the furthest reach of rocks and caves. It would be impossible to tell if it was Wren but for the two specks of dog that trickle along the sand beside her, casting tiny black shadows in their wake. But she's heading away from home, not towards it, and Laura has no way of knowing how much longer she'll be gone for. What to do?

Laura's phone buzzes in her coat pocket: a message from Rob.

Flight

We're in Padstow. Just checking in at the Metropole.
How far away are you? Call me in ten minutes?

Looking back out at the retreating figure of Wren, Laura makes a decision. She'll go to Rob. She'll go to Rob and together they will bring Phoebe to her mother.

When she thinks of all those years she wasted on Doug, Laura could weep. The memory of it turns in her stomach like a forgotten anxiety, like waking each morning after a bereavement, only to experience the grief all over again. Seven years of her life given to the wrong man – seven years when she might have been growing a little family of her own, instead of watching it pass by as Doug allowed their future, their security, to disappear in a toxic cloud of the white stuff. He was a good enough man, kind, funny, talented. But he was self-obsessed too, driven only by his desire to 'make it', to practise his art, his music – and for the first couple of years Laura effectively funded his lifestyle. While he'd go through long phases off the drugs, it would only take some small disappointment – a rejection from a record producer, a poorly attended gig, *another* miscarriage – to send him reeling, trigger him to seek out his old familiars, and the cycle would begin again. As if what he was doing to himself wasn't bad enough, there was her career to think of; if her colleagues had ever had their suspicions about Doug's extracurricular habits, had ever called at their flat and seen the undesirables knocking at their door at all hours, her teaching life would have been over in a minute. After three years, quite out of the blue, they had moved from his horrible squat into a stylish apartment, and seemingly overnight an endless supply of cash appeared from nowhere. Yet, officially, they were still just living off Laura's own modest salary. It didn't add up. She never asked him outright if he was dealing, but in the stark light of hindsight how could he not have been?

For years after they split up it would keep her awake at night, agonising over what her father would have thought if he'd ever learned the real reasons for the failure of her relationship. He'd have had kittens. He'd have said, *That's what happens when you give it away – you end up with a wrong 'un.* Despite not being a religious man, he'd never got over the fact that she was 'living in sin' with Doug, that Doug hadn't made an honest woman of her – a *housewife* of her, no doubt.

Poor Dad, Laura thinks now, recalling his deathly pallor towards the end, long after she had left Doug and started anew with Rob and Phoebe. He was dying, though it was not something Laura and her mother ever discussed in honest terms, behaving as though it was business as usual as he battled against the crushing weight of his illness, gasping for every one of his last breaths. On the final day, sitting beside his makeshift bed in the parlour while Mum was off brewing another round of tea, Laura had lied to him, knowing it was the end. However skewed his view of the world, of women, still she longed for his approval.

'Rob and I are getting married,' she'd whispered close to his face, before kissing him on the brow. 'His job's going well, and Phoebe needs someone to look after her until she starts at school. And all being well, Dad, you'll be there to give me away?'

A flicker crossed his face; almost a smile. She forced a small laugh despite her tears, tears he would never see through his mask of agony.

'I'll have to get a few housekeeping tips from Mum, eh? You know how hopeless I am.'

With unbearable labour he spoke, his voice a rattle. 'You'll do fine, love.'

Laura squeezed his hand and left the room, to lock herself in the bathroom, where she sank to the floor and sobbed for the relationship they might have had, in another time, another place.

The route to Padstow is uncomplicated, and soon after she enters the town Laura swings into the car park at the front of the Metropole hotel, feeling a surge of relief as she spots Rob's silver car parked in the far corner. She pulls up in a free space and switches off the engine, sitting for a few moments beneath the shade of a tree, her hand still resting on the wheel as she wonders what to tell him – to tell Phoebe – and feeling more uncertain than she's ever felt about where this will all lead. She contemplates backing out again and driving home, back to the London suburbs, without stopping to say goodbye to Wren. But then what? The stuff of this weekend can't be simply undone; they've opened the lid of this box now – surely they owe it to themselves, to Phoebe, to finish what they started… to look inside.

Laura arrived at Robert's just before seven that evening back in 1994, and he stepped out on to the path before Laura had even come to a stop, his eyes unreachable. Laura drew him close, cradled his head to her shoulder and cried with him. Not in their entire history together had he needed her like this, called for her in his hour of desperation. It had always been the other way round, always Laura leaning on *him*, and, as she stood in the cold autumn glow on his doorstep, the unfamiliar sensation of his need for her was crushing in its intensity.

Inside, the house seemed wintry, uninhabited, as if, in the few short hours since she'd gone, Wren had robbed the house of its light and warmth. The silence felt like a death. Phoebe was lying on her play mat, tugging at her socks. Laura went straight to her, lifting her high and smothering her in kisses; the baby girl laughed and waved, oblivious to the great hole in the room, the seismic shift casting fractures through their cosy world.

'She's bottle-fed now, isn't she?' Laura felt desperate to do something practical, to snap him from his darkness.

Flopping back on the sofa, Rob ran his hands over his trousers, his face in turmoil as he tried to retrieve the answer to her question. 'Yes, mainly,' he eventually said. 'Wren's been weaning her off over the past few weeks. Except for the last one of the day – she's still breastfeeding at bedtime.' Fresh horror crossed his face as he tried to anticipate the difficulty of getting Phoebe to take the bottle at night instead.

Laura raised a hand, urging him to calm down, and she shifted the baby to her other hip as she headed for the door. 'She'll be fine, Rob. You stay where you are, rest your eyes for a bit. I'll take care of Phoebe.'

In the kitchen, she found clean bottles in the steriliser and carefully followed the pack instructions to make up some milk, while Phoebe watched from her bouncer chair, chewing on a finger rusk. Upstairs Laura bathed her, kissing her tummy as she dressed her in a fresh babygro, before turning the light low to settle in the feeding chair of Phoebe's nursery room. At first the baby resisted the synthetic teat of the bottle, grizzling and wrestling her head inwards as she sought her mother's breast, confused by the change in routine. But eventually she took the bottle, and after five or ten minutes rocking gently in the darkness Phoebe allowed Laura to lay her in her cot, where she found her special cloth and the comfort of her thumb.

Softly treading down the stairs, Laura returned to Robert where he sat on the sofa, staring at the blank screen of the TV, his face scored in concentration. 'There must have been something, Rob,' she said. 'Some clue that she wasn't happy?'

He tore his gaze from the screen to look at Laura, now perched on the corner of the coffee table, and shook his head.

'Did you argue?'

'No.' Robert closed his eyes and dropped his head against the back of the sofa. '*No.*'

Laura took his hand and kissed it, before opening the drinks cabinet to take out two crystal tumblers. She fetched ice from the kitchen and returned, pouring generous quantities of scotch and sitting at the opposite end of the sofa, pushing the glass into Robert's resisting hand. 'You're in shock. Just have a drink, Rob. *Go on.*'

He drank the whisky, and several more afterwards, until his dazed façade began to slip, and the words came. Upstairs, Phoebe slept peacefully. Laura brought a tray of cold food to the coffee table, to sit cross-legged beside Robert, passing him crackers and Stilton and listening to him talk.

Rob pushed the crumbs around his plate, gathering them into a small mound. 'Remember that first day in the canteen? Remember what she was like? Her quiet eyes – her laugh. Her laugh is still the most beautiful sound to me, Laur. I miss it. I miss her laugh.'

'Rob, she's only been gone a few hours. You'll hear her laugh again soon enough.'

He rapped his knuckles on the glass of the table. 'No. *I miss her laugh*. I haven't heard it in months.'

Laura frowned, poured him another drink.

'She stopped laughing, Laur – that's the difference. She hasn't laughed for the longest time. Since the baby. You tell me when you last heard her laugh.'

He must be wrong, Laura thought, though she struggled to remember Wren being anything other than distant and humourless in more recent times. 'Tell me about the last time you remember her laughing,' she said, hoping he'd realise he was wrong, that things weren't really the way they seemed right now.

'I know exactly when it was. It was the day before she went into labour. We walked along the river – trying to bring the baby on – and we were talking about college and that party we had at Victoria Terrace right before we all moved out.'

Laura smiled, conjuring up an image of Mad Benji squatting in the flowerbed with his trousers round his ankles and a knitted tea cosy on his head. 'It's just as well we were moving out; they'd have evicted us otherwise. The mess we made of the flower borders!'

'Wren said she'd gone into our bedroom to look for someone's coat and found Professor Waite under a donkey jacket with Matthew Truss.'

'No! Wren said that? She'd have told us, surely? Wasn't the prof a married man – and I'm sure Matt had a girlfriend!'

'They begged her not to tell, and, Wren being Wren, she didn't say a word till years later when we heard that Waite had died. When she walked in on them at the party, old Waite was apparently wearing nothing but his beard and horn-rimmed specs – and Michael – well, she said she'd never seen such an enormous appendage in her entire life.'

Laura screamed with laughter. 'But Matthew was a tiny little man! He was nearly as small as me!'

'She said it was like a third leg.' Rob smiled, his eyes filling up with tears. 'And the thing is, Laur, we laughed when she told me this story; we leant on the railings looking down at the ducks bobbing along on the water, and we laughed so hard she thought her waters might break. And that was the last time. I haven't heard her laugh like that in over six months.' He looked into Laura's eyes as she placed a light hand on his wrist. 'I knew she was changing, saw it happening in front of my face, and I did nothing to help her, nothing to bring her back. I just got up each morning and went to work and came home as if everything was just the same as ever. But it isn't – it wasn't – and now she's gone. I'm a fucking idiot.'

'She'll be back, Rob,' Laura said, but in her heart she couldn't be sure it was true. If it had been anyone else she'd have believed it, but not Wren. Not calm, consistent Wren. Everything she ever undertook, she did it with such certainty and resolution; and now she had gone. 'And, until she does, I'll be here for you. OK? I can let the agency know I won't be back for a while – and I'll be here to look after Phoebe until Wren comes home. OK, Rob?'

Robert placed his hand over hers and blinked once, a shattered, scotch-soaked curl touching one corner of his mouth. Laura helped him to bed, slipping in beside him and breathing in the ghostly scent of Wren as she drifted into dreams of lost children.

A rap on the passenger window startles her and she slaps the key-bunch to her chest with a gasp. It's Phoebe, and she looks friendly at least. She cocks a thumb, telling Laura to get out of the car. Laura doesn't move for a few seconds, noticing again how grown-up Phoebe has become, how self-assured and calm. In that tranquil, determined way she has about her, she looks so like Wren, it's uncanny. Laura steps out of the car and walks around the rear and into Phoebe's arms, holding her tight.

'I'm so sorry, Phoebs. It was selfish of me, running off like that.'

Phoebe pushes her away to look into her face, before grabbing her back more fiercely than before. When she eases away, Laura takes her hands and lowers her voice. 'Phoebs – there's so much we need to talk about.'

'I know, I know,' Phoebe says. 'Dad and I talked all the way here in the car – he told me so much about my mum, stuff he's never talked about before. About how you met, all those years you three lived together – about you and him growing up in Gatebridge. He even gave me this – ' She reaches into the back pocket of her jeans to produce a passport photograph, the one taken near Camden Lock in their first year at college. 'He's got two – one of his own, and one – you won't believe this – that he found under the floorboards in your old flat. Isn't that amazing? He said I can keep this one, so now we all have one each. You, Dad, Wren and me.'

Laura smiles blankly, baffled by the idea of Robert returning to their old flat, to dig up their old photo. Why would he do that – why would he go there and not tell her, not take her too? It seems like weeks since they were last together, when in fact it's been no more than a weekend. *So many secrets between us*, she thinks, *so many half-truths*. Her pulse races at the thought of that letter he tried to conceal, and she recalls his startled expression while he sat and read it in the car… the lie he told when she asked him about it. She knows Wren isn't telling her everything either, one moment warm and yielding, the next a closed door. And Phoebe – well, Phoebe is protecting another secret altogether. She focuses in on her goddaughter, who's now looking at her with confusion and concern.

'Laura?'

'Phoebs, you're going to have to tell your dad, you know. You have to tell him about the baby.'

Phoebe tries to break away, the colour rising to her cheeks, but Laura holds tight of her fingers, refusing to let her go.

'Phoebe, *please*. I know about this. I've been there myself – just like you, pretending nothing's going on, that everything's fine – and in my experience these things rarely go away by themselves.'

Beyond Phoebe, across the drive, Rob appears in the hotel entrance. When he spots them, his face lights up and he breaks into a jog, his delight at seeing Laura clear. '*Shh*,' Laura whispers locking eyes with Phoebe. 'We'll talk more later. OK? Don't worry. You're not on your own.'

This time it's Phoebe who won't let go, and when Rob sweeps Laura into his embrace Phoebe remains attached, allowing herself to be gathered up into the loving arms of her parents, back together again.

ROB

'We have to talk.'

It's the first thing Rob can think to say, and he immediately realises it's a horrible cliché.

'You don't say, Rob.' Laura pulls back and looks meaningfully at Phoebe, who laughs nervously, gives her dad a little shove. There's something childish in their awkwardness, as they stand in a rigid huddle beside Laura's car, three strangers to Cornwall gathered in a hotel car park. The autumn sun is high in the blue sky, and the smell of the coast is in the air.

Rob tries to smile, but finds his mouth won't do what he wants it to. 'So, you've seen her?' He glances at Phoebe; she knows they are here to find her mother, it's what Phoebe wants, but still, it feels unsettling to be talking about her so openly. 'You've been with Wren?'

Laura looks from Rob to Phoebe, her expression that of stunned surprise. 'I can hardly believe it myself, but she's here. I stayed with her the past couple of nights. She's only a few miles away, along the coast, living in a little cottage overlooking the sea – just her and her dogs.'

The heat drains from Robert's skin, and he's shocked by the power of his reaction. 'She's really here?' He stares into Laura's face; she looks drawn. 'Did she ask about me? About Phoebe? Was she pleased to see you? Does she know – ?'

'Does she want to see me?' Phoebe cuts in, her fingers reaching out to tug at Laura's sleeve, childlike. 'Can we see her?'

Laura backs up against the side of the car. She turns her face towards the sky, releasing a slow breath. 'Christ.' After a pause she runs the heel of her hand up over her brow, appearing distracted by the passing traffic. She turns her attention back to Rob and Phoebe as she twirls her hair into a rope, casting it over her shoulder. 'I haven't thought this through at all. *We* haven't thought this through, Rob. Phoebs, she doesn't even know you're here – in fact, as far as she knows, it's just me. She's different, Rob – she's the same in certain ways, but she's so different. I don't know – I don't know how she'd react if you just turned up. These past couple of days it's been like chipping away at stone – and no, I haven't told her everything about you and me. She knows we're living together, and that I've been around for Phoebe – but I've been nervous about saying too much too soon. We need to be really careful not to scare her off.'

As Rob waits for Laura to continue, his phone buzzes inside his breast pocket, instantly bringing Ava to mind. He fumbles for the phone and looks at the message: *20% off this weekend at Pizza Express.* 'Listen, Laur. We *really* do need to talk,' he says again, 'and not just about Wren.' His mind is bursting with new information; he's struggling to hold on to what matters most – to separate all these things, to pull together and pick apart the connections that thread between them. He has to talk to Laura about Ava, but he knows it will have to wait until he has her alone. Phoebe can't hear this, not yet.

'We *are* talking,' Laura replies. She turns to Phoebe, confused.

'No. *Us.* We need to talk. You and me.'

Phoebe's eyes fill with fear and she crosses her arms, pulls in her chin. 'What is it?' she asks, lowering her voice.

'What do you need to talk about? You two are OK, aren't you? Dad?'

As one, Laura and Rob turn towards Phoebe, both reaching out to reassure her.

'We're fine, really,' says Laura. 'We're all just a bit strung out. Right, Rob?'

Rob nods. 'Right.'

'We've been through worse, haven't we? And we survived.'

Rob nods again, struck mute with the fear of their future, his senses returning to trespass on the raw wounds of those early days after Wren had gone.

For the first few weeks after Phoebe was born Laura visited every weekend without fail, and, while Rob could tell she was eager to bond with her baby goddaughter, he suspected she wasn't exactly sorry to get away from Doug either. Weekends, she'd confided several years earlier, were Doug's low point, the time when all restraint was abandoned, when his demons were most likely to make themselves known. It wasn't as if he even had a proper occupation, a Monday-to-Friday job like the rest of them, yet still the weekend was when he was most likely to go on a bender, and Laura was only too glad of an excuse to be out of it.

'At any rate, Robbie, you need me more at the moment,' she told him as she emptied her rucksack out on to the spare bed, organising her few belongings before deftly taking over Phoebe duties.

And she was right: Rob did need her. What he probably didn't entirely appreciate was that Wren's need for Laura was even greater than his; he barely allowed himself to acknowledge the weak relief in Wren's face every time her best friend reappeared in their front doorway. Even a couple of weeks after Phoebe's birth Wren was shadowy and slight, but the health visitor was encouraging, quick to put it down to the demands of breastfeeding and mild anaemia. She left them with iron pills, leaflets and a well-practised hug, and then they were on their own. And so, when Fridays came around and Laura arrived on the doorstep in a flurry of auburn locks and good humour, Rob couldn't have been happier. Together they glossed over Wren's passive mood, answering for her, telling her not to expect to run before she could walk, and during Laura's visits at least she seemed to pick up a little. Simultaneously there grew an unspoken agreement that they would no longer discuss Laura's own want of a child; while Phoebe was there to glue them all together, the system worked. Between them, the collusion was almost flawless.

When Phoebe was just over a fortnight old, Rob went back to work, having taken all the additional leave he could possibly afford in his position at the school. Laura stayed on for an extra night to help ease Wren into her first day without Rob, and that morning he left them together at the breakfast table, kissing each before pausing in the doorway to study them for a moment, his two oldest friends passing baby Phoebe between them as they ate. Together they sat, beautifully make-up-free in their dressing gowns, and they smiled, waved him away, told him to forget about them, to have a good day.

'It's like having two wives,' he joked, and Laura told him to think again, threatening to lob the sugar bowl at him if he didn't hop it quick.

As he eased out into the Monday morning traffic, and drove along the well-travelled route towards school, his relief was overwhelming. He was out – out from beneath the stifling blanket of home life – of feeding and cleaning and changing and caring, of fretting and checking and making the best. Of broken sleep and unspoken fears. For those brief hours, from Monday to Friday, Rob felt entirely free.

Eventually, Laura takes control, and the three of them retreat inside for a hurried tea in the hotel bar, while they devise a plan for the afternoon ahead. Rob agrees easily. Somehow he senses he's on Laura's territory here, even though she only arrived in Cornwall a short while before him. But those few hours, those two nights make all the difference to their roles here. She's seen Wren – talked to her – and with that advantage Laura is best placed to lead the way.

Phoebe is insistent that she will see her mother, no matter how she is received. 'She owes me that much, doesn't she?' she asks Laura across the bright cotton tablecloth of their window seat. The waitress places tea for three on the table between them, along with a plate of biscuits. Phoebe reaches for one. 'What's the worst that can happen? She's rejected me once. It's not going to kill me if she does it again.'

Rob looks aghast at the thought. 'Sweetheart? I know you're putting on a brave face, but – '

Phoebe stirs her tea with some force, and he knows to give in.

'Eat something, Dad,' she says. 'You barely touched the sandwiches I made on the way here.' And for the next ten minutes a silence falls over the table, as they eat their biscuits and drink their tea, each lost in their own private thoughts.

By mid-afternoon, under Laura's guidance, Rob is driving them back along the coastal roads, in the direction of the cottage, where they will deliver Phoebe, like a parcel, to Wren's front door. Rob's heart is pounding, his knuckles stretched pale at the wheel, and he searches his mind for something, something useful, *anything* reassuring to say to Phoebe, who sits in the back seat, gazing serenely from the window at the fields and coastline passing by. His eyes return to her in the rear-view mirror, and he knows from her resolute avoidance that she is aware of him looking, as she stoically buttons herself up to cope with whatever may come. She's so like Wren in that way, it almost breaks him to see it. Some fifteen minutes later they turn into the narrow track leading towards Wren's place and Laura indicates to pull over a little way down the lane, where she knows the car won't be seen. The blue eaves of the cottage are just visible, peeking over the top of the hedgerow, the only indication that there's a house there at all. The unfamiliarity of it all opens up inside him like a wound: to think that Wren is just beyond that border, that she's been here, without them for all these years. Alone.

'She won't like it,' Laura warns, twisting in her seat to face Phoebe. 'Don't let her – her seriousness – put you off. She'll be shocked. She might even refuse to talk to you at all. Phoebs? Can you cope with that? Because we're going to leave you here on your own.'

'*Laura*, I'm an adult. I'll be fine.' As she says this, Rob detects the uncertainty in her voice, sees the tiny furrow of anxiety in her smooth young forehead.

Laura pauses to look at Rob in the seat beside her. He feels exposed, useless. She squeezes his hand before turning back to Phoebe. 'OK,' she says. 'So, I'll take you to the door, then your dad and I are going to carry on down this path to the car park at the end. We'll walk out to the rocks, give you as long as you want, or need – but if you've had enough, if it doesn't go well, head down that way and we'll meet up one way or another. You can't go wrong; it's just one road, straight down to the beach.' She rummages about in her bag and hands Phoebe a ten-pound note. 'Get yourself a hot chocolate if you have to wait around for us. There's a kiosk in the car park.'

Phoebe takes the money. 'Hopefully *she'll* make me a drink, and then I can give this back to you.'

'Hopefully,' says Laura. She purses her lips decisively and opens the passenger door. 'Let's go.'

Rob remains in the driver's seat as, hand in hand, Laura and Phoebe take the short walk towards Wren's cottage. They hesitate just before the opening in the hedge, to turn and wave, and Rob notices for the first time just how much Phoebe has changed. She's right, of course: she's all grown up, and with some small sadness he realises that baby Phoebe is now head and shoulders above little Laura. The thought of Wren rejecting her now, of her not reaching out to gather her up as a mother should – it's almost more than he can bear to contemplate. How, Rob wonders, will Wren see the infant in her now – how will she know that she's hers?

Visions of newborn Ava expand in Rob's mind, an infant discarded on a hospital ward, motherless, fatherless, a secret hidden across the years. He watches a line of birds as it slices the sky, and he cries out in self-loathing at the wall he has built up against the idea of her. This is his child; if he were to deny Ava, as Wren has denied Phoebe, how could he live with himself? The thought of her out in the world all this time, robbed of knowledge, is too cruel, too unjust. Slamming the car door, Rob heads down the sand-blown dirt track, scrolling through his phone until he locates the email with Ava's number attached. The wind snaps at the back of his neck and he pulls his collar up against the cold, dialling the number, keeping watch on the path behind, in case Laura should reappear.

Ava answers on the third ring. 'Hello?' she says.

'Ava? This is Robert Irving.' He's aware how formal he sounds, so startled is he that she should have answered at all.

There's a pause on the line before she responds. 'Oh, my God! Oh, my *God*! I can't believe it's actually you!' Ava sounds young, so much younger than the written voice of her emails. She can hardly contain her excitement, and Rob feels the thrill of her delight rushing at him. 'Talk to me, so I can hear your voice!'

He laughs; it's like talking to Phoebe at her most playful, or a couple of years back, before she headed off to university. 'Goodness, this feels strange, doesn't it?' he says, suddenly self-conscious. They will remember this conversation forever; the sun is high and bright in the sky, the wind biting cold, every word they speak loaded with expectation. The enormity of the moment is not lost on him. 'I meant to reply to your email earlier – you know, about meeting up some time?'

'Yes?'

'I'd like that, of course.'

'You would? Oh, that's such a relief to hear – I can't tell you – I was really worried I might have scared you off, asking so soon after making contact. I mean, I've had my whole life to get used to the idea that I've got other parents out there – but you – well, you know what I mean?'

She sounds so gentle, so generous, and Robert feels like a self-centred idiot for fearing this contact, for his initial dread. 'I was so sorry to hear about your mum, Ava. That's tough when you're still so young. But it sounds as if she's done a wonderful job raising you.'

'Well, you know.' She laughs again, this time awkwardly, nervously. 'She was pretty ill for a long time, and I'd been wanting to track down my birth parents for years, but was too worried about how she'd feel. Not that I – '

'No, no, of course. It's terrible to watch a loved one get ill like that. What about your dad – is he still around?'

'Oh, yeah, I've still got my dad. He's found it quite hard, since Mum, so I've been helping him to go through her things this weekend as he couldn't face it. I'm actually up in the spare room going through one of her old suitcases now – that's how I managed to get hold of that photograph.'

Rob's stomach flips. 'Photograph?'

'Didn't you get my last email? The one with the picture of you attached – at least that's who I'm hoping it is! It's the photo my birth mother left with her letter.'

Instinctively Rob turns back to look up the path for Laura, the shame of his deceit rearing its head again. 'No – no, the last one I got was about meeting up. I haven't seen one with a picture.'

'Well, look out for it – and phone me when you get it? I'm desperate to know if it's you or not.'

'Will you resend it? I'm not at home but I can pick up emails on my phone now – resend it now, will you?' He can hear the pace in his voice accelerating; they're running out of time before Laura returns for him.

'OK, I'll do it straight away. So, about meeting up? What do you think?'

To Rob's alarm the figure of Laura reappears in the distance, just beyond the bonnet of his car. She raises an arm to wave. 'Ava, can I call you back later?' he says.

'What? Oh, yes – about meeting up? OK, you've got my number?'

'Yes,' he whispers, turning away from Laura as she now approaches, his pulse hammering. 'It's just I need to tell my family about you first, you understand?'

'Of course! Just so you know, I'm sending that photo now – '

'Ava, I've got to go – ' and then Laura is right beside him, and he panics and snaps shut his phone. Shutting off the phone; shutting off Ava.

'Who was that?' Laura asks, slipping her arm through his and steering them back towards the car.

'Oh, another one of those poxy PPI claims companies.' He stops in the road and turns Laura towards him. 'Is she alright? Phoebe – is she going to be alright in there?'

Laura kisses him and jerks her head towards the car. 'She's going to be just fine. She's made of stronger stuff than you and I, Rob. Your daughter's a bloody trooper.'

Jane Pearson, one of Wren's colleagues, had a baby just a couple of weeks after Phoebe arrived, and so it seemed natural that they should meet from time to time, for afternoon tea and 'play'. Rob always thought this was a great laugh, the concept of these tiny babies playing, when they couldn't yet sit up.

'What do the babies do? Lie there pulling each other's ears while you two drink coffee and natter?'

'Pretty much,' Wren replied.

One Friday evening, Rob arrived home just as Jane and baby Jacob were leaving, and, riding in on his end-of-the-week high, he invited her and husband Graham to join them for Sunday lunch that weekend. As soon as Jane was safely off the front drive, Wren let her dismay be known.

'Sunday lunch?' she asked. She dropped her shoulders, appeared smaller still.

'You're getting awfully thin,' Rob replied, as if that was a suitable response.

Wren lowered her eyes, handed him the baby and spent the rest of the evening in the spare room, sleeping on the single bed beside Phoebe's crib.

When Sunday came around, Rob cooked, busying himself in the kitchen in the hours before the Pearsons arrived, while Wren took care of Phoebe. Somehow, they had managed to avoid talking about the impending lunch; over the past few months they had lost the ability to disagree out in the open, and instead Wren's deep dread of the occasion steeped away beneath the surface, as Rob chattered about his work, and behaved as if everything was just fine.

'Are they drinkers?' Rob asked. He was standing in the doorway to the lounge, holding aloft one bottle of red wine, one bottle of white.

Wren looked up from Phoebe, who was tucked beneath her blouse, feeding. She shrugged. 'I don't know Jane all that well. Maybe.'

He knew she was criticising him, passive in her deflection. 'Really? You seemed pretty chummy to me.'

Wren lifted Phoebe from her breast, adjusted her underwear and switched sides. 'Well, I can tell you what washing powder she uses to reduce her eczema – and how long her labour was – and how many hours Jacob slept on Thursday night. But as for her drinking preferences, Rob, I really haven't a clue.' Her eyes remained fixed on the back of Phoebe's head.

Rob lowered the wine bottles and smiled blankly. 'I'll stick the white in the fridge, then, just in case.' He left her feeding and returned to the reassuring warmth of the kitchen, to potter about checking the lamb and singing along to The Clash until the doorbell rang at midday on the dot.

Jane and Graham breezed through the hallway in a flurry of goodwill, bringing with them the soft scent of Johnson's baby powder and a bottle of Australian white. Jane handed Jacob to Rob as they returned to the front drive to ferry in a seemingly endless supply of baby paraphernalia, amid comradely laughter and eyes raised to the heavens.

'He can't go anywhere without Buns!' Jane apologised as she lugged in Jacob's enormous blue rabbit. She wiggled Buns in the baby's direction to demonstrate. Jacob returned a flatulent blink, before extending a tiny hand, clenching and flexing his fingers towards the toy.

'See?' Jane laughed, and she scooped up the baby and left Rob and Graham in the kitchen as she went to seek out Wren. 'There you both are!' Rob heard her exclaim from along the hall, and he shuddered at the thought of Wren sitting on the sofa loathing Jane, loathing him. This whole thing had been a stupid idea. A stupid, *stupid* idea.

'Jane's the designated driver,' Graham said as he handed over his bottle. 'And in any event she won't drink a drop while she's breastfeeding. Probably why the little bugger keeps us awake half the night!'

Rob laughed and poured them both a drink.

'I've told her – give yourself a break! A glass of wine won't hurt; in fact it might do both of them a bit of good to loosen up a bit. But she won't listen – determined to be Mum of the Year in everything.'

Rob offered George a stuffed olive. 'An impossible task.'

'You'd think, wouldn't you? So, how's yours? Phoebe? Does she sleep?' He leant in, in an instant betraying his exhaustion. The circles under his eyes were puffy and grey.

'She's not too bad,' Rob replied, erring on the side of vagueness. The truth was that she had been sleeping fairly well since she was a month old, but what new parent wanted to hear that? He indicated for them to move through to join the others. 'Highs and lows, you know. I'm sure little Jake will be sleeping right through before you know it!'

'It's Jacob,' Jane corrected him as they entered the living room. She was sitting on the rug with the baby, the coffee table having been pushed to one side to make room for Jacob and his vast array of multicoloured toys.

'Like the cream cracker?' Rob asked with a smirk. Wren met his eye, and he nearly, so very nearly detected a glimmer of a smile in the white of her eye that he was tempted to carry on. 'Like David – '

'No,' Graham and Jane answered together.

'After the Old Testament,' Jane said. After a tense pause, she broke into a wide smile and loomed over the infant, grabbing at his round tummy. 'And what a fine little Jacob he is!'

Jacob gasped, startled, and for a moment Rob actually hoped he would cry. Instead, the baby gurgled happily and sicked up a thin dribble of breast milk. Rob glanced at Wren, saw her staring fixedly at the milky trail as it ran from Jacob's mouth and pooled on the rug beside his ear. She looked appalled.

When the doorbell rang Rob was almost grateful. 'Excuse me,' he said, placing his glass on the mantelpiece and leaving the group listening to Jane's plans to breastfeed for a minimum of two years. He was still grimacing as he opened the door, where he found Laura standing on the doorstep, blessedly familiar in her parka and boots, her army surplus kit bag at her feet.

'Room for a small one?' she smiled, reaching out for a hug. 'I was missing Phoebe, so I thought I'd surprise you!' She inclined her head, tuning in to the strange voices along the hall. 'Oh, God! You've got guests – I should have called!' She dropped back down off the step as if to leave.

Rob reached out and grabbed her by the sleeve, dragging her over the threshold and scooping up her bag in one swift movement. 'You're not going anywhere,' he said, in hushed tones, nudging her along the hall. 'You were sent to save us. I want you to meet Graham and Jane. They're a brilliant advert for not having kids.'

At the beach kiosk, Rob asks for two teas and thumbs through his old phone messages as they wait – there's definitely no sign of that email and photograph from Ava. Ava… How in hell's name is he going to broach the subject with Laura, with *Phoebe*?

'This is Arthur,' Laura says, breaking into his muddled thoughts.

'Oh?' he replies. He takes a good look at the chap pouring hot water into their cardboard cups and wonders how he is of significance to Wren. He's in his late sixties, weathered and slightly tatty, with a sharp intelligence shining from his eyes. Rob offers his hand. 'Rob. Glad to meet you. So – so, you must know Wren?'

Arthur hands them their teas, gestures towards the milk and sugar. 'I do,' he replies.

'We don't really – ' Rob starts to say, but Laura stops him with a touch to his wrist and he takes a small step away from the counter, feeling like a foreigner in a strange land. He looks out over the car park, where a group of surfers are congregated, unstrapping their boards and zipping themselves into wetsuits.

'We don't get to visit very often,' Laura fills in, and Rob turns back to her, to watch her speak. She lies so easily, he observes. An unbidden thought rushes into the front of his mind: what if she were to leave him again? Would he see the signs; would he see it coming? He didn't spot the signs with Wren, and she was gone in an instant. Suddenly he feels cold to the bone and he wraps his fingers around the corrugated cup, brings it close to his lips, draws in the heat.

Arthur hands Laura her change. 'I can't say I've ever known Wren to have visitors,' he says, 'so you must be special guests.'

'We are!' Laura replies, sounding high-spirited. 'Have you known her very long, Arthur?'

'Ever since she got here. I don't know, nearly twenty years – gawd, that makes me realise how old I'm getting. I see her most days, though, with the sausages. She's not much of a one for chitchat, but she's a sturdy walker.'

'Sausages?' Rob asks, trying to bring his thoughts back into order.

'Dogs.' Laura laughs. 'Dachshunds. Badger and Willow – you'll get to see them later on, Rob. They're lovely – makes me feel quite tempted to get one myself!'

'So you haven't seen her yet?' Arthur leans back on to his stool, addressing Rob. 'She was out on the rocks this morning as usual. I'm surprised you didn't call in on her on the way past?'

Laura blows on her hot tea. 'Rob's only just got here, so we thought we'd take a walk on the beach after his long drive. Stretch our legs!'

Rob's had enough of the lies and subterfuge. He just wants the truth to out. 'We've just dropped Phoebe at Wren's, so they can catch up.'

Laura stiffens visibly.

'Phoebe?' Arthur says, folding his arms, displaying rough fingers covered in newsprint.

'Her daughter,' Rob replies, ignoring Laura's silent fury. Has Wren never mentioned her child to this friend of hers, not once in twenty years? He looks back along the coastal path, in the direction of the little stone cottage and wonders if Phoebe's alright up there, alone with Wren.

Laura hooks her arm beneath his elbow and draws him away. 'She was probably trying to avoid the subject of family. You know what she's like. She's very private.' She raises a hand and calls back over her shoulder. 'We'll see you later, Arthur!'

They walk away, down through the car park to the wide expanse of sand below, feeling the heat of Arthur's gaze on their backs.

Laura's yearning for a child was a faceless beast, something Rob felt keenly in the silent moments when she was visiting, swooping Phoebe from Wren's arms to cradle her gently, gazing down at her with an expression of love more profound than he had ever seen from Wren. Looking back, it was as if she, Laura, had always been Phoebe's real mother. It was just that she hadn't carried her in her womb, delivered her into the world. And it was this that she longed for, that she wept for behind the closed door of the spare room, where she thought Rob and Wren couldn't hear her. It pained him so deeply, this loss in her, this emptiness, and yet, from the moment Phoebe arrived, it became the thing they couldn't talk about, the creature they couldn't look in the eye.

In the October before Wren left, Laura arrived late one Friday night after an absence of over a month. She had been staying away, she said, because she didn't want to jinx it by telling them too soon – and she knew she wouldn't be able to keep it from them for even a minute if she saw them. But in the end she couldn't wait a second longer, needed to share her joy with the two most important people in her life. She was pregnant – just eight weeks, but it was the longest she'd ever held on to a child in recent years, and she felt good about this one, felt sure everything was going to work out. After all, how unlucky could one woman be? Wren's spirits soared at the news, and she persuaded Laura to stay for the weekend, fussing over her like a mother, insisting that Laura have lie-ins as she brought her breakfast and newspapers in bed. Rob watched Wren, entranced. The life flooded back into her features, the light growing bright behind her eyes.

'I'm not ill!' Laura complained, as Rob and Wren sat at the foot of the single bed, pinching her toes, delighted at her news.

'We'll be in it together,' Wren said as Rob left the room to respond to Phoebe's cries from the kitchen. He returned with her in his arms and stood in the doorway, swaying her to sleep. 'We'll be the best parents,' Wren said, 'and Rob of course.'

Laura and Rob laughed; Wren always used to say it was more like *they* were the married ones, with Rob thrown in to balance them out. Laura picked up her mug and took a swig. 'So what do you think I'll have?'

'I think you're having a girl,' Wren replied resolutely, and she moved up the bed to pull Laura against her body, to cup their chins over one another's shoulder like two parts of the same person.

Rob watched them together, at the fresh glow radiating from Wren, and he wished Laura could stay, wished she could move in with them and stay forever. Only in the times when Laura was around could he fully acknowledge the steep decline he'd been witnessing in Wren; she grew fainter with every passing day, her vibrancy fading like a candle in a room with no air. When Laura returned, the flame would flicker to life, increasing in strength and luminosity, and Wren would return to their home, to him and Phoebe. He studied Laura's face as she held on to Wren, her eyes closed, the creases of her forehead smoothed out in peace, and he thought about asking her: *Move in with us, Lolly, just like before – at college – remember how happy we were?* He imagined her reply, her delight – Wren's delight – as they hatched their plan, filled up his car with her belongings, settled her into her new room. He saw Laura and Wren strolling through the park with their pushchairs, feeding ducks at the river, the three of them taking holidays together; growing old together.

Phoebe whimpered in his arms, bringing him back to the present. He knew it was a childish notion and one he would never voice; there was Doug, of course, it was his baby too – and soon, Rob feared, Laura would be swept along with her own concerns, bogged down in the mire of new parenthood, something he knew about only too well. Broken nights and nappies and fear and exhilaration and washing and shopping and anxiety and love, love so huge it could break you in two… There was so much to think about now that Laura was to be a parent, now that they were all to be parents. So much to live for.

Three weeks later, shortly before her twelve-week appointment with the midwife, Laura miscarried. After the medics had performed a D&C and put her in a taxi home with painkillers and leaflets, Doug embarked on a forty-eight-hour binge of self-medication, leaving Laura at home alone with her grief. She phoned Rob to break the news, telling him that she hoped he understood, but she wouldn't be round this weekend, or the next, as she had to rest. And it was just too painful for her at the moment – to see Phoebe – to see Rob and Wren and Phoebe. She didn't want any visitors, any fuss. Would he tell Wren, would he explain to her?

For the next few days, Wren was inconsolable. It was as if it were she who had lost a baby. She couldn't speak to him, couldn't handle Phoebe, couldn't go to the phone. And then, just as quickly, she was out from the hole again, back to her regular subdued state, back to the way things were before Laura had announced she was pregnant. They didn't discuss it, didn't mention Laura at all, but as far as Rob was concerned things were functioning again: they rose in the mornings, he went to work, and when he returned each evening Wren was there on the sofa with Phoebe and everything was just fine.

A fortnight later, she was gone.

Laura leads Rob up through the rocks until they reach a large pool at the top of the formation. It's huge, draped in seaweed and mussels and thick plates of barnacles that spread up over the edges and out across the stone bank. They stand at the pool's edge, looking out over the beach and ocean. Laura takes his hand.

'Are you sure she'll be alright?' Rob asks again, feeling the power slip from him.

'Of course. I wouldn't take any risks with Phoebe, would I? I've been with Wren for the past few days, and yes, she's changed a lot – but it's nothing to be concerned about. She's not a danger, Rob, if that's what's worrying you.'

He squeezes her fingers, looks up into the blue sky above, his eyes following the movements of a large bird heading out to sea. 'God, Laura, I don't know what I'd do without you right now. This whole thing, it's just a bloody great mess.'

'What do you mean?' Her red curls lift and hover in the bright breeze. 'How's it a mess? Finally Phoebe's getting to meet her mother. Surely that's got to be a *good* thing?'

'Wren's not her mother, Laur, not really. Not like you. You're the one who was there for her first day of school, her first words, her first exam. Not Wren.'

Laura reaches behind her head to gather up the tangle of hair that whips about her face.

'It's not the same, Rob. I love her like my own, you know that. But Phoebe needed to find Wren eventually – she needed to know where she came from. Wouldn't you, if your mother had given you up?'

Rob narrows his eyes, tries to make sense of her words, her actions. She stands before him, her hands thrust in deep pockets, her sturdy little boots planted firmly against the rock. He wishes he could burrow down inside her thoughts, to seek out her truth, uncover her secrets.

'What?' she asks. 'Why are you looking at me like that?'

Rob

Inside his jacket pocket, Rob's phone vibrates, and he reaches for it with fumbling fingertips. He opens his inbox as a backup of delayed messages floods in. Most are junk, but finally, here is the one he is expecting from Ava. Rob turns away from Laura, walks slowly around the edge of the rock pool so that he can stand facing out to sea, his back to her. He opens the message:

Hi Robert,

It was so great to speak to you! Thank you for phoning. We got cut off, but as promised here is that photo. I'm pretty sure it's the one mentioned in my mother's letter. Is it you? I hope so!

Ax

Rob can barely hear the crash of the waves over the roaring in his own head. With fear and anticipation rushing through his veins, he clicks to open the attachment, and waits, waits, waits as the little green arrow on the screen rotates and the image loads.

WREN

Wren didn't acknowledge the first shifts in her perspective until several months into her pregnancy with Phoebe. The early weeks were a rush of exhilaration, mostly Rob's, as they kept a lid on the news, waiting as advised until they crossed the line into the twelve-week safety zone. Never before had Wren seen such excitement coursing from him, and he talked at length about all the things they would all do together, the places they would see.

'I know we're going to be the best parents ever,' he told her, his gentle palm circling her still flat stomach. 'And I know we're going to make the most beautiful baby the world has ever seen.'

What he didn't know, and what would have hurt him deeply him if he had, was that he wasn't the first to find out.

On a late summer morning in September, just before the schools returned for the new term, Wren had met Laura at the station where they caught the train to Camden, for a day trip to mark their last days of freedom from the classroom. Rob stayed at home, preparing for the new term, having 'a mountain' of forms and assessments to complete as part of his fast-track programme. Since they'd moved into their new family home in Peynton Gardens a year earlier, he had been working harder than ever, to secure their future with his plans to scale the career ladder.

'*Yawn*,' Laura laughed as Wren told her about Rob's progress so far. They were sitting at table seats, their bags and coats spread out beside them to put other passengers off joining them. 'I know I should be more ambitious, but really, I think I'd die of boredom doing all that paperwork, jumping through all those hoops. Now I've got used to it, I'm quite enjoying the freedom of supply teaching.'

'Rob would hate that – you know what he's like about having things "settled". He's obsessed with security. You know: pensions, savings plans, mortgage rises and falls. I wish he'd lighten up a bit. He's turning into an old man before he's even thirty.' Wren sifted through her bag, searching for the cereal bar she had packed for the journey. She tore open the packet and held it up, poised to break it in half. 'Want some?'

Laura wrinkled her nose – 'Rabbit food!' – and waited for the tea trolley to come by with its biscuits and crisps.

At Camden Lock, Laura left Wren at the canalside while she went in search of a cashpoint before they decided on somewhere for lunch. The sun was high and bright over the water, and Wren wandered alongside the railings to look out across the water, where sparkling white shards dipped and rolled with the movement of the canal boats that daytripped along the waterway. There was still heat in the air, and across the lock families and couples reclined on the benches and low walls, turning their faces to the sun, feeling its rays warm their skin. Wren was struck by the serenity of the vista, and how, all at once, every one of them – the mothers, children, lovers, friends – every last one of them was here in this moment with her, feeling this sunshine, not thinking of the future, nor the past. Like Wren, they were simply *here*.

'Woohoo!'

Wren was plucked from her warm trance by Laura's cry, and she spun around to see her friend jogging across the stone path, a silk Paisley scarf flowing from her fingers.

Laura gently wound it around Wren's neck and gave her a peck on the cheek.

'What's this for?' Wren asked.

'I must have lost at least three of your scarves when we were living together at Victoria Terrace. I'm making amends.'

Wren laughed, smoothing the silk through her palm. 'You didn't lose them,' she said, giving Laura a little shove as she leant over the railings to peer into the water below. 'You kept giving them to your delinquent boyfriends. I remember Jack coming on stage one night with my favourite houndstooth print wrapped round his head like a school tie. That was the last I saw of that!'

'I was always stupid around boys. In my defence, I was usually so drunk when I gave your stuff away that I really believed it was mine to give. Bloody hell – Jack! I haven't thought of him in years. I wonder what he's doing these days. Probably a bald banker by now.'

'And fat. In my mind's eye, all my exes are fat and bald and miserably married with kids.'

'While, of course, we both just get better and better with age.' Laura flicked her hair self-indulgently and hooked her arm through Wren's.

They chatted and walked alongside the water, enjoying the bustle and flow that spilled out from the shops and bars that edged the busy pathway, eventually deciding on a café for lunch, where Laura set off to find a table in the sun while Wren visited the Ladies'. Once inside the cubicle, she leant against the back of the door and opened her bag, drawing out a pharmacy pack containing the pregnancy test she had bought in the high street on the way down. She hadn't wanted Laura to see, so she'd purposely lost her at the perfume counter of Boots, sprinting off to make her purchase and exclaiming her relief at having found her again minutes later. Now, she unwrapped the testing stick and shoved the wrappers in the bin, rapidly double-reading the instructions to make sure she did the test properly. She was only a couple of days late, but so certain she'd felt a little different when she woke this morning – somehow *outside* of herself – that she'd known she couldn't wait a moment longer to take the test. With care, she held the tip of the tester in her urine stream and sat watching as the liquid blotted through the stick. Checking her watch, she waited and counted and then turned her eyes back to the stick, and there it was, quick and clear and without delay or doubt – a double bar. Her stomach flipped over – a rush of adrenaline, and what? Happiness? Fear? All those things and more.

Outside, Laura had found them a table beneath a bright Orangina umbrella, and she waved Wren over just as the barman turned up with two large cocktails.

'Margaritas!' Laura announced, lifting her glass and holding it up to the light. 'Remember? For old times' sake.'

Wren sat down, stared at the frosted lime drinks and frowned. 'I'm not sure – ' she said, grasping for words. 'I – '

At first Laura looked perplexed, but quickly her expression changed to one of shocked comprehension. 'Oh. My. God.' Her eyes sparkled, blinking hard at Wren as she lowered her glass, her mouth opening like an 'O'. She leant in close to the table, her hand sliding across to grip Wren's. 'You are, aren't you?'

Wren's gaze fell on their entwined hands, their fingers tangled together like a stack of slipper limpets and her face shifted into a slow, shy smile as her eyes met Laura's. She nodded, hushing her voice, feeling almost fraudulent as she spoke the words. 'I just did a test, Laur. It's *positive*.'

Laura clapped a hand to her mouth, rushing around the table to crush Wren in her embrace. Waving excitedly, she called over a new waiter and returned the margaritas, claiming they'd been sent the wrong drinks. 'We'll have a large freshly squeezed orange juice, please. And a huge glass of champagne. We're celebrating.' She smiled proudly. 'We're having a baby.'

Willow and Badger sense the alteration in Wren as they scurry ahead of her through the meadow, halting to check back every once in a while for reassurance that she's following. When Willow turns, the soft dome of her head wrinkles, causing her dappled brow markings to incline in an exaggeration of concern.

'On,' Wren says, with a sweep of her hand.

The dogs wriggle beneath the low bar of the stile, stopping to sniff at the salt-split fence post on the other side. As Wren climbs over, she glances back towards the house, at the upper gables just visible beyond the wall of hedge, and wonders if Laura is still standing in the garden, waiting for her to change her mind and return.

Her own anger has taken her by surprise. The rational part of her recognises the guilt and dread she's pushing down inside herself, and she'd known it was only a matter of time before Laura demanded some answers, but anger isn't her usual response. In the absence of other human contact, Wren has, until now, found it entirely possible to blank out unwanted emotion, to stuff it down and muffle its voice. To function and to exist, neither happy nor sad, but at some level of peace. But now Laura – she's forced her way in, and she's given this blank space a voice, and a face, and Wren hates her for it, hates her for trespassing on her life, for peeling back the corners of her past and forcing her to look in. The things she said last night in the cave – about Phoebe and the baby, about Rob – they seem unreal now, like one of her dreams. *But she's only a baby herself*, Wren had replied, unable to process the news, unable to shift her thoughts forward, to think of her infant as now grown. And what about the rest of the story? Surely Laura's not telling her the whole story. There has to be more to tell. There *must* to be more to tell, or else Wren doesn't know how she can go forward from here, how she can bear to keep going with all that Laura has told her, and all that she has not. *What else?* she wanted to scream at her in the darkness, but she dared not for fear of the reply. When Laura had told her that she hadn't seen Rob for a full year after Wren had gone, that he had spent all that time alone with Phoebe, her heart had shrunk, injured. *You should have been there, Laura,* she thinks now. *You were meant to be there*. Perhaps then it would have all come together in the way she had dreamed for them, Rob and Laura and Phoebe, and, soon afterwards, a child of their own.

Poor Laura, poor wonderful, beautiful Laura. How Wren has missed her, deep in that locker of buried feeling. What must she make of all this? What does she see when she looks at Wren, at the plainness of the small stone cottage, at the bonfire debris of the garden and the dogs who sleep on the bed. What must she make of the transformation in Wren? She doesn't even own a mirror, save the small broken compact mirror she digs out when she cuts her own hair. These days she only knows herself from the most practical of distances, observing the turn of her skin as spring gives way to summer, or the hardening of her thumb pads as the digging of the autumn soil gets under way. The absence of clutter is soothing to her; gone are the beauty-seeking lotions and potions of her youth, the constrictions of fashion, the exhaustion of vanity. But now, something about opening the door to Laura – to the past – uncovers that long forgotten self-consciousness in her, and she wonders how her looks are holding up in this, the year she turned fifty. *Fifty*. Her father didn't even make it that far, she realises, and it saddens her all the more as she looks out across the bay and sees a young family stooped at the water's edge, filling a bucket, a parent on either side of a yellow-anoraked toddler. He would have made a good grandfather, given the chance.

The grip of Wren's pregnancy was a stealthy thing, like a slowly tightening fist, whose pressure increased so gradually that no real pain was felt, yet the restriction grew steadily, intensifying, smothering, until one day she woke up hardly able to breathe.

At twelve weeks, Rob was ready to announce their joy from the rooftops.

'I'd take out an advert on the side of a bus if I could,' he declared over breakfast, patting down his muesli and smiling to himself in anticipation of telling his colleagues. 'So, are you going to phone your mother tonight?'

Wren unwrapped a new packet of Weetabix and put two biscuits in her bowl, feeling troubled that they didn't fit perfectly, wouldn't quite lie flat. 'One thing at a time,' she replied, gesturing for the milk. 'I'll get work out of the way first.'

Rob passed the carton down the table, and fetched the sugar bowl for her. 'You make it sound like an arduous task. Aren't you excited about telling everyone?'

She shrugged. 'I feel a bit embarrassed, if I'm honest.'

'Embarrassed?' Rob sat down again, raised his spoon. 'Why on earth would you feel embarrassed?'

'I don't know. They'll make a fuss – stop talking to me and start talking to my stomach. I saw it with Tracey Bell and Shelley Cowley when they were expecting. Everyone starts speaking all sing-song, like you've had a bash on the head. *So, how's the new mum, then? Ooh, aren't you getting big? Look at you – blooming!* I even did it myself. I don't want all that.'

Rob shook his head, spooning muesli into his mouth and checking his watch. 'You old grouch. They'll be delighted for you, and there's nothing wrong with that. As will your mother, if you'll ever get around to letting her know. Shall we ring her tonight?'

Wren forced a tight smile and took her bowl to the sink, abandoning the second Weetabix, mushy now at the bottom. 'OK,' she said with her back to him, 'we'll phone her tonight,' and she left him at the table while she headed up to the bedroom to get ready for work.

At her dressing table she reached for her hairbrush then stopped, alarmed by her reflection. Since discovering she was pregnant she had been almost constantly queasy with morning sickness, and only in the past week had she started to feel better, physically. But now that the nausea was gone she was left with something else, something below the surface that she couldn't quite articulate. The circles below her eyes were dark, haunted-looking, the corners of her mouth downturned. Far from 'blooming', she looked terrible.

It's the baby. At once she understood: *there must be something wrong with the baby.* Standing, she allowed her dressing gown to drop to the floor, and stood before the mirror in her underwear, slowly moving her fingers across the gentle new shape of her waist and stomach, concentrating, squeezing her eyes shut as she tried to communicate with the foetus growing inside – tried to glean some greater perception of the crisis that raged within.

'Wren?' Her eyes snapped open and there in the doorway, reflected in her mirror, was Robert, concern visible on his face. His fingers held on to the doorframe. 'What's wrong?'

She stared at him, momentarily unable to respond, before breaking away from the mirror to retrieve her dressing gown, to cover her changing form. 'Nothing,' she said, her eyes darting to his. 'I'm fine.'

He remained in the doorway a few moments longer, a strange expression fixed in his eyes. 'OK,' he finally said, and reached out to snatch his tie off the wardrobe door. 'Sure you're OK? Well – I'd better get a move on or I'll be late for work.' Pausing in the hallway, he looked back at her, awkwardly winding the tie around his hand. 'Good luck with telling your workmates,' he said, and then he vanished down the stairs like a stranger.

Wren got dressed for work, where she would successfully conceal her pregnancy for another two long weeks, before being outed by Shelley Cowley who had observed her ongoing abstention from tea and coffee, and who *knew all the signs*. Shelley, as it turned out, was the first to tell Wren she was blooming, but she would be by no means the last.

Blooming, Wren thinks now as she follows Willow and Badger along towards the beach. *Flowers bloom, not women.* She rests against one of the rocky boulders at the mouth of the cave, scooping up a large nugget of polished glass from the sand as her eyes travel across the merging panorama of sky and sea. The glass pebble appears to be the very colour of the sea today... could almost be the essence of the ocean, made solid. She pushes it into the palm of her hand; it's just the kind of trinket she would have collected up and taken home as a child, a totem of time and place, a souvenir. She unfurls her fingers and lets the nugget drop to the sand between her boots. She's been out here for hours, where it's safe, where she doesn't have to think, to speak, to face Laura's questions and challenges. Badger and Willow are having a mad five minutes, chasing each other in wide galloping circles, coughing out barks of excitement and kicking up the sand in their wake. Occasionally they halt at a distance, tails waving stiffly, their wrinkled mouths turned up in anticipation as they wait for the other to begin again. Wren wonders at the joy of a dog's life, the art of simple pleasure. Given the same circumstances, were all dogs happy, did they all share the same capacity for inner calm? Or were they like people, some born with bottomless wells of cheer, others with innate fear or disquiet lurking in their depths?

She recalls the morning Arthur stopped her at the beach kiosk to first tell her about the pups: the gentle pressure he exerted, how he tenderly cupped his hands to illustrate the tiny size of them.

'They're old enough to go to new homes this week,' he said.

He had tried to persuade her to take on a pup before, a few years back, after Kelly died. But she wasn't ready then, didn't want the responsibility, the risk of another loss. Kelly had only been with her for a year, wandering in off the beach in a state of neglect, and Wren had had no idea where she came from or how old she was, though it was clear she was getting on in years. She was a mix of all sorts, the size of a cocker spaniel, with a terrier face and shaggy matted hair.

Her eyes were the colour of Laura's and Robert's, warm and intelligent, and Wren had felt obliged to let her stay, to ease her passage in her elder years.

'You know I don't want another dog,' she had replied. Arthur simply nodded, dropping her money in the cash box. 'What kind are they?' she asked, immediately vexed at herself.

'Sausage dogs – miniatures. Mostly chocolate and tan, and a couple of dapply ones too.'

'My dad had a dachshund when he was a boy,' she said. The image of an old photograph came to mind, of her father, then a young boy in shorts and side-slicked hair, sitting on a beach with his dog between his feet. 'Sacha, they called it.'

Arthur eased back in his camping seat. 'The thing is, Rosie's loath to let 'em go, so she's insisting that they go in pairs.'

Wren took a sip of coffee from the polystyrene cup and studied his face. 'Have you seen them?'

He nodded. 'I could fit the whole litter in one of my shoes.' A rumble of laughter threatened to escape, lighting up his eyes. 'You'd like 'em, Wren.'

She knew what he was doing; he was a wily old man. He fiddled with his coffee machine, opening it up to empty out the filter, glancing at her furtively to gauge her reaction.

'I could take you to have a look, if you wanted. Be a shame to miss 'em when they're so small. Grow up quick. I don't mean to keep – just for a look.'

Wren scowled at him and started to walk away across the car park and towards the beach, irritably chewing the inside of her lip. She stopped to turn back, to where Arthur was standing behind his counter, his hands cupping his elbows. 'What time?' she shouted over.

'I'll stop outside yours on my way past at two. No pressure. Just a little look!'

She raised a hand and headed out to her rocks, feeling momentarily lifted from her solitude. That evening, she returned to her cottage carrying a cardboard box containing two dachshund puppies and a month's supply of puppy food.

Now, as Willow and Badger return from the water's edge, she realises another decade has passed, without her noticing. If Laura hadn't reappeared like this, would she have just gone on, not noticing the passing of time, other than the changing of the seasons, and the gradual decay of her body and home? The dogs will mark time, she supposes, when they pass on, and she will miss them. And what will that leave her with, living alone in a tiny stone cottage at the edge of the world?

Snapping her fingers lightly, she rises from her boulder seat and starts to make her way back home.

Eliza Adler wasn't able to talk for long when Wren phoned to deliver the news that she was about to be made a grandmother. Some important guests were expected at her Paris apartment in the next half-hour or so, and she still hadn't polished the glasses.

'Would you mind awfully if we talked about this some other time, darling? Of course, it's lovely news – wonderful! It's just I'm in a bit of a tizz at the moment, what with this dinner we're hosting tonight. Listen, I'll be in London next week – how about a quick get-together then? We could have tea at Claridge's, like we used to?'

'Next week? I didn't think you were in the UK again until the autumn.'

'Oh, well, it's only a fleeting trip – I didn't mention it because I wasn't sure we'd have time for anything other than Siegfried's business – anyway, we'll *make* time, won't we?'

They fixed a date, and Wren hung up the phone, feeling, as always, crushed by her mother's levity. The following Wednesday, she took a day off school, claiming she had an antenatal appointment, and took the bus into central London, checking her reflection and powdering down the perspiration shine of her forehead before stepping off at her final stop outside Claridge's.

She had visited the tea room many times as a child – it was her mother's celebration spot of choice – and after all these years she still felt awed as she entered the elegant art deco foyer, as grand and resplendent as it ever was. Her mother was at her favourite table on the far side, having arrived, as always, ahead of Wren. She liked to sit at a distance from the entrance, Wren remembered, where she might *watch the comings and goings – and avoid anyone we'd rather not see!* Now, as Wren raised a hand and made her way over, she realised they had never once bumped into anyone they knew in the swanky hotel. Like so much else, it was all just elevated bluster, Mother trying to construct an image of a loftier lifestyle than the one they really lived. When Dad was alive Mother had always been saying snooty things of that kind, but with a smile and a kiss he would put it down to her unfortunate downwardly mobile marriage, at which Eliza would coyly smack him away and flutter her eyelashes. They had been so completely in love. Wren missed the mother she had been in those days.

'Darling – look at you!' Her mother rose from her seat and clasped Wren to her shoulder, pushing her back at once to run her eyes over her, assessing her head to toe. 'My goodness, you look – you look – '

Wren pulled out a chair. 'Please, don't tell me I look blooming.'

'Actually, I was going to say *exhausted*! Are you looking after yourself?'

Wren laughed, relieved for once at her mother's honesty. 'I'm fine, really. I've been queasy for these first two or three months, but – touch wood – I'm over the worst. Perhaps I really will be blooming the next time you see me.'

Her mother ordered afternoon tea, and a glass of champagne for herself, Wren having declined one several times before she would take no for an answer. Once the waiter had laid out their spread and checked that they had everything they required, they were left alone, and Wren began to fret about all the things she wanted to say to Eliza, to ask her, to discover. She was edgy, awkward in her mother's unflappable presence, and she feared she might let the meeting pass in a shallow whirlwind of small talk, only to watch her sail off again, once more absent from their lives until long after the baby had arrived.

'Are you sure you're alright, darling? You look terribly distracted.' Eliza poured their tea and served Wren a selection of sweet pastries from the tower of confection that dominated the table.

Wren broke the corner off an apple scone and popped it in her mouth.

'Do use a knife, dear,' her mother said, tapping the white tablecloth next to Wren's setting of silver cutlery.

Unfolding a starched napkin, Wren draped it over her lap and studiously smoothed out the creases.

'Mum, I've always wondered why it was just me – why you and Dad never had any more children?' There, it was out.

Her mother paused, a piece of pastry midway to her mouth. She returned it to her plate. 'Goodness, what's brought this on?'

'I've been thinking – I suppose since I discovered I'm expecting myself – I was thirteen when Dad died, so I'm guessing you must have decided long before that that you wouldn't have any more children. I was just curious. I would have loved a brother or sister.'

'Sometimes these choices are made for us,' her mother replied.

'You *couldn't* have any more?' For some reason, this explanation had never occurred to Wren.

Her mother appeared to study her shell-coloured fingernails, her hands resting decorously either side of the striped china plate.

'Were there complications with me? Maybe I should know about it – the midwife asked me what I knew about my own birth – it often follows a family pattern, you know?'

'There were no complications, Wren; I had a perfectly acceptable birth – rather good compared to many other young mothers I knew. I... well, I just wasn't terribly well *suited* to it.'

'To what?'

The waiter passed alongside their table, discreetly checking that everything was in order.

'I struggled a little, after you were born. I was never really the Earth Mother type – as you know.' She smiled indulgently, brushing Wren's wrist with the lightest of touches. 'Do you remember Anouk, who looked after you were little?'

Anouk. Lovely Anouk, with her soft, yielding bosom, her attentive blue eyes and patient warmth. She had been too young to be a mother figure; Wren had always imagined her as a big sister, or a young aunt – until she'd left suddenly during the heatwave summer, when her own mother took ill in Holland. She'd sent a postcard, a picture of a tulip field spreading out in a rainbow of colour, but after that Wren had never heard from her again.

'We hadn't planned on a nanny but I found the whole thing very trying – the feeding, the crying and so on. I was just shattered, I suppose, completely tired out – and Daddy and I decided that it wasn't a good idea to go through that again, not when we were perfectly happy just the three of us. That's why we had Anouk to live in for the first few years, to take some of the strain.'

Wren tried to picture her mother 'shattered', and she couldn't bring it to mind, simply couldn't envisage it in any way. 'But you're so in control, Mum. I can't begin to imagine you not managing. Remember those huge parties you used to throw on my birthdays – all those children running around, shouting and crying and making a mess. When Tommy Mann threw up Wotsits on your Chinese rug, you just shrugged it off and gave him a winner's rosette.'

'Yes, but it was *Anouk* who had to clear it up, darling.'

Her mother's transparency, her easy admission of imperfection, was deeply unsettling.

'But all my friends thought you were brilliant! You were a great mum!' The words came out in a rush, and as a complete surprise to Wren. She had had no idea she felt like this about her mother; as a teenager, and as an adult, she'd always had her down as a rather selfish woman, distant and uninterested.

'Oh, I was good at the showy stuff – still am! That's why Siegfried snapped me up so quickly: I'm a wonderful organiser! But the baby phase... I'm sorry to say, it almost finished me off.' A shadow passed across her composed features, a wrinkle of pain pricking at her mouth.

'Was it depression, Mum?' At once Wren wanted to spill out everything – to speak aloud, for the first time since the day she'd conceived, about the darkness that had blanketed her light, about the fear and futility that crept across her thoughts in the waking hours, about the certainty that it *wouldn't* be alright, that this whole thing was a huge, huge mistake. 'Was it postnatal depression?'

Eliza laughed, a controlled tinkling sound. 'Goodness, darling – our generation weren't as keen to stick labels on everything as you youngsters! It was something and nothing – over in a flash – and it all turned out fine in the end, didn't it?'

Wren picked up a scone and broke it in two, sending tiny crumbs ricocheting across the perfect white tablecloth.

Laura's car is gone, and Wren finds herself rushing to the rear of the cottage, to let herself in through the unlocked door, checking for signs that she'll be back. She is shocked at the surge of horror she feels at the thought of never seeing Laura again, a feeling so conflicting with her craving to be left in peace.

In the bathroom, Laura's toothbrush has been left on the shelf, but that doesn't mean anything. Wren goes from room to room, trying to remember what Laura brought with her – a rucksack, a coat, a pair of gloves? There's nothing of Laura's to be found, but Wren can't allow herself to think this is the end of it. The essence of her still hangs in the air – the promise that she's coming back, that she won't be gone for long. Willow and Badger stand on the threshold between the living room and the kitchen as Wren stands beside the sofa, slowly scanning the room for clues. She marches past the dogs, opening a cupboard and snatching up a couple of rawhide strips, which she throws far out on to the sunlit grass, closing the door behind the dogs as they chase down through the garden to sniff out their treats, their heads low to the ground, their tails erect.

Wren sets to work in the kitchen, distractedly chopping vegetables and loading the bread machine, her one concession to modern living, for tomorrow's loaf. It was Arthur who talked her into getting the machine a couple of years back, after waxing lyrical about the bread he produced from his own. She resisted, told him no, until some weeks later, when she arrived at his kiosk to get her morning coffee and there it was under his counter, a brand new machine, shiny and persuasive in its carrier bag. She was cross with him, told him so, and the stubborn old mule said, 'It's not a gift, so don't go getting any ideas about not paying me. You take it home and give it a go – and if you still think you want to do it the hard way, you bring it back to me. But, if you like it, it'll cost you sixty quid.' A week later, Wren stopped by for her coffee. As he handed her her cup, she pressed three twenty-pound notes into his hand and strode on, and not another word was said on the matter.

While the soup cooks, Wren sets about tidying the house. She must look a fool, she knows, rushing around the place as if she's expecting royalty, but Laura didn't give her any warning last time and had to take it as she found it, shabby and neglected. Alone, Wren has no cause for pride when it comes to her home. It serves its purpose – keeps her warm in the winter, provides her with heat to cook, with water to drink, with a roof for shelter. The dogs and she have no need for anything more, but here she is, running around, fluffing up dusty old cushions and straightening the ash-marked rag rug before the fireplace.

After half an hour, she's had enough and is beginning to think that Laura's not going to return at all. She lies on the sofa and closes her eyes, embracing the heat of Willow as she clambers up and curls her face into the crook of her neck, their breaths rising and falling as one. Her velvet head smells like freshly baked biscuits, smooth and unsullied as an infant's. Wren slips into watery dreams of summer youth, of Cornish caves, of the slip and plop of starfish returning to their salty pond. She's soothed by the warmth of toddler summers, the sun's rays soaking into the soles of tiny upturned feet; yet all the while the anxiety of loss bubbles like an underground earthquake at the bottom of the ocean.

On their first night home from the maternity hospital, Robert set Wren up in the bedroom so that everything she and the baby needed was within easy reach. He'd bought a brand new portable TV, spending several harassed hours installing it before hospital visiting time started, the time when he would collect Wren and the baby, and bring them home at last. On the bed was a special V-shaped cushion – a 'nursing pillow', the woman in the baby shop had called it – and a freshly ironed pile of muslin cloths, although Rob wasn't entirely sure what they were for. He had followed the list from the *Mother & Baby* magazine Wren's colleagues had included in her leaving hamper. He spent a small fortune on every item the experts considered to be an essential, and another small fortune on most of those they thought were not.

As she sank back against the puffy pile of pillows, Wren instinctively cupped the loose husk of her abdomen, smiling wanly at Rob through her fatigue. He stood at the foot of the bed, gazing into the rustling Moses basket beside her, his eyes lit up with wonder as he offered Wren tea. She declined, but when she noticed his lost expression, his need to do *something*, she congratulated him on the freshly laundered sheets, and thanked him for the efforts he'd made to get the house looking so nice.

'It was Laura mostly,' he confessed. She'd only returned to her own home that morning, three days after Phoebe had arrived in the world, bruised and crying. While Wren had been sitting alone at the edge of her hospital bed, shedding tears at the needle-sharp bursts of first milk, Rob and Laura had toasted her, as they shared a good couple of nights wetting the baby's head over takeaway curries, and exchanging emotional homilies regarding the majesty of Nature's creations.

'I'm so glad she saw Phoebe on her first day,' Wren said, as she settled against her new pillow and breathed in the warm scent of her daughter's softly domed head, marred as it was by the angry indentation of the ventouse cup. The horror of that moment jolted her thoughts, and she blinked it back, forcing it deep into the damp cellar of her troubled memories. 'Though part of me feels sick with guilt that we did it first, that we did it without her. It should have been *her* first, not me.'

Rob's expression fell, and he moved to sit at the edge of the bed, worry working through the lines of his forehead. 'Laura's happier for you – for us – than anyone. She couldn't be more ecstatic if Phoebe were her own baby. She wasn't ready for a baby before, when she – well, you know – lost it.

It wasn't planned.' He leant in and kissed Wren on the lips, pulling back and squinting at her as if she were the most beautiful woman in the world. Wren felt wretched, squeezed out, less than a woman. The gap where her baby had been left a crater of loneliness behind, and she closed her eyelids against Rob, desperately trying to recall how it felt just days ago, to feel the undulating tide of another life nestling beneath her skin.

Rob's voice startled her.

'Who knows if it'll even be with Doug, but until Laura does have kids she's quite happy playing the role of Best Godmother in the World.'

'Why isn't she here?' Wren asked, her voice betraying her sudden panic. She wanted Laura more than any other person, more than Rob or the baby or her mother. 'I thought she'd be here when we came home.'

'She had to get back, Wrenny. She couldn't stay on any longer; she'd already taken a couple of days off work just to be here for the big day. You know she's starting a new supply job on Monday, and to be honest she was a bit worried about getting in the way here, with the new baby. That reminds me – she wanted me to give you this.' He opened the drawer of the bedside cabinet and took out a small gift-wrapped bundle. Inside was a painted Russian doll, not ten centimetres in height, beautiful and perfect, containing doll after doll, all the way down to the tiniest little seed doll at the heart of the woman. *Take care of your precious girl*, the gift card read. *With all my love, Laura x*

Badger barks, scratching at the back door, waking Wren with a start. She wonders how long she has slept, and leaps up to check that the pan hasn't boiled dry. It's fine: the soup is still bubbling and the sun hasn't moved far in the sky; she can only have dozed off for a few minutes. She takes the saucepan off the hob and leaves it to cool, shooing Willow out into the garden to follow her brother. The little dogs sniff around in the overgrown grass, before starting on a game of hunt and roll, their excited yaps rising, muted through the salt-streaked windows of the cold kitchen.

Over at the bench, Laura's coffee cup sits on the wooden arm, with Wren's balanced on the opposite side, abandoned when they went their separate ways this morning. Was she coming back? Surely she wouldn't go without saying goodbye, without saying *something*? They've never before had a disagreement, not a real one, and Wren couldn't stand it if they left things on a bad note.

She balks at her own sentimentality, something which is so completely absent in this life that it troubles her with its unbidden appearance. She finds herself in a limbo of nervousness, uncertain what to do next, and again she trails from room to room, checking on the tidying she carried out before her unplanned nap. The only room she hasn't looked in is the boot room at the back, and as she opens the door she is alarmed to see the contents of the trunk still spilled out across the floor and organised into piles for disposal – for the charity shop, for the bin, for burning. She kneels beside the trunk, and stays there a few minutes, her silent gaze moving over the strange antiquities of her past. The sleeve of the orange silk shirt hangs from the mouth of the bin liner and she brings the garment up her face, to feel the peach-soft slip of the fabric brush against her cheek. In a jolt of craving for material things, she strips off her upper clothes – the fisherman's jumper, the mannish grey thermal vest with its long sleeves and ribbed cuffs – and eases her arms into the blouse, taking her time to fasten the tiny shell buttons, a skill her rough fingers seem to have forgotten. She extends her arms to inspect the drape of the sleeves, the way in which they puff at the wrists before ending in delicate button-studded cuffs. Still inside the trunk is her old jewellery box; why she had thought to pack this when she left she has no idea, as she hasn't worn a single item of jewellery since she arrived here. Within days of moving in, along with the clothes and bags, the shoes and fripperies, all these things had been consigned to the trunk, shoved beside the coat rack and concealed beneath a layer of practicality – of boots and tools and winter supplies.

Opening up the jewellery box, she sees that the 'jewels' are laughable now. A large collection of hangover trinkets from the 1980s, from her student days – plastic hoops in a variety of acid colours, a handful of cheap filigree danglers bought from Camden Market, and an arm's length of bashed silver bangles, found in various hippy gift shops and festival bazaars. There's a garnet ring in a tiny embossed jeweller's box, gifted to her by her father, having belonged to his aunt, and a silver brooch her mother had given her on her sixteenth birthday, a wreath of daisies. At the time, Wren had been irritated that her mother knew her so little that she could even think she would want an old lady's gift like this. Looking at it now, she sees it really is a small thing of beauty, with each tiny daisy head perfectly crafted to form a circle of flowers, rather like the daisy chains she used to make for her mother as a young child. Was that her mother's intention? To reflect back to those summer picnics of childhood – to the fleeting beauty of daisy tiaras and necklaces and anklets; to Wren adorning her reclining madonna with floral celebrations, as father poured elderflower fizz and handed out sandwiches, reciting half-remembered snippets of Wordsworth beside the stream. What a fool she was, not to have seen it. And how like her mother, to not point out the significance, even when faced with Wren's sullen lack of appreciation. She unhinges the clasp and pins the brooch to the breast of her silk shirt.

The remaining snaggle of old jewellery is poured on to the charity shop pile. Maybe some of these things will be in fashion again; maybe someone will enjoy them. Mother used to say that bad fashion always came back round again, like a bad penny. Wren lifts the top layer from the jewellery box and fishes out the contents below: a collection of obsolete coins – some ha'pennies and old shillings her father had given her to play shop with; a purple hair bobble fashioned into a ring; and a small hoard of cracker toys, tiny plastic horses and dogs in an array of colours, each with a hoop in its back for dangling, perhaps from keyrings or neck chains. She can't bring herself to part with these little animals, amassed as they were over several happy Christmases, when all the cracker tokens would be gathered up and added to Wren's collection at the end of the festive lunch. Her favourite was a tiny black dog – a wiry terrier with the kindest expression cast in its face. It was the type of dog she'd always thought she might have one day, when she grew up, a scruffy little terrier with keen black eyes.

She really has no use for a jewellery box, she thinks, and she returns the top layer and snaps the lock shut, putting the empty case on the 'donation' pile. Inside the trunk, only one item remains, and Laura reaches in and retrieves that last thing, tucked into the far corner, small and bright and perfectly formed: Laura's Russian doll. She'll show it to Laura, she decides. If she ever comes back, she'll show it to Laura.

Outside, the dogs are barking wildly. She'd forgotten about them in the garden, and she pushes herself to her feet, heading for the kitchen, where she sets the doll down on the side and opens the back door to let them in. In a rush of exuberance they bound across her sandy boots and race through the house to scratch at the front door of the cottage.

'Slow down,' she murmurs, perplexed by their frenzy, following them and scooping Willow under one arm. As she turns back towards the kitchen, the front door knocker raps against the old wooden exterior, startling her to her very core.

Shifting Willow to her shoulder, she feels rooted to the spot, and as she slowly turns her eyes towards the small front window she catches a glimpse of Laura's red hair, blowing about in the breeze as she stands on the doorstep. 'She's come back,' Wren whispers into Willow's neck.

She's come back to say goodbye.

When Phoebe was two or three months old, Laura made her a velour comforter fringed with garment labels she had carefully snipped from her clothes, hand-sewing each to the blanket's edge with tiny, precise stitches. Phoebe loved it, instantly bringing her thumb to her mouth and turning her face into the soft, silky bundle in a rapture of delight. It was an inspired gift, conceived one hot afternoon in July while Laura sat on a picnic blanket in Wren's back garden, watching Phoebe in the shade of a parasol as Wren took down laundry from the washing line. Phoebe had almost mastered rolling over, and she lay on her back tugging at her own toes, restlessly flip-flopping from side to side in the fitful way babies did before an overdue nap. Her chest rose and fell, and she rubbed her head from side to side, her fists working away at her face, her mouth turning downwards. '*Argh-argh-argh-argh*,' she began, her chest revving up as she built momentum. Her legs stiffened, rising up, thumping down against the blanket in frustration. Wren continued to fetch washing from the line. It was such a beautiful, clear-sky day; she had hoped they could stay outside for a picnic lunch, for egg sandwiches and strawberries and Pimms in the sunshine. She had hoped that Phoebe would sleep.

Laura shifted position, coming up on to her knees to make soothing noises and perform *peep-bo* behind her hands in an attempt at distraction. 'She's getting a bit grizzly,' she called over, laying a hand gently on the rising dome of the baby's bright white vest. Phoebe kicked out and her whining intensified, shattering the peace of the sheltered garden, the serenity of the imagined picnic. 'Shall I put her in her pram? I can rock her off to sleep if you like.'

'You stay there,' Wren said, trying to keep the tension from her voice as the pressure travelled along the base of her neck, fingering out around her jaw. 'I'll be finished in a sec.'

When she was alone with Phoebe she was able to shrink the more demanding elements of their existence together, but in company she felt them with all the more force, all the more clarity. It was as if the volume increased when there were others there; as if Phoebe's presence swelled into the room, using up the air, making Wren smaller, making her fade. But no, this was a wrong thought: Wren loved Phoebe limitlessly, loved her soft chubby creases and her tiny shell-like fingernails, loved the way she pressed her face into the curve of her neck, unsteadily digging perfect toes against her thighs to burrow in closer, to gum her mouth against her ear, her cheek, her chin. So close that she might almost crawl beneath Wren's skin and become part of her again, reabsorbed into her mother's body until she no longer existed in the world, her presence nothing more than a myth.

Wren unpegged the last pieces of underwear from the line and dropped them into the laundry basket that sat beside the picnic blanket. A bra – an ugly great maternity bra with clumsy popper fixings – landed on the blanket at Phoebe's side, and in a heartbeat the baby grasped it in her fist and brought it to her mouth. As the label brushed her upper lip, her thumb found her mouth, and the infant's eyes closed. Her fidgeting ceased and she was lulled into a soft murmur of suckling contentment.

'Did you see that?' Laura laughed, looking up at Wren in wonder. 'It's a bloody miracle!' She pressed her face against Phoebe's soft belly and blew a raspberry, provoking a gurgle of happiness from her thumb-plugged little mouth.

Wren stood at the edge of the blanket, in awe of the physical ease they shared, at the invisible bond between the two. Laura's hands roamed over the baby's body, tugging her legs, smoothing her fine hair, tickling her pudgy hands, and Wren looked on, with no envy at all. What she felt was bewilderment: why should *she* be the mother, when Laura was the one who knew how it worked – the one who wanted it so much? Laura was a natural.

'I've got Pimm's,' Wren said, trying to be visible again, to find her voice. 'Do you fancy a glass?'

Laura turned her attention from the baby, her face a delight. 'You *really* need to ask?' She flopped back against the blanket, throwing her arms wide, stretching out in the sunshine, the bright light bouncing off her sunglasses. 'Pimm's and sunshine and my two favourite girls in all the world. Life doesn't get much better than this.'

PHOEBE

Phoebe is not all that certain what she was expecting. Perhaps the Wren of Laura's old black and white college photographs – the slender student with shiny long hair and china-doll shoes? Perhaps the pale and enigmatic mother cradling her baby bundle in a hospital bed, a muslin cloth draped over her shoulder? Or the 1960s child on a beach, so like Phoebe herself it's startling, bucket dangling at her side?

Whatever it was she anticipated, the woman who answers the door doesn't correspond at all.

Wren – for Phoebe can't yet begin to think of her as 'Mum' – faces them blankly, her eyes locked on Laura, seemingly refusing to turn them in the direction of Phoebe. She's dressed in a bizarre combination, as if the top half of her is going somewhere nice for afternoon tea, while the bottom half is dressed for armed combat. Her closely cropped hair stands in irregular greying peaks that suggest she may have cut it herself, and there's so little left of the Wren Phoebe knows from the family history that she is momentarily convinced Laura has got it all wrong, brought them to this stranger's house in error. But the tension between the two women suggests otherwise: in this, there is history.

Two dogs accompany her. One sits at her feet, sweeping the floor with its tail and panting up at Laura; the other is curled over Wren's shoulder like a newborn baby. The second dog shifts in her arms, tucking its head beneath her chin to gain a better view of the visitors.

'Wren,' Laura says.

'I thought you'd gone,' she replies, her focus still firmly fixed ahead. Her voice is soft and hesitant, as if speaking takes great effort.

Laura reaches out, lightly touches her elbow, trying to steer her attention.

'This is Phoebe, Wren. Your daughter.' She speaks kindly, allowing her fingers to linger a moment on the orange silk of the blouse.

Resolutely, the woman anchors on Laura, moisture rising to her eyes for lack of blinking. 'You shouldn't – ' she begins, and she takes a small step backwards, sand sprinkling from her heavy boots with the movement.

Phoebe turns to Laura, tries to speak for herself, but no words will come. There was always the chance that Wren would turn them away, that she wouldn't want to know. But still, this moment has taken her by surprise. *Don't expect too much*, Laura had warned. *In fact, don't expect anything – and if she does welcome you, it'll be a bonus.* Phoebe had told her she wasn't afraid of Wren's response: if she didn't want to know, wasn't it her loss, not theirs? But standing here in the crisp sunlight of Wren's front door, faced with the alarm in her birth mother's eyes, with the prospect of being sent away empty-handed (or empty-hearted, if such a concept existed) – she finds she *does* care; she *is* afraid. What would she tell Dad? That she failed, that it's *her* Wren ran away from, not him – no matter how many years he has spent trying to convince her otherwise?

The little dog takes a step forward and sniffs the toe of Phoebe's boot. She stoops to scratch it under the chin. 'Is it a boy or a girl?' she asks without looking up.

'A boy. Badger.'

Phoebe

Phoebe remains on her haunches. The dogs seem to be a safe subject. 'I always wanted a dog, didn't I, Laura?' She inclines her head, still concentrating on Badger.

Laura nods. 'She wanted one like that, actually.'

'Really?' Wren replies, and Phoebe stands, encouraged, holding out her wrist to show off her bracelet of silver charms, one of which is a tiny short-haired dachshund.

Wren leans in very slightly, her attention on the bracelet, her expression sharp, mistrusting. She reminds Phoebe of a wild goat, edging forward to take food from an outstretched hand. For just a second she raises her eyes to meet Phoebe's, then instantly retreats as if burnt. Phoebe turns to Laura, silently implores her, *What do we do?* Laura must know. Laura is the one with the answers, surely.

They stand there, either side of Wren's threshold, each searching for some clue as to what happens next. What to say next…

The first time Phoebe became aware of her unusual family situation was when a little boy called Jacob Pearson informed a group of their classmates that Phoebe's mummy had run away 'like a thief in the night'. By the time it had passed through the playground tom-toms and reached the six-year-old Phoebe's ears, it had translated as 'Phoebe's mummy ran away because she's a thief.'

'Your mother didn't run away,' Laura reassured her as she tucked her into bed that night, after an evening of sobbing in her arms, 'and she certainly wasn't a thief!'

'If she didn't run away, where is she?' Phoebe asked, her chest still rising and falling in small juddering breaths.

Laura smoothed the hair from her damp face.

'She just had to go and live somewhere else for a while. That's not the same as running away.'

'Where did she go?'

Phoebe recalls Laura's puzzled expression, the way she appeared to scan the edges of the ceiling in search of an answer. 'Well, I'm not sure, but I expect it's somewhere exciting, like America or France.' She left the room and returned holding a photo album. Phoebe scooched along and they sat together on the bed, turning the pages as Laura pointed out pictures of her mother – Mummy with Laura, Mummy with Daddy, Mummy standing at the edge of a river, on the steps of a library, drinking tea in a café. Phoebe stops at a picture of Wren sitting up in a hospital bed wearing a baggy white T-shirt, holding a small pink baby in her arms.

'Has she got a new baby?' Phoebe asked, pleased and surprised, her little finger coming down on the photograph.

Laura laughed, cradled Phoebe's head and kissed her hair. 'That's you, you nincompoop! That's your mummy, and that's baby Phoebe – the day you were born.'

Phoebe drew the album closer, to better study the picture, her eyes wrinkling up in fierce concentration. It didn't even look like her. 'I don't remember,' she said sadly, wishing she knew how to miss her mother, and she curled against the soft warmth of Laura's body and fell asleep.

In a sudden burst of action Laura is inside the cottage, sweeping the dog up off the floor and depositing him into Phoebe's inexpert arms. Wren bites down on her lower lip, like a person trying to stop words from flying out into the room, and Phoebe looks on, shifting the dog up over her shoulder to stop him from wriggling.

'OK, Wren, you won't like this, but I can't see any other way to deal with it except head-on. I've got Rob outside in the car, and we're going to leave now – just for a couple of hours – and Phoebe's going to stay here with you.'

Wren opens her mouth to object, but Laura blocks her with a flat hand, already stepping out through the front door, nudging Phoebe over the doormat and into the cottage. 'We'll be down on the beach. *OK*?' She gives Phoebe one final nod of support, and pulls the front door shut with a soft thud.

In the dim light of the living room Phoebe stares at the inside of the door, her heart pounding beneath Badger's soft heat. She commands herself to look at Wren, at her mother, and when she turns to face her she sees they are just two women, as alike as they are different, each cradling a small form; benign as new mothers meeting in the park.

Wren gazes at Badger, her attention appearing to linger on Phoebe's fingers as they gently stroke the velvet fur under his chin. Phoebe waits, waits, waits for Wren to say something, while the silence of the room throbs like white noise.

'You've got my hands,' Wren finally says, and she lowers her dog to the carpet and heads into the kitchen, where she busies herself at the stove.

On her eleventh birthday, Phoebe took the bus with Laura to Claridge's, where she was to meet her grandmother for afternoon tea. She had no strong memories of her, this woman – mother of her own absent mother – and had put up a good fight when the invitation initially arrived.

'I don't even know her!' she'd ranted, as her dad went to great lengths to put across the positive reasons she should meet with her maternal grandmother. 'Why does she suddenly want to meet me now? She's never shown any interest before!'

Laura had eventually talked her round, telling her inflated stories of previous visits, reminding her of the few gifts she had sent her: a Lalique mermaid, some monogrammed handkerchiefs, a bag of bonbons from Paris. On the afternoon of her birthday, as they stood at the entrance to the hotel, Phoebe clung to Laura, scared. 'What if she hates me?' she asked. 'What if she's disappointed?'

Laura ran her thumbs over Phoebe's cheeks, wiping away the tears. 'Now you're being ridiculous, pumpkin. How could she not fall in love with you? I did! Come on, I'll walk you up to the tea room, make sure she's there – and then I'll be back for you at four, just like we arranged. OK?'

Her grandmother was already there, seated at a far table, facing out towards the door. Laura raised a hand to gain her attention, and gave Phoebe a little push in the small of her back. Feeling suddenly self-conscious, Phoebe moved towards the table, her limbs stiff with apprehension, waiting for the elderly lady to smile, to acknowledge her in some way. When she arrived at the table, the woman looked at her with what seemed a critical and studied expression, and nodded, giving her permission to speak.

'I'm Phoebe,' she said, her fingers feeling for the silky shop label beneath the hem of her new blouse.

Her grandmother rose from her seat and held out her arms, briefly drawing Phoebe to her chest and smiling approvingly. 'Phoebe, my darling! What a beautiful young lady you've turned into!' She indicated the seat beside her. 'My goodness! Just look at you. Now, I've been giving this some thought, and I think you should call me Grandma Ellie. How does that sound?'

'OK. *Grandma Ellie.*' Phoebe smiled, tucking her knees underneath the white tablecloth, relieved that her grandmother seemed so warm and welcoming.

The waiter brought a tower of tiny cakes and pastries, and a pot of tea for two.

'Help yourself – use those silver tongs – anything you like, it's all for us!' Grandma Ellie poured the tea, and told Phoebe tales of her life in Paris, her life with Siegfried 'who is now sadly passed', a whirl of dinner parties and diplomats and springtime walks beside the Seine. She regaled her with stories of the holidays they'd taken – to Vienna and Sydney and Montreal, and so many other places – painting pictures so clear that Phoebe could almost imagine she had been there herself. She loved hearing these stories, and yet she longed to ask her, *And what about my mother? Tell me about her, tell me what she was like as a little girl, as a young woman, as a mother to me?* But Phoebe suspected the subject was off limits, noticing the way that Grandma Ellie steered the conversation towards only the positive and the elegant; towards herself.

As they neared the end of their time together, she asked Phoebe to pour them a last cup of tea, instructing her to first add the milk, and how to tilt the teapot gently without overextending her elbows. Phoebe felt her eyes on her, studying every movement, and hoped she was getting it right. She slid the cup and saucer towards her grandmother with a shy smile.

'Well, fancy that!' Grandma Ellie said. 'You've got my hands!'

The other dog scratches at the back door.

'Can I take a look around your garden?' Phoebe asks, placing Badger on the floor. 'I think the dogs want to go out.'

Wren nods and continues to stir the soup, and Phoebe is grateful for an excuse to escape the silence. Is this what she expected to feel? Wren's manner – her coolness – is shocking to Phoebe, and her own emotions feel muted in response. Does Wren regret leaving – is she glad to see her daughter, after a lifetime apart? Is she disappointed or pleased to see how Phoebe has turned out? Phoebe has no way of guessing, and no way of knowing what to do or say next.

She closes the back door behind her and follows the dogs down through the garden, past the vegetable patches and over the lawn towards the bench and sea view. On the lawn, she picks up a windblown wisteria vine, season-dried and gnarly, which she trails across the grass to amuse the dogs, who run in wide circles as they try to catch their fast-moving prey. Round and round Phoebe spins, laughing at their yapping excitement, then dizzily giving in and throwing them the vine. They set to work on either end, emitting low growls of contentment and destroying it in moments, sending dusty flakes tumbling across the garden.

Looking out across the bay, Phoebe wonders how Laura is feeling right now, having left her here – surrendered her to the woman who left her behind. What does Laura feel towards Wren? She's protective as a lioness at times, if she fears for Phoebe's safety or happiness, and this is surely one of those occasions when she'll be biting down on her tongue, trying not to wade in and spill out all the things that have been playing on her mind during the past twenty years – all the criticisms and disappointments she must have felt towards Wren for leaving them behind. Phoebe knows that Laura's love for her is unconditional; she knows it in her patience and forgiveness, in the quiet way she listens, advises, steps back. She knows it in her warm embrace, her boisterous banter; in the imperfect home-made fairy cakes that would appear on the kitchen counter every Friday after school, and which still make the occasional appearance to this day. Car-crash cakes, Dad calls them. 'They may look like hell, but they taste like heaven.'

Phoebe turns back towards the house, and there is Wren, framed in the window, watching her. Her expression is distant and Phoebe can't be sure if she's even aware of her returning gaze. What would Wren want to be called? Mother? Mum? Phoebe wouldn't be comfortable with that, and she's certain that Wren wouldn't want it either. More than that, she wonders how Laura would feel, after all these years of mothering and care. Phoebe couldn't do that to her; she won't. But never mind – soon there will be a new baby, who will call her Grandma or Nana or Gamma or whatever Laura chooses, and this boy or girl will be Laura's first grandchild, and Phoebe's heart leaps at the preciousness of the gift, at the wonder of her secret.

In all but name, Laura Self was Phoebe's mother. It was Laura who took her to buy her first pair of shiny school shoes from Russell and Bromley, who hovered at the end of the path waiting to catch her when Dad launched her, pedalling like fury, on her brand new big-girl bicycle; Laura who showed her how to brush her teeth properly, who patched up her grazed elbows, her playground tiffs, her infrequently broken heart. When Phoebe needed a starter bra, when she was doubled over with those first monthly cramps that seemed to knock the life from her, it was Laura she turned to: her supporter, her guardian, her voice of reason. *And what's in a name, anyway?* That was what Dad said, when as a teenager Phoebe asked why they had decided against Laura becoming 'Mum'. She had, Phoebe argued, been there from the start, had taken on the mother role – so why not take on the title?

It was the summer holidays, shortly before Phoebe returned to school for her final year and GCSEs. Dad was reading a book in the garden, stretched out on a sun lounger, and Laura – where was Laura? Perhaps she was doing the food shopping. Or volunteering at the youth centre in town; she did that for several years, Phoebe recalls, helping out with teenage kids who weren't as lucky as her, who didn't have a secure home and family. Kids who were there to *escape* home and family. The older she got, the more it struck her as a terrifying and alien concept; Phoebe couldn't imagine the fear and isolation of needing to escape from home. Home was her haven, a warm and worry-free zone, where nobody judged her, where she was at liberty and cushioned all at once. It was the world outside her home where fear lived, in the wide spaces inhabited by other people; in the media, in the too-cool kids who draped themselves over the leatherette booths of the Youth Club, in the lager-swilling, cigarette-smoking clusters that flanked the entrances of pubs and clubs of town. Fear lived in what to wear, how to speak, how to dress your hair – in walking into a classroom, late, suspecting you didn't belong, feeling like a fraud. Fear was hating yourself for feeling fear at all, when you had no right to it, when you had parents who loved and protected you, and a home that was a place of safety. Safety was the holidays, in the comfort of home.

Phoebe dragged the second recliner across the grass and positioned it beside her dad in the sunshine. She was wearing cut-off jeans and a sleeveless vest, her skin having deepened to a warm honey over the past weeks of freedom. During the holidays she had managed to do just about nothing of note: no job, no homework, no revision, no demands. It had been the perfect summer, spent lounging around the house and garden, baking cakes with Laura, listening to music in her room or chatting with friends on the phone. Life felt good. As she stretched out on the sunbed next to Dad, the heat of the sun in the breezeless sky felt like warm silk on her skin.

Seeing that he was paying no attention to her arrival, she tapped the metal frame of his lounger, two little raps with her fingernail.

'You know my friend Melissa? She has a stepdad, and, even though he only moved in with them when she was ten, they call him Dad, not John.'

'Uh-huh,' her dad replied, turning the page of his book. It was a dog-eared copy of *High Fidelity*, a book she'd seen him read several times before.

'And Bethan was adopted when she was four, and she calls her parents Mum and Dad.'

Her dad lifted his sunglasses and peered beneath them. 'What's your point, Phoebs?'

'Well, I just wondered why it's different with us. With Laura. She's been here since I was a baby – longer than Mel or Bethan's parents – well, you know what I mean.'

'You're asking why Laura never became "Mum"?' He shifted position so that he was facing her up on the lounger beside him.

She nodded.

'But she is a mum to you, isn't she? She's your mum in everything but the word. That's what counts, isn't it?'

Phoebe knew it shouldn't matter, but it did. The absence of that label had always, would always keep them one small, inarticulable step apart from being mother and daughter. Phoebe wished that she didn't feel it so keenly, but she couldn't shake it off.

'I would have liked it, though. When my friends all talk about their mums and dads, I talk about "Dad and Laura". It's not the same.' She felt a pang of guilt for putting him on the spot. 'I know it's too late to change it now – I just got thinking about it, I suppose. That's all.'

Dad closed his book and placed it on the grass between them. 'It wasn't so straightforward with Laura, love. When your real mum left, we honestly had no idea how long she would be gone for. She wrote a letter saying she wasn't returning, but I suppose we didn't want to believe it. We never really talked about it, but I think we both felt that we couldn't just give her name – her *role* away – not without knowing what the future held. There was every chance that she'd change her mind and come back.'

'But she didn't come back.'

'No, she didn't.'

Phoebe thinks of the photograph of her mother holding her in the hospital bed, just hours after her birth. 'How soon after she went did you and Laura get together?'

A ripple of defensiveness registered between Dad's eyebrows. 'What do you mean, how long?'

'Well, was it weeks, months – years?'

He linked his hands behind his head on the recliner, retreating behind his sunglasses, his face turned towards the sun. 'Let's see. It was November when your real mum left – '

'*Wren*. Just call her Wren, Dad.'

Her father frowned, surprised by her adult tone. 'OK – when Wren left. I remember it was November because it was desperately cold, a hard frost on the windscreen every morning, ice hanging from the holly tree at the front. Anyway, Laura came straight away – as a friend – and she must have stayed... maybe a fortnight? While I got back on my feet.'

'Then what?' Phoebe glanced towards the back of the house, hoping that Laura wouldn't arrive home yet. Dad would never talk as openly if she was there; although she wouldn't speak of it, Phoebe knew that Laura still harboured some misplaced guilt about stepping into Wren's shoes.

'Then she went off travelling for a year, and we didn't see her again until the following Christmas – which was when we got together as a proper couple.'

'What did people think?'

'People?'

'Your friends – Auntie Lily – Granny and Gramps? They must have thought it was all a bit weird, what with you and Laura being best friends since you were little.'

Dad smiled, rubbed the side of his nose with his knuckle. 'I was *petrified* of telling them. It was bad enough the year before, having to break it to them that Wren had left me, and I knew there'd be raised eyebrows over me and Laura. You know, Lily actually asked me if that was why Wren had left in the first place – if Laura and I had been having an affair behind her back.'

'Were you?'

'No! Of course not!' He lifted his glasses again, reached out with his other hand to turn her chin. 'I adored your mother, Phoebs. Don't ever be in any doubt about that. She was a wonderful woman – a kind, funny, beautiful person. I would never have done anything to jeopardise our life together.'

'So why did she leave, then?'

For a while, he didn't speak at all. Dropping his head back against the recliner, he let his eyes scan the borders of the leafy garden, rising and falling over shrubs and trees, over ancient rose bushes and withered alliums, making a full sweep of their surroundings.

'Sometimes, for whatever reason, these things just fall out of balance. I guess in the end, Phoebs, she didn't love me as much as I loved her.'

The kitchen is small, basic, the single decorative thing being a little Russian doll that's perched on the edge of the worktop. Other than that it's spartan, with neither frill nor comfort beyond the table, chair and stool at the centre of the room. Laura said the journalist mentioned a Lottery win but he must have got it wrong – this tiny cottage didn't look anything like the home of a jackpot millionaire.

Phoebe waits uncertainly at the back door, watching her mother as she stirs a large pan of soup, adding a pinch of salt, a grind of pepper, dipping in a teaspoon to check it for flavour. She must be almost exactly the same build as Phoebe, but leaner, more efficient-looking. Phoebe lowers Badger to the floor and he pads across the tiles to stand beside Wren, raising his muzzle hopefully, before patting her boot with one of his oversized paws.

'Are you hungry?' Wren asks, without turning round. Phoebe assumes she's talking to the dog, until she raises her wooden spoon like a conductor's baton. 'I've made soup. Do you want some?'

'Oh,' Phoebe replies, feeling foolish, feeling useless. 'Yes. Oh, yes. I'll pretty much eat anything, any time!' She laughs a little forcedly, brushes her hands down the front of her jacket and looks around the kitchen, desperately searching for prompts with which to start a conversation. 'Can I help at all?'

Wren takes a sideways glance, still not facing her full on, and indicates with her wooden spoon towards the wall cupboards. 'Bowls and plates,' then down towards the drawers, 'knives and spoons. There's bread on the table. You could slice the bread.'

Phoebe is relieved to have something to do, to fill the great gaping silences that push out against the walls and windows of this claustrophobic cottage. What must Wren do all day, in this small space? The garden is a fair size, much of which is taken up with the vegetable patch, and gardening tools lean up against the bench, suggesting she's been out there digging recently. Does she have friends? A partner, even? Somehow that seems unlikely. What is she interested in? What does she do in the evenings – where does she go on holiday? Phoebe knows nothing about her – not this new version of her mother, so unlike the Wren of Laura's photo albums. That Wren looked directly into the camera lens, and, even when her mouth wasn't smiling, her eyes were. Except in the birth photo, she realises now; in that picture, it seems there's nothing behind her eyes at all.

She lays out a bowl and a plate on either side of the small table, and saws at the bread to produce two slightly wonky slices, placing one on each plate. 'Sorry. I'm not very good at cutting bread. Dad says I'm cack-handed.'

Switching off the gas, Wren transfers the pan to the table and ladles out the soup, returning it to the hob before pulling out her chair. Phoebe sits on the stool opposite and waits for Wren to start before picking up her spoon and following her lead. She hopes conversation will follow naturally enough, but, after several moments filled with nothing but the sound of spoons against china, Wren has still said nothing, still not looked Phoebe full in the face.

Phoebe lays down her spoon and runs her hands over her jeans, gathering courage. Despite the chill of the cottage, there's a film of perspiration building in the creases of her palms and a hot flush has crept up over her neck. She thinks of asking about the dogs, about living in Cornwall, of enquiring whether Wren has a job or not; they might be good conversation starters. Or maybe she should tell her a bit about herself, about her plans to study gardening at college – ask her about her own garden? Quite unexpectedly, Wren looks up, now square-on, her eyes traversing the contours of Phoebe's face. Her expression is not harsh; there's kindness behind it, a curiosity of sorts.

'Laura tells me you're expecting a child.' Releasing her gaze, Wren picks up her bread and tears off an edge. She dunks the crust into her soup and brings it to her mouth, glancing at Phoebe's startled face as she does so. 'How far gone are you?'

Phoebe is frozen in her seat, unable to look away.

She knew she was expecting from almost the moment of conception. The changes showed themselves so starkly – the metallic taste in her mouth, the fierce aversion to fish and tea, the swelling tenderness of her breasts. The lightheaded otherness of walking beneath the spotlights in Top Shop or H&M, where she stole furtive glances at the mother-to-be ranges, hoping that soon she might buy things from those rails. Taking the pregnancy test was really nothing more than a formality, proof that she wasn't imagining the whole thing.

In part she supposed she was attuned to the alterations of her body, since the pregnancy had been carefully planned. She had spent a considerable number of hours online, searching the parenting forums for advice on conception and healthy living in the run-up to pregnancy. She'd been taking folic acid for a couple of months beforehand, as well as exercising regularly and living cleanly, until really the last remaining obstacle had been to find a suitable man to provide her with the necessary fifty per cent required for fertilisation to take place.

Esteban had seemed perfect. He was handsome, funny and intelligent – and, better still, he had had no intention of staying in the UK after his summer working holiday. When Phoebe met him on their first day of tomato-picking at Vale Farm, she knew she had found her man, and by the end of just one week toiling side by side in the sweltering heat of the greenhouse they were a firm item. Every evening after work, they would stop off at the Barleymow for a pint of orange juice and lemonade (Esteban had a small beer), leaning their bicycles against the garden bench while they drank in the sunshine, before continuing on to his digs at the edge of town, where they would work out the last of their energies beneath the musky haven of his bright cotton sheets.

Phoebe had told him she was on the pill, that he had nothing to worry about on that count, and she surprised herself at the easiness of the lie, how unabashed she felt about the whole deceit. He was only there for the summer months, to experience London (though he rarely ventured beyond the suburbs), to make a bit of money on the farm, and to practise his English – and his reluctance to talk in any depth about matters of home left Phoebe more than certain that he had a girlfriend back in Spain. Why wouldn't he have? He was gorgeous. He made love with a studied seriousness, and even now she thrilled at the memory of his lean torso rising and falling above her, gleaming with exertion.

She had had no plans to become entangled, and she'd thought she had it all under control. But by the time she fell pregnant, by the time she realised that she was smitten, that she had fallen for him completely and utterly, he was off. They stood together on Platform 7 at Clapham Junction, oblivious to the waves of rush-hour passengers coursing by, and kissed, a bottomless embrace of tongues and lips, and she wanted that kiss never to end. As the train to Gatwick was announced over the tannoy, Esteban tugged her to him by the small of her back and murmured, 'I will never forget you, Phoebe Irving,' and in that moment she understood. She loved him more than he loved her.

'Laura said that?' she eventually answers, retrieving her spoon and tackling her soup with exaggerated concentration.

'She did.'

'She had no right to say that to you. I haven't even – she doesn't – '

Wren picks up her empty bowl and places it on her plate, sliding them both to one side. 'Why haven't you told them? It's not the kind of thing you can keep concealed for very long. You're starting to show.'

Phoebe's jaw drops; for a woman of so few words, Wren is alarmingly direct. But, finally, she's looking at Phoebe as if she's there, as if she exists as another human being in the room.

'I know that. I wanted to tell Laura straight away – but then, I just couldn't find the right words for it, and weeks turned into months. I'm three months gone.'

'What about your dad? Surely he'd want to know.'

Phoebe merely nods, her mind racing over the possible reactions she might face from Dad, from Laura. She thinks about the secrets Dad has been keeping, the questions he evaded as she prodded away at him in the car this morning, as he sat with his eyes resolutely on the road ahead, careful to deflect her truth-seeking glare.

'Why are you so afraid of telling them? They're good people. You're lucky to have good people in your life.'

How do you respond to something like that? Phoebe wonders. 'She's been like a mother to me,' she says, expecting to wound Wren, to see her balk. But she doesn't; instead her face relaxes, and she almost smiles.

'If Laura's been as big a part of your life as I suspect, it looks as if she's done a very good job with you.' Now she smiles, nervously, moisture rising to her eyes.

'You call this a good job?' Phoebe laughs, fighting the tears herself, smoothing her sweater tight across her abdomen. 'Twenty, single, and knocked up!'

Wren clears the table, turning away to swipe at her eyes. Phoebe sees this, and is thankful that they've broken through the silence, the formality; that Wren appears to be human after all, not so much the strange, spooked creature who met them at the door. She runs hot water into the sink, noisily dropping their dishes into the suds, working the dishcloth over the worktops, over the table.

'It was planned,' Phoebe says as the dishcloth gathers up the crumbs from the space in front of her.

Wren stops, cloth held in one hand.

'I wanted a baby. I know I'm only young – and I'm not in a stable relationship – but this was something I wanted more than anything. Everyone else – all my friends, my teachers,

Dad and Laura – they go on and on about university, about how bright I am, how I should use it – about how important a degree is in securing my future – but none of that is *my* dream. It's all over the TV and internet, how much it costs to send your kids to uni, how so many finish their degrees and it's all "sorry, no jobs" or "sorry, you'll have to work for nothing for a year before we'll even think about employing you" – and, even though I went along with the whole thing for a long while, it just wasn't for me. You know, I sat in that miserable student room in Hull and I thought, what am I doing here? I'm lonely, I hate the course, I miss my family, my home – I cry myself to sleep every night, and for what? And then there was Laura, and everything she's done for me, and everything she's missed out on, just to be there for me and Dad – '

Wren lowers herself to her seat, pushes the cloth to one side. 'Is she not happy?'

'She's happy enough – she adores Dad, and she loves her work, and me – but she's made so many sacrifices, and I just thought, this, this is the one thing I could do for her, for Dad, for all of us.' Phoebe brings her elbows to the table, drops her face against her knuckles. 'I'm sorry, I'm just rambling on. You must think I'm a bloody nightmare.'

She feels fingers at her wrist, the gentle tug of Wren's hands, forcing her to look up.

'Phoebe, why are you having this baby?'

Phoebe gazes into Wren's eyes, and there, something like a long buried dream rises in her, recognition of a kind, and she knows she can trust her with this thing, with this secret that can't be kept.

'I just wanted something for myself. Something to care for, to love and hold – and to be loved, unconditionally.' She hesitates, holds Wren's gaze, and for a split second – more than anything – she wants to hurt her for leaving her behind. 'I want to know how it feels to be a mother.'

ROB

On that November morning after Wren had vanished, Rob came round from a deathlike sleep, his body sluggish with hangover, and he started in horror at the sight of Laura's face on the pillow beside him.

'Are you OK?' she asked, her face betraying hurt at the shock so visible on his.

He stared at her for a moment, the connections in his brain firing off as he put it all together.

'What – ?' He tried to speak, pushing himself up to a slumped sitting position, cradling his banging temples between the knuckles of his fists as the memory of Wren's absence rushed in.

'We didn't *do* anything, you idiot,' Laura said, and as she swung her legs off the bed he felt foolish at the sight of her fully clothed body. She scowled back at him and bent down to retrieve her balled-up socks. '*As if.*'

Phoebe's bubbling chatter drifted in from the room next door, and Laura disappeared into the hall, leaving Rob to welter in his throbbing misery, rising only to follow the aroma of bacon and coffee and the promise of paracetamol. In the kitchen, Phoebe was already installed in her high chair. At the sight of Daddy in the doorway her chubby heels battered out an animated beat against the padded vinyl as her arms pumped the air in a halting wave. He gaped at his delighted daughter, the implications of Wren's actions gaining clarity and speed in his waking mind.

'What if she doesn't come home?' Rob said, his voice hushed as if Phoebe might understand. His eyes shifted to meet Laura's, as she pointed to a chair and, with a single motion of her extended finger, ordered him to eat.

'She *will* come home, Rob.' She poured herself another coffee.

Rob picked up his cutlery, studying his autumn-dappled reflection in the knife's silver. The distorted image seemed a perfect reflection of the surreal sense he felt now, the way in which his life had become blurred and strained at the edges. 'But, if she doesn't? Then what?'

'Then you'll get through it. *We'll* get through it. You're not on your own here. I'm here – and I'm not going anywhere until we get you all through this. You *and* Wren. You, and Wren, and Phoebe.' She snatched the knife and fork from his hovering hands and cut a slice of bacon, holding it up to his mouth with a fierce frown. 'Eat, you fool! You're hungover, and you've got responsibilities. Now, *get on with it*, Rob.'

Running a damp cloth over Phoebe's eggy face, she cast Rob a businesslike nod, and left the room to phone her agency, to tell them she wouldn't be able to fill in at Leverside Comprehensive after all. 'It's a family emergency,' Rob heard her say. Shakily, he stood and crossed the room, standing just within the doorframe to listen in on her conversation, unearthing the buried shame of childhood eavesdropping but lingering all the same.

'Yes, I realise it's late notice,' Laura said, 'that's why I'm phoning you so early. So you can make alternative arrangements.' There was a pause, while the speaker on the other end of the line responded. Rob could hear the irritation in Laura's silence, the impatience she felt at having to explain further. Finally, she spoke again. 'It's a death, if you must know. Close family. I'm sorry, Monica – I really don't want to go into any more detail right now, but I'll be in touch.'

In that moment, inexplicably, Rob knew for certain that Wren would never be coming home.

Ava's message and the photograph within still haven't loaded when Laura reaches out and takes the phone from Rob's hand. She flips it shut and hands it back to him. 'Rob? Are you alright?'

Panic surges through him. The picture timed out before he could see it – Phoebe's up in that little stone cottage with Wren – and he hasn't even started to work out how to broach this with Laura –

'Rob? You look terrible; you're as white as a sheet. Come on, let's take a walk along the beach? You've got to stop worrying. You'll hear the phone if she calls.'

'Who?' he stammers, feeling the heat rise into his face. Despite the cool breeze in the air, he's sweating.

'Phoebe, of course! You need to calm down a bit – you'll give yourself a heart attack at this rate.'

Laura leads the way back through the rocks as Rob follows, gingerly clambering down to the sandy shore, accepting her hand as she steers him towards the water's edge where a group of sanderlings runs in and out of the shallows, taking to wing as they draw near. He follows their progress as their shadows flutter like static across the sand, and is seized by the same helplessness as that he experienced when Wren left, feeling as powerless as a small boy. He must find a way to talk to Laura about Ava. But how? How did you ask someone, *Did you have my baby? Did you abandon her at birth? Did you conceal it from me for all these years?* He studies her face, the curve of her cheekbones, the arch of her brow, the wild beauty of her hair, still her crowning glory. Is he insane? How could he begin to imagine that Laura was capable of such cruel deceit, that she could keep this one huge thing from him, when they've already spent a lifetime together, sharing everything? He has to be wrong; perhaps the whole thing is wrong, and it's simply some big, terrifying mistake.

'You're looking at me in that strange way again,' she says, giving his arm a little shake. 'What's on your mind?'

They reach the sandy stretch leading up to Arthur's kiosk and the car park, passing it by as they follow the rippling line of the water's edge. Rob looks towards Wren's cottage and breathes deeply, trying to stay located in the present. He turns back to Laura, thinking of all those lost babies, and wondering, would that grief have made it more difficult or easier to give another away?

'Do you regret never having a baby of your own, Laur?'

'You know I do.' She fixes on the landscape ahead. 'But I had Phoebe. She was like my own.'

'I wonder why we never – I mean, you never wanted to discuss it as an option. We were young enough, when we got together. When Wren left, you were, what twenty-nine, thirty? We could have had a child together, if we'd wanted.'

A knot of tension ripples along Laura's jawline, the set of her mouth clenching hard. She turns her eyes on him, and there's sadness in them. 'Can you imagine – if Wren came back after a year, two years, and found you, me and Phoebe, and another child. *Our* child – can you imagine what that would have done to her, Rob? To us?'

Rob stops, pulls her into his arms, smoothes his hand across the warm nest of her hair.

'You always thought she'd come back, didn't you?'

She shakes her head against his chest. 'No. But I always *hoped* she'd come back – that she'd want to come back – and I needed to be ready for everything to return to normal if she ever did.'

'To normal?' Rob holds her at arm's length, so she's forced to look at him. 'How could we ever have returned to normal? After she'd left me, and Phoebe – after she'd left you? What – you would have moved out, content for me and Wren to try happy families again, with you visiting at weekends and holidays as if nothing had changed?'

Laura shakes free and continues along the beach, her stride gathering force. 'Obviously not. But I could never really think of you as mine, could I? Even in our happiest times, Rob, the ghost of Wren was there. The unfinished business. You know, in all these years, not once have I heard a knock at our door without jumping, without wondering, however briefly, if it might be Wren come home. Not once.'

Rob slides his hand inside her coat pocket, wrestling her resisting fingers back into his. 'But we *could* have had a child together – you and me – if we'd wanted.' He's testing her, watching for her reaction.

'It would never have worked,' she replies, and it's like a door closing. She drops his hand and gestures towards the terrace of rocky caves ahead of them, breaking into a loose jog as she heads in the direction of the largest.

'You should see this,' she calls back to him, the ease returning to her voice. 'It's Wren's cave. We came here last night – I think she'd want you to see it.'

During that first fortnight, Laura moved herself into the spare room, and she and Rob gradually worked out a rhythm to help him through the fog of everyday life. After a week, she managed to persuade him to return to work while she stayed at home with Phoebe and took care of the house, and the mood of the home shifted as his confidence gradually rose and his attention was diverted from the horror of his abandonment. At the end of his first week back at school, Laura prepared a celebratory curry, and sent him upstairs to shower and change while she set out the table and got Phoebe off to sleep.

'Tell me about your week,' she asked when he returned to join her at the table, smelling of alpine shower gel and fresh skin. '*Darling*,' she added, passing down the mango chutney and pouring him a glass of wine. They laughed properly for the first time since she'd arrived.

Rob snapped a poppadom in two, spooning chutney on to the edge in a small, neat heap. 'You know what? It was OK. No, better than that – it was good. It was really good to get out of the house.' Still holding on to his poppadom, he rubbed his nose with the knuckle of his right hand, at once self-conscious. 'Not away from you and Phoebe, you know – '

'Of course I know, Rob. Away from the thing we can't seem to talk about. *Away from Wren* is what you mean – or at least the bloody great hole she's left.'

He watched as she pushed her chair out from the table and went to the sink to run herself a glass of water, tensely flexing her shoulders before turning to rejoin him at the table.

'I'm sorry,' he said. 'I miss her. I don't know what else to say. I love her. I miss her. I'm terrified that she's gone for good. What else is there to say? What use is there in saying it over and over?'

'No, I'm sorry,' she said. 'I know I shouldn't, but I feel so angry at her. And confused. What she's done, Rob – *running away* – it's not what Wren does. It's not the Wren we know, is it? She's just not that selfish.'

An image of Eliza Adler filled his mind. 'A singular kind of gal', Wren had called her, but Rob couldn't agree, couldn't concur that it was alright for a mother to dump her daughter in a boarding school just because she had better things to do. Surely Wren of all people would know that this was the wrong solution, no matter what was going on, no matter how unhappy she might have become? Hadn't her own experience of abandonment been enough to show her how not to parent, how important a mother's presence was in a child's life?

For the first time since Wren had left, he started to allow his own feelings of anger to break through, and he stared at Laura across the table, watching as her eyes brimmed with tears and she reached again for the bottle. Rob drained his own wine glass and nodded for her to pass the bottle down. He couldn't speak, fearful of betraying Wren with his words; if he started to express the rising heat of his feelings he would never be able to take it back – it would be out there in the world, as real as if he had said it to Wren herself. He must keep it down, he knew, lest speaking it gave it life. For some time, they continued to eat and drink in silence in this way, spooning up the tikka, polishing off the wine as they each dwelt on the situation in their own private space.

Eventually, Laura laid down her fork and pushed her empty glass away, just a fraction. 'Rob,' she said, 'I would do anything to make things better for you. But she hasn't only walked out on you, she's walked out on Phoebe. She's walked out on her mother. And she's walked out on *me*.'

Her voice faltered at this last, and in reflex she covered her mouth with a hand as if to swallow the words back up, to wish them gone. From across the kitchen table Rob watched as her tears bounced like raindrops against the edge of her dinner plate. His eyes roamed over the half-empty dishes laid out across the table – dishes she'd spent all afternoon preparing for the end of his week back at work. It was, he was suddenly and acutely aware, an unintentional copy of the first meal they had all shared together, after that chance meeting with Wren in the college canteen queue of 1982.

'The curry's quite good,' he said, faintly hoping to raise a glimmer of a smile as he quoted the very words Wren had spoken to Laura as she held up the line.

'Is there anything we could have done?' Laura asks, guilt in the wet of her eyes.

Rob's gaze dropped from hers. 'Like what?'

'Do you think she was OK? I – I don't think she was OK, Rob. I'm not sure that we did everything we should have done.'

Rob pushed back his chair, dropped his napkin to his unfinished plate. 'She was fine, Laur – everyone gets a bit blue after a baby – it's normal. Most of the time, she was just fine.'

'What about the cleaning thing? You told me she'd be up at two in the morning some nights, bleaching the kitchen units – rewashing Phoebe's clean clothes. You told me that.'

'Yes, but that's not – that's not depression, is it? That's not going to bed and not getting up, or suicidal thoughts or – I don't know, but it's not that!' His voice had risen with the colour in his neck, and he stood anchored to the space opposite Laura and didn't know which way to turn.

Laura left her seat and went to him. 'I'm not blaming you, Rob. No one's to blame for this. I'm just sounding off –

trying to blame myself if anything – I'm just trying to work it all out.'

His face crumpled, unable to hold it all in, and Laura pulled him close, where he clung to her fiercely, sobbing great racks of anguish against her neck, his tears spilling into the warm refuge of her fragrant curls. The smell of her skin and the pressure of her fingertips as she cradled his head in her hand, the welcome taste of his tears as they passed from his eyes to his lips... he was moved by these sensations, stirred by her affection. Their breathing fell into one rhythm, and he barely knew how to move away from her, to release her small, soft frame from the cage of his hands, hands that rested and clung to the curves of her waist. 'Stay with me,' he whispered, drawing her tighter, reading the subtle turn of her face, the brush of her chin below his. She couldn't speak, was as powerless as he to let go. Without a word, they abandoned the kitchen and the debris of their meal for Laura's single bed, where under the glare of the overhead light they made love in an urgent tangle of anguish, startling to them both in its brevity and force.

The following morning, wreathed in shame and regret, Laura packed her bag and left. As she drove away, Robert stood in the icy doorway with Phoebe in his arms, watching as her car disappeared behind the frosted box hedges of Peynton Gardens, leaving nothing but a plume of white exhaust. Laura was gone, and he wasn't to see her again for another full year.

At the mouth of the cave, Rob stoops to pick up a large, smooth nugget of glass. It's bright, blue as the Cornish skyline; Phoebe will love it. She'll add it to her glass collection at home, stored in an old Kilner jar that sits on her bedroom windowsill, beside the Lalique mermaid shipped over from Grandma Ellie in Paris to mark Phoebe's tenth birthday. She hardly knew her grandmother, but still she loved it, perhaps all the more for their infrequency of contact. Eliza had selected the statuette having admired the polished glass collection when she'd last visited Phoebe around the age of five or six. 'Wren loved polished glass,' Eliza had said, running a manicured finger down the contours of the jar. She did that – talked about Wren as if she were dead, almost from the moment she left. Rob hated her insensitivity, and he'd retreated to the kitchen, leaving Laura to manage the small talk required to get them through the one or two hours she would stay. *Treasures* was what Phoebe called the glass pebbles, laying them out across the carpet of her bedroom, separating them into swirling groups of colour, the blues being the smallest collection, and her favourite. Phoebe, Phoebe, how on earth will she take the news of Ava? Laura will help him, he knows; Laura will know what to do. But first, he needs to work out how to tell Laura...

He slips the blue treasure inside his jacket pocket and follows Laura into the cool tranquillity of Wren's cave.

After Laura walked out on him too, something shifted in Rob. She had helped him through the worst of it, through the first shock and sickness of desertion, and then, just as he'd started to see the way forward, to *feel* again, she was gone. He didn't blame her; he was as wretched and ashamed as she was about their night together. But, as wrong as that had been, he knew that their brief and unexpected rush of intimacy had restarted the beat of his heart and it felt like awakening. In truth, he believed Laura would be back in just a few days, after she'd had a chance to get over the shock of what they'd done. After all, they had never spent more than a week or two apart since childhood, and it must take more than this – however deplorable it was – to break them apart.

At first, as he waited for her return, he threw himself into the mechanics of caring for Phoebe, enlisting the help of Fiona next door, who agreed to have Phoebe during Rob's working hours, on a cash-in-hand, week-by-week basis. His parents visited, offering to help out on occasional weekends in the event that Wren didn't return soon; they were *there for him*, they stressed in voices weighted with concern; he only had to ask. The general tone of sympathy, as if he were a widower not an abandoned spouse, was almost more than Rob could take, and he fixed his mind on showing them all how well he could cope – that he was stronger than any of them gave him credit for. He pushed his anger down, desperate not to give way to the fierce swell of anxiety that constantly threatened to engulf him and sully the life he had once shared with Wren.

Part of him hated her for leaving him; for leaving Phoebe. How could she go, without a word – how could she leave the child she had brought into the world, the child she had nourished and loved and cradled to sleep? Did he really hate her? He knew that wasn't the truth. He couldn't hate her, not really, not when in his darkest moments he felt certain that it was he who was to blame, he who had driven her away. He would do this, he told himself; until Wren returned he would care for his daughter alone. He would do this, and, for now, he would put thoughts of Wren out of his mind, certain that soon she would make contact, when she was ready to come home. Gradually his friends and colleagues began to comment on how well he was doing, how healthy he looked, and for a short while he managed to convince himself that it was enough for him: his daughter, his home, his work.

But in his private moments, in the dim pools of his dreams and his foggy waking thoughts, Rob was consumed by recollections of that single night with Laura. He replayed it like a video on constant loop, gathering up every sensory detail – the glare of the overhead light, the tiny golden freckles that covered her winter-pale skin, the scent of cooking spices hanging in the air. It haunted him and yet he longed for her again, longed to relive the force of Laura's passion as her hip clashed with his, to look into the gleam of her eyes, to see the pain and hunger within. He had never thought of Laura in that way – in any way other than as his closest friend, his ally, his pal. But now, this thing had passed between them, and the power of his need for her was so strong that it felt as if it had lived inside him always, buried deep and, until that night together, denied air. And amidst all of this he missed Wren so deeply, missed her like a man who had lost a limb. When he closed his eyes at night and flexed the imaginary digits of that missing limb, he could feel it still there, feel *her* still there. Just as for an amputee, the morning would inevitably arrive, and every day he would reel with the fresh shock of loss when he saw the space beside him lying empty.

A week after Laura left, a formal solicitor's letter arrived on Wren's behalf, stating her intention to remain unfound, and it was as though Rob had been expecting it all along. Instead of the shock he should have felt, he experienced its reverse, a calm acceptance, and he began to deal with the longer-term practicalities of her vanishing, making lists of people to contact – doctors, dentists, health visitors, neighbours. Jim from two doors down suggested he inform the local police, just to be sure there was no suspicion of Rob attached to her disappearance. Rob was alarmed that he hadn't thought of this himself, and immediately wheeled Phoebe down to the station, only to be surprised by the lack of curiosity once he produced the solicitor's letter.

'It certainly looks like she doesn't want finding.' The duty officer nodded as he took down the details.

'I just thought I should let someone know,' Rob replied. He felt suddenly foolish. Perhaps they thought he was a time-waster. Phoebe lay in her recliner pram, bashing the string of toys that ran across its hood. 'I mean, she left nearly three weeks ago – and she left a brief note, saying she'd be in touch. I didn't come earlier as I'd hoped she'd be home by now.'

'I think her intentions are reasonably clear, judging by this letter. Did she take anything notable with her – passport, etcetera?'

'She didn't take much, but all her documents have gone. Birth certificate, driving licence, passport. She left our wedding certificate.' Of course this wasn't relevant. He just felt the need to say something, anything that might make some sense.

The police officer tapped his chin with his pen. 'Well, Mr Irving, I've made a note of all this and taken a copy of your letter. We'll follow up with the solicitor as a matter of routine, but in the meantime I think the best advice I can give you is to carry on as normal – and, if your situation changes, just let us know. We'll give you a call to let you know what we find out. How does that sound?'

Rob reached across the counter to shake the officer's hand, thanking him effusively before backing out of the double doors into the dull drizzle of the day. He turned his collar up and jogged the pram home to Peynton Gardens, dodging the puddles that had gathered overnight. *Carry on as normal*, the police officer had said. Easier said than done.

A week later, Rob drove over to Gatebridge to drop Phoebe with his parents, before speeding back along the M3 to join colleagues for his first night out since Wren had gone. It was the staff Christmas party at the White Hart inn, and for the first time in all Rob's years at the school the social committee had decided on a no-partners event. Rob was relieved, having already decided he wouldn't attend if husbands and wives were included.

At the bar he was greeted by Ruth, the school secretary, with a tray of 'champagne' cocktails and an unfastened smile. 'Rob! I'm so glad you came.'

He took a glass and kissed her cheek. 'Wouldn't miss it for the world.' He noticed the dip of her green dress, the string of fake jet that disappeared into a cleavage she kept well under wraps in the school office. 'You look great,' he said, his attention dwelling on her unpierced earlobes for a moment too long; they reminded him of Laura's.

Ruth's eyes sparkled; she put down the tray and took a drink for herself, leading him through to the chatter of the main dining area where most of his colleagues were already standing around, several drinks in, and letting their hair down. He followed Ruth through the party, stopping to shake hands and kiss cheeks, his gaze drifting to the wide curve of her green satin backside, as she led him towards the rear of the room and a giant horseshoe arrangement of tables.

'I'll show you where you'll be sitting,' she said, 'so you won't have to hunt around when they call us to eat.' She stopped at a place-setting towards the centre of the room, and pointed out his name tag, attached in bold letters to a bright festive cracker.

He checked the labels of the settings to either side of his. 'I'm next to you,' he said.

'There's a coincidence,' she said, laughing, and she turned on her high shiny heels and started towards the crowd, looking back over her shoulder with a conspiratorial smile. 'We'd better join the others, before they start wondering where we've got to.'

The next morning, Rob awoke in one of the guest rooms at the White Hart, lying naked on a double bed beside Ruth, who was passed out on the pillow beside him. Her mouth was slightly open, the skin above it chapped-looking where her crimson lipstick had smudged in their haste. This close up he could see every pore in her skin, the margin of regrowth in her hair where the dark roots pushed through, and he ran his hands across his face, wincing in recollection at the events of the night before.

'It was my idea, to not have partners this year,' she had told him, leaning close to his ear as she slid back into her seat. She'd looked up to thank the waitress for the tray of coffees she had just delivered.

'Really?'

She nodded. 'I thought it might be easier on you.'

Rob had stared into his coffee, given it an unnecessary stir. 'That was kind of you.'

Crossing her legs slowly, she'd twisted in her seat, her face falling into an expression which told him her motives had not been purely selfless. 'Now tell me, Mr Irving,' she'd said, her fingers twirling around the jet beads at her throat, 'would you care to join me for a tequila?'

With the stale taste of tequila still on his tongue, Rob shuddered and eased himself off the bed, stealthily pulling on his clothes, careful to gather all his belongings before he slipped from Ruth's room. He strode through the corridor, down the stairs, out across the breakfast room and into his car as fast as he could move without running. '*Fuck*,' he muttered, fumbling with the ignition and snagging the seatbelt as he pulled it across his body, pushing thoughts of Wren and Laura from his mind. Catching his reflection in the rear-view mirror, he recognised the disgust in his own eyes, and struck out at the dashboard with the heel of his hand as he threw the car into gear and headed back to his empty home.

Inside the cave, Rob's eyes are rendered momentarily blind. He stands in the shadows blinking as Laura rummages in her coat pocket, bringing out the small Maglite she keeps attached to her key fob. 'It's not as powerful as Wren's, but it's better than nothing.'

They proceed further into the cave, Rob's eyes gradually growing accustomed to the gloom, and stop at a raised rock pool, draped in thick ropes of seaweed. Laura shines the light beam across the water, angling it to pick out the tiny life forms that dart in and out of crevices and creep along the floor of the pool.

'Phoebe will love this,' Laura says, pleasure written on her face. 'Remember that summer holiday on the Isle of Wight? What was she – four or five? There was that fabulous heated pool back at the hotel, but Phoebe just wanted the beach every day. Hours we spent in those rock pools, picking out crabs and guppies.'

Rob

Rob recalls the holiday as if it were last year. Laura had given up work the year before, to be around for Phoebe once she started at big school, and by the time the summer holidays came round she had been stir-crazy with too much time spent around the house. Rob had booked them into a five-star hotel near Ventnor, with breathtaking coastal views across the channel. The sun had seemed to shine without pause. For two blissful weeks, the three of them had embraced island life, harmonious in their family of three. Even now, he can see the tiny shape of Phoebe running ahead of them in a swimsuit printed with seahorses and urchins, an orange bucket swinging in one hand, a net dragging along the sand in the other. Laura chasing after her with a white sunhat in her hand, trying to fix the strap beneath Phoebe's soft chin as she wrestled and complained; later, laughing together as they watched the hat drifting out on the tide. An accident, Phoebe said, as she poked at a pale shrimp wriggling in the palm of her hand.

'We talked about moving there,' he says, following the trail of a pool shrimp that moves in and out of the dark weed. 'We even stopped outside estate agents' windows in Newport to compare house prices. You were really keen, I seem to remember.'

'*You* were worried about work opportunities, *I* seem to remember.' She continues to swirl the torchlight around the pool, dipping her hand to cause a crab to skitter along the bottom. Her fingers appear to wobble and bend, distorted by the ripples and curves of the water.

'I was probably right to be cautious,' he replies, hating how jaded he sounds. 'It would have been a bit risky. House prices in London are generally a lot more stable than the rest of the country. We'd have been giving up that security.'

'Haven't you ever wanted to do something reckless, Rob? To throw caution to the wind and just go for it – do whatever the hell you want for a change?'

He doesn't know how to reply. He's on the brink of confessing to her the living, breathing outcome of his recklessness – of implicating her in it too – and yet he stands weak in the shadows of this dark cave, barely able to speak. 'Like what?' he asks, his voice quiet and still.

'Like – like anything! Like, jacking your job in and travelling the world? Like, cashing in your savings and moving to France? An adventure! A risk!' She waves her arms about, the way she does when she's building up to an argument, building up towards her point. 'An affair?' Now she looks angry.

'What?' Rob pulls back his chin as if he's been slapped.

'An *affair*. Maybe you're not as squeaky clean as you make out, Rob. You've been keeping secrets, I know that much. Since when do we keep secrets from each other?' She shines the torch at his face, lowers it again when he flinches. 'The letter, Rob?'

'The letter,' he echoes, and anxiety floods back in, waiting as it was for a crack in his armour. He takes out his phone, opens Ava's message and tries on the link again, groaning inwardly as the green arrow returns, waiting to load. 'Listen, Laur, I do want to tell you about the letter – about everything. But first, can we get out of this bloody cave?' he asks. 'It's giving me a headache.'

In the bright light of the bay, Laura stands waiting, her arms folded, the wide blue horizon of sea and sky stretching out behind her for miles. 'I'm listening,' she says.

Rob glances at the spooling image on his phone, before fixing Laura firmly and holding her gaze. 'Just tell me one thing,' he says. 'If we had had a child together, what would you have called it?'

Laura pulls a face and turns away from him to face the water. For a moment he thinks she plans to ignore his question, and he turns back to his phone to see the scrolling image as it finally fills the screen, at last revealing the photograph in clear and certain detail. Rob's breath catches like a choke in the back of his throat. The picture on his phone is one he's seen before, one of a set of four: a passport photo taken at Camden Market – of him, and Laura, and Wren.

'Ava,' Laura replies, spinning on her heel to face him, bringing him back to the moment as his eyes follow the spray of sand kicked up around her boot.

He looks up from his phone.

'What did you say?'

Laura shakes her head, as if she's dealing with a madman. 'You asked me what I would have called our child. I said Ava. If we'd had a girl, I would have called her Ava.'

For a few brief weeks after the Christmas party Rob made the most of his Friday nights, either joining his colleagues for after-work drinks or heading up west alone to take relief in the anonymity of the city wine bars, where, if he was lucky, he might find himself numb in the arms of a stranger for the night. It was unhappy sex, he recognised that much, but in those vital moments the obliteration of thought and solitude was so complete that, for a brief interlude at least, he was soothed. Afterwards, however, his self-loathing was all-encompassing, and the next day he would drive along the motorway towards his parents' house, berating himself with thoughts of his baby daughter, who he knew needed him to be as good as he could be.

Several months passed, and still Laura made no contact, sent no forwarding address. It was as if, just like Wren, she had simply vanished. As if she had never been there in the first place. In the shortest space of time he had lost them both, the two people he cared for most in the world, the two people who cared most about him. By Phoebe's first birthday in May, Wren had been gone for six months, and as he marked it off on his calendar Rob resolved to turn his back on the thankless pleasure-seeking of the past half-year, to dedicate himself to his work, his health, and his family. He enrolled Phoebe in a full-time nursery, where she thrived in the company of other children, and within weeks he was back on track, and being urged by his head to apply for a new deputy head post due for consideration in the autumn. Life was more than tolerable; he had found his way to some kind of peace.

And so, when Laura reappeared just days before Christmas, one full year since she had left, he almost turned her away.

'Can I stay?' she asked him. Her skin was tanned, her eyes dark with exhaustion.

'Can you *stay*?' he repeated, astounded at the casual tone of her opening words. His fingers gripped the edge of the door frame, his body barring the entrance as his heart hammered against his ribcage. He fought to keep the emotion from his voice. 'Laura, it's been over a year. You haven't phoned, or written – not a word from you to ask how we're doing!'

'I'm sorry, Rob. I'm so, *so* sorry. You're right to still be angry at me.'

'Angry? Laura – you're a year too late for anger.' Rob spoke softly, conscious as he was of Phoebe napping in the living room just along the hall. 'I did all that in the weeks and months after you disappeared on me. I'm not angry about it any more – just sad.'

She shook her head, tears coursing down her cheeks. 'I was so ashamed after what we did – everything changed in that instant, Rob, and I couldn't...' Her words trailed off as she swiped at her face and reached down for her old army rucksack in a move to leave.

Rob stared at Laura's face, so familiar and reassuring, and silently urged her to raise her eyes and meet his. 'We needed you, Laur,' he said, his tone softening as his own tears threatened to break through. 'We missed you.'

'Let me come in, Rob, please? Just let me explain? Let me see Phoebe?'

When it came to it he couldn't send her away. Despite everything, he couldn't shut her out; he wanted her there more than he wanted her gone. 'Let's talk,' he replied, and he stood aside to let Laura through, and she fell back into his life.

'Ava...?' Rob stands on the beach, feet planted wide, anchoring him to the earth lest he lets go and the whole world unravels. He grips his phone in one hand, still reeling from the image on the screen, the fingers of his other hand holding tight to the blue glass pebble in his pocket. 'Why Ava?'

Laura looks tiny against the backdrop of the empty beach. Out above the rocks, sea birds float and soar between coast and field, casting their cries out into the wide sky. This is a beautiful place; he understands how Wren might have found her peace here.

'Why? I don't know – something about bird names, I think. Like Phoebe – Phoebe's a bird name too.'

Rob cannot pull his eyes from her face. She looks puzzled as she stares back, hands thrust into the pockets of her oversized parka, hair coiling around her head like fire. 'What is it, Rob?' she asks, the concern in her voice rising. 'I know this is stressful – worrying for you. But you look as if you've got the weight of the world on your shoulders.'

A group of surfers appear on the beach between them and the rocks, jogging across the sand with boards under their arms. They wade out into the sea, launching on to their surfboards, swimming out with powerful strokes to reach the deeper waters where the tide rises and falls.

Rob holds out a hand to Laura and leads her back to the small mound of rocky boulders surrounding the entrance to the cave, where they sit together, with the view of the beach and rocks before them. He slides the blue pebble from his pocket and places it in her hand, folding her fingers over it, wanting her to hold tight to its reassuring smooth edges. 'I'm going to tell you about the letter,' he says. 'But first, I want you to tell me about that year you spent away. After Wren had gone, after we had – ' He breaks off, unable to finish the sentence, the guilt of their actions capable of such power even after all these years.

Laura turns the pebble over in her hands, her eyes downcast. 'You know about that year, Rob. It wasn't a good one for me.'

'You said you went travelling. Island-hopping, you said?'

'At first I went back to my parents' for a time, while Doug and I put the flat up for sale. When it was sold, I couldn't contemplate staying around, and my head was all over the place, after… well, you know.'

'You were distraught, when you left.'

She flips the pebble over, slips it in her pocket. 'Of course I was – we both were! We would have been no better than monsters if we hadn't been. After all those years of friendship? I'd always loved you, Rob – I mean, properly loved you – but I understood that it was meant to be you and Wren, and I would never, ever have made my true feelings known.'

She turns to face him for a moment, to check his response. He nods for her to continue.

'And Wren – I loved her so much it hurt. She was more than a sister to me; I can't explain it. After she'd gone, I was incomplete. I was rootless, I suppose, and that's why I went travelling. To *find myself*.' She says these last words with irony, trying to make light of it, but it's not light; it's not ironic.

'So you went travelling, for the whole year?'

'Well, not the whole year, but yes, I went travelling. You know this! Look, Rob, what's with all the questions? I don't understand why you're so interested after all these years. It's a long time ago.'

Rob reaches inside his jacket and brings out the folded letter, offering it to Laura between two fingers. Dark smudges run along the creased edges and scored folds, where he's carried it around with him, terrified to let it far from his grasp.

'The letter?' she asks, looking at him cautiously as she takes it from his hand. 'The one from your "old college pal"?'

'Read it,' he replies.

For a few minutes they sit in silence, Laura bent over her knees, fingers pressed against her mouth, her eyes scanning the words as she reads and rereads the letter. She turns to look at him, her stunned expression asking all the questions she can't find the words for.

'Did you see the name at the foot of the page?' he asks.

'Ava,' she whispers, her eyes locking on the surfers as they cross the horizon, silhouetted shape-shifters standing tall. 'You have another daughter – *called Ava?*'

'That's right, *Ava*. We've emailed each other, and she's given me a few details of her birth – where she was found, her birth date and so on.'

'And?' Laura asks. Her skin is ashen.

'She was born on the first of August 1995. She could have been born several weeks early or late – but it means that anyone I was with around that time could be the mother.' He hesitates, his eyes roaming her face for signs of acknowledgement. 'Laura – *you* could be her mother.'

With a gasp Laura thrusts the letter back at him, her eyes wide. 'Are you seriously asking me if I'm the mother of this girl? And, what – I just gave her away and jumped on the first plane to Greece?' She rises, steps away from the rock, sweeps her hands over her face. 'How could you – how could you even think that, Rob? Do you have any idea what I would have given for a child of my own?'

Rob stands, passes her the phone. 'Just take a look at this, Laur. This is the photograph Ava's mother left with her.'

Staring at the image, she shakes her head in disbelief, looking from the screen to Rob's face as she processes the information. She pushes the phone back into his palm and starts to rummage in her pockets, bringing out her leather wallet. 'I can't believe – ' Laura sighs, more to herself than to Rob, and she crouches over the sand, opening the wallet, flinging out credit cards and loyalty cards and stamps and receipts and vouchers, until eventually she unearths it. It's tiny and tatty and rough at the edges but it's the real thing, held out to him in trembling fingers – it's her copy of the photograph.

Rob's thoughts whirl, as he too retrieves the picture stored in his wallet, identical to the one he gave to Phoebe just this morning. He holds it up beside Laura's. Exactly the same. Photograph number three.

Far out in the bay, two figures appear from beyond the craggy rocks, their figures gaining shape and clarity as they come out of the shadows and on to the beach. As the pair walks towards them across the sand, silhouettes against the purpling sky, their posture and gait is almost indistinguishable from one another, and it's only when Phoebe raises her hand, waves to them in a wide arcing motion, that Rob knows for sure which is which. Rob and Laura stand on the beach, transfixed by the image of Wren walking towards them at Phoebe's side. Their hands feel for each other as Rob watches her, watches Wren – really, truly, Wren, walking towards him again, after all these years.

'It's Wren's photograph,' Laura murmurs, her voice low and composed. '*Wren* is Ava's mother.'

WREN

The morning it dawned on Wren that she was pregnant again, thoughts of suicide passed through her mind like fast-moving clouds in a dark sky. In the months since Phoebe had arrived, she had separated so far from her original self that she had no way of knowing if these thoughts were serious or real; they simply appeared as clear and rational possibilities streaming through her consciousness on a spinning reel.

She hadn't taken a test and she didn't need to – the signs were all there, recognisable from the first time round. It was a Saturday morning and she was standing in the bathroom, her arms huddled about her as she listened intently to the tinny sound of the rain driving hard against the window that looked out over the lawns of their lovely garden. She had been in there a while, avoiding Rob and Phoebe, who were in the kitchen taking their time over breakfast, peppering the air with cheery sounds. Were weekends worse? she wondered. Were the days worse when there was company, or were they better? Fuller, or lonelier still? She couldn't say. Time had become an endless foe, stretching out in long chunks of emptiness, in which she could sit for unknown lengths, simply thinking – or not thinking, focusing on the strange details of the objects in a room, wondering what could be considered real, what a figment of her imagination. The shadows of the shifting day moved things; she watched as the light and shade slipped around the kitchen, altering those objects, causing her to suspect them to be phantoms, seen only by her. Sometimes she would sit and watch for hours, sure that she might catch them out with her stealth and resilience. Now, she stood at the washbasin, scrutinising her dark-eyed reflection in the mirror, her pulse throbbing low as her mind lurched across the thought of bringing a new child – *another baby* – into this house. It was a madness, a horror, an unthinkable scenario.

She harboured no delusions about her condition and accepted it as some kind of depression, though she had never voiced as much, for fear of alarming Robert and making things worse. Six months had passed now, and still she was in this trough of unspoken despair – yet Phoebe was a happy, healthy baby, all smiles and affection, and Wren *did* love her. That much she knew: she felt love for her, even if it was on a subdued plane of emotion. Why did it all feel so very wrong? It had to be something in her, something that was in her mother too, and maybe on and on, travelling backwards throughout their maternal history. Perhaps they shared a recessive gene that meant mothering was outside of their sphere of capabilities? Was it mothering that was the problem – or home-making – or simply the act of loving? How could she know the answer to these things; how could she *ever* know?

She ran cold water over her hands and drew them across her face, pushing cool fingers up into her hairline, rapt at the sweep of her eyebrows, brushing up and out in a mask of surprise. When would the fog lift, she wondered; when would she start to feel like herself again, to experience living in the moment instead of through a screen, like a spectator in a cinema audience, watching at a distance?

Drying her hands on the towel, she kept an eye on the mirror, trying to catch out her reflection. The copy of her never looked away, eyes remaining locked no matter which way she moved her head, left, right, up and around – she wouldn't be tricked. Wren moved closer to the mirror, breathed on the glass to generate a circle of mist and stepped back to watch it disappear again like a ghost. *That's what I am*, she thought. *A ghost. I drift about this place like mist, seen by few, heard by none. Dear God, how would I cope with a second child?*

When Robert knocked on the bathroom door Wren almost screamed, so astonished was she by the reminder that she was not alone. She clasped the towel to her chest, unbolting the door and throwing it back with more force than she knew she had in her, causing it to crash noisily against the shower screen. Robert recoiled as if expecting an attack. Did he fear her? That wasn't possible. She blinked at the small dot of shaving tissue he had stuck to his jawline and repressed a nervous smile, grateful that he could not gain access to the jumble of words and images inside her head.

'That was Laura on the phone,' he said, his expression grave.

Of course! Here was her answer, her salvation – how could she not have thought of it before – here it was, in the shape of Laura and her unborn child. Laura who had come to them so recently with the news of her pregnancy, joyous and hopeful that this would be the one that made it, the child that would make her a mother at last. This was how it was meant to be – *this time* Wren wouldn't be alone. She would have Laura by her side, going through the same alterations and uncertainty. A baby, something Laura had longed for so deeply and for too long, and now Wren would be able to share it with her, and they would be together. In a rush of exhilaration she shifted her gaze to meet Robert's eyes square-on.

The tiniest bob of his head told her that he understood the answer too, that she only had to say the words and they would make it all right again, the three stooges united once more: three leaves of a clover, three legs of a stool. Her words rushed from her like spilt milk. 'We must get her to move in, Rob. There's plenty of room, isn't there? And she won't miss Doug – he's a waste of space, even Laura says so. You know about the drugs, don't you? You can't bring a child up in that kind of environment. God, she must be desperate to get out of there! I think this baby is just what she needs to climb out of the rut she's in, and we could help – '

'Wren, stop,' he said, reaching out a hand to slow her down.

'What?' She took a step back to avoid his touch.

'There is no baby, Wren. That's why she was calling. She's just come back from the hospital – she lost the baby.'

Wren sank to the floor like a carcass, her arms curling up over the back of head, her hands clamping against her ears. From far, far away the sound of keening was drifting towards her, a high, animal cry of grief and longing. How could Laura go on after this, after such endless loss, so unfair, so cruel? Wren retreated deeper inside herself and dreamt of death, of delirious, dark, infinite death.

The girl, for Wren can't yet begin to think of her as 'Phoebe', sits at the table watching her stir the soup. She feels her eyes on her back, can almost hear the tick and whirr of her mind as it races about the room, searching for prompts to start conversation. *Conversation.* What a strange concept that is to Wren nowadays, for a woman who can go for days on end – weeks sometimes – barely exchanging more than the briefest 'good morning' or 'thank you' with the man who serves her coffee at the beachside. Even down by the water, when she passes fellow walkers or the surfers who frequent her golden bay, nothing more than a nod is ever required, and that's the way she likes it. That way peace lies. She thinks now of Arthur, of him watching Laura and Robert pass by his kiosk on their way down to the beach. If they stop for a drink, she knows he'll chat, and she hopes Laura takes care to be discreet, to protect her anonymity in this small corner of her world.

The girl cuts bread, making a hash of the job, and apologises, calling herself cack-handed. That's one of Robert's expressions; he's passed it on. Back in their old student flat it was always Robert or Wren who sliced the bread, or served up the cake, as it would end up in bits if left to Laura. 'You're cack-handed,' he'd say, taking the knife from her and righting the damage she'd done. Laura would stick her fingers up, or snub her nose, and Wren would laugh at the pair of them bickering like siblings. The memory is like an old film in her mind's eye, in which the three of them, Wren, Rob and Laura, sit on upturned fruit crates in the garden of Victoria Terrace pouring tea and serving up marble cake, the light catching in the gleam of Laura's smile, in the gloss of Robert's floppy fringe. They were so happy, for such a long time.

Wren serves up the soup and takes a seat on the other side of the table. She glances up at the girl, at Phoebe, and sees her fully for the first time, sitting across from her, startled as a deer. This means a great deal to her, Wren can see; she can't allow the meal to continue in silence in this way – it would be unkind, unfair. She wishes she could find it in herself to send the girl away – it would be the easiest thing, the *safest* thing – but she simply can't, and in her deepest reserves she knows she doesn't want to. It's wrong, this selfish desire to be near her, when she has neither claim nor understanding of the emotion, no right to feel anything towards her at all – and she searches the face that looks back at her for signs of anger or resentment, wondering just what it is she can do for her or say to her to ease her anxiety. Despite her discomfort the girl doesn't look away, but Wren barely notices, so transfixed is she by her features, which appear at once familiar and alien, like some half-remembered dream. She has sprung from Wren, it's clear, and yet there's much of her that is Robert. There's something else in there too, another element that reflects outwards in the steadfast glint of her eyes and the pucker of her lips, and with a silent lurch of exhilaration Wren recognises it for what it is. It's Laura: she has Laura's spirit, and it radiates from her like a shaft of morning light.

'Laura tells me you're expecting a child,' Wren says. She dunks the crust into her soup and brings it to her mouth, trying hard to read the expression on the girl's face. 'How far gone are you?'

The colour drains from Phoebe's face. She feels for the scarf around her neck, instinctively searching for the silky care label that nestles between its folds, smoothing it between crossed fingers like the hand of a child protecting itself against a white lie. Wren feels helpless as the girl's eyes fill with moisture. She's really not very good at this kind of thing. She takes a deep breath. Maybe they could start again.

The purchase of Tegh Cottage was fairly quick and simple; it was a vacant property, and Wren was a cash buyer. In the couple of weeks prior to completion she stayed at the

Metropole hotel, where she slept late in the mornings and ate meals in her room. In the afternoons she would stroll through the tranquil streets of Padstow, taking comfort from the sights and sounds of industry around the lobster hatchery and harbour, resting on the bench at the old pier to watch the autumn sun as it sank beyond the horizon. By the time she took possession of the cottage she had erased all thoughts of her old life, of Robert and Phoebe – of Laura – and the baby growing inside her was denied acknowledgement.

Her new home was just right for her needs, overlooked by no one, its only neighbour the meadow and the dirt path that ran alongside the front hedge. To begin with she was glad of her car, as she trekked to and from Constantine and Padstow, organising supplies and following up contacts suggested to her by the man at the beach café. It was a hard winter, and for Wren a period of toil unlike anything she had ever experienced before – the tough physical graft of digging out her vegetable patch in readiness for the spring, of stripping and sanding and painting, of shoring up the perimeters of her home to make it secure. Arthur helped to organise a small chest freezer to be delivered, along with a washing machine and a second-hand oven, and she spent several consecutive days driving back and forth between garden centres, building up a stock of tools, how-to manuals and early seeds. But before long it became clear she had everything she needed and the car, with all its cheery echoes of domesticity from a time before, became a source of anxiety to her, filtering into her thoughts and dreams, and threatening to bring unwanted complication to her door. It was the paperwork that would create the real problems, she realised – when the tax and insurance ran out, she'd have to fill out new paperwork, and that was something she simply couldn't do. She had gone to great lengths to erase her trail, changing her surname, and giving her childhood family address when asked for previous residences on deed and utility documents. This car was an impediment, and it had to go.

The dilemma came to a head when she awoke in the early hours of a frosty December morning, disturbed again by the incessant night anguish fuelled by the presence of that car. She rose from her bed, pulling on thick socks to protect her feet from the ice chill of the flagstone floor, and padded through to the living room. At the front window she peered out into the darkness, where her eyes were drawn to the distinctive shape – the tail end of the car – visible through the bars of the front gate. It had to go *now*. Dressing rapidly, she pulled on jeans, sweater, boots and winter coat, and packed a bag with food and water, uncertain how long she might be gone. In the back room she dragged out the wooden trunk and rummaged through the paraphernalia of the time before, carefully reading labels and selecting a handful of items to drop in her bag, before dashing to the back of the house to snatch up the box of cook's matches from beside the hob. Silently, she slipped from the house.

Out on the main road in the black of early morning, she had no plan as to where she was heading, so she followed her instincts and drove west along unfamiliar coastal paths, keeping an eye on the dashboard clock, wanting to be sure she had driven a safe distance from her new home in the bay. After twenty minutes or so, she picked up signs to Mawgan Porth and left the main route to follow the dark country lanes until she came out at a small beach resort and a cluster of cafés and bars overlooking the water. By now it was coming up for five, and as she slowed the car to pass through the resort she could see already there were signs of life inside some of the buildings, small flickerings of light and movement, the hum of generators cranking up for the day. She kept driving, passing through the small community, up and round the winding roads, onwards without thought, until eventually she spotted a dirt layby at the side of the road, in a secluded spot overlooking nothing but fields and hedgerows. Wren wound down the front windows and turned off the engine, grabbing her bag and stepping out of the car. Unlocking the boot, she checked to make sure there was nothing left behind, before opening the passenger door to search through the glovebox. She retrieved a small hand torch and ice scraper, stuffing them inside her bag as things of use, and continued pulling out scraps of paper and old maps, which she bunched up and discarded on the back seat. At the very bottom of the glovebox was a favourite old Paisley scarf of Wren's, one she'd spent hours searching for previously, and she pulled it out now, wondering what it was that connected people so irrationally to *things*. Things that meant nothing. As the scarf unravelled, a small mitten dropped from its silky tangle, and it lay on the passenger seat, its tiny woollen thumb pointing at Wren like an accusation. In a breath, she gathered the mitten up in a ball of scarf and threw them atop the paper pyre on the back seat, on to which she poured the remains of a bottle of nail polish remover, and the highly scented contents of an expensive *eau de parfum*. Standing back, she hoisted her bag over her shoulder and lit a match.

The back seat went up like a bonfire, its efforts accelerated by the high coastal wind that whipped through the open windows of the small family car. Wren stepped back and watched for long enough to be sure that the fire had taken, then she turned on her heel and ran without looking back, down and round the winding country paths until she reached the sand in time to see the sun coming up over the deserted holiday cottages and headland of North Cornwall.

After they've eaten, they take mugs of tea into the garden, and Wren leads Phoebe around the vegetable patch in the fast-fading light, pointing out her neat lines of digging, showing her where the courgettes will go, the curly kale, the carrots and beans. The potatoes have a large plot all of their own, beside rhubarb plants and a small blackcurrant bush, and this year she plans to grow butternut squash as they keep so well for soups and stews. There's nothing much to show now – November is a month of preparation and thought – but there will be: come spring and summer there will be more vegetables and salad than Wren will have use for.

She watches in wonder as her daughter picks up a hard clod of earth and crumbles it in her smooth white hands. *A baby*. Wren tries to suppress the rushes of adrenaline she's been feeling since Phoebe sat across from her and talked about the baby that grows and turns within her. To hear her anticipation, to feel the joy and endless love that pours from her as she speaks of the child and the life ahead of her – it feels like a gift. It feels like hope.

'I'm going to college to study landscape gardening in April,' Phoebe says, and the expression she turns on Wren seems to seek her approval. 'I dropped out of uni in May, and I've been trying to work out what to do with myself ever since. I think gardening might suit me.'

Wren gestures towards the bench, where they sit looking out to sea, much as she and Laura had done early this morning, just those few hours ago. Who would have thought life could shift so completely within such a short space of time? That Wren's world could become so crowded, so full of questions and sensations in a matter of days.

'There's something soothing about it,' Wren says, 'about working the land.'

She feels Phoebe's eyes on her, can make out the slight nod of her head from the edges of her vision. 'I worked in a greenhouse picking tomatoes this summer. It was exhausting – so hot! And backbreaking too, but you know, I felt happier in those few weeks than I had for that whole year at university. Where I was meant to be *fulfilling my potential*.'

'Why weren't you happy?'

Phoebe turns her palms over, appearing to study them where they rest on her knees. Wren is aware of how close their bodies are, how easy it would be to wrap her arms around Phoebe and draw her close, to smell her skin and smooth her soft forehead; to close her eyes and imagine her an infant again.

'I guess I just couldn't hack it. I don't know if it's something about me – if I'm just not degree material – but I couldn't do it. It was the most horrible experience of my life, and if Laura hadn't come and got me like she did, I don't know what I would have done.'

When Wren doesn't respond, Phoebe continues talking, filling the empty spaces just as Laura had done before her.

'I was in student halls, so it's not as if I was completely alone. But the rooms are singles, and every night I could hear the other students coming and going – laughing, calling out to each other up and down the corridors, having a good time – and I just didn't fit in. University was like this enormous place where everyone else was in on the secret, and I was on the outside without the VIP pass.' She fixes her gaze on the horizon beyond the meadow, her brow crinkled against the dusk. 'I tried to get on with it, to "cope" like everyone else, but in the end – I honestly thought I was losing my mind or something. Have you ever had that – where you *actually* think you're going mad? I stopped going to lectures and I just lay in bed and cried and slept for days on end – and *nobody* noticed me missing, no one came looking for me. One day I got up and looked in the mirror and I knew I had to phone Laura.' She glances at Wren, embarrassed. 'I don't know why I'm – I mean, I've never told anyone this before. Except Laura. Even Dad doesn't know the whole story.'

Wren experiences a sudden tug of protectiveness towards the girl, and she covers her mouth to prevent her words flying out into the world, to stop herself from saying all the things a mother should say, when she has no place doing so. She has no right.

'Is that why *you* left, I wondered?' Phoebe asks, leaning on to her knees, turning her face towards Wren's. 'Because you felt alone?'

Wren steels herself, desperate to compose her thoughts, to pull her emotions into check, and she wonders how this girl has the power to cut through it all in one short hour, to peer into Wren's hidden well and draw deep of the water. Glancing up at Phoebe, she can detect the healthy smoulder of her pregnancy in the fullness of her lips, in the gleam of her eyes. So, this was what they talked about when they said 'blooming'; it was more than just a physical reaction to the condition, it was from within – from the heart, the mind, the soul. Wren struggles to recall a clear sense of her own experience, and the deepest sadness resurfaces in her. The word *confinement* springs from somewhere as she pictures her state of airlessness, of drowning even, and with relief she understands that this is *not* something passed on through the generations, like some long-unacknowledged family flaw. Phoebe wants this baby – wants to be a mother – and she will be wonderful and giving and capable and warm. Just like the woman who raised her; just like Laura.

Without answering, Wren gathers up their cups and starts back towards the house, indicating for Phoebe to follow as she steps in through the kitchen door and pauses beside the sink. 'I'm sorry,' she whispers as they face each other in the fading daylight of the kitchen window, each searching the other for some comfort.

Phoebe turns to look out over the garden, where the shapes of shrubs and wooden trellises are outlined against the darkening sky. 'I know,' she replies, and she steps into her mother's arms and weeps.

The first signs showed themselves in the early hours of a sweat-soaked night in late July, waking Wren from a fitful sleep in slow, rolling waves that stretched out through the daylight hours and into the evening. These early contractions were mild enough that Wren was able to convince herself she had eaten something bad, that the low, clawing cramps were nothing more than the symptoms of food poisoning; that they would pass in time, given some bed-rest and plenty of water. By the time evening came around, the griping had settled to a low, imperceptible throb, and, despite the glaring heat of the day just past, she lit a fire in the living room and set to work on her rag rug, a project she had begun some months earlier and meant to complete. Through high fever and chills, she hooked and tugged strips of fabric into the early hours, pausing only to douse her face and neck in cold water, or to slip into a restless slumber on the sofa. There, she drifted through nightmarish dreams, underwater scenes in which the faces of her past rose up through cloudy pools of salt water, their features streaming like tangleweed on the sucking current. She was late, running across the beach, racing to catch Laura as she pushed a wooden dinghy on to the water. Wren watched her getting further and further away, following the swell of the tide, until she was waist-deep and the water lapped at the lower coils of her auburn hair, pulling her head back with its weight. Laura hoisted herself up and over the boat's edge, to be with her child, and Wren called to her, waving both arms above her head, trying to prevent her from sailing out into the black sea that churned and broiled like the very surface of hell. But Laura didn't turn her head, didn't look back, and Wren could only stand and watch, as the scorching heat of the summer sun burnt the vision from her mind and she woke, drenched in perspiration, uncertain, for those brief heart-thumping moments, what she was doing alone in this strange place. What time was it? Gone midday, judging by the position of the sun that poured through the windows; as late as mid-afternoon, even. As she rose, she fought the fainting sensation that pressed down on her clammy skin, and slumped back against the cushions, breathing long and slow, trying to establish whether the cramps had subsided altogether, whether the sickness had passed its worst.

A knock at the door corresponded with a dazzling wave of pain, more powerful than any before, rising up like a sleeping beast from the lowest reaches of her belly, causing her to gasp, her fingers clawing at the fabric of the sofa. Now louder – *bang, bang* – and a man's voice; Arthur's voice. 'Wren? It's Arthur here. Just checking you're alright, love?'

The panic that rushed through Wren's veins was paralysing. Why was he here? What did he want? She had to get rid of him, send him away and shut out the light. It took every last breath of effort for Wren to push herself up out of the sofa, to shuffle slowly towards the front door, where she paused to compose herself, straightening out her shoulders as she unlatched the lock.

'Hello, Arthur,' she said, desperately conscious of the heat of her body radiating towards him, furnace-like.

His eyes did a rapid scan of her face and form, concern etching his features. 'Wren, love – haven't seen you for a couple of days. Thought I'd better check, what with – well, you know.' He jerked his chin towards her stomach. 'Everything alright?'

A film of sweat beaded up in her hairline, across her temples, and Wren resisted the temptation to swipe it away, fearful of drawing attention to her distress. 'I'm fine,' she replied. The sensation of passing out was threatening to overcome her again, to envelop her in its welcome embrace.

'Listen, love – I know you don't like me prying, but you must be just about fit to burst. How long have you got to go? You don't look all that good, Wren.'

Drawing a breath, she dug her fingernails into the soft pad of her hand, willing herself to stay in the present, to draw enough strength to send him away, to leave her in peace. 'I said I'm fine, Arthur.' She felt her body swaying slightly, and she began to close the door on him, so she could return to the safety of the sofa, to sleep and block out the tremors that were now rising up through her core.

Arthur's face was uncertain, streaked with concern, his voice hesitant. 'Alright, love. I'm heading back home now, but I'll look in on you in the morning. Just to be sure?'

Flight

Closing the door, Wren sat on the windowsill, unable to move in the grip of a forceful seizure. If Arthur was on his way home it was past six o'clock, and the morning was a full half-day away. She was safe for the time being, she thought. As she hobbled slowly across the living room floor, fluid rushed from her in a torrent, bringing with it a current of pain so profound she fell to her knees, clasping the unfinished rag rug to her cheek. The truth was, this baby was more than two weeks overdue, and, one way or another, it would find its way into the world; it would be born.

Wren leads them along the overgrown footpath, walking in silence down through the rocks and gorse that line the little-used route. There's an aged bench at the path's edge, and Wren leans against its wooden back as Phoebe pauses to take in the landscape. As she looks across the sun-dappled horizon, Wren's thoughts are on Ava, out there somewhere in the world beyond the bay. But where? Over the years Wren's conscious mind has barricaded itself against thoughts of her life before, of what she has done and not done. But in her dreams... she cannot control her dreams, and at times they have been the source of great trauma, chasing her through the night and holding her face towards her fears. In her dreams, Ava, more than Phoebe, has returned to haunt Wren, bringing visions of the infant disappearing into the abyss of darkness, vanishing like mist. In nightmarish clarity Wren has seen herself sliding the swaddled baby into the well of a fishing boat as she wades deep and pushes her out to sea. Through a window she has spied her lying in a crib behind a clinical curtain, undiscovered and fading away; she has unearthed her, face-down in the vegetable garden on a late summer afternoon, rotting like a marrow. Rarely has she dreamt of the child safe in the embrace of Robert and Laura, the one place her deepest hopes would have had her be. Wren's sleeping mind knows that there was every chance that Ava did not make it home; her waking mind has never trespassed on the idea.

'The views are beautiful,' Phoebe says. The last rays of daylight fall on her skin, illuminating the youth of her, the future of her, and for a moment Wren must remind herself which one this is, which spectre from her past. The girl shows no signs of animosity towards her, despite Wren's silence, her lack of voice. 'It must be a calming place to live,' Phoebe continues. 'You seem like a calm person – not like me.'

Wren thinks of the times she has heard this; her reputation for serenity lives on. Throughout childhood, college, work, everyone described her in those terms. Capable, unflappable, composed. If you wanted a job done, you could rely on Wren. She was the kind of friend you wanted around in a crisis, clear-thinking and self-possessed – broad-shouldered and mature. They had no idea of the turmoil beneath the surface, her crippling fear of death – not of her own, but of those she held dear, those who might slip through her fingers like the powder-blonde sand of a Cornish beach. They couldn't imagine the restless anxiety that chased her waking moments and those of her sleep, couldn't see into her thoughts and dreams, claustrophobic nightmares that tightened around her and crushed her soul. How could she have told them any of this? They would never have believed her. They didn't believe her.

'*I feel like I'm fading,*' she had whispered into the phone, speaking to Laura several months after Phoebe was born. 'Sometimes I look in the mirror and I'm barely there.'

Laura told her that she was just tired out; that she should tell Rob how she felt, get him to help out a bit more with the baby. 'All new mothers get tired like this, Wrenny. Honestly, it will pass.'

Wren hung up and went to Rob, who was sitting in the living room watching some American sitcom, laughing hard as he massaged a foot through his sock. 'You should watch this,' he said, 'it's very funny.'

'Can you see me?' Wren asked.

Rob took a second to look away from the screen. 'Huh?'

'*Am I fading?*' She knew how mad she sounded, could hear it from far away; she could even see herself, pale and dishevelled, viewed from a distance: like watching some strange play.

'Fading? Don't be daft!' He rose from his seat and wrapped his arms around her. 'How could you fade – you're as beautiful now as the day I met you. *More* beautiful.'

'I don't mean – ' she tried to say, but her voice was muffled against his cable-knit jumper, and at any rate she couldn't get the words out if she tried.

Phoebe closes her eyes and takes a long, deep breath. She turns to look at Wren with a smile, her face wide and trusting. 'You know, I think I'd be a calm person if I lived somewhere like this. If I walked on the beach every day the way you do, to have time alone with my thoughts.'

Wren's timelines are tangled, thoughts and memories tumbling across one another in cables of disorder. Gulls fly overhead, towards the ocean, their sharp eyes on the water, on the feast below. It's hard to know what's real and what's not – whether Phoebe is really standing here beside her, gentle in her tone. In the distance a figure clambers up the rocks, the old ghost of her, out on her daily walk, having come the right way, the usual way, along the path and across the sand. She reaches the upper pool and rests her hands on her thighs, peering into the rippling water. She's looking for starfish, Wren knows. Bloody Henries, cushion stars, spinies and brittlestars. Black ones and orange ones and yellow and red. They were all in there if you searched long enough, if you kept your eye on the shadows.

Wren looks back at the girl – at Phoebe – her eyes searching for the gentle curve of her pregnancy, hidden beneath layers, a life waiting to happen. She sees herself cradling an infant; is it Phoebe, or Ava, or the new child? The thought of the new child fills her with light. 'It is calming,' she eventually manages, plucking deep to come back into the foreground again. 'I've walked almost every single day since I arrived here twenty years ago. The same route, the same distance, every day. Even when I was expecting you, right till the end, I still walked.'

The girl's expression crumples in confusion. 'Me? But you'd already had me by the time you came here.'

The fog of Wren's mind clears and she blinks at Phoebe, looking back out towards the horizon where she had once stood on the rocks. Out across the wide expanse of beach she sees them, Laura and Rob, and she knows it's time to face them, time to face her past. More than that, it's time to face her future, whatever that might bring. She rises and holds her hand out to Phoebe, a mother to a daughter. 'There's so much to tell you, Phoebe,' she says. 'There's so much to tell.'

Helpless to fight back, Wren clung to the rear seat of Arthur's truck as he pleaded with her to put her head down, to calm herself and let him help. The sky was dark, dotted with summer stars; he must have come back for her, she managed to piece together as she drifted in and out of conscious thought. Her rucksack landed in the footwell below her head, hastily thrown together by Arthur. She could hear his words breaking through her dreams: *What do you need, love? I've packed your keys – your purse – a few clothes. What else?*

'You need help, love,' he insisted, pulling a rough blanket from the parcel shelf and tucking it around her shaking body. And he was right: she was ill, her fever so high she couldn't speak coherently, and she couldn't make him understand that she had to stay put, that the only course of action was for her to crawl back inside her fortress and pull up the drawbridge.

Arthur's truck started away from the house, kicking up gravel against the stillness of the humid night. 'I'll die if you take me,' she screamed like a crazy woman.

'You'll die if I leave you,' he replied.

At the hospital he drew up at the emergency entrance, wanting to go in with her, pleading with her to let him stay, to make sure everything was alright. But as the porter helped her into a wheelchair she turned her eyes on him, ferocious clarity shining through. 'Go, Arthur,' she said, her voice now low and controlled. '*Go.*'

The child was born not an hour after Wren arrived on the maternity ward, and despite her late appearance she was fine: a daughter, seven pounds, one ounce. The place was overrun, so none of the nurses or midwives on duty were around for long enough to notice Wren's silent tears, or to check on the false details she gave them when filling in their forms. She was there on holiday, she said, and her name was Anne White. Her husband would be coming with her antenatal booklet soon; he'd been called away to London on business and hadn't been able to make it back in time.

'What a shame he missed the birth!' the midwife said as she completed the initial paperwork. 'You poor love. Still, he's on his way, that's what matters. So, do we have a name?' she asked, pointing a pen towards the baby she had deposited in Wren's arms just moments before. She was scribbling down details at speed, checking her watch fob, whispering to her assistant to check what time her replacement would be coming on duty.

'Anne White,' Wren repeated, swallowing back the raw terror that she wasn't believed.

The midwife laughed, a full-bellied guffaw.

'Not you, Mummy! We know your name. I meant the *baby*.'

'Oh,' Wren replied in a whisper. 'It's Ava.'

'Very nice – like the actress.'

'It's a bird name.'

'Lovely. Unusual.' Without warning, the midwife put down her papers and crossed the room to Wren's bedside, where she began wrestling the baby's head into a feeding position, delivering practical instructions on how to angle her nipple towards the infant's mouth.

'I can't – ' Wren tried to object, but the midwife had zoned out as she grappled with her hand, forcing her to cup her own breast, the baby to suckle. In a gulp of air the baby was latched on, drawing deep, sharp tugs that blunted Wren's mind and left her numb with shock. She sank back against the hospital-starched pillow and gave in, helpless. Over the next few hours she was visited constantly, as the baby was checked, as she was checked – blood pressure, pulse, temperature, stitches, cord stump, vitamin jabs, hip tests – endless prodding and poking, endless questions. These things appeared to be happening to someone else, and Wren was quite separate from events, floating nearby, responding to all that was asked of her, lifting her shirt here, rolling back a sleeve there, her mind as blank as a smooth pebble. By early afternoon a student doctor was perched at her bedside, talking her through handfuls of leaflets and explaining how it was now their policy to send new mothers home as soon as possible, for the health and happiness of both mother and baby.

'Do you have someone to pick you up, Anne? We're happy that you're both fit and well enough to go home this afternoon – as soon as we've seen your antenatal booklet and filled in all the relevant sections.'

Wren was still in the crumpled shirt she had arrived in, and she rummaged through her rucksack to see what Arthur had packed during their hasty departure last night. To her relief she discovered a fresh set of clothes: a sleeveless vest, shirt and leggings, along with her wallet and keys. She nodded. 'My husband's coming with the book. I'm going to meet him where the taxis pick up. Do you know where that is?'

'We'd like him to come up to meet you in the ward. So we know you're in good hands. Why don't you get yourself dressed – no rush – and, once he's here, we'll finish up the forms and get you and baby off home!' The young doctor provided her with a small supply of maternity pads and left her behind the curtain to change.

Alone behind the screen, Wren glanced down at the loose folds of skin that hung from her torso. It seemed to belong to someone else, silvery and thin as petals. There was now a lightness in her movement, as she raised a knee to step into the disposable maternity knickers the midwife had left for her, able to twist and stoop properly for the first time in weeks. Her lungs were fuller, her breathing deeper, and for a moment her mind cleared. As she paused to gaze into the face of the sleeping infant, a bolt of fresh understanding shot through her like a sign, and it became clear what she had to do – she knew why this baby had been brought to her. This beautiful child wasn't hers at all; this baby was Laura's – long-awaited, dreamed-of, lost already many times over – and Wren must send her home. Smoothing out the clean white napkin that came with her breakfast toast, she leant against the bedside cabinet and wrote, her words bumpy and uneven on the rough grain. As her pen raced across the paper she fought the mental paralysis that threatened to seize her, finding herself unable to draw on some of the simplest of details from her past, from the past she'd once lived. Her old address, the name of her husband's school – these things were quite inaccessible to her in the driving urgency of the moment. She did the best she could, writing down her message in heart-shuddering haste, her hand shaking every time she heard footsteps behind the screen. Reaching inside her bag for her wallet, she retrieved her most treasured photograph, taken in a passport booth in Camden a lifetime ago. These two things she slipped inside the child's bedding, visible enough to be seen between the clear plastic cot and the hospital regulation blankets.

With Ava asleep in her crib, her letter and photo in place, Wren placed a hand on the child's head and prayed to all the powers on earth and in the universe and the heavens above that this baby would make it home – that she would be returned to the heart of her people, to Laura and Rob, a family at last. With a single last glance, Wren slipped through the curtains that surrounded her bed, to vanish along the bleach-scented corridors and stairwells, out into the light beyond.

The meeting place Robert suggested is just over an hour away, in the tea rooms of the Metropole hotel in Padstow. It's a place I've never been to before, and last night I checked and double-checked the route on Dad's road map to make sure I know exactly where I'm going today. When I start off from home, the midday sun is high and bright in the sky, and I drive up the coast from Gwithian, overlooking the clean light of St Ives bay until it drops away from view, and all I see ahead is the journey I'm making to meet my family. *My family*. What strangely ordinary words for something so completely extraordinary. *To meet my family*.

Every day I feel something different. I'm a bundle of nerves one minute, an excited child the next. Dad says I'm driving him bonkers, but I know he's pleased for me all the same, glad that I will get to learn more about my birth parents – about where I come from. I would have tried earlier, if it hadn't been for Mum. She couldn't bring herself to talk about it when I broached the subject on my birthday all those years ago, and so I never mentioned it again. And for a long time I didn't mind. I was lucky they chose me, and, although I could never have put her through that while she was still here, now that she's gone I don't feel guilty or disloyal, not even a little bit. I feel excited, and hopeful, and certain that Mum would be OK with it if she could see what this means to me. I think about Dad, hugging me fiercely before I got in the car to leave. 'Go knock 'em dead,' he told

317

me, his voice muffled in the pink wool of my scarf. 'They'll love yer!'

Will they love me, though? Or will they be disappointed? I've watched enough films and documentaries on this subject to know it's not always straightforward – and I've braced myself for the possibility that it might not work out, that the reconciliation could be an anticlimax. But some kind of faith drives me on, even after all these months of waiting since first finding Robert. He's stalled over meeting face to face, but we've never broken contact, and I feel as if I will know him the moment we meet. We've spoken on the phone just about every week, gradually growing more familiar, until now, on this mild June day under a mackerel sky, we will see each other for the first time, for real. *What will I call you?* I asked him in one email. *Let's decide when we meet*, he replied, and I was glad of that, not in any hurry to use the word 'Dad' for anyone other than the man who hugged me on the doorstep this morning.

Robert has answered the endless questions I have about my sister – about Phoebe – and we've exchanged stories of her childhood and mine: compared holidays, pets, school achievements, birthdays, Christmases. He says she's kind and warm, and sometimes a bit stubborn; that she's desperately clever, but often wilfully absent-minded. I told him my dad says she sounds a bit like me. I talked about my friends and past boyfriends, about my relatives in Penzance and Bude, about how my parents couldn't have children and so they chose me – and, after a couple of months of communicating like that, he told me that Phoebe was pregnant. The strangest thing: I felt a sharp pang of envy. Why? The last thing I'd want is a baby myself, and yet the news pricked me, and I felt bad for feeling that way. Perhaps I wanted Rob and Phoebe to myself for a while. The baby is here now, though, born just last month, and I cried when Robert phoned to tell me I was an auntie. It's incredible to me that soon I will hear Phoebe's voice and thoughts, this person who shares my genes, who shares a father *and* a mother with me.

My mother is the one who is still a mystery.

Every Sunday I look forward to Robert's emails, filling me in on the news of his week, but in particular I love to read the stories of his past, the past he shared with my mother and with Laura. Sometimes those stories are so funny and touching, they make me want to cry. I seem to do a lot of that lately. It makes me ache to meet Wren, to look into her eyes and know her for myself. But there's so much to fear in this too. Robert has told me about their history. From our emails and conversations I know this has been difficult for him, as he tries to come to terms with what she did, not just leaving him like that, but taking me, robbing him of my childhood. It's something he can never forgive, he says, and I understand that, although I wish it wasn't that way. If I can come to terms with all this, I hold out hope that they might also make peace – that we might in some way, even at a distance, share our lives. But so far, he says, they've barely spoken a word, apart from the one occasion, when he confronted her about leaving, and about me. I phoned him when I read that, desperate to know what was said, how she reacted. Was she sorry? Did she ever think of me? Was I the reason she left? *Was it my fault?* Robert was horrified to think he might have put those thoughts in my head, and in the end he told me all about the argument.

The first time they spoke was at her cottage, when Robert drove down to deliver Phoebe for a visit, perhaps a month or so after they'd found her. He asked Phoebe to wait in the car while he went ahead to see Wren, but he said when she answered the door she treated him like a stranger. To me, Robert seems so calm and rational, but he told me he said things she didn't want to hear, that it got heated when she wouldn't acknowledge him, or the things she had done. Apparently he demanded answers, some kind of explanation, but Wren could barely look at him, let alone talk. *I was expecting Phoebe,* was all she said in return, and she left him standing in the kitchen as she went out to her garden. Robert told me it left him feeling as if he had meant nothing. As if my life, given away, had meant nothing. I didn't know how to respond to that. Perhaps things might improve, given time, but Robert's not so sure. He's certain she will be different with me, just as she has been with Phoebe, but all this unfinished business makes me nervous about meeting her, more than I ever thought I could be. Yet despite my nerves I'm glad he has told me the full story; it makes me feel closer to him, to know his anger and distress and to see how he feels for Phoebe, how I hope he will feel for me. I know he wants to see me, and there's a warm certainty about being welcomed in. But Wren sounds unpredictable; a closed book. My fear, my greatest fear, is that she'll reject me too and I can't say how I'll cope with that.

Now, the grand shadow of the Metropole looms over me as I pull into the driveway and park the car, switching off the engine and breathing deeply as I look out across the harbour and gather my courage. At last, I am here. I'm afraid, but finally, I'm here.

Robert must have been watching out for me, because he appears in the hotel entrance, his expression transparent, and when he wraps his arms around me it feels like being welcomed home. Somehow I know his face, his voice, his arms, and we shed tears together and laugh, and when we pull apart we find it hard to keep from reaching out to touch one another, to check that we're both really there.

'You've got my eyes,' he says, looking at me intently, swiping away the tears that streak his face. 'You're a lot like my sister.'

'Sorry about the hair – ' I feel embarrassed and run my hands through the rough crop that's grown back through over the past few months, since I shaved it on an impulse soon after Mum died. Dad went mad at me; I only regretted it when I realised we'd found Robert a few days later.

'I like it,' Robert replies, and he leads me to a bench at the side of the hotel, overlooking the beach. 'We're all here,' he says. 'Phoebe, Wren, Laura – baby Bobby. Everyone is so excited about meeting you. *So* excited, but naturally a bit nervous too.' He laces his fingers, pressing his thumbs together until the nails turn white, and a small crinkle appears between his eyebrows. 'I'm sorry it's taken so long, Ava. I hope you understand? There's been so much to get our heads around – all of us.'

I nod, anxious to race inside to find the rest of the family, but at the same time wishing I could just stay here like this, listening to Robert's voice, taking in the details of his face.

'After you'd made contact it seemed my whole world turned upside down, for all sorts of reasons – finding you, finding Wren, discovering Phoebe was pregnant. Don't they say these things come in threes?' He hooks an arm over the back of the bench, shifting his position to face me full-on. 'I wanted to make sure things were sorted with Phoebe first, and the baby, so that I could really focus on getting to know you when the time came. It's meant so much, talking with you on the phone and sharing emails...'

He reaches out to me again, and I see the pain behind his eyes, fresh and sharp.

'How are things now with Wren?' I ask.

'She still behaves as if I'm not in the room. It's strange, but I hope some day we'll get past it. She's not the same person she was – but then I suppose neither am I. When we go inside, you're bound to notice some tension between us, and it's important you know it's not aimed at you, Ava. Wren's been living alone for the past twenty years, and she's out of practice with all the social stuff, so don't be surprised if she's not as upbeat as the rest of us. Remember, Phoebe has just been through the same thing as you, meeting her mother, and she says you just have to go slowly.' Robert lays a hand on mine, and looks at me steadily through his amber eyes. 'Now, speaking of Phoebe, she'll skin me alive if I keep you from her any longer. Ready?'

My heart races. 'Ready.'

The hotel lobby is quiet and Robert tells me we have a room off the café to ourselves. At the entrance he hugs me once more, before standing aside to let me enter first.

So here they all are; my family, a portrait of anticipation and uncertainty in the soft blue light of the room.

Time seems to stand still; my hearing is muted, like the colours of the room, and my movements feel slow as I take in the faces of the two women who sit at either end of the sofa, their amazed eyes fixed on me, and Phoebe, my sister, who springs up from the armchair, to throw her arms around me and clasp me tight. When she releases me she doesn't say a word, just takes my hand and steps back to look, to really look at me, as if I'm a rare creature of great interest, and I laugh as I realise I'm doing the same in reflection. I see my mother, Wren, who remains seated; I feel the distance between her and Robert as their eyes meet in a flash of shared hurt, and I know that somehow they're held together by this other woman on the sofa: Laura. I recognise her from her curls, just as she looked in the passport photograph, and as she smiles at me I feel her warmth.

Wren appears startled, ready to bolt from the room, and she holds tight to the tiny baby swaddled in her arms, glancing at me intermittently, though her focus is drawn to the safety of the child.

'Wren?' Phoebe says, stepping back, her fingers still looped over mine.

Robert moves away from me, his hand rising to pinch at his lower lip as he perches on the arm of the sofa beside Laura. The room feels as if it might explode with the pressure of so much feeling, and, just as I think Wren might never stir, Laura turns to her, and scoops the baby from her arms. With a gentle jerk of her head she indicates for Wren to stand, and after a pause she does, cautiously, as I release Phoebe to extend a hand, wanting Wren to come to me; wanting her to want it too. In a moment we are in each other's arms, and I feel the rise and fall of her breathing as she clings to me, her wet cheek pressed to mine.

'*Were you happy?*' she whispers so that only I can hear, and I pull back and look into her eyes, so full of hope and longing, and I nod. That's all, I nod my head, and through her tears and pain Wren's face breaks into a smile that lights up the room.

Acknowledgements

My list of thanks grows longer with each new book – my family, friends, readers, champions – my superb agent and first-rate publishing team – you know who you are and I appreciate you all so very much.

Above all else, a special mention must go to my husband, who has loved me and supported my ambitions from the start, to help make all of this possible. Colin, my love – thank you.

A F T E R W O R D :

BOOK GROUP GUIDE :

1. *Flight* shifts between different viewpoints and between the past and the present. Do you have a favourite character, or feel more sympathy for one over the other?

2. Wren is a complex personality. Do you feel you understand her motivations for her actions? Did your view of her change as the novel progresses?

3. Can Wren ever be forgiven for what she's done? Can leaving a partner and child in this way ever be justified?

4. Would you feel differently if the 'leaver' were the father?

5. Would Wren have left if she hadn't come into money?

6. It would be easy to attribute Wren's state of mind to postnatal depression alone, but do you think there were earlier indications of her fragility – or her need to escape?

7. Is there such a thing as a 'natural mother'?

8. What does the novel seem to say about nature versus nurture?

9. How do you feel about Wren's mother, Eliza?

10. What is your opinion of Robert as a character?

11. What do you make of Laura's relationship with her parents?

12. Were Robert and Laura always meant to be together?

13. Laura has sacrificed a lot to live the life she does. Is she the real hero of the story?

14. How does the North Cornwall setting affect the mood of the novel?

15. Did the truth about Ava come as a shock to you?

16. What does the novel – and Phoebe's experience in particular – make you think about the extent to which we are our parents' children?

17. Does Wren, Robert and Laura's story reveal anything about the nature of love, both in terms of friendship and romantic love?

18. What does the novel tell us about the ways in which the past haunt us?

19. How satisfying did you find the ending of the novel?

20. What does the future hold for the family?

Read on for an extract from Isabel Ashdown's critically
acclaimed novel *Hurry Up and Wait*.

Sarah waits at the kerbside, her winter coat buttoned up tight against the cold night air. The tang of sea spray whips through the lamp-lit High Street, as the distant rumble of clawing waves travels in from the dark shoreline, up and over the hedges and gardens of East Selton. It's an ancient echo, both soothing and unsettling in its familiarity. She checks her watch. She's early.

At the far end of the Parade, an old Citroën turns the corner and rattles along the street, drawing to a stop alongside her. She stoops to peer through the window, and sees John Gilroy smiling broadly, stretching across to open the passenger door, which has lost its outside handle. She slides into the seat, pulling the door shut with a hollow clatter.

'It's good to see you, John,' she says, returning his smile, not knowing whether to kiss him or not. She runs her fingers through her hair. 'This is a bit weird, isn't it?'

John pinches his bottom lip between his fingers and frowns. 'Yeah, *really* weird.'

There's a moment's pause as they look at each other.

'I suppose we'd better get it over with, then?' he says, releasing the handbrake and pulling away.

They cruise slowly along the deserted Parade as the wind buffets the faded canvas roof of the car, whistling out across the night. Sarah draws the seatbelt across her body, clunking it into place between the seats. A disquieting recollection rattles her, a sense of having been here before, with John at her side.

She studies his face as he struggles with the gear-change from second to third, a slice of mild irritation still lodged between his black eyebrows. 'Sticky gearbox,' he mutters as it grinds into gear.

Sarah gazes out at the shop windows as they pass through the High Street. She remembers old Mr Phipps from the tobacconist's. Every Saturday morning Dad would take her there on the way back from the paper shop, and she'd choose something from the jars at the back of the counter. It was a tiny vanilla-smelling store, its walls adorned with framed black and white photographs of the screen greats: Clark Gable; Bette Davis; Victor Mature. She notices the estate agent's, on the corner opposite the war memorial, although the name over the top has changed.

'I couldn't believe it when I got your email,' she says. 'It's been years.'

'Twenty-four years,' John replies.

She nods.

'I worked it out. It was just before your sixteenth birthday, wasn't it?'

'You've got a good memory.'

He keeps his eyes fixed on the road ahead. 'Well, one minute you were there, and the next you'd gone. It sort of sticks in your mind.'

Sarah shivers against the cold. 'The town gives me the creeps, to be honest. When I checked into the B&B this afternoon, the woman who owns it seemed familiar, but I don't know why. I guess she's just got that Selton look.'

'What's a "Selton look"?'

'Don't know. But it puts me on edge, whatever it is.'

John scowls, feigning offence.

'Not you, though!' she says quickly. 'You don't count.'

She notices he's wearing a knitted waistcoat under his jacket. It's a bit hippyish but she's pleased to see he's no longer in the black prog-rock T-shirts that seemed to be welded to his torso throughout the eighties.

They turn into School Lane.

'So, who are you dreading most tonight?' John asks.

'Oh, God, what a question! It would be easier to say who I'm not dreading.'

'OK, then. Who?'

A light mist of freezing fog has started to descend, and the windscreen wipers squeak into action.

'Actually it's the same people. I'm looking forward to seeing certain people but dreading them at the same time. Tina and Kate are the obvious ones.'

'Dante?' John asks, briefly turning his eyes on her with a small smile.

She blinks. 'He probably ended up in some rock band in LA. That was the trouble with Dante. Too cool for school.'

John laughs, rubbing his chin.

They pull up in the new car park at the rear of the girls' building, a few rows back from the large open double doors of the gym. Sarah scans the area, trying to make sense of the layout. 'This bit used to be the netball court,' she says. 'Can you believe they've built a car park on it?'

John shrugs. 'Well, I suppose the schools are even bigger now than in our day. I'm surprised they haven't merged the boys' and girls' schools into one. It would make sense, wouldn't it?'

Sarah's fingers fiddle nervously with the charm bracelet beneath the sleeve of her coat. She rolls a small silver conch between her thumb and forefinger. 'Do you mind if we just sit here a moment?' she asks.

John shifts in his seat. 'We can sit here as long as you like.' He reaches inside his jacket and brings out the postcard-sized invitation. 'I wonder who designed the cheesy invites? Look at this: "*Wanna know what your old school friends have been Kajagoogooing? Then put on your leg warmers and Walk this Way for a Wham Fantastic night out...*"'

'Stop!' Sarah laughs, clapping her hands over her ears. 'I can't believe I let you talk me into coming.'

'It'll be fine,' he says, slipping the card back in his jacket.

A taxi pulls up outside the entrance to the gym and a small group of men and women disembark. The men are clutching cans of lager, and they stumble on to the pavement, laughing and shouting to each other. Sarah recognises one of the women as a girl from her class, but she can't quite grasp the name. Melanie? Or perhaps it was Mandy.

'Bloody hell,' says John, grimacing. 'Look at the state of them.'

Sarah blows air through pursed lips, watching her white breath slowly drift and disperse inside the car. Her eyes rest on the funny little gearstick, poking out of the dashboard like a tiny umbrella handle. 'Is this a Citroën Dyane?'

John leans into the windscreen to wipe the moisture away with a sponge. It's a stiff synthetic sponge, and all it does is turn the condensation to water, which runs into a pool on the dashboard. 'Yep. My trusty old Dyane. It's a bit of a renovation project.'

'Thought so,' she says. 'It's freezing. Just like my dad's old car.'

He sticks the sponge under the dashboard. 'I know. I really liked his car. Used to see it chugging through the town sometimes, and I thought, one day, when I've got a bit of money, I'd like one of those.'

Sarah leans across and kisses him on the cheek. It takes them both by surprise, and she draws her hand to her mouth.

'Sorry,' she says from behind her glove. 'I'm a bit nervous.'

John shifts in his seat so he's facing the windscreen. 'Me too.'

Two screaming women run down the side of the car towards the school, click-clacking on high heels. Sarah tries to make them out, but they're strangers to her. She draws a smiley face on her misted side window.

'We'd better go in,' says John, 'before the car steams up completely.'

Sarah stares ahead, her fingers curled around the still-buckled belt strap. 'Just five more minutes.'

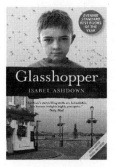

WINNER OF THE *MAIL ON SUNDAY* NOVEL COMPETITION

At once troubling, funny and joyous, Isabel Ashdown's debut is the intimate, lyrical and deeply moving story of an ordinary family crumbling under the weight of past mistakes.

In this intense novel of secrets and simmering passions that takes us back to the legendary heatwave of 1976, Isabel Ashdown once again unravels the complexity of her characters' lives – and reveals what really lies beneath the surface.

MORE FROM MYRIAD

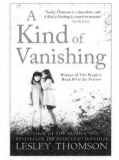

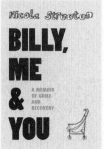

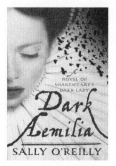
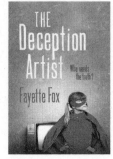

MORE FROM MYRIAD

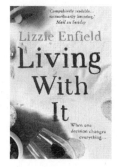

MORE FROM MYRIAD

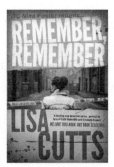

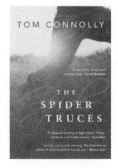

Sign up to our mailing list at
www.myriadeditions.com
Follow us on Facebook and Twitter

Isabel Ashdown is the author of four critically acclaimed novels: *Flight* (2015), *Summer of '76* (2013), *Hurry Up and Wait* (2011) and *Glasshopper* (2009). Her first novel, *Glasshopper* (*Observer* Best Debuts, *Evening Standard* Best Books of the Year), won the *Mail on Sunday* Novel Competition. She lives in West Sussex with her husband and two children.

To find out more, visit:

www.isabelashdown.com
Facebook: /IsabelAshdownBooks
Twitter: @IsabelAshdown